SATIRICAL STORIES
OF
NIKOLAI LESKOV

SATIRICAL STORIES
OF
NIKOLAI LESKOV

Translated and Edited by William B. Edgerton

PEGASUS   NEW YORK

Copyright © 1969 by
Western Publishing Company, Inc.
Library of Congress Catalogue Card Number 69–27987
All rights reserved.
This book, or parts thereof, may not be
reproduced in any form without permission
of the publishers.
Printed in the United States
of America.

Dedicated
in love and gratitude
to my Father and Mother,
who have shown the way
by continuing to grow
throughout the years.
—W. B. E.

CONTENTS

INTRODUCTION

With most of the great Russian writers of the nineteenth century one or two or three works are sufficient to give the reader a fairly adequate notion of their genius. Read *War and Peace* and *Anna Karénina* and you will know why Leo Tolstóy towers above the common run of nineteenth-century European realists. Read *Crime and Punishment* and *The Brothers Karamázov* and you will understand, even before you go on to *The Idiot* and *The Devils*, why Dostoévsky still excites passionate discussion in the second half of the twentieth century. Read Turgénev's *Fathers and Sons*, Gógol's *Dead Souls*, Púshkin's *Eugene Onégin*, or Goncharóv's *Oblómov*, and you will know each of the authors well enough not to be greatly surprised by anything you find in the rest of their works.

But when you turn to Nikolái Leskóv, your plight is comparable to that of the blind men in the fable about the elephant. If you read his most widely published work in English, "Lady Macbeth of the Mtsensk District," you will conclude that Leskóv wrote stories in a sober, restrained style about crimes of passion. And yet no other work of Leskóv is comparable in either style or theme. Turn then to *The Cathedral Folk,* and you will conclude that Leskóv wrote leisurely, rambling novels, not devoid of humor, giving a sympathetic view of the provincial Russian Orthodox clergy. This conclusion is indeed a little closer to the truth, because Russian religious life—Orthodox as well as unorthodox—did provide Leskóv with material for many of his most important works. Leskóv virtually disowned it, however, within three years after its first publication in Russian. Turn next to *The Enchanted Pilgrim*, and you will place Leskóv among the writers of picaresque novels, but with a peculiarly Russian type of good-hearted, simple-minded hero in the place of the traditional rogue. In its structural pattern as a frame story, its humor, its riotously colorful pictures of Russian provincial life, and the overarching religious sky under which this earthy and exuberant narrative takes place, *The Enchanted*

Pilgrim does reveal several important characteristics of Leskóv's genius. Still, much remains undiscovered by the reader who knows only these three works. For example, there remains the vast territory covered by what Leskov called his "retrospective stories," in which he so successfully blurred the line between truth and fiction as a means of attaining verisimilitude that most of his biographers have been trapped into accepting Leskóv's persuasive fiction as if it were actual fact. Likewise there remains Leskov's gallery of "Righteous Men," those quixotic positive heroes whom he made convincing by making them just a little ridiculous. There also remain Leskov's legends of the early Christian era, such as "The Mountain" ("Gorá"), "The Juggler Pamfalón" ("Skomorókh Pamfalón"), and "Beautiful Aza" ("Prekrásnaya Aza"), not one of which has yet been translated into English. Further aspects of Leskóv's genius are represented by his beautifully written story about the Russian Old Believers, "The Sealed Angel" ("Zapechatlénny ángel"), which still awaits adequate English translation; his "Life of a Peasant Woman" ("Zhitié odnói báby"), an early novelette giving a sympathetic account of a sensitive peasant girl driven insane by the brutality of her environment; his Christmas stories, which in his work assumed the character of a fairly distinct genre; his stories for children, such as "The Beast" ("Zver") and the gently ironical "Scarecrow" ("Púgalo"); and "The Sentry" ("Chelovék na chasákh"), a story in which the soulless bureaucracy of the age of Nicholas I is subjected to bitter satire by Leskóv in a style that is appropriately and ironically bureaucratic.

The aspect of Leskóv's works that is the most striking of all, however, and the one that the mention of his name will immediately bring to the mind of any native Russian, is his highly original language. Scarcely any of Leskóv's best stories are written in the kind of unobtrusive standard literary style that is assumed to be characteristic of the main stream of nineteenth-century Russian realism. Leskóv's writing requires a special kind of partnership between reader and author, and the effect they jointly achieve might be compared to counterpoint in music. The reader, for his part, must provide a knowledge of standard literary Russian, which echoes in his ear as a background melody; and Leskóv achieves his peculiar contrapuntal effect in the mind of the reader with a dazzling medley of variations on standard Russian. Leskóv's contribution to this joint production may include words and phrases from numerous Russian dialects, a wealth of proverbs and folk expressions, jargon drawn from almost every conceivable stratum of Russian society, quaint old-fashioned Church Slavonic forms, Ukrainianisms, Polonisms, Germanisms, comically distorted French, and—most characteristic of all—his own Leskovian kind of malapropisms, which almost invariably carry a punning satirical sting created on the pattern of folk etymology.

The most famous story illustrating this Leskovian language is "The Steel

Flea," which has been translated into English more often than anything else Leskóv ever wrote. Unfortunately, none of the six English versions preceding the one now published here succeeded in creating any English equivalent to the contrapuntal effect of Leskóv's original Russian. Translating Leskóv without finding esthetic equivalents for his style is like translating Púshkin's *Eugene Onégin* into prose, or reproducing the paintings of Monet in black and white. Leskóv himself once told the first German translator of his works that he did not believe it was possible to convey the tone of "The Steel Flea" in another language. The translations published here of "The Steel Flea" and also of the similarly dazzling "Night Owls" represent the stubborn efforts of two of Leskóv's admirers to prove that he was wrong. Whether they have succeeded is of course a question that can be answered only by the readers of this book.

The circumstances of Leskóv's birth and early years in Oryól Province provided him with a store of material upon which he was to draw for his literary works throughout his life. He was born on February 4 (Old Style), 1831, in the village of Gorókhovo, a few miles south of the provincial capital. Through family connections he had an opportunity to become acquainted with practically every class in Russian society. His father was the son of a village priest and had been educated in a seminary but had gone into government service instead of following the family clerical tradition. One of his mother's sisters was married to a wealthy landowner whose estate was a family center for his mother's side of the house. Another aunt married a Scotchman named Alexander Scott whose father had moved his family to Russia some time before 1825 and had taken over the management of the enormous estates belonging to the wealthy Peróvsky and Narýshkin families. Thanks to this Scottish uncle (Leskóv always referred to him as an Englishman) within the family circle, Leskóv had an opportunity almost from his earliest childhood to look at his native Russia through the eyes of an outsider and to compare Russian culture with the culture of Great Britain. There are references to his uncle in a number of his fictional and journalistic works, including two of the stories included in this volume, "The Archbishop and the Englishman" and "A Product of Nature."

One of the hardiest myths about Leskóv's biography grew out of a story he wrote in 1892 called "Vale of Tears" ("Yudól"). The heroine of the story was a certain "Aunt Polly," who had taken an English Quaker girl as a governess for her daughters and had herself begun to follow the Quaker way of life. In D. S. Mirsky's classic history of Russian literature Leskóv's legendary Aunt Polly became the wife of Alexander Scott; and in at least one subsequent biographical sketch which elaborated upon Mirsky's legend the fictitious Quakeress of this literary creation of 1892 became a dominant influence upon the boyhood of Nikolái Leskóv, and accounted for the equally fictitious gentleness of spirit bestowed upon him by the biographer.

Another myth concerns the explanation for Leskóv's scanty formal education. Two different autobiographical notes in his own hand declare that he was left a helpless orphan at the age of sixteen, when his father died and his family lost all its property in the great Oryól fires, and that he then had to leave school and go to work. The facts are that he quit school at the age of fifteen in 1846, two years before his father's death and the Oryól fires—which could scarcely have affected the Leskóv family property because by that time they were living in the country.

Thanks to his keen mind and his voracious appetite for reading, Leskóv eventually managed to educate himself remarkably well, but he never overcame his embarrassment over the fact that the whole of his formal education was limited to five years at the Oryól Secondary School, which he left without even taking the examinations for the third class.

After working for a time as a clerk in the Oryól Criminal Court, Leskóv got himself transferred in 1849 to a minor government post in Kíev. The seven years and a half that he spent in the ancient capital of the Ukraine played a role of very great importance in his cultural formation. He learned the Polish language, which at that time was still the language of the Kíev aristocracy, and he acquired an enthusiasm for Polish literature. He likewise came into contact there with Ukrainian cultural nationalists, and through them he became interested in the general Slavic renaissance movement that had begun a generation earlier among the Czechs. Through his governmental post he gained an entrée into the social life of Kievan officialdom; and through his mother's brother, who was then a professor of medicine, he also became acquainted with a number of his uncle's scholarly friends at the university.

In 1857 Leskóv joined a new commercial firm organized by his uncle Alexander Scott and another Briton named Wilkins. Married by then to Olga Smirnóva, the daughter of a wealthy merchant in Kíev, Leskóv moved his wife and baby daughter to the Scott estate in Pénza Province and spent three years traveling all over European Russia as the chief Russian representative of his uncle's company. In his old age he looked back on that as the happiest period in his life. The wealth of impressions he stored up in his memory during those years of travel furnished him to the end of his life with material for his literary works. Indeed, it was his letters to Scott reporting on his journeys that first called attention to Leskóv's literary talent; and soon after the Scott and Wilkins company went bankrupt in 1860, he moved to Petersburg and plunged into full-time work as a crusading journalist, in the spirit of the age of reform that began in Russia with the death of Nicholas I and the advent of Alexander II to the Russian throne.

Leskóv quickly made a wide circle of acquaintances among Petersburg writers, but several things set him apart from them. Even though he was a native of the very heart of Russia, the same general region south of Moscow from which Turgénev and Tolstóy had sprung, Leskóv was culturally an outsider: he lacked a university education, he owed his intellectual formation largely to the half-Polish capital of the Ukraine, and he was greatly influenced in his outlook on life by his long association with his Scottish uncle and his wealth of experiences in government service in Kíev and in commercial travel as an agent of Scott and Wilkins. Leskóv's greater age and experience (he entered Petersburg literary life at the age of thirty) made him skeptical of the despotic young revolutionaries then dominant in Petersburg journalism. His own fiery temper eventually brought him into such violent conflict with them that a notorious campaign of vilification poisoned his life, closed all but the most conservative Russian publications to him for some fifteen years, and so firmly fastened the term "reactionary" upon him that it continues to turn up to this day in conventional histories of Russian literature.

This literary boycott left him literally *Nowhere to Go (Nékuda)*—the title of his most sensational novel—except to the conservatives, and for a period of some five years he published his literary works largely in the most prominent conservative journal in Russia, *The Russian Herald (Rússki véstnik)*. In 1874, however, Leskóv broke with this journal over arbitrary changes the editors made in *A Family in Decline (Zakhudály rod)* which biased the text in favor of the editors' conservative policy.[1]

In the summer of 1875 Leskóv took his second trip to Western Europe. During his visit he got acquainted with a number of Catholic and Protestant religious leaders and with a great deal of religious and political literature forbidden in Russia. As a result, this visit marks a turning point in Leskóv's whole life. "In general," he wrote to an old friend on his way home, "I have become a 'turncoat,' and I no longer burn incense to many of my old gods. Above all, I have broken with ecclesiasticism . . . had I read all that I have now read on this subject and heard all that I have now heard, I would not have written *The Cathedral Folk* as it is now written. . . . Instead I am itching now to write about a Russian heretic—an intelligent, well-read, and freethinking *Spiritual Christian,* who has passed through all doubts in his search for the truth of Christ and has found it only within his own soul. I would name such a story 'Fornósov the Heretic,' and I would publish it—where could it be published? Oh, these political tendencies!"[2]

Leskóv never got around to writing "Fornósov the Heretic," but this statement foreshadows the new direction that his literary career was to follow to the very end of his life. Before the year was out he had written "At the Ends of the Earth" ("Na kraiú svéta"), a story whose heretical implications were so generally overlooked that it was published in perhaps the most conservative periodical in Russia, *The Citizen (Grazhdanín)* and was recommended to the Tsar by no less a pillar of Orthodoxy than Pobedonóstsev himself, the Chief Procurator of the Holy Synod. Two years later Leskóv published "The Unbaptized Priest" ("Nekreshchóny pop"), a deceptively comical story that criticized conservative, ritualistic Orthodoxy in the name of a religion of the spirit that impelled men to live good lives. In 1880 he began publishing a series of stories about "Righteous Men," taking as his epigraph the Russian saying, "Without three righteous men no city shall stand," which is based on the Old Testament account in Genesis 18 of Abraham's bargaining session with the Lord God Himself.[3] Three of the stories in the present collection deal with comical heroes that are generally classed among Leskóv's Righteous Men: "The Steel Flea," "Singlethought," and "Figúra."

It is common knowledge that one of the most difficult tasks in literature is to create a convincing positive hero. Leskóv succeeded by following the example of Cervantes in *Don Quixote*. Leskóv's Righteous Men are believable because only their goodness sets them apart from the rest of us. Except for their goodness they may be as simple-minded, as naïve, as ridiculous and full of idiosyncrasies as all the rest of mankind. But the light of their goodness shines all the brighter because it shines forth in the most unexpected nooks and crannies of humanity.

In the new direction he took after 1875 Leskóv anticipated the inner religious revolution that Leo Tolstóy went through toward the end of the 1870's. "I 'fell in step' with Tolstóy rather than being 'won over' by him," Leskóv wrote in 1893. "I did not imitate him; I was saying the same thing *before* he did, but without eloquence or self-confidence, shyly and awkwardly. When I perceived his great power, I laid aside my flickering lamp and followed after his great torch."[4] From the mid-1880's until his death on February 21 (Old Style), 1895, Leskóv found his way in large measure through both literature and life by the light of Tolstóy's "great torch." He was neither dogmatic nor uncritical in his attitude toward Tolstóy's teachings, but to the very end of his life he revered Tolstóy as "the most important man of our time."[5]

Leskóv's greatest achievement in the period after 1875, however, was his satire, and the stories in the present collection have been chosen especially with a view to illustrating the range of his satirical attacks and the variety and subtlety of his satirical methods.

Leskóv's satire is essentially moral in nature, but its reverberations leave scarcely any aspect of social or political life untouched. Leskóv himself referred to his satirical manner as "crafty." His most famous device is what Russian critics refer to as *skaz*, the use of a narrator who is limited not only in language but also in his outlook. By allowing this limited narrator to express blatantly conventional opinions about the story he is telling, Leskóv accomplishes two things: he throws dust in the eyes of the censor, and he gives his reader the pleasure of perceiving Leskóv's irony for himself. Examples of this technique in the present collection are to be found in the old gunsmith who tells the story of "The Steel Flea," the unknown cleric who laboriously comments in "Notes from an Unknown Hand," and the utterly unprincipled Márya Martýnovna in "Night Owls," who provides her own comments as she goes along in her story about the confrontation of the Tolstoyan girl and the powerful Orthodox evangelist John of Kronstadt.

The new direction that Leskóv's writing took after 1875 was not slow in arousing the suspicion of the Russian authorities. In 1883 he was dismissed from a minor position in the Ministry of National Education, in 1884 a Moscow periodical was halted for publishing works by Leskóv that the censors found unacceptable, and in 1889 Volume Six of Leskóv's collected works was ordered seized and burned by the censors. Finally, in 1895, less than a month before his death, perhaps the supreme irony of his whole career occurred when one of his finest works, "The March Hare" ("Záyachi remiz") was rejected as too dangerous by one of the same progressive editors who a few years earlier had taken part in the campaign against Leskóv for allegedly being a reactionary.

Leskóv has been called the most Russian of Russian writers, and his satirical stories are aimed squarely at the weaknesses and evils he saw in his own Tsarist Russian society. What gives his satire its universal appeal, however, is the fact that it transcends the nineteenth-century Russian conditions that called it forth. Arrogance, corruption, inhuman callousness, personal and national self-righteousness, prejudice, dogmatism, hypocrisy, and love of power are not confined to Russia and are not greatly affected by revolution. They are a part of the human clay out of which all men are fashioned. Hence Leskóv's satire, like Gógol's, is unlimited by geography or time. Haughty archbishops and hysterical nihilist-hunters can be found as readily today (under other labels, of course) in the Soviet Union or the United States as they could under the original labels in Tsarist Russia.

Apart from "Deception" and "Fish Soup Without Fish," all the stories in the present collection are taken from the eleven-volume Russian edition of Leskóv's selected works and letters published in Moscow in 1956–58. Two of these stories, "Administrative Grace" and "About the Rooster and His Children," were never allowed by the censors to be published in Leskóv's lifetime. "Deception," which has never been republished in Russian since the Soviet Revolution, is translated from the thirty-six volume edition of Leskóv's works published in 1902–03. "Fish Soup Without Fish" made its original appearance in 1886 in the periodical *Nov*, No. 7, and it is translated from that source.

Much of the information given in the footnotes to this collection is taken from the notes to the eleven-volume Soviet edition mentioned above. The editor wishes to acknowledge his indebtedness to the Russian scholars who annotated the volumes from which these stories were translated, and in particular to B. Ya. Búkhshtab and S. A. Réiser and to the late B. M. Eikhenbáum, the fruits of whose long study of Leskóv are to be found not only in the eleven-volume edition they helped to edit but also in a number of other valuable studies dealing with Leskóv.

All the translations in the present edition are published here for the first time. With the exception of "The Steel Flea" none of these stories has ever appeared before in English translation. I am particularly happy to acknowledge my indebtedness to Hugh McLean, whose writings on Leskóv are known to every Leskóv scholar, for allowing me to include two of his translations in this volume, and especially for giving me the opportunity to collaborate with him in the final stages of work on his remarkable translation of "Night Owls."

I conclude with an inadequate word of appreciation to my wife, whose partnership in this undertaking has assumed forms ranging from constant personal encouragement to serving as chief critic, typing the whole manuscript, and contributing English equivalents for several of Leskóv's most perplexing malapropisms.

William B. Edgerton

---

[1] An examination of the original manuscript some years ago in Leningrad by the author of this article revealed that among the editors' omissions was a passage Leskóv had written in favor of broad religious tolerance and among their insertions was an anti-Semitic remark.

[2] Letter of July 29 (August 10), 1875 to P. K. Shchebálsky, printed in N. S. Leskóv, *Sobránie sochinénii* (Moscow, 1956–58), X, 411–412.

[3] This saying provides an interesting link between Leskóv and the present-day Soviet writer Alexander Solzhenítsyn, whose remarkable story "Matryóna's House" ("Matryónin dvor") contains the same quotation about Righteous Men.

[4] Letter of November 12, 1893, to M. O. Ménshikov, quoted in Andréi Leskóv, *Zhizn Nikoláya Leskóva* (Moscow, 1954), p. 605.

[5] Letter of February 15, 1894, to M. O. Ménshikov, quoted in *Zhizn Nikoláya Leskóva*, p. 594.

THE SOUNDS AND SPELLING OF RUSSIAN

The near anarchy of English spelling makes it impossible to represent the sound system of Russian in an orderly way within the spelling system to which speakers of English are accustomed. Consequently, three different systems of transcribing Russian are in common use in English. The best of the three is very simple and very exact but has no more relation to the English spelling system than Czech spelling does. As a result, its usefulness is largely confined to specialized works designed for an international scholarly audience.

The so-called Popular System used in this book has the advantage of giving the general reader a reasonably clear idea of how Russian words should be pronounced within the limits of the English sound system (which does not contain all the sounds in the Russian language). On the other hand, it has the disadvantage of being too inexact to permit completely accurate transliteration back into Russian characters.

Here are its main features:

All the vowels are pronounced separately.

A—always like the *a* in "*f*a*ther.*"

E—In words of foreign origin, such as *éra*, like the *e* in "m*e*t." Otherwise, like the first two letters in "yes," e.g., Dostoévsky (Dos-to-YEV-ski).

I—like the *i* in "mach*i*ne" when accented; otherwise, as in "hab*i*t."

O—like the *o* in "n*o*se" when accented; otherwise, as in "*o*ccur."

U—like the *oo* in "f*oo*d."

Y—approximately like the *i* in "m*i*ll"; before vowels, as in "*y*am." Note: *y* never has the sound of the *y* in "fl*y*."

I or Y following a vowel has the semivowel sound of the *y* in "bo*y*." For example:

    ai—like the *i* in "wr*i*te."
    oi—like the *oi* in "v*oi*ce."
    ei—like "*yea.*"

KH—approximately like the *ch* in German. (Pronounce a heavily aspirated *k* without initially closing the air passage in the throat.)

ZH—like the *s* in "mea*s*ure."

SHCH—like the *sh-ch* in "fre*sh ch*eese."

The stress in Russian, which can fall on any syllable, is regularly marked in this book.

It must be borne in mind that this is *not* a guide to the pronunciation of Russian, nor even to the transliteration of Russian into English letters. It is solely a guide to the pronunciation of Russian words in English.

A NOTE ON RUSSIAN NAMES

The peculiar and interesting Russian system of names is so firmly imbedded in the fabric of Russian culture that even the great upheaval of 1917 left the traditional Russian forms of address untouched.

Understanding the Russian usage in names is essential for savoring the full flavor of Russian literature, and is actually far simpler than is commonly supposed. "Mr." and "Mrs." as forms of address in prerevolutionary Russia were as cold and impersonal as the Russian word for "Citizen" is today in the Soviet Union. The most respectfully friendly way to address a Russian has always been to use his first name and a special form of his father's first name, called his patronymic. A Russian named Pável (Paul) whose father's name is Iván (John) will be known as Pável Ivánovich. If he has a sister named Anna, she will be called Anna Ivánovna. Every Russian is given only one name, and his patronymic automatically becomes his middle name. Masculine patronymics usually end in -ovich or -evich (shortened in rapid speech to -ych and -ich), and feminine patronymics usually end in -ovna or -evna.

This usage is so common among Russians that it is hard for a Russian adult to speak very long with a new acquaintance before asking what his first name and patronymic are.

Within one's family and among close friends the first name and patronymic are replaced by some familiar form of the first name alone. Here the Russian love of diminutives does complicate matters, for almost every Russian first name has a number of diminutive forms that can express a wide variety of emotions. Perhaps the best way to understand this in English terms is to compare the possibilities offered by such a name as John: "Johnny," "Jack," "Jackie," "Jack darling," "Jack dear," the small boy's "Old Jack Jones," and the wife's reference to "my Jack."

In "Superfluous Mother Love" the assessor's widow calls her son Ignáty by the diminutive form "Ignásha." If she had ever allowed him to play with other boys, they would very likely have called him Ignáshka, since the forms ending in -ka tend to imply familiarity without any particular affection. The hero of "Singlethought" was called "Alexáshka" (translated here as "Aleck") until he became a town official, and then his neighbors paid him added respect by using his first name and patronymic—"Alexander Afanásyevich." Within her family the heroine of "Night Owls," Klávdia, was affectionately called "Klavdyúsha" and "Klávdinka." Since her uncle, Nikolái Stépenev, was called "Nikolái Ivánovich," we know automatically that his father's first name was Iván. His son Peter ("Pyotr" in Russian) is called within the family by the familiar forms "Pétya" or "Pétinka," but once he settles down and becomes, like his father, "the outstanding member of his family and a loyal putriot," people will no doubt respectfully call him by his first name and patronymic, "Peter Nikoláevich."

Occasionally the patronymic is used alone in a spirit of comradely informality, sometimes with a touch of affection. Figúra, for example, in the story that bears his name, at one point refers to General Dmítry Eroféevich Osten-Sacken as "Eroféich." In "Night Owls" Klávdia's mother familiarly calls Márya Martýnovna by her patronymic alone, "Martýnovna," and then toward the end of the story she expresses her disdain for the meddlesome old woman by adding a disparaging ending and making it "Martýnikha."

Literary translation, like politics, involves perpetual compromise; and it is fair to warn the reader that one of the points at which this translator has compromised with strict consistency is in giving some Russian first names in their original form (e.g., "Márya" instead of "Mary" and "Nikolái" instead of "Nicholas") and using the English equivalents for certain others (e.g., "Peter," "Paul," "Alexander," and "Luke" instead of "Pyotr," "Pável," "Alexándr," and "Luká"). The reader should look for no underlying principle governing this inconsistency apart from the translator's own feeling for what seemed to place the lesser obstacle in the way of a direct response to the esthetic values in the original Russian text.

SATIRICAL STORIES
OF
NIKOLAI LESKOV

NOTE TO "THE STEEL FLEA"

When Nikolái Leskóv first published this story in 1881, he claimed in a foreword that he had heard it from an old Túla gunsmith, then living in Sestrorétsk, who "liked to recall old times, revered Emperor Nicholas the First, was an Old Believer by faith, read religious books, and raised canaries." According to Leskóv the comical distortions in the old storyteller's language were the result of his effort to imitate the conversational style of the social classes his characters represented. Not knowing just how tsars, courtiers, and Englishmen spoke in real life, the old gunsmith thought his characters would appear more lifelike if he made their speech as different as possible from his own everyday language.

Leskóv's account of the storyteller was so convincing that it backfired. The public was taken in completely and gave all the credit for the story to the old Túla gunsmith, not realizing that he was entirely the product of Leskóv's creative art. Leskóv was dismayed over losing the credit for his own story to a character he himself had put into it and wrote a letter to the leading Petersburg newspaper admitting that he had made up the whole account from beginning to end—Túla gunsmith, canaries, and all. And in subsequent editions of "The Steel Flea" he omitted the foreword containing his fictitious competitor.

However, even without the foreword and even though he is no longer mentioned, the old Túla gunsmith is still present. "The Steel Flea" is his story, told in his own preposterously original language; and only in the twentieth and final chapter does he retire, still unseen, to his religious books and his canaries and let Leskóv come forward with a bow to ring down the curtain.

The Russian language has no word for "malapropism," and there is no evidence that Leskóv had ever heard of Richard Sheridan or the play in

which he created the famous Mrs. Malaprop. Nevertheless, Russian malapropisms are the nails that hold the structure of "The Steel Flea" together.
The translator who turns this story into straightforward literary English,
taking no account of Leskóv's droll distortions of Russian, will convey
only a part of the meaning that lies in the Russian original.

The true malapropism, in Russian as in English, must fit the rhythm
and the sound pattern of the word it distorts. Its comic effect is achieved
through the incongruity between the meaning of the malapropism itself
and the meaning of the word intended by the speaker. For example, some
years ago in a university town in Pennsylvania there was a locally famous
handy man who was a direct descendant of Mrs. Malaprop. After the death
of a relative he told one of the university confessors: "But she didn't suffer
none—she just slipped into a trench and quietly passed away." Leskóv
would have understood that man.

Underneath the deceptive gaiety of Leskóv's prose there runs a caustic
commentary on Russian social and political life. Its effect is all the more
powerful because it is ironically placed in the mouth of a narrator who is
a staunch supporter of things as they are. This so-called *skaz* manner, the
device of telling a story through one of its characters and in his own
peculiar language, is the most prominent feature of Leskóv's storytelling
technique. He almost always uses it ironically; and his malapropisms and
other deformations of language reinforce his satire.

Much of the delight that generations of Russian readers have found in
"The Steel Flea" arises from the fact that Leskóv puts only a part of his
verbal effects out in plain view. He hides many others in the bushes of
innocent-looking prose or camouflages them to make them look so familiar
that the unsuspecting reader may pass them by completely before he
realizes that crafty old Leskóv has put one over on him again.

For the translator who ventures to turn "The Steel Flea" into English
it is not enough merely to find true English equivalents for Leskóv's malapropisms. He must also cultivate Leskóv's subtlety. If his translation of the
Russian verbal effects is so obvious that the reader becomes aware of them
all on his first trip through the story, then the translator has failed to
convey the full effect of Leskóv's wily genius.

THE STEEL FLEA

*(The Tale of the Cross-Eyed, Left-Handed
Gunsmith from Túla and the Steel Flea)*

CHAPTER ONE

When Emperor Alexander the First had finished the Council of Vienna
he decided he would like to take a trip around Europe and look at the
marvels in the different countries. He traveled through all the nations,
and everywhere his friendliness always helped him get into the most intimidating conversations with all kinds of people, and everybody would
amaze him with one thing or another and try to win him over to their
side. But along with him was the Don Cossack Plátov,[1] who didn't like
all this persuasion; he hankered to get back to his farm, and he kept trying
to talk the Emperor into going home. And if Plátov noticed the Emperor
getting really interested in something foreign, then just as soon as all the
guides stopped talking for a minute, Plátov would pop up and say this,
that, and the other, telling them ours at home was just as good, and one
way or another he would get their minds onto something else.

The Englishmen knew this, and they thought up all kinds of shifty
tricks for the Emperor's visit, so as to get him in their power with their
outlandishness and get his mind off the Russians, and in a lot of cases
they managed it, especially at their big meetings, where Plátov couldn't
say everything completely in French. But then he was not very much
interested in that, since he was a married man and looked on all French
conversations as trifles not worthy of serious imagination. And when the
Englishmen started inviting the Emperor into all their store houses, gun
works, and soapy-rope factories, so as to show how much better they were
than us in everything and then brag about it, Plátov said to himself:

"Well, this has gone far enough. I've put up with it so far, but I can't
take any more. Maybe I'll succeed and maybe I'll fail, but at least I won't
go back on my own people."

And he had no sooner said this to himself than the Emperor told him:

"Tomorrow you and I are going to look at their military museum. There
they've got such natures of perfection that just as soon as you've seen them
you'll agree that we Russians with our significance don't mean a thing."

25

Plátov said nothing in reply to the Emperor but just stuck his hump-backed nose down into his shaggy felt overcoat and went to his room. He told his orderly to get a bottle of Caucasian grape vodka out of their traveling supplies. He gulped down a big glassful, said his prayers before the folding traveling icon, covered himself with his overcoat, and started snoring such a tune that none of the Englishmen in the whole house could get any sleep.

He thought: "Wait until the morning light; it's always wiser than the night."

CHAPTER TWO

The next day the Emperor and Plátov went to the museums. The Emperor took none of his other Russians with him, because the carriage they gave him was only a two-sitter.

They came to a great big building, with an entrance beyond description, corridors beyond measure, and one room after another, until at last they came into the biggest hall of all, with tremendulous estuaries, and right in the middle, under a canoply, stood the Apollo Velvet Ear.

The Emperor glanced around sideways at Plátov to see what he was looking at and whether he was very much amazed; but Plátov was walking along with his eyes looking down at the ground as if he didn't see anything, and he was only winding his moustaches into rings.

The Englishmen started at once to show off all sorts of marvels and explain how everything in them was fitted together with everything else for military circumstances. There were nautical whether-meters, gamble-hair coats for the infantry, and waterproof rein coats for the cavalry. The Emperor was glad to see all this, and he thought everything looked very good; but Plátov held his impatience and said it all didn't mean a thing for him.

The Emperor said:

"How is that possible? How can you be so unfeeling? Doesn't anything at all impress you here?"

And Plátov replied:

"Just one thing impresses me here: my Don River boys fought without all this and drove out old Bony Part."

The Emperor said:

"That's just prejudunce."

Plátov answered:

"I don't know what to call it, but I ain't allowed to argue so I'll keep quiet."

The Englishmen, seeing this exchange between the Emperor, at once took him up to the statue of Apollo Velvet Ear itself and took a Mortimer rifle out of one hand and a pistol out of the other.

"Here's the kind of production we've got," they said, and they handed him the rifle.

The Emperor looked calmly at the Mortimer rifle, because he had some like it at home in his Summer Palace, and then they handed him the pistol and said:

"This is a pistol of unknown and inimitable workmanship. Our admiral snatched it off the belt of a robber chieftain at Candelabria."

The Emperor fastened his eyes on the pistol and couldn't get enough of looking at it.

He oh-ed and ah-ed something awful.

"Oh! Oh! Oh!" he says. "What do you know about that! How is it possible to do such fine work!" And he turned to Plátov and said to him in Russian: "Now if only I had just one craftsman like that in Russia I would be a very happy man; I'd be so proud I would make a nobleman of him on the spot."

At these words Plátov stuck his right hand into his big wide trousers and pulled out a gunsmith's screwdriver. The Englishmen said: "This won't come open," but Plátov, paying no attention to them, started tinkering with the gun-lock. He turned it once, he turned it twice—and the gun opened up. Plátov showed the Emperor the trigger, and right there in the crook was a Russian inscription: "Iván Moskvín in Túla Town."

The Englishmen were amazed and nudged each other:

"Uh-oh!" they said. "We slipped up that time."

But the Emperor said sadly to Plátov:

"Why did you have to embarrass them so much? Now I feel very sorry for them. Let's go."

They got into their two-sitter again and started off, and the Emperor went to a ball that evening, but Plátov downed a still bigger glass of grape vodka and slept the sound sleep of the Cossacks.

He had been glad to put the Englishmen to rout and attract contention to the Túla gunsmith, but he had been put out as well: why did the Emperor have to feel sorry for the Englishmen in a case like this?

"Why did the Emperor feel bad about it?" thought Plátov. "I can't figure it out at all." And in this consideration he got up twice, crossed himself, and drank vodka until at last he forced himself into a sound sleep.

At that same time the Englishmen were not asleep either, because their heads were spinning, too. While the Emperor was having a good time at the ball, they cooked up such a new marvel for him that they completely knocked the imagination out of Plátov.

CHAPTER THREE

The next day, when Plátov reported to the Emperor to say good morning, he told Plátov:

"Have the two-sitter carriage hitched up, and let's go to look at some more museums."

Plátov even made bold to ask the Emperor whether they hadn't looked at enough outlandish products, and wouldn't it be better to get ready to go back to Russia, but the Emperor said:

"No, I wish to see still other novelties here; they have boasted to me about how they make sugar of the very highest quality."

They started off.

The Englishmen showed everything to the Emperor—just how many different highest qualities they had—and Plátov looked and looked, and then suddenly he said:

"But won't you show us your factories where you make Molvó sugar?"

The Englishmen didn't know what "Molvó" was.[2] They whispered back and forth to each other, winked back and forth to each other, and repeated to each other: "Molvó, Molvó," but they couldn't understand what kind of sugar that was that we made in our country, and they had to admit that they had all kinds of sugar—but no "Molvó."

Plátov said:

"Well, then, you haven't got anything to brag about. Come to our country and we'll fill you full of tea with genuwine Molvó sugar from Bóbrinsky's[3] factory."

But the Emperor tugged him by the sleeve and said quietly:

"Now, please don't go and spoil my politics."

Then the Englishmen invited the Emperor to their very latest museum, where they had brought together mineral stones and nymphusorias from all over the world, beginning with the most enormous Egyptian hobble lists and coming down to the hide-bound flea, which you can't see with your eyes but can only feel when he bites you between your hide and your body.

The Emperor set out.

They looked at the hobble lists and all kinds of stuffed animals, and then came out and Plátov thought to himself:

"There now, thank the Lord, everything is turning out all right: the Emperor hasn't marveled at anything."

But as soon as they got to the very last room, there were workmen standing around in everyday jackets and aprons holding a tray that had nothing on it.

Then the Emperor really did marvel because they offered him an empty tray.

"What does this mean?" he asked, and the English craftsmen replied:

"This is our humble offering to your Highness."

"But what *is* it?"

"Well," they said, "does your Highness kindly see this little speck?"

The Emperor took a look and saw that there really was the tiniest little speck lying on the tray.

The workmen said:

"Be so kind as to spit on your finger and pick it up and put it on your hand."

"What good is that speck to me?"

"That," they answered, "is not a speck but a nymphusoria."

"Is it alive?"

"No, sir," they answered, "it's not alive. We made it in the shape of a flea out of pure English steel, and inside it is a motor and a spring. Be so kind as to wind it up with the key: then it will do a little *dansez*."

The Emperor got curious and asked:

"But where is the key?"

The Englishmen replied:

"Here is the key, right in front of your eyes."

"Then why can't I see it?" asked the Emperor.

"Because," they said, "you have to blow it up in a nitroscope."

A nitroscope was brought in, and the Emperor saw that a little key really was lying on the tray beside the flea.

"Be so kind as to take it in your hand," they said. "There's a hole in its belly for the key, and the key will take seven turns. Then it will start its *dansez*."

The Emperor could barely pick up the key and barely hold it in his fingers. He took hold of the flea with his other hand and hadn't hardly stuck the key in before he felt the whiskers move, and then the legs started working, and at last it suddenly jumped up and in one bound did a straight *dansez* and two fairiations to one side and then to the other, and danced like that through a whole cod drill in three fairiations.

The Emperor gave orders on the spot to give a million to the Englishmen in any kind of money they wanted—either in silver five-kopeck coins if they wished, or else in small bills.

The Englishmen asked for it in silver, because they couldn't make heads or tails out of paper money, and then right off they pulled another one of their shifty tricks: they handed over the flea as a gift, but they hadn't brought any case for it. Without a case you couldn't keep either the flea or the key, because they would get lost and thrown out with the trash. But they had made a case out of a diamond in the shape of a nut, with a hole dug out of the middle for the flea. They didn't make a gift of this, because they said the case was government property, and they are very strict over there about government property, even for the Emperor—you can't give it away.

Plátov was about to get hot under the collar, and he said:

"What's the idea of all this swindle! They gave us a gift and they got a million for it, and still that isn't enough! The case," he says, "always goes with such things as these."

But the Emperor said:

"Leave off, please, this isn't your affair—don't go and spoil my politics. They have their own customs." And he asked: "How much does that nut cost that the flea fits into?"

The Englishmen reckoned that would be five thousand more.

Emperor Alexander said, "Pay them," and put the flea in that nut himself, and the key along with it, and so as not to lose the nut he put it into his gold snuffbox, and he ordered the snuffbox put into his little traveling casket, which was all covered with the mother of pearl and fishbones. The Emperor dismissed the English workmen with honor and said to them: "You are the finest workmen in the whole world, and my men can't do anything compared to you."

They were very pleased with this, and Plátov could say nothing against the words of his Emperor. Only he took the nitroscope and slipped it in his pocket without saying anything, because "it goes with it," he says, "and you've taken a lot of money from us already."

The Emperor knew nothing about that till he got to Russia. They left right away, because military affairs had filled the Emperor with melancholy and he wanted to go to spiritual confession before Father Fedót in Taganróg.° On the way he and Plátov had a mighty unpleasant conversation, because they had entirely different ideas in their heads: the Emperor thought nobody could come up to the Englishmen in art, and Plátov begged to report that our people could make anything once they got a good look at it, only they didn't have any useful training. And he pointed out to the Emperor that the English workmen have completely different rules of life, science, and production for everything, and every man among them has all the absolute circumstances before him, and for that reason he has a completely different meaning.

The Emperor would not listen very long to that, and when Plátov saw this he didn't insist. So they rode along in silence, only Plátov would get out at every station and in his aggravation he would drink up a big glass of vodka, eat a little salt mutton, light up his enormous pipe, which was big enough to hold a whole pound of Zhúkov's tobacco, and then take his seat and sit without saying a word beside the Tsar in the carriage. The Emperor would look off in one direction, and Plátov would stick his chibouk out the other window and smoke into the wind. This was how

---

°"Father Fedót" was not made up out of thin air. Before his death in Taganróg Emperor Alexander the First did go to confession to the priest Alexéi *Fedótov*-Chekhóvsky, who was known after that as "Confessor to His Majesty" and loved to call everybody's attention to this completely chance occurrence. This *Fedótov*-Chekhóvsky is apparently the legendary "Father Fedót." *(Leskóv's note.)*

they rode all the way to Petersburg, and when the Emperor went on to see Father Fedót he didn't take Plátov at all.

"You," he said, "are intemperate in spiritual conversation, and you smoke so much that my head is full of soot from your pipe."

Plátov felt insulted and he lay down at home on his bed of ire, and just kept on lying there, smoking his Zhúkov tobacco without intercession.[4]

CHAPTER FOUR

The marvelous flea of blue English steel remained in Alexander the First's little fishbone casket until he died in Taganróg, after turning it over to Father Fedót to pass on to the Empress when she calmed down. Empress Elizabeth Alexéevna looked at the flea's fairiations and smiled, but she didn't take an interest in it.

"My affairs now," she said, "are widow's affairs, and no amusements can win my attention," and when she got back to Petersburg she handed over this wonder with all her other valuables as an inheritance for the new emperor.

In the beginning Tsar Nicholas the First also paid no attention to the flea, because there was trouble at the time he got up on the throne, but after that one day he started looking through the little casket that had come down to him from his brother, and he took out the snuffbox, and out of the snuffbox he took the diamond nut, and in it he found the steel flea, which had not been wound up in a long time and for that reason was not moving, but lay there quietly like it was numb.

The Emperor looked at it in amazement.

"What can this trifle be, and to what purpose did my brother preserve it in this way?"

The courtiers wanted to throw it out, but the Emperor said:

"No, this must mean something."

They called a druggist from the pharmacy effacing the Ánichkin Bridge, who weighed poisons in the very finest scales. They showed it to him, and he took the flea and put it on his tongue, and said: "I feel something cold, like strong metal." And then he mashed it a little with his teeth and announced:

"Say what you please, but this is not a genuine flea but a nymphusoria, and it is made of metal, and the work is not ours—not Russian."

The Emperor ordered that inquiries should be made at once about where it had come from and what it signified.

They plunged into an examination of the records and the lists, but nothing was written in the records. They began asking this one and that, but nobody knew anything. By good luck, though, Plátov the Don Cossack was still alive and even still lying on his bed of ire and smoking his pipe. As soon as he heard about all that disturbance at the Court, he rose up from his bed, threw down his pipe, and reported to the Emperor with all his decorations. The Emperor said:

"What need have you of me, courageous old man?"

And Plátov answered:

"I need nothing for myself, Your Majesty, since I eat and drink all I want and I'm satisfied with everything. But," he says, "I have come to report about that nymphusoria they found. This is the way it was," he says, "this is how it happened right before my eyes in England, and right here beside it is the key, and I've got their own nitroscope, that you can use to blow it up and look at it, and with this key you can wind up the nymphusoria through its belly, and it will hop around in any space you want and do fairiations to each side."

They wound it up, it began to jump, and Plátov said:

"You're right, Your Majesty," he says, "that the work is mighty fine and interesting, only it's not right for us to marvel at it with nothing but the rapture of our feelings. It ought to be submitted for Russian inspection at Túla or Sesterbék (at that time Sestrorétsk was still called Sesterbék), to see whether our craftsmen can't outdo it, so that the Englishmen won't keep lording it over us Russians."

Emperor Nicholas had great confidence in his Russian men and didn't like to yield to any foreigner, and so he answered Plátov:

"You speak well, courageous old man, and I charge you with the task of proving this matter. With all my cares I do not need this little box. You take it with you, and lie no more on your bed of ire, but go to the silent Don, and strike up intimidating conversations there with my Don people about their life and devotion and what is pleasing to them. And when you go through Túla, show this nymphusoria to my Túla craftsmen, that they may ponder over it. Tell them from me that my brother marveled at this thing, and he praised above all others the foreigners who made this nymphusoria, but I place my hope in my own people, that they are surpassed by no one. They will heed my word and will do something."

CHAPTER FIVE

Plátov took the steel flea, and when he went through Túla toward the Don, he showed it to the Túla gunsmiths and passed the Emperor's words on to them and then asked:

"Now what can we do about it, Orthodox brethren?"

The gunsmiths replied:

"Worthy old man, we feel the gracious word of the Emperor, and we never can forget it, because he puts his hope in his own people, but what we can do about it in this here case we can't say in just one minute, because the English nation ain't stupid either; they're even sort of cunning, and their art is full of horse sense. We mustn't go out after them till we've pondered about it and got God's blessing. Now, if you have confidence in us like the Emperor, then journey hence to your home upon the silent Don, and leave us this here little flea just like it is, in its case and in the golden snuffbox of the Tsar. Make yourself merry along the Don and heal the wounds you have suffered for our fatherland, and when you return through Túla, tarry and send for us: by that time, God willing, it may be that we'll have something thunk up."

Plátov was not completely satisfied because the Túla workmen demanded so much time and didn't talk very clearly about just what they hoped to make. He asked them this way and that, and using his Don Cossack cunning he talked with them in every sort of way, but the Túla men were no less cunning than he was, because they already had thought up such a plan that they couldn't really hope even Plátov would believe them, and they wanted to carry out their bold idea right away and then hand it over.

They said:

"Even we ourselves don't know yet what we'll do, but we'll only rest our faith in God and trust that the Tsar's word won't be put to shame through our doings."

Plátov kept twisting and turning this way and that, and so did the men from Túla.

Plátov wriggled and wriggled till he saw that he couldn't outwriggle a Túla man, and then he handed over the snuffbox with the nymphusoria and said:

"Well, there's nothing to do. Let it be your way," he says. "I know you—what kind you are. Still, there's nothing to do—I believe you. Only take care and don't try to swap diamonds on me, and don't spoil the fine English workmanship, and don't fool around very long, because I travel fast. Two weeks won't go by before I return again from the silent Don to Petersburg. At that time see to it that I have something to show the Emperor."

The gunsmiths reassured him completely:

"We ain't going to harm the fine workmanship," they said, "and we won't change diamonds on you, and two weeks are enough time for us, and by the time you come back you will have *something* worthy to be shown to his Imperial Splendor."

But exactly *what* it was they just wouldn't say.

CHAPTER SIX

Plátov departed from Túla; and three of the gunsmiths, the most skillful of them all—one of them a cross-eyed left-handed man with a birthmark on his cheek and bald spots on his temples where the hair had been pulled out when he was an apprentice—these three bade farewell to their fellow workmen and their families, and without saying anything to anybody they took their bags, put what food they needed into them, and disappeared from town.

The only thing anybody noticed was that they didn't go out through the Moscow gate but through the one on the other side, in the direction of Kíev, and people thought they had gone to Kíev to bow down before the saints resting there in peace or to take counsel with some of the holy men still alive there, who were always available in abundance in Kíev.

But this was only close to the truth and not the truth itself. Neither time nor distance allowed the Túla craftsmen in three weeks to walk to Kíev and then on top of that to make something that would put the English nation to shame. They might have done better to go and pray in Moscow, which was only "twice fifty miles away," and a good many holy saints rest in peace there too. In the other direction too it was "twice fifty miles" to Oryól, and then another good three hundred from Oryól to Kíev. You won't get over that much ground in a hurry, and even when you've done it you won't get rested in a hurry: for a long time your feet will feel as numb as glass and your hands will tremble.

Some people even thought the craftsmen had bragged a little too much to Plátov and then after they thought it over had got scared and run away for good, taking along the Tsar's gold snuffbox, and the diamond, and the English steel flea in its case that had brought them all the trouble.

However, this supposition too was completely unfounded, and was unworthy of the clever men on whom the hope of the nation now rested.

CHAPTER SEVEN

The inhabitants of Túla, who are intelligent people and knowledgeable about metal work, are also well known as the finest experts in religion. Their fame in this connection has spread all over their native land and has even reached Mount Athos: they are not only masters at singing their fancy trills; they also know how to paint the picture "Evening Bells," and if any of them dedicate themselves to greater service and enter monastic life, they become famous as the best managers of monastery household affairs, and they make the most capable collectors of alms. On holy Mount Athos everybody knows that the Túla inhabitants are a most remunerative people, and if it wasn't for them, most likely the dark corners of Russia would not see very many holy relics from the distant East, and Mount Athos would be deprived of many useful contributions from Russian generosity and piety. Today the "Túla men of Mount Athos" carry holy relics all over our native land and skillfully collect contributions even where there is nothing to collect. The Túla man is full of churchly piety and is highly practical in this matter, and so the three master craftsmen who took it on themselves to uphold Plátov, and with him all Russia, made no mistake when they headed south instead of toward Moscow. They didn't go to Kíev at all but to Mtsensk, to the district town of Oryól Province in which there stands the ancient "stone-graven" icon of Saint Nicholas, which was brought here in the most ancient times along the river Zúsha on a large cross, likewise made of stone. This icon is "awesome and most terrible" in appearance. The sainted archbishop of Myra in Lycia is represented on it full-length, clothed all over in silver-gilt clothing, swarthy of face and holding a temple in one hand and the sword of "Military Conquest" in the other. It was just this "Conquest" that held the meaning of the whole thing: Saint Nicholas in general and "Nicholas of Mtsensk" in particular was the patron saint of commerce and warfare, and so the Túla gunsmiths went to make their bows to him. They held their prayer service right in front of the icon, and then in front of the stone cross, and finally, returning home by night and saying nothing to anybody, they set about their work in awful secrecy. All three of them got together in Lefty's house; they locked the doors, boarded up the windows, lighted a lamp before the icon of Saint Nicholas, and started to work.

One day, two days, three days they sat without going out anywhere, all of them tapping away with their hammers. They were making something, but what it was they were making nobody knew.

Everyone was curious, but nobody could find out a thing, because the workmen said nothing and never stuck their noses outside. All sorts of people would go up to the little house and knock on the door with all sorts of excuses, to ask for fire or borrow some salt, but the three experts would not open up for any kind of request. Even how they got food nobody knew. People tried to scare them, and pretended that the house next door was on fire to see whether they wouldn't run out in fright and give away the secret of what they were making, but nothing could take in those shrewd workmen. Lefty stuck his head out only once and shouted: "Go ahead and burn up; we ain't got time," and then he drew in his plucked head, banged the shutters tight, and got to work again.

Through the tiny cracks people could only see the glitter of a light and hear the ringing blows of tiny hammers tapping on anvils.

In a word, the whole thing was handled in such awful secrecy that there was no way to find out anything about it, and it lasted right up to the return of the Cossack Plátov from the silent Don on his way to the Emperor, and during all that time the craftsmen saw nobody and said nothing.

CHAPTER EIGHT

Plátov traveled in great haste and ceremony: he himself sat in the carriage, and on the coach-boxes two Cossack scurriers holding whips sat on each side of the driver and poured it on him unmercifully so as to make him hurry. If either one of the Cossacks dozed off, Plátov would give him a kick from inside the carriage, and they would tear along even more wildly. These measures worked so well that there was no holding back the horses at a single station anywhere; they would always gallop on a hundred paces past the halting-place. Then the Cossack would work on the driver once more in the opposite direction, and they would go back to the entrance.

That was the way they rolled into Túla: there too at first they flew a hundred paces beyond the Moscow gate, and then the Cossack worked on the driver with his whip in the opposite direction, and at the entrance they started hitching up fresh horses. Plátov didn't get out of the carriage but only told his scurrier to go as fast as possible and get the craftsmen he had left the flea with.

One scurrier dashed off to get them to come as fast as possible and bring him the work that was to put the Englishmen to shame, and that scurrier had run only a short distance when Plátov sent first one and then another after him so as to speed things up.

He sent off all his scurriers and then began dispatching ordinary people from the curious crowd, and in impatience he even stuck his own legs out of the carriage and was about to start running impatiently himself, and he gritted his teeth because they were all so slow in coming into sight.

In those days everything had to be done just right and very fast, so as not to lose a minute that might be useful to Russia.

CHAPTER NINE

At that very moment the Túla craftsmen who were making the marvelous thing had finished their work. The scurriers ran up to them puffing and blowing, and the ordinary people from the curious crowd—well, they didn't even get there at all, because their legs, being out of practice, scattered and fell all along the way, and then in terror, for fear they might catch sight of Plátov, they lit out for home and hid wherever they could.

As soon as the scurriers ran up, they gave a shout, and when they saw that nobody opened up, they jerked at the bolts on the shutters, but the bolts were so strong they wouldn't give at all; they pulled at the doors, but the doors were fastened from the inside with heavy oak bars. Then the scurriers picked up a beam from the street and stuck it under the eave of the roof the way firemen do, and in one blow they prized the whole roof off the hut. But as soon as they got the roof off, they themselves keeled over, because the workmen with their unceasing labor in their crowded little shanty had expired so much that a man who wasn't used to it, coming right in when the wind was dead, instinkly choked.

The messengers cried out:

"What are you doing, you so-and-so's, you swine? What do you mean by knocking us over with that expiration? Or ain't you got any fear of

God left in you?"

And they answered:

"Just a minute, we're driving in the last nail, and as soon as we hammer it down we'll bring out our work."

The messengers said:

"He'll eat us alive before then and won't even leave our souls for the funeral."

But the craftsmen answered:

"He won't have time to gobble you up, because we drove the last nail in while you were standing there talking. Run and tell him we're bringing it right now."

The scurriers dashed off, but their hearts weren't in it, because they thought the craftsmen might fool them, and for that reason they ran and ran but kept looking back. But the craftsmen were coming along behind them, and they had hurried so fast they hadn't even got dressed quite the way they ought for a meeting with an important person, and while they ran they were still fastening the hooks of their kaftans. Two of them had nothing in their hands, but the third one, Lefty, had the Tsar's jewel casket wrapped in a green cloth cover with the English steel flea inside.

CHAPTER TEN

The scurriers ran up to Plátov and said:

"Here they are in person!"

Plátov barked at the craftsmen:

"Is it ready?"

"It's all ready," they answered.

"Give it here."

They handed it over.

The carriage was already hitched up, and the driver and postilion were in their places. The Cossacks at once took their seats beside the driver and raised their whips over his head and held them brandished there.

Plátov snatched off the green cover, opened the little casket, took the gold snuffbox out of its padding and the diamond nut out of the snuffbox. He saw the English flea lying there just the way it had before, and apart from it nothing else was there.

Plátov said:

"What's the meaning of this? Where is your work that you wanted to console the Emperor with?"

The gunsmiths answered:

"Our work is right there."

Plátov asked:

"What kind of work?"

The gunsmiths answered:

"What's the use of explaining? Everything is right there in front of your eyes. Just take a look at it."

Plátov squared his shoulders and shouted:

"Where's the key to the flea?"

"Why, it's right here," they answered. "Where the flea is, there the key is—in the same nut."

Plátov tried to take hold of the key, but his fingers were too stubby. He grabbed and grabbed but couldn't catch either the flea or the key to its bellyworks, and suddenly he burst out and started swearing with colorful Cossack words.

He shouted:

"You scoundrels, you've done nothing at all, and on top of it you've probably ruined the whole thing! I'll take off your heads!"

But the Túla men answered him:

"There ain't no use insulting us. From you, as the Emperor's messenger, we've got to put up with all insults, but just because you wouldn't trust us and thought we were the kind that would even cheat the Emperor hisself, we ain't going to tell you the secret of our work now; just be so kind as to take it to the Emperor, and he'll see what sort of men he's got in us, and whether we've done anything to make him ashamed of us."

Plátov shouted:

"You're lying, you scoundrels, and I won't let you get away from me like that. One of you will go with me to Petersburg, and there I'll get out of him what kind of scullduggery you've been up to."

And with this he reached out, grabbed the cross-eyed Lefty by the collar with his stubby fingers, so that all the hooks flew off his kazakin shirt, and pitched him into the carriage at his feet.

"Lie there like a puddle," he said, "till we get to Petersburg. You'll answer to me for all of them. And you," he said to the scurriers, "get a move on! Look sharp now, and see to it that I'm in Petersburg at the Emperor's the day after tomorrow!"

The craftsmen stuck their necks out for their comrade and asked how he could be taken away from them like that without his grasp port. Then he would have no way to get back! But instead of answering them Plátov just showed them his fist—a frightful one, all knotty and hacked apart and somehow grown back together again—and waving it in front of them he said: "There's a grasp port for you!"

And he said to his Cossacks:

"Let's go, boys!"

His Cossacks, drivers, and steeds all started working at once and they whisked Lefty away without his grasp port, and two days later, just as Plátov had ordered, they rolled up to the Emperor's palace, arriving at such a properly furious gallop that they drove right past the columns.

Plátov stood up, hooked on his decorations, and went in to the Emperor, telling his Cossack scurriers to keep watch at the entrance over cross-eyed Lefty.

CHAPTER ELEVEN

Plátov was afraid to report to the Emperor in person, because it was awful how noticeable and memorable Tsar Nicholas was—he never forgot anything. Plátov knew he was bound to ask him about the flea. And even though he was afraid of no enemy on earth, right here he got cold feet: he carried the little casket into the palace and very quietly laid it down in the hall behind the stove. With the box hidden he presented himself to the Emperor in his office and quickly began reporting on the intimidating conversations he'd had with the Cossacks on the silent Don. He figured he would try to keep the Emperor busy with this. Then if the Emperor remembered and started talking about the flea, he would have to hand it over and answer, but if the Emperor didn't say anything about it, he could just keep quiet. He would tell the Emperor's servant to hide the little casket and lock up Lefty in a fortress cell so as to keep him handy in case he might be needed.

But Emperor Nicholas forgot about nothing, and Plátov had barely finished about the intimidating conversations when he asked at once:

"And how about it—how did my Túla craftsmen justify themselves against the English nymphusoria?"

Plátov answered the way the matter looked to him.

"Your Majesty," he says, "the nymphusoria is still lying in that same space, and I have brought it back, but the Túla craftsmen couldn't make anything more marvelous."

The Emperor replied:

"You are a courageous old man, but what you report to me cannot be so."

Plátov tried to convince him and told him how the whole thing had happened, and when he got to the part where the Túla workmen asked him to show the flea to the Emperor, Tsar Nicholas slapped him on the back and said:

"Give it here. I know my men won't let me down. Something has been done here that is past all understanding."

CHAPTER TWELVE

They brought the little casket out from behind the stove, they took the cloth cover off, they opened the gold snuffbox and the diamond nut—and there the flea was, lying just the way it had before.

The Emperor took a look and said:

"What a misfortune!" But his faith in his Russian craftsmen didn't slacken, and he sent for his favorite daughter Alexandra and commanded her:

"You have slender fingers: hasten, take that little key and wind up the bellyworks of that nymphusoria."

The princess began to wind it up, and the flea at once started wiggling its whiskers, but it didn't move its feet. Alexandra pulled on the whole works, but still the nymphusoria wouldn't do a single *dansez* or fairiation, the way it used to.

Plátov turned green all over and shouted:

"Oh those rascally dogs! Now I understand why they wouldn't tell me anything. It's lucky I brought one of their blockheads along with me."

With these words he ran out to the entrance, grabbed Lefty by the hair, and began to swing him back and forth so hard that tufts of it started flying. When Plátov had stopped beating him, Lefty straightened himself out and said:

"That's the way all my hair got pulled out while I was an apprentice. I don't know what need there is now to go through all that again."

"That's because I'd counted on you and vouched for you," said Plátov, "and then you went and spoiled that rarity."

Lefty answered:

"We're mighty glad you vouched for us, and as for spoiling—we didn't spoil nothing. Just blow it up in your strongest nitroscope and take a look."

Plátov ran back to tell them about the nitroscope, but to Lefty he only warned:

"I'll give you this-that-and-the-other even yet."

He ordered the scurriers to twist Lefty's arms even harder behind his back, and he himself went up the steps, puffing and blowing and repeating the prayer, "Blessed Tsar's Most Blessed Mother, immaculate and pure," and so on, as needed. And the courtiers who were standing on the steps all turned their backs on him. They thought, "Plátov is done for now, and he'll soon be chased out of the palace," because they couldn't stand him on account of his bravery.

CHAPTER THIRTEEN

As soon as Plátov reported Lefty's words to the Emperor, he said full of joy:

"I know my Russian men will not let me down." And he ordered the nitroscope to be brought forward on a pillow.

The nitroscope was brought forward that very minute, and the Emperor took the flea and laid it under the glass, first on its belly, then on its side, and then on its back. In a word, it was turned in every direction, but nothing could be seen. Still the Emperor didn't lose faith even now. He only said:

"Bring hither at once that gunsmith who is waiting below."

Plátov reported:

"They'd have to dress him up. He's still got the clothes on he was caught in, and now he's in bad shape."

But the Emperor replied:

"Never mind; bring him in just as he is."

Plátov said:

"Come in here, now, you so-and-so, and answer to the Emperor before his eyes."

Lefty replied:

"Why, sure, I'll go like this and I'll answer."

He went like he was: in ragged boots, with one trouser-leg tucked in and the other dangling, with an old jacket that wouldn't fasten because the hooks were lost, and with the collar that was torn; but it didn't matter—he wasn't embarrassed.

"What of it?" he thought. "If the Emperor wants to see me, I've got to go, and if I ain't got a grasp port, it ain't my fault, and I'll tell him how it happened."

As soon as Lefty came in and bowed, the Emperor said to him:

"What does this mean, my good man? We have looked this way and that and have blown it up in the nitroscope and we still can't find anything remarkable."

Lefty answered:

"Did Your Majesty be so kind as to look at it the right way?"

The nobles motioned to him to tell him that was not the way to talk, but he didn't understand how to talk courtier language—with flattery or cunning—and he kept on talking simply.

The Emperor said to them:

"Stop making things complicated for him; let him answer as he knows how."

And then he explained to Lefty:

"This is the way we laid it," he says. And he put the flea under the nitroscope. "Look at it yourself," he says. "You can't see a thing."

Lefty answered:

"You can't see nothing that way, Your Majesty, because our work is a lot too secret for that size."

The Emperor asked:

"Then how *do* we manage it?"

"You have to put just one of its feet in detail under the whole nitroscope, and look one at a time at each foot it walks on."

"Goodness Gracious," said the Emperor. "That's powerfully small."

"But what else can you do," answered Lefty, "if that's the only way you can get a look at our work? Then you can see the whole amazement."

They laid it down the way Lefty said, and as soon as the Emperor looked in the upper glass, he beamed all over. He grabbed Lefty just the way he was—dirty, dusty, unwashed—and put his arms around him and kissed him on the cheek, and then he turned to all the courtiers and said:

"You see, I knew better than everybody that my Russians would not let me down. Just look: why, the rascals have taken the English flea and nailed flea-shoes on its feet!"

CHAPTER FOURTEEN

They all came up to look: all the flea's feet really were shod with genuine flea-shoes, and Lefty reported that this was not the only marvel.

"If you had a better nitroscope," he said, "one that would blow it up five million times, then you could be so kind as to see that a craftsman's name was put on each shoe, so as to show which Russian gunsmith made that shoe."

"Is your name there too?" asked the Emperor.

"No, sir," answered Lefty. "Mine is the only one that ain't."

"Why isn't it?"

"Because I did smaller work than these flea-shoes," he said. "I made the nails the shoes were fastened on with, and they are too small for any nitroscope to blow them up."

The Emperor asked:

"But where is your nitroscope, which you used to produce this marvel?"

Lefty answered:

"We are poor people—too poor to own a nitroscope, so we just sharpened our eyes."

Seeing that Lefty's business had turned out well, the other courtiers began to kiss him, and Plátov gave him a hundred rubles and said:

"Forgive me, brother, for dragging you around by the hair."

Lefty answered:

"God will forgive you—it ain't the first time that kind of snow has fallen on my head."

He would say no more—and he didn't even have time to say more, because the Emperor ordered the iron-shod nymphusoria to be packed up and sent back at once to England, as a sort of gift, to make them understand that it wasn't any marvel to us. And the Emperor ordered the flea to be carried by a special courier who was learned in all languages, and ordered the left-handed smith to go with him so that he himself could show their work to the Englishmen and show them what kind of craftsmen we have in Túla.

Plátov made the sign of the cross over him.

"Blessings be upon you," he said. "I'll send you some of my own grape vodka for the journey. Don't drink too little and don't drink too much—drink middlesome."

And so he did—he sent it.

Count Nestlebroad[5] gave orders to wash Lefty in the Túla Public Baths, cut his hair in a barber shop, and deck him out in the full-dress coat of a singer in the royal choir, so that he would look like he had some kind of paid government rank.

As soon as they had worked him over this way, they filled him with tea and Plátov's grape vodka, drew up his belt as tight as possible so that his guts wouldn't shake, and sent him off to London. That is when foreign sights started happening to Lefty.

CHAPTER FIFTEEN

The courier traveled powerfully fast with Lefty, so that they didn't stop to rest anywhere between Petersburg and London, but only drew their belts another notch tighter at every station, so that their guts wouldn't get mixed up with their lungs; but since Lefty on Plátov's orders was allotted as much government vodka as he wanted after he had been presented to the Emperor, he kept up his strength on this alone, without eating anything, and he sang Russian songs all the way through Europe—only adding a refrain of foreign words:

> *Aye loolee*
> *Say tray Joe Lee*

As soon as the courier got him to London, he reported to the proper authorities and handed over the box, and then put Lefty down in a hotel room; but there he soon began to get restless, and besides, he was hungry. He knocked on the door and pointed to his mouth when the servant came, and the servant took him right off to the feeding room.

Here Lefty sat down at a table and waited. He didn't know how to ask for anything in English. But then he figured it out: again he just tapped on the table with his finger and pointed to his mouth; the Englishmen guessed what he meant and served him, only they didn't always bring what he wanted. But he wouldn't take anything that didn't suit him. They brought him their kind of hot glum pudding in flames. He said: "I don't see how anybody can eat that," and he wouldn't take a bite. They exchanged it for him and brought him something else to eat. He wouldn't drink their vodka, either, because it was green—like they had flavored it with sulfuric acid. He picked out the plainest stuff they had, and waited in the cool with his canteen for the courier.

And the people the courier had handed the nymphusoria over to looked at it that very minute through their strongest nitroscope and sent a description right off to a calumnist on the *Daily Telegraft,* so that he could tell everybody about it the very next day.

"And as for that craftsman," they said, "we want to see him at once."

The courier took them to the hotel room and from there to the feeding room, where our Lefty had begun to glow very decently, and said: "There he is."

The Englishmen slapped Lefty on the back right away and took him by the hands just like their own equal. "Comrade," they said, "comrade, you're a good craftsman. We'll talk to you afterwards when there is time, but now we want to drink to your prosperity."

They ordered a lot of wine and gave Lefty the first glass, but out of politeness he wouldn't be the first to drink. He thought: "Maybe you're so aggravated you want to poison me."

"No," he said, "that's not the way to do it. Even with a Polish thirst, you have to let the host drink first. You yourselves drink on ahead."

The Englishmen tasted all their wines in front of him and then started filling his glass. He stood up, crossed himself with his left hand, and drank to the health of them all.

They noticed that he had crossed himself with his left hand, and they asked the courier:

"What is he—a Lutheranian or a Protesterian?"

The courier answered:

"He's not either a Lutheranian or a Protesterian; he belongs to the Russian faith."

"But why does he cross himself with his left hand?"

The courier replied:

"He's a left-handed man, and he does everything with his left hand."

The Englishmen marveled even more and started pumping both Lefty and the courier full of wine, and kept on this way for three whole days, and then they said: "Now that's enough." They symphonied some water out of a bottle with impressed air, and when they were refreshed all over they started asking Lefty all about where had he studied, and what had he studied, and how far had he gone in arithmetic.

Lefty answered:

"Our learning is simple—according to the Psalter and the *Dream-Book.* We don't know no arithmetic at all."

The Englishmen looked at each other and said:

"That's amazing."

And Lefty answered:

"It's that way all over in our country."

"But what sort of book is that in Russia," they asked, "that dream-book?"

"That book," he said, "refers to if King David didn't reveal some fortune-telling clearly in the Psalter, then you can get some extra fortunes out of the *Dream-Book*."

They said:

"That's too bad. It would be better if you at least knew the four rules of arithmetic; that would be a lot more utilifying to you than your whole *Dream-Book*. Then you would be able to understand that every machine has its balance of forces. As it is, even though you are mighty skillful with your hands, you didn't realize that such a little machine as the one in the nymphusoria was calculated for the most accurate exactness, and it can't carry the flea-shoes. That's why the nymphusoria won't jump or dance any *dansez*."

Lefty agreed.

"About that there ain't no argument," he said. "We didn't get very far in book-learning, but only faithfully serve our fatherland."

And the Englishmen said to him:

"Stay here with us; we'll give you a big education and you'll turn out to be a superbluous craftsman."

But Lefty wouldn't agree.

"I've got my parents at home," he said.

The Englishmen offered to send his parents money, but Lefty wouldn't take it.

"We are devoted to our country," he said, "and my daddy's an old man and my mother's an old woman, and they're used to going to church in their own parish, and it would be mighty lonely here for me all by myself, because I'm still a bachelor by calling."

"You'll get used to it," they said. "You'll accept our laws, and we'll get you married."

"That can never be," answered Lefty.

"Why not?"

"Because," he answered, "our Russian faith is the rightest one, and the way our forefathers believed is just the way their dissentants have to believe."

"You don't know our faith," said the Englishmen. "We've got the same Christian law and hold to the same Gospel."

"It's true," said Lefty, "that everybody's got the same Gospel, but *our* books are thicker than yours, and our faith is fuller."

"How can you judge that way?"

"We've got all the evident proofs of it," he answered.

"What kind?"

"Why, we've got God-wondering icons and prism-working relics, and you ain't got nothing—except for Sunday you ain't even got any special holidays. And the second reason is that even if I was married in the law to an English girl it would be confusing to live with her."

"How's that?" they asked. "Don't turn up your nose at our girls—they too dress neatly and they're good housekeepers."

But Lefty said:

"I don't know them."

The Englishmen replied:

"That's no problem—you'll get to know them. We'll fix up a roundy-view for you."

Lefty started blushing.

"What's the use of stringing the girls along for no reason?" he said, and he wouldn't budge. "That's something for fine gentlemen. It wouldn't suit us. And if they found out about it at home, in Túla, they'd make fun of me something awful."

The Englishmen got curious:

"Then suppose we did it without a roundy-view," they said. "How do you manage in your country so as to make a favorable choice?"

Lefty explained our way to them.

"In our country," he said, "when a man wants to reveal a circumstantial intention in regard to a girl, he sends over a conversational woman, and when she has made a preposition, they politely go to the house together and look the girl over without concealment, and in front of all the relationships."

They understood, but they answered that they had no conversational women and followed no such custom, and Lefty said:

"That's all the better, because if you go in for that kind of thing you have to do it with a circumstantial intention, and since I don't feel none towards a foreign nation, what's the use of stringing the girls along?"

The Englishmen were pleased with him for these opinions too, and so they started off again in their friendly way, slapping him on the back and the knees, and they asked:

"Just out of curiosity," they said, "we'd like to know what signs of defects you've noticed in our girls, and why you keep away from them?"

At this Lefty answered them frankly:

"I don't mean to run them down; I just don't like the way their dresses sort of swish back and forth, so that you can't make out just what they've got on and what it's for. There'll be one thing here, and below something else will be pinned on, and on their arms they'll have some kind of socks. In them velveteen coats of theirs they look just like capuchin monkeys."

The Englishmen laughed and said:

"Why does that get in your way?"

"It don't get in my way," answered Lefty, "only I'm scared I'd be ashamed to look and wait until she got untangled from all that stuff."

"But do you really think your fashions are better?" they asked.

"Our fashions in Túla," he replied, "are simple: every girl is dressed in her own lace. Our lace is worn even by fine ladies."

Then they showed him off to their own ladies, and there they served him tea and asked him:

"What are you frowning for?"

He answered that "we ain't used to drinking it so sweet."

Then they served it to him in the Russian way, with a lump of sugar to suck.

This didn't seem to be as good to them, but Lefty said:

"To our taste this way it's tastier."

The Englishmen couldn't find any bait at all that could make him take to their life. They could only talk him into staying with them for a short while as their guest, and said they would take him to all sorts of factories and show him all their arts.

And after that, they said, they would put him on their own ship and "deliver him safe and sound in Petersburg."

He agreed to that.

CHAPTER SIXTEEN

The Englishmen took charge of Lefty and sent the Russian courier back to Russia. Even though the courier had government rank and was learned in various languages, they weren't interested in him, but they *were* interested in Lefty, and they set out to take Lefty around and show him everything. He looked at all their production: he really liked their metallic mills and their soapy-rope factories, and the way they managed things— especially the way they took care of their workers. Every one of their workmen was always well fed, none was dressed in rags, each one had on a capable everyday jacket and wore thick hard-nail boots with iron caps, so that he wouldn't stump his toes anywhere on anything. Along with his work he got teaching instead of beatings, and he worked with comprehension. In front of each one, hung up right in full view, was a stultification table, and within arm's reach was a racing slate. Whatever any craftsman did, he would look up at the tables, and then check it with comprehension, and then write one thing down on the slate, race another thing, and put it together accurately: whatever was written down in the figures really came out that way. And when a holiday came, they would all get together in couples, each one would take a walking stick in his hand, and they would go for a walk in a proper way, all proud and polite.

Lefty got a good look at all their life and all their work, but above all else he paid attention to something that surprised the Englishmen a lot. He wasn't interested so much in how they made new rifles as in how they took care of the old ones. He would walk around everything and praise it and say:

"We can do that too."

But whenever he came to an old rifle, he would stick his finger in the barrel, rub it around inside, and sigh:

"That is way yonder better than ours."

The Englishmen couldn't figure out what Lefty noticed. He asked them:

"Might I know whether or not our generals have ever looked at this?"

They answered:

"Those who have been here must have taken a look."

"But when they were here," he asked, "did they have gloves on or not?"

"Yours are full-dress generals," they said. "Gloves come with them, so they must have had them on here."

Lefty said nothing. But suddenly he began to feel an uneasy homesickness. He pined away and pined away and said to the Englishmen:

"I thank you kindly for your entertainment, and I like everything in your country, and I've seen everything I needed to see—and now I'd like to go home in a hurry."

They couldn't hold him back any longer. There was no way to let him go by land because he didn't know all languages, and it was a bad time to go by sea because it was the fall of the year and stormy, but he insisted: "Let me go."

"We've looked at the whether meter," they said. "A storm is coming; you could drown; after all, this is not like your Gulf of Finland—this is the real Militerranean Sea."

"It's all the same where a man dies," he answered. "It's all God's will alone, and I want to get back home in a hurry; because if I don't, I might get a kind of craziness in the head."

They couldn't hold him back by force. They fed him till he creaked, they rewarded him with money, they gave him an alarmed gold watch as a souvenir, and for the cold weather at sea on the late fall voyage they gave him a woolen overcoat with a windy hurricane hat for his head. They dressed him warmly and took him down to the ship that was sailing for Russia. There they gave Lefty the very best cabin, like a real nobleman, but he felt ashamed and didn't like to sit shut up with the other gentlemen, and he would go up on deck and sit down under the tar poling and ask: "Where is our Russia?"

The Englishman he asked would point or nod off in that direction, and then Lefty would turn his head that way and impatiently look for his native land.

When they sailed out of the bay into the Militerranean Sea, his longing for Russia became so strong that there was no way to calm him down. The rolling and pitching was awful, but Lefty still wouldn't go down to his cabin; he sat under the tar poling, pulled his hurricane hat down over his eyes, and kept looking toward his homeland.

Often the Englishmen would come up and invite him to a warm spot down below, and he even began to lie his way out so that they would stop bothering him.

"No," he would answer. "I feel better out here; if I went inside with all this rolling and pitching the sea wretch would get me."

And so the whole time he would never go below until he had to for special reasons, and because of this the thirst mate took a liking to him. This thirst mate, to the misfortune of our Lefty, knew how to talk Russian, and he couldn't get over marveling that a Russian landlubber could hold out like that through all the rough weather.

"Good lad, Russ!" he said. "Let's take a drink!"

Lefty took a drink.

And the thirst mate said:

"Another one!"

So Lefty took another one, and they drank themselves tight.

The thirst mate asked him:

"What kind of secret is it you're taking to Russia from our country?"

Lefty answered:

"That's my business."

"Well, if that's the way it is," answered the thirst mate, "then let me make an English bet with you."

Lefty asked:

"What kind?"

"That we'll never drink alone and will always drink the same—one just as much as the other—and whoever drinks the other one down will win."

Lefty thought: "Dark skies, bellies rise; the boredom's strong and the way is long. We still can't see the homeland beyond the waves—it *will* be merrier after all to make the bet."

"All right," he said. "It's a bet."

"Only let it be honest."

"As far as that goes," he said, "you ain't got no worry."

They agreed and shook hands on it.

CHAPTER SEVENTEEN

Their bet began in the Militerranean Sea, and they drank all the way to the Riga Dünamünde,[6] but they ran neck and neck, and neither one fell behind the other, and they kept so strictly even with each other that when one of them looked down into the sea and saw a devil climbing up out of the water, the very same thing immediately appeared to the other one. Only, the thirst mate saw a red-headed devil, and Lefty claimed it was dark, like a blackamoor.

Lefty said:

"Cross yourself and turn away; that's a devil from the deep."

But the Englishman argued that it was only a "deep-sea driver."

"If you want me to," he said, "I'll pitch you overboard. Don't be afraid—he'll bring you right back to me."

And Lefty answered:

"If that's true, then pitch me over."

The thirst mate picked him up by the shoulders and carried him to the rail.

The sailors saw this and stopped them and reported it to the captain. He ordered them both to be locked up below and kept on rations of rum and wine and cold food, so that they could both eat and drink and stick to their bet, but he gave orders that they were not to get any hot glum pudding in flames, for fear the spirits in their innards might catch fire.

So they traveled locked up all the way to Petersburg, and neither one of them won the bet. There they were spread out in separate sleighs, and the Englishman was sent to the embassy on the English quay and Lefty to the police station.

From this point their destinies became very different.

CHAPTER EIGHTEEN

When the Englishman was brought to the Ambassador's house, they at once called in a doctor and a druggist for him. The doctor ordered him put into a warm bath on the spot, and the druggist right away rolled up a gutta-percha pill and personally stuck it in his mouth, and then both of them together took and laid him on a feather bed and covered him over with a fur coat and left him to sweat; and to keep anyone from disturbing him the order was sent out through the whole embassy to let nobody sneeze. The doctor and the druggist waited till the thirst mate went to sleep, and then they made another gutta-percha pill for him, laid it on a little table at the head of his bed, and went off.

But at the police station they threw Lefty on the floor and started questioning him:

"Who was he, and where was he from, and did he have a grasp port or any other kind of document?"

But he was so weak from his illness and the drinking and the rolling and pitching that he didn't answer a word, but only groaned.

Then they searched him right away, relieved him of his colorful clothes and his alarmed watch, and fleeced him of his money; and the police officer gave orders that the first passing sleigh-driver should take him free to the hospital.

The policeman took Lefty out to put him into a sleigh, but for a long time he couldn't catch a single one, because sleigh-drivers avoid policemen. Lefty was lying all this time on the cold depravement. Then the policeman caught a sleigh-driver, only, one without a warm fur lap-robe, because in cases like that they hide the fur lap-robe by sitting on it, in order to make policemen's feet freeze faster. So they carried Lefty in an open sleigh, and whenever they transferred him from one sleigh to another they would keep dropping him, and when they picked him up they would pull his ears to make him come to. They got him to one hospital, but there they wouldn't accept him without a grasp port; they took him to another, and they wouldn't accept him there either; and then to a third, and a fourth. All night long they kept dragging him through all the little winding alleys and transferring him over and over, until he was half dead. Then one doctor's assistant told the policeman to take him to the Obúkhvin Public Hospital, where everybody of unknown social class was taken in to die.

There they gave orders to write out a receipt and deposit Lefty on the floor in the corridor till they could inspect him.

And at that very same time the next day the English thirst mate got up, swallowed the second gutta-percha pill down to his innards, ate a light breakfast of chicken and rice, took a drink of impressed air, and said:

"Where is my Russian buddy? I'm going to look for him."

He got dressed and off he ran.

CHAPTER NINETEEN

In some amazing way the thirst mate found Lefty very quickly; only, they hadn't yet put him on a bed. He was still lying in the hall on the floor, and he complained to the Englishman.

"I've just got to have two words with the Emperor," he said.

The Englishman ran off to Count Kleinmichel[7] and ripped and roared:

"Really, now, this is the limit!" he said. "Though only a sheepskin coat it be, in its wearer a human soul we see."

For this statement the Englishman was turned out at once, so that he shouldn't dare mention the human soul again. After that somebody said to him: "You'd do better to go around to Plátov the Cossack; he's got simple feelings."

The Englishman got hold of Plátov, who by this time was lying again on his bed. Plátov listened to his story and remembered Lefty.

"Why, of course, brother," he said. "I know him very well. I've even dragged him around by the hair. Only, I don't know how I can help him in this kind of trouble, because I've served out my time and got a full apple plexy—now they don't pay attention to me any more. But you just run over to the Commandant Skóbelev;[8] he's in full force, and he's also had experience in this line—he'll do something."

The thirst mate went to Skóbelev and told all about what sort of illness Lefty had and how it had happened. Skóbelev said:

"I understand that illness; only, the Germans don't know how to treat it; here you have to have some kind of doctor from the spiritual profession, because they have grown up with these cases and they can help; I'll send over the Russian doctor Martýn-Sólsky right away." [9]

But when Martýn-Sólsky got there, Lefty was already dying, because he had cracked open the back of his head when they dropped him on the cold depravement; and he was able to say only one thing clearly:

"Tell the Emperor that the English don't clean their rifles with brick dust, and we must stop it too, or else God save us from a war, because they won't be any good for shooting."

And with this loyalty Lefty crossed himself and kicked the bucket.

Martýn-Sólsky went out at once and reported this to Count Chernyshóv,[10] so that he could tell the Emperor, but Count Chernyshóv shouted at him:

"Look here now," he said, "your job is laxatives and purgatives. Don't stick your nose into other people's business: in Russia we've got generals for that."

So nothing was said to the Emperor, and the cleaning went on in the same old way right up to the Crimean War. At that time when they started loading their rifles, the bullets just rattled around in them, because the barrels had been cleaned out with brick dust.

Then Martýn-Sólsky reminded Count Chernyshóv about Lefty, and Count Chernyshóv said:

"Go to the devil, you public enema, and don't stick your nose into other people's business or I'll deny I ever heard about that from you, and then you yourself will catch it."

Martýn-Sólsky thought: "And he really will deny it." So he kept quiet.

But if only they had reported Lefty's words in time to the Emperor, the war against the enemy in Crimea would have taken an entirely different turn.

CHAPTER TWENTY

Now all this is "affairs of long-gone days" and "traditions of yore," [11] even though this yore is not very old. But there is no need to be hasty about forgetting these traditions, despite the incredible nature of the legend and the epic character of its principal hero. Lefty's real name, like the names of many of the greatest geniuses, has been lost to posterity forever; but he is interesting as the embodiment of a myth in the popular imagination, and his adventures can serve to remind us of an epoch whose general spirit has been portrayed here clearly and accurately.

It goes without saying that Túla no longer has such master craftsmen as the legendary Lefty: machines have evened up the inequalities in gifts and talents, and genius no longer strains itself in a struggle against diligence and exactness. Even though they encourage the raising of salaries, machines do not encourage artistic daring, which sometimes went so far beyond ordinary bounds as to inspire the folk imagination to create unbelievable legends like this one.

The workmen, of course, can appreciate the advantages they have gained through practical applications of mechanical science, but they still recall those olden times with pride and affection. These memories are their epic—an epic that has a genuinely "human soul."

NOTES FOR "THE STEEL FLEA"

[1] Matvéi Ivánovich Plátov (1751–1818) was a historical figure, a general in the Russian army and a Cossack hetman, who actually accompanied Emperor Alexander I to London.

[2] At the beginning of the nineteenth century there was a sugar factory in Petersburg owned by a certain Ya. N. Molvó. Apparently this name was a Russified form of the French name Mollevaut. If this supposition is true, then the irony of Plátov's patriotic Russian defense of "Mollevaut" sugar becomes all the sweeter.

[3] Count A. A. Bóbrinsky owned a sugar refinery in southern Russia during the 1830's.

[4] Zhúkov tobacco, a popular brand in Russia during the first half of the nineteenth century, was manufactured in Petersburg in a factory owned by Vasíly Zhúkov.

[5] Count Karl Vasílyevich Nésselrode (1780–1862) was Minister of Foreign Affairs from 1822 to 1856.

[6] A port town at the mouth of the Western Dvina river.

[7] Count Peter Andréevich Kleinmichel (1793–1869) served from 1842 to 1855 as Chief Administrator of Highways and Public Buildings.

[8] General Iván Nikítich Skóbelev (1778–1849), was commandant in 1839 of the Fortress of Peter and Paul in Petersburg, which was used as a prison.

[9] Martýn Dmítrievich Sólski (1798–1881) was an army doctor and a member of the medical council of the Ministry of Internal Affairs.

[10] Alexander Ivánovich Chernyshóv (1786–1857) served as Minister of War from 1827 to 1852.

[11] Echoes of Púshkin's poem "Ruslán i Lyudmíla."

NOTE TO "THE ARCHBISHOP AND THE ENGLISHMAN"

This little story was first published in 1878 as one of a series of apparently innocent sketches that Leskóv wrote under the general heading of *Trifles from the Life of Archbishops*. When they were published in book form in 1879, Leskóv wrote a preface for them in which he declared that he had tried to say something "in *defense* of our ecclesiastical rulers, who find no other defenders than narrow and one-sided persons in whose opinion any statement at all about archbishops is an affront to their dignity."

Leskóv's lively sketches in "defense" of archbishops scaled them down to such human proportions that few of them got through his defense unscathed. In 1889, when he attempted to republish the sketches in Volume Six of his collected works, the volume was condemned by both the civil and the ecclesiastical censors and the whole printing of 2200 copies was confiscated. Apparently no more than eight complete copies escaped when the stock was burned by order of the censors in 1893. Even the earlier editions were not permitted to circulate in public libraries until after the 1905 Revolution, and in 1891 a cadet in a military school was placed under arrest when an officer reported that he possessed a copy of *Trifles from the Life of Archbishops*. The complete work was not republished until 1957, seventy-seven years after the last complete edition of 1880.

Despite the furor it created among high officials of church and state, *Trifles from the Life of Archbishops* was by no means an attack upon either religion or Orthodoxy. The real targets of Leskóv's satire were the unchristian vices that almost invariably creep in and corrupt even Christians when they get into positions of power. There were humble members of the lower ranks in the Orthodox hierarchy who welcomed Leskóv's book, and he claimed that even one archbishop had criticized him for representing the archbishops as "better than they are in actual fact."

"The Archbishop and the Englishman" is a typical example of Leskóv's effort to achieve verisimilitude by deliberately erasing the line that separates fact from fiction. Whether this story actually happened—and it is quite possible that it did—is almost beside the point. What is important is that Leskóv deliberately sets out to make us believe it happened.

Nothing that Leskóv ever wrote about his Scottish uncle illustrates so clearly as this story just how important a role the Scott family played in the formation of Leskóv's intellect. Alexander Scott's encounter with Varlaám was more than the amusing collision of an arrogant archbishop with an independent-minded Scot. In the eyes of Scott's young Russian nephew from Oryól Province it took on the proportions of a confrontation between Russian and British culture.

"The Archbishop and the Englishman" is the title given by the translator to Chapter III of *Trifles from the Life of Archbishops.*

THE ARCHBISHOP AND
THE ENGLISHMAN

A chapter out of
Trifles from the Life of Archbishops

One of my aunts was married to an Englishman named Scott, who managed the enormous estates of the Counts Peróvski, in the eastern part of Russia. The Englishman Scott was a man of great nobility and kindness, but he had his peculiarities. He was very courteous, but if he met with rudeness and effrontery on the part of anybody at all, he would never let the man get away with it. Even as a youth in Oryól Province he had an incident with a certain colonel in the cavalry, to whom Scott gave a thrashing, pure and simple, for his insolence. In this respect he did not change even with the approach of old age. When I lived in Pénza Province, at the time when he was sixty years old, he challenged Arápov, the provincial marshal of the nobility, to a duel, and Arápov took fright. Only death prevented Scott from settling his accounts with Arápov. Today they are both dead.

Once in summer—now I don't remember just which year—Uncle Scott, who built the *first* steam mill in Pénza Province, bought in the village of K. some enormous French millstones for it, which had been made in pieces and then welded together with strong metal bands. We were very reluctant to take them apart and have to weld them back again. We decided to roll them along in one piece, and we sent specially prepared equipment, horses, and men to do it; but suddenly we received news that our stones had scarcely rolled six miles from K. when they *broke through a bridge* and settled on the piles below.

Scott and I set off at once for the site of the accident, and arriving late in the evening at K., we stayed overnight in the home of the local priest, then still a very young man, who was both glad and sad to see us. Because of his good personal relations with Scott he welcomed us very cordially, but he was anxious and upset because the Right Reverend Varlaám, who at that season was making a tour of his diocese, had stopped for the night only six miles from K. and was to descend upon him the next day with that whole horde of guides whom Peter the Great in his regulation on church affairs had called "insatiable swine." The priest, of course, had reason to be worried: he had to provide both food and lodging for "those insatiable swine." He was especially troubled by the second, since his little village house was very small, and the damaged bridge with the mill-stones stuck in the piling gave no hope at all that the archbishop's car-riage could soon be transported to the other side of the stream.

To a certain extent we were responsible for the priest's distressing com-plications. We felt this, too, but there was no way for us to help him except by not laying claim to the hospitality of his house, which was already pre-pared for "His Eminence"; and so we settled down for the night in the hayloft. We got up the next day at the crack of dawn and went down to the broken bridge, which there was no hope of repairing until we found some way to pull out the millstone that was stuck fast in a hole in the planking, between the supports.

It turned out, however, to be completely impossible to remove the stone, and after thinking it over a great deal we decided to cut through the iron bands that held it in one piece, after which it would come apart and the pieces would fall into the brook. Then we would have to drag them out and carry them across on handcarts.

After giving orders for this work and leaving our men there on the job, we went back to the priest's house about ten o'clock in the morning, went bathing in the river, ate some fried eggs, and, all tired out, tumbled into the hayloft and went to sleep. But we were scarcely asleep when suddenly there arose a great clamor: we were awakened by the deafening sound of bells that poured forth over the parish house, and by the shout: "He's coming! He's coming! The archbishop is coming!"

It was very curious to observe just how "he was coming."

Still only half-awake, with tousled heads, sleepy faces, and in our damp and muddy traveling clothes, we went out to the wicket-gate and saw that he was coming rather poorly—astride Shank's mare. To put it bluntly, *he was walking*, because his carriage had not been able to get across the bridge. The worthy reverend walked along surrounded by a crowd of some twenty clerics and members of the laity, among whom two old peasant women were particularly remarkable. One of these zealous Chris-tians kept spreading a towel out in front of the reverend and he would step on it for her satisfaction, while the other woman was even more pious and kept trying to throw herself down before his feet, very likely in order that the reverend father should walk on her; but he did not grant her this pleasure. He himself was a person with a reddish, hemorrhoidal face, in which there flashed two angry little gray eyes, separated by a thick, cudgel-shaped nose. In the whole appearance of the archbishop there was not only nothing saintly; there was not even anything imposing. He appeared merely pained and angry. His troubled countenance seemed to be asking each and all: "What is the meaning of this? Why is it that *I* have to walk?"

Uncle Scott was a religious man and even went to the Russian church, to which his wife and children belonged; but unfortunately at that time he had it in for archbishops. This had come about because of an incident that had taken place not long before with the daughter of his British friends, Miss Sp--ng. What had happened was that Miss Sp--ng had become ill while visiting friends of hers and ours in Oryól Province, and since she was a religious girl she had sent for the only ecclesiastic in the village—the parish priest. And the good country father had not only anointed her with consecrated oil and given her the sacraments but had also anointed all this into her papers, that is, he had inserted an inscription about this in her passport.

Meanwhile, after the last sacraments had been performed over the dying Miss Sp--ng, she not only got well but soon became engaged to the son of the well-known English merchant in Moscow, Mr. L--vy. And then, when the time came for the wedding, the English pastor in Moscow came upon a most unexpected surprise: the bride turned out to be "Orthodox"! Both of the English families, and the whole English parish in Moscow, were unable to account for this circumstance and found themselves in the most bewildering confusion and horror. Then the pastor and my uncle went to Metropolitan Filarét Drozdóv[1] and asked him to "give back" the English girl who had been joined to the Orthodox Church without knowing it, but the Metropolitan refused. Then they straightened the matter out another way—much more easily and simply. Their sorrow was assuaged in this case by a certain Moscow policeman, who pointed out a way to transfer the Orthodoxicated bride back to her old heretical Anglicanism. His secret consisted, as far as I recall, in merely *losing* the English girl's passport with its inscription about her salvation through Orthodoxy, and then requesting a new one—in which there would be no inscription about her salvation. And so she was married off as "allegedly an Englishwoman," although the blessings of Orthodoxy have naturally continued to rest upon her up to this very day. But just the same, the Moscow English inhabitants of Leóntyev Lane[2] became furious over all this trouble, and my Uncle Scott, according to his words, was "down on archbishops," and he swore he would never have anything further to do with them. However, the following incident forced him to break his word.

We knew a little about the local Pénza archbishop, Varlaám, but what we knew was chiefly comical.[3] He was distinguished for his independence in manhandling his subordinates, and in general he showed a variety of eccentricities. For example, he kept the cathedral archpriest O--n in his own bedroom for a whole winter so as to break that old man from the habit of taking snuff even at night. It is true that the obituary-writers say various things about that archbishop, but in Pénza he had the reputation of being rude, arbitrary, and annoying.

Needless to say, we were not particularly interested in him at all, but now we felt like taking a look to see whether he might not reveal some wondrous eccentricity in this case. And so my Uncle Scott and I followed the procession into the church, not expecting, of course, that His Eminence would try to lord it over one of us.

When we entered the church, the archbishop, dissatisfied with his journey, was up at the altar raking somebody over the coals, and he was shouting so interestingly that we tried to get closer and walked over and stood in the left choir. The middle doors in the iconostasis were open, and we clearly heard the words: "Dog! Fool! Blockhead!" which seemed to be falling principally on the head of the chief priest, but perhaps in part also upon other personages of the cloth. Then at last, having inspected everything and given all his orders in the altar-room, the archbishop came out in front of the iconostasis, where the cantor and two or three other clerics were standing. The wife of the chief priest was also standing there, having come to ask His Eminence to tea.

The archbishop was still scowling; and giving his hand in blessing to everybody, he asked each one in turn: "Whose man is that?" or "Whose man are you?" And after giving out all these blessings he answered the low bow and greetings of the priest's wife with:

"Be off, now, and get ready. I'll come along."

Then he turned unexpectedly to us, standing meekly in the left choir, and called out with a roar:

"And what are you? Whose men are you? Why don't you say something, you old codger, there?"

My Englishman started wagging his head, which was usually a sign that he was dissatisfied, and suddenly answered for everybody:

"And you there, old codger, what are you shouting for?"

The archbishop actually jumped back in surprise, and shrieked:

"What! Who do you think you are?"

"And who do you think *you* are?"

The noisy archbishop seemed completely flustered by this, and pointing his finger at us he shouted to the priest:

"Speak up! Who is that lout?"

"I may be a lout, but I'm not a blockhead," answered Scott, forestalling a reply from the embarrassed priest.

The archbishop turned as red as a beet, and drumming on his cane with his fingers he wheezed rather than spoke:

"I want to know at once: *what is that thing?*"

He was told that *that thing* was A. J. Scott, the general manager of the estates belonging to the Counts Peróvsky.

The archbishop calmed down at once and inquired:

"But why is he dressed like that?" Then without waiting for any kind of answer to his question he went straight up to my uncle.

This was the most decisive moment of all, but it ended with the archbishop's holding out his hand to Scott and saying:

"I have great respect for the English nation."

"Thank you."

"It is a nation of character."

"It's not bad," answered Scott.

"Now, what has just happened here—I beg of you—let it remain just between ourselves."

"So be it."

"Now let me ask you to join me at the priest's and share my tea with me."

"Why not?" my uncle answered. "I like tea."

"You mean you've turned Russian?"

"No. I mean I like tea."

His Eminence gave my uncle a comradely slap on the back and exclaimed once more:

"What a nation of character, man alive! Let's stop being angry!"

And after that he turned to all the people who were standing around and added:

"Now, you go your ways."

And after filling each other with compliments the Englishman and the archbishop had a nice little time taking tea together and enjoying a snack from the archbishop's "travel supplies," during which His Eminence time and again would slap Scott on the back, and he in his turn, not letting such a favor go unanswered, would poke him in the stomach. They remained so well satisfied with each other that on saying farewell they kissed each other three times in brotherly fashion, and when the archbishop gave him his hand Scott grasped it so firmly that he winced and cried out once more:

"Ow! what a healthy nation!"

And so this fleeting encounter between the archbishop and the Englishman ended in a peaceful and friendly fashion. Nevertheless, this same archbishop was represented by other contemporaries of his as a man both spiteful and jaundiced, and even later the writers of his obituaries could not agree in their evaluation of him. For my part I am more inclined to agree with those who try to prove that Archbishop Varlaám was very good-hearted. In any case I can see no reason why I should not conclude that this man had the happy ability to become very meek and mild *if* he felt that he was dealing with a man who belonged to a "healthy nation." And in that case it is quite possible that those who thought he was indomitable very likely did not know how to behave before him. The old rule must never be forgotten: "If you want others to respect you, you must first respect yourself."

It even seems to me that for a Russian His Eminence had a rather high ideal of civic responsibility, and precisely for that reason he allowed himself to be irritated by the contemptible obsequiousness and flattery of those who surrounded him. He wanted to see more fortitude in people and that is why it immediately gave him a gratifying sense of satisfaction to meet a man from a "healthy nation." If he had previously met with something similar on the part of Russians, very likely they would have had the same kind of good effect on his disposition. This is perhaps the most successful way to characterize him, and the ecclesiastical apologists of Archbishop Varlaám missed an opportunity when they failed to make use of it.

NOTES FOR "THE ARCHBISHOP AND THE ENGLISHMAN"

[1] Filarét Drozdóv (1783–1867), the Metropolitan of Moscow, about whom unfavorable references are frequent in Leskóv's writings.

[2] According to official Moscow records, the Scott house on Leóntyev Lane remained in the possession of members of the Scott family from about 1825 to 1913. At least two descendants (now known as "Shkott") were still living in Moscow as late as 1955.

[3] Varlaám (Uspénsky, died in 1876) was archbishop in Pénza from 1854 to 1862.

NOTE TO "SINGLETHOUGHT"

This story, the first in Leskóv's cycle about "Righteous Men," can have no better introduction than the one Leskov himself provided when he first published it in book form in 1880. A complete translation of his own introduction is given here. The "dying writer" is his hypochondriac old friend A. F. Písemsky.

> *Without three righteous men no city*
> *shall stand.*

For the forty-eighth time a certain great Russian writer lay dying before my eyes. He is still alive, just as he remained alive after his forty-seven previous deaths, which took place under other auspices and in other circumstances.

He lay alone before me, stretched out full-length on his unencompassable sofa, and was getting ready to dictate to me his last will and testament—but instead of that he started swearing.

I can relate without any embarrassment just how it happened and what the consequences were.

The writer was threatened by death through the fault of the theatrical censorship committee, whose unflinching hand at that time had just killed his play. There was not a single pharmacy that had any medicine for the tormenting pains this had inflicted upon his authorial health.

"My soul is poisoned, and all my guts are tangled up in my belly," said the sufferer, looking up at the ceiling of his hotel room. Then, turning to me, he suddenly cried out:

"Why don't you say anything? You act as if your mouth were stopped up with the devil knows what. You Petersburg people have some kind of nastiness in your souls; you haven't got a word of consolation for a man even when he lies dying right here before your eyes."

This was the first time I had been present at the death of that remarkable man; and failing to understand his death throes, I said to him:

"How can I console you? At least I can tell you one thing: everybody will be extremely sorrowful if this harsh decision by the theatrical censorship committee cuts short your precious life, but—"

"That's not bad for a start," the writer interrupted. "Keep on talking, please, and maybe I can get to sleep."

"Go right ahead," I answered. "And so, are you really sure you are dying?"

"Am I sure? I tell you I'm just about to croak!"

"Excellent," I answered, "but have you thoroughly considered whether this vexation is really worth dying over?"

"Of course it is!" groaned the dying man. "It's worth a thousand rubles."

"Yes," I answered. "Unfortunately, your play would scarcely have brought in more than a thousand rubles, and so—"

But the dying man would not let me finish. He quickly jumped up from the sofa and shouted:

"What sort of disgusting talk is that! Just let me have a thousand rubles and then you can talk any way you please."

"But why should I pay for other people's sins?" I asked.

"And why should I take the loss?"

"Because you, who know the conditions in our theaters, described nothing but upper-class people in your play and made each one of them out to be worse and more disgusting than the next."

"Ye-e-es. So that's your kind of consolation. I take it that you think we should describe nothing but good people. Well, brother, I write about what I see, and I see nothing but filth."

"That shows your eyesight is bad."

"Maybe so," the dying man answered, now completely furious. "But what can I do when I can see nothing but abomination in either your soul or mine? And for that may the Lord God truly help me to turn my back on you and go to sleep with a clear conscience, and I will leave tomorrow full of scorn for my native land and your consolations."

And the prayer of the sufferer was answered: he truly got an excellent night's sleep, and I took him to the station the next morning. But then his words caused me in my turn to be seized by pangs of uneasiness.

"What!" I thought. "Is it really possible that nothing but filth can be seen in my soul or his or the soul of any other Russian? Can all the goodness and kindness that has ever been noted by the artistic eye of other writers really be nothing more than nonsense and fabrication? That is not only sad, it is frightful. If no city can stand without three righteous men, as the folk saying goes, then how can a whole country survive with nothing but the filth that lives, dear reader, in your soul and mine?"

I found this frightful and unbearable, and I set out to look for righteous men. I set out with the solemn vow not to rest until I should find at least that small number of three righteous persons without whom "no city shall stand." But no matter where I turned and no matter whom I asked, everybody answered to the effect that they had never seen any righteous men, because all men were sinful. Still, here and there I would run across somebody who knew a few good people, and I started taking notes. This would all have to be collected and examined, I thought to myself, in order to see whether they were righteous or unrighteous, and to find out "what rose above the level of simple morality" and therefore was "holy in the sight of the Lord."

And so here are some of my notes.

SINGLETHOUGHT

CHAPTER ONE

During the reign of Catherine the Great, in the family of a certain government clerk by the name of Ryzhóv, there was born a son by the name of Aleck. This family lived in Soligálich, a district town of Kostromá Province that lay between the Kostromá River and Svétitsa. According to Prince Gagárin's Encyclopedia that town contains six stone churches, two religious schools and one secular, seven mills and factories, thirty-seven shops, three inns, two taverns for the sale of liquor, and 3665 inhabitants of both sexes. The town has two yearly fairs and a weekly bazaar; besides this it is recorded that there is "a rather active trade in lime and tar." At the time when our hero was alive there were salt works here as well.

It is necessary to know all this in order to get some idea how such a person as our insignificant hero Aleck—or as he was later called, Alexander Afanasyevich Ryzhóv, nicknamed "Singlethought"—could really have existed.

Aleck's parents had a home of their own—one of those little houses in that wooded area which were worth nothing at all but at least provided a shelter. Apart from Aleck the government clerk Ryzhóv had no other children, or at least I never heard of any.

The clerk died soon after the birth of this son and left his wife and son with nothing except that little house, which, as stated above, was worthless. But the clerk's widow was herself worth a lot: she was one of those Russian women, who

> *Unflinching in disaster saves the day;*
> *Dashes into the furiously burning house,*
> *And bravely stops the horse that runs away.*[1]

—a simple, healthy, sober-minded Russian woman, with strength in her body, with courage in her soul, and with a tender capacity for loving deeply and truly.

When she became a widow she still had features that were attractive enough to suit unpretentious tastes, and several matchmakers were sent to call on her, but she declined all further matrimony and began to spend her time baking pies. On ordinary days these pies were made of cottage cheese and liver, and on fast days of porridge and peas. The widow would carry them to the square on peddler's trays and sell them for five copper kopecks apiece. With the income from her pie production she fed herself and her son, whom she turned over to a "schoolmarm" for some learning. The schoolmarm taught Aleck what she herself knew. Further and more serious learning he got from a deacon with braided hair and a leather pouch in which he carried snuff without any snuffbox, for use in the well-known way.

After he had finished off Aleck's learning, the deacon took his pot of porridge in payment,[2] and thereupon the widow's son set forth in the world to earn his living and receive all the benefits that were destined for him in this life.

Aleck was then fourteen years old, and at this age it is time to introduce him to the reader.

Physically, young Ryzhóv took after his mother: he was tall, broad-shouldered—almost an athlete—with unbounded strength and indestructible health. In the years of his boyhood he was stronger than everybody else, and he presided so successfully over the troops in fist fights that whichever side Aleck Ryzhóv happened to be on was considered invincible. He had spare time and he loved to work. The deacon's school had given him excellent, flowing, clear, and beautiful handwriting, in which he wrote out for old women a great quantity of prayer lists for the dead, and thereby laid the foundation for his own bread and butter. But more important than this were the qualities his mother gave him through her own living example, transmitting her austere and sober disposition to his healthy soul, living in its healthy, powerful body. Like his mother, he was moderate in everything and never resorted to any outsider for help.

At fourteen years he already considered it a sin to live off his mother. The prayer lists did not bring in very much; and besides, that income, depending as it did on chance, was irregular. Ryzhóv had an innate aversion to trade, and he would not leave Soligálich, so as not to be separated from his mother, whom he loved very much. For this reason it was necessary to dig up a job right there, and he dug one up.

At that time regular postal service was just getting started in our country. A system of messengers was established between neighboring towns, and once a week they would make the journey on foot, carrying mailbags with packages. This was called "walking mail." The pay for this service was not set very high: a ruble and a half a month "on your own food and in your own shoes." But those who found such maintenance tempting still hesitated to undertake carrying the mail, for the sensitive Christian conscience of Russian piety found something suspicious in all this, and feared

lest such a vain enterprise as the carrying of paper should contain something heretical and contrary to the true Christian faith.

Everyone who chanced to hear about it pondered over how to avoid
losing their souls thereby, so that they should not miss eternal life for
the sake of temporary recompense. At this point the compassion of the
neighbors fixed up Widow Ryzhóv's son Aleck.

"He," they said, "is an orphan: the Lord will forgive more in him—
especially since he's so young. If a bear or a wolf chews him up on the
road while he is carrying the mail and he gets called before the Judgment
Seat, all he will have to answer is, 'I didn't understand, Lord,' and that
will be all there is to it. Even then there won't be anything to take away
from him. And if he should get through it alive and live to a ripe old age,
then he can go into a monastery and pray it all off very well—and he
won't even have to pay for the candles and incense. For an orphan like
him what more could he expect?"

Aleck himself, who was more affected by this than anybody else, had
nothing against the world but was not beholden to it, as the saying goes.
With a firm hand he picked up the mailbag, threw it over his shoulder,
and started carrying it back and forth from Soligálich to Chúkhloma.
Service in the walking mail was perfectly suited to his taste and nature:
he went alone through the forests, fields, and swamps, and would think
his orphan thoughts to himself, just as they came to him under the stimu-
lation of everything he met and saw and heard. Such circumstances might
have made a poet out of him like Burns or Koltsóv, but Aleck Ryzhóv
had another turn of mind—neither poetic nor philosophical—and he became only the remarkable eccentric "Singlethought." Neither the fatigue
of the distant road, nor heat, nor cold, nor wind and rain could frighten
him. His mailbag was so insignificant for his powerful shoulders that in
addition to that one he always carried another too, a gray canvas bag, in
which there lay a thick book that had an irresistible influence over him.

That book was the Bible.

CHAPTER TWO

I do not know how many years he served in the walking mail, continually
lugging his mailbag and his Bible, but it seems to have lasted a long time
and it ended with the replacement of the walking mail by postmen on
horseback, and Ryzhóv was awarded a government rank. After these two
important events in the life of our hero his fate underwent an important
turning point. He liked carrying the mail so much on foot that he refused
to ride on the post wagon and started looking for another job—again by
all means there in Soligálich, so as not to be separated from his mother,
who by now was very old and had lost so much of her eyesight that her
pies had deteriorated.

Judging by the fact that government ranks were not given quickly to the lower postal employees, usually not till after some twelve years of service, we may suppose that Ryzhóv at that time was about twenty-six years old, or even a little older. During all that time he had only walked back and forth between Soligálich and Chúkhloma, and while he was walking and resting he read nothing but his Bible in its shabby binding. He read it to his heart's content, and he got from it the great and solid ideas that formed the basis of the original life he led later, when he had begun to reason things out and apply his Biblical views to his affairs.

And there really was much in all this that was original. For example, Ryzhóv knew all the writings of many of the prophets by heart. He especially loved Isaiah, whose deep knowledge of God corresponded to his spiritual nature and constituted his whole catechism and his whole theology.

An old man who in his youth had known the eighty-year-old Ryzhóv after he had become famous and earned the name of "Singlethought," told me how old Ryzhóv recalled some sort of "oak tree in a swamp," where he especially liked to rest and "shout into the wind."

"I used to stand up on it," he said, "and howl into the air:

" 'The ox knoweth his owner, and the ass his master's crib, but my people doth not consider. A seed of evildoers, children that are corrupters! Why should ye be stricken any more, ye will revolt more and more: the whole head is sick, and the whole heart faint. To what purpose is the multitude of your sacrifices unto Me? I delight not in the blood of bullocks, or of lambs, or of he-goats. Do not come to appear before Me. Bring no more vain oblations; incense is an abomination unto Me; the new moons and the sabbaths, I cannot away with the great day. Your fasts and your appointed feasts and your new moons My soul hateth. And when ye spread forth your hands, I will hide Mine eyes from you: yea, when ye make many prayers I will not hear. Wash you, take away the evil from your souls. Learn to do well, and come let Us reason together, and though your sins be as scarlet, I will make them white as snow. But thy princes are rebellious, and companions of thieves; every one loveth gifts, and followeth after rewards. Therefore saith the Lord of hosts: Woe unto the mighty. My fury shall not cease against mine adversaries.' " [3]

So the little orphan boy would shout this, "Woe, woe unto the mighty!" over the empty swamp, and it seemed to him that the wind would catch up the words of Isaiah and carry them off to where the dry bones that were seen by Ezekiel lay motionless; no living flesh would grow upon them, and no corrupt heart came to life in their breast.

The oak and the serpents of the swamp listened to him, and he himself became half a mystic and half an agitator in the Biblical sense; according to his words he "breathed love and daring."

All this had ripened within him long before, but it came to light only when he received his government rank and began hunting for another job, not overlooking the swamp. Ryzhóv's development was completely finished, and the time was approaching for action in which he could apply the rules he had worked out for himself on his Biblical foundation.

Under the same oak and above the same swamp where Ryzhóv shouted in the words of Isaiah, "Woe unto the mighty," he waited until he received the inspiration that gave him the idea of becoming mighty himself, so that he might put to shame those who were the mightiest of all. And so he accepted this consecration and bore it up to the grave that ended the almost one hundred years of his life, never once having stumbled or faltered to the right or to the left.

Now before us lie several examples of his astonishing power, which was stifled in its cramping confinement; and at the end of this tale there is an unexpected act of audacious fearlessness, which crowned his chivalrous head with a chivalrous reward.

CHAPTER THREE

In that distant period from which my tale about Ryzhóv has come down, the most important person in every Godforsaken little town in Russia was the town governor. It was frequently asserted and disputed by no one that in the opinion of many Russians the town governor was the "third person in the realm." In the mind of the common people the governmental authority branched out from its primary source, the monarch; in this way the first person in the state was the emperor, who ruled the whole country; after him came the provincial governor, who had charge of the province; and then right after the governor came the third person, the town governor, who "sat on the town." At that time district police officers did not yet exist, and for that reason they were not included in this division of authority. For that matter, things remained this way even afterwards: the district police officer was a traveling man, and he thrashed only the country people, who didn't yet have their own conception of the hierarchy, and no matter who thrashed them, they always kicked out their legs the same way.

The introduction of the court system, which put a limit on the former theocratic authority of those village administrators, rather spoiled all this, especially in the towns, where it contributed a good deal to the decline in the prestige of both the town and the provincial governors. It was impossible to raise this prestige to its former level, at least as far as town governors were concerned, because their high position was replaced in the new order of things.

But at the time when Singlethought was considering and determining his fate, all this was still flourishing in good order. The governors sat in their capitals like little tsars. It was hard to gain access to them, and an audience with them was accompanied by fear and trembling. They showered their haughtiness on everybody, and everybody bowed down before them to the waist, and some—through particular zeal—even to the ground; the archpriests would greet them at the door of the church with crosses and holy water, and the second-rate gentry would honor them with expressions of humble servility and barely found the courage to ask them, through a few carefully chosen intermediaries, to "stand at the baptismal font as godfather." And even when they condescended to come down to such a level of kindness, they conducted themselves regally: they would not go to the baptism themselves but would send their adjutants or administrative assistants as substitutes, bearing the baptismal cloth and receiving the honors "in the name of him who had sent them." In those days everything was majestic, sedate, and serious, in keeping with those serious, good old days, which are often contrasted to our present times, neither good nor serious.

An excellent opportunity turned up for Ryzhóv to get close to the source of city authority and take a position at the fourth level of the empire without leaving his native town. In Soligálich the old policeman died, and Ryzhóv got the idea of asking for his job.

CHAPTER FOUR

Although the policeman's position was not very high, despite the fact that it occupied the first level just below the town governor, still it was rather advantageous if only the man who occupied it was adept at pulling a log of wood, a couple of beets, or a head of cabbage off every wagon. But if he was not skilled at that, it would go hard with him, since the official salary for that fourth highest position in the empire was fixed at only ten paper rubles a month, in other words, about two rubles and eighty-five kopecks according to our present figures. Out of this the fourth most important personage in the empire had to maintain himself and his family in a proper manner, and since that was impossible, every policeman squeezed a little out of everybody who came to see him about something "on business." It was impossible to make ends meet without this "squeezing," and even the Voltaireans offered no objection to that.[4] The thought of an "unaccepting" policeman had never occurred to anybody, and so if all policemen "accepted," then Ryzhóv would have to accept too. The authorities themselves could not wish or allow him to corrupt the established procedures. About this there could be no doubt whatever, or even any discussion.

The town governor to whom Ryzhóv applied for the policeman's job naturally did not even ask himself about his ability to take bribes. Very likely he thought that on this point Ryzhóv would be like all the rest, and so there was no special agreement between them on this point. The governor took into consideration only his enormous height, his physique, his well-known strength, and his tirelessness in walking, which Ryzhóv had shown through his delivery of the mail on foot. All these were qualities well suited to the police work for which Ryzhóv had applied, and so he was made the Soligálich policeman, and his mother continued to bake her pies and sell them in that same market where her son was to establish and maintain good order—observing true weight and full measure, shaken down.

The town governor gave him just one suggestion:

"Beat them without maiming them, and don't grab anything that belongs to me."

Ryzhóv promised to fulfill this and entered into action, but soon he began to raise strange doubts about himself, which started troubling that third person in the empire; and the former Aleck himself, or Alexander Afanásyevich, as people called him now, was exposed to very painful ordeals.

From the very first day of his work Ryzhóv proved to be diligent and careful in his duties. When he came to the market square he assigned a place to each wagon, and he set out the women and their pies without giving the best place to his own mother. As for the drunken peasants, he made some of them see reason and he taught the rest of them a lesson with his authoritative arm, but in a pleasant way, and so well that you might think he was doing them a favor—and he took nothing in return for his lesson. On that same day he refused an offering from the cabbage women, who had come to bow down before him on business, and he informed them that nobody owed him anything on business, because whatever he had coming to him on business "would come from the Tsar, and God forbids taking bribes."

The day went well for Ryzhóv, and the night went even better: he walked around the whole town, and whenever he met anybody wandering around at that late hour he would ask where they were from, and where they were going, and what for. If it was a good person he would talk with him a little, and even walk along with him and give him some advice, but he gave a good yank on the ears of one or two drunkards, and he took a watchman's wife who had gone out to cast a spell on the cows, and he locked her up in the clink, and the next morning he reported to the town governor that the only hindrance he had in his work was the watchmen.

"They spend their time in idleness," he said, "and then they walk around half asleep for no reason. They are always pestering people on business, and they themselves go to the dogs. The best thing is to turn them out for their empty-headed laziness and send them off to pull weeds in Your Excellency's garden, and I'll manage the whole thing myself."

The governor didn't see any objections to that, and his thrifty wife thought it was a fine idea; only the watchmen may not have liked it, and it didn't exactly fit the law—but who would ever think of asking the watchmen? And as for the law, the governor judged that with good Russian judgment:

> *Just saddle the law like a horse, you know,*
> *It'll take you wherever you want to go.*

But Alexander Afanásyevich placed above everything else the law that says to "Eat thy bread in the sweat of thy brow," and according to that law it turned out that every unnecessary "hireling" was a useless burden that ought to be dropped and assigned somewhere else to some real work— the sweaty kind.

So this matter was arranged the way Ryzhóv indicated, and it was pleasing in the sight of the ruler and the people, and it turned the hearts of the grateful toward Ryzhóv. Ryzhóv himself walked about the town by day, and he walked alone by night, and little by little his good, thrifty supervision began to make itself felt everywhere, and again this was pleasing in the eyes of all. In short, everything went well and promised imperturbable peace—but right here was where the trouble began:

> *Peaceful people? Nothing's worse!*
> *Who'll then line the judge's purse?*

Nothing at all came in from any direction on business, and except for the harvesting of his garden the governor received no profits—neither large, middle-sized, nor small.

The governor waxed wroth in spirit; he went to the heart of the matter, saw that this could not be, and started a bitter persecution against Ryzhóv.

He asked the archpriest to find out whether there was not some kind of un-Orthodoxy in the unbusinesslike Ryzhóv; but the archpriest answered that he could discern no manifest un-Orthodoxy in Ryzhóv, but he did notice a certain pride in him, which of course came from the fact that his mother baked pies and turned some over to him.

"I would counsel that this commerce be halted, since it ill becomes her now because of her son's position, and then that excessive pride within him will be destroyed, and he will become businesslike."

"I will halt it," said the governor, and he told Ryzhóv: "It is not suitable for your mother to sit in the market place."

"All right," said Ryzhóv, and he took his mother and her trays away from the market, but he persisted as before in his blameworthy conduct: he remained unbusinesslike.

Then the archpriest pointed out that Ryzhóv had not acquired a uniform, and on the day of our risen Lord, having stingily exchanged the triple Easter kiss with only a few intimate friends, he had not appeared with Easter greetings before any of the town's leading citizens—which had led none of them, it must be said, to lodge any complaints.

These two matters were mutually dependent on each other. Ryzhóv never went out on festive occasions and therefore he had no occasion to dress up in a uniform, but a uniform was required, and the former policeman had worn one. Everybody had seen his full-dress coat and collar, his riding-breeches, and tasseled boots, while Ryzhóv still dressed in what he had worn when he carried the mail—a quilted jacket make of striped mattress-ticking, fastened together with hooks, tan nankeen trousers, and a simple peasant cap, and for the winter he had a sheepskin coat with the wool turned inside out, and he got himself nothing else, nor could he get anything else on the salary of two rubles and eighty-seven kopecks a month on which he lived, performing his duties faithfully and justly.

On top of that something happened that required money: Ryzhóv's mother died, having nothing on earth to do when she could no longer sell pies on it.

Alexander Afanásyevich buried her very "stingily," according to the general opinion, thus showing his lack of love for her. He paid a bare trifle to the clergy for her, but for the pie-seller herself he didn't even bake a pie, and the forty-day prayer for her soul he didn't order at all.

A heretic! And this was all the more certain because, even though the governor didn't trust him and the archpriest had his doubts about him, the governess and the archpriestess stood up for him to the hilt—the former because he had herded the watchmen into her garden and the latter for some secret reason that lay in her "oppositional character."

In these two personages Alexander Afanásyevich found defenders. The governor's wife sent him two measures of potatoes from her earthly harvest, but without untying the sacks he carried the potatoes back on his shoulders and said tersely:

"I thank you for your kindness, but I don't accept gifts."

Then the priest's wife, a suspicious lady, presented him with two calico shirt fronts of her own handiwork, made in the early days before her archpriest had been ordained; but the cranky fellow would not accept that either.

"I can't take gifts," he said, "and anyhow, since I wear plain clothes, I haven't got any use for that sort of finery."

Thereupon the priest's wife made a spitefully cutting remark to her husband:

"That's the kind of man who ought to be standing before the altar," she said, "and not you spiritual fleecers."

The archpriest got angry and ordered his wife to shut up, and he himself kept lying there and thought:

"This is some new-fangled kind of freemasonry, and if I keep an eye on it and expose it, I may win special distinction, and I may even get transferred to Petersburg."

And so he worked himself into a fever over this, and in his fever he devised a plan to lay Ryzhóv's conscience so bare that it would separate his soul from his body.

CHAPTER FIVE

Lent was approaching, and the archpriest saw as clearly as if it were right before his eyes just how he would lay Ryzhóv's soul bare to the separation point, and then he would know how to deal with him for straying from the truths of Orthodoxy.

Thereupon he advised the governor to send him the striped policeman for confession during the very first week. And he promised to work on him thoroughly at confession, and worm all his innermost secrets out of him, and find out why he shied away from everything and wouldn't take gifts. And he added: "By the looks of his conscience when we have laid it bare through fear, we shall see to what powers he is subject, and then we shall subject him to them for the salvation of his soul."

Having mentioned the words of Paul, the archpriest waited quietly, knowing that each one could find what he needed in them.

The governor also did his part.

"You and I, Alexander Afanásyevich," he said, "must set an example for people in religion and pay our respects to the Church."

Ryzhóv said he agreed.

"Now, brother, do fast and go to confession."

"Agreed," said Ryzhóv.

"And since we are both in the public eye, we ought to do all this in a public way, and not as if we were somehow trying to be secret about it. I myself go to the archpriest for confession; he is the most experienced of all the clergy—now, suppose you go to him too."

"I'll go to the archpriest."

"Yes—you go during the first week and I'll go during the last week. In that way we'll divide it up between us."

"And I agree on that too."

The archpriest confessed Ryzhóv thoroughly and even boasted that he had scolded him for all he was worth, but he found no mortal sin in him.

"He confessed to first one thing, then another, then a third; he wasn't innocent in the slightest, but his sins were all simple and human, and he thinks no evil against the authorities, and he has no thought of reporting either you or me on business. And as for his 'not accepting gifts,' well, that is purely because of his harmful notions."

"So he does have harmful notions just the same. And what kind of harmful notions are they?"

"He's filled his head with Bible-reading."

"So that's what the fool has got into!"

"Yes. He read it out of boredom, and now he can't get it out of his mind."

"The blasted fool! But what can we do with him?"

"You can't do anything: he's pretty far gone by now."

"Has he already gone as far as 'Christ'?"

"He's read it all—all of it."

"Well, in that case it's all up with him."

They felt sorry about it, and they became more charitable toward Ryzhóv. In our ancient Russian land every Orthodox knows that whoever has read the Bible all the way through and "even got to Christ" can no longer be held strictly responsible for his actions; but such people are like the well-known "fools of God"—they will do queer things but they won't harm anybody, and no one is afraid of them. But just to be more certain about Ryzhóv's strange corrigibility on business, the reverend archpriest gave the governor some wise but harsh advice: to get Alexander Afanásyevich married.

"A married man," the archpriest explained, "has trouble maintaining his honesty even if he has 'read up to Christ'; his wife will keep after him like the itch, and one way or another she'll so wear him out that he will finally give in and let the whole Bible slip out of his head, and then he'll become receptive to gifts and devoted to the authorities."

This advice fitted in with the governor's own ideas, and he ordered Alexander Afanásyevich to go about it any way he liked but by all means to get married, because bachelors were unreliable in political positions.

"You can say what you will, brother," he told him, "but I like your way of reasoning about everything, except that your reasoning about one thing just won't do."

"How's that?"

"You're a bachelor."

"What's wrong with that?"

"What's wrong is that you might do something treacherous and run off to somebody else's province. After all, what's holding you here? You grab your Bible and you're gone."

"Yes, I'm gone."

"Don't you see? That's unreliable."

"But would a married man be any more reliable?"

"Why, there's no comparison. I can twist a married man around my little finger. He'll put up with anything, because he'll have his brood to raise and his wife to love; but a bachelor is like a bird—you can't trust him. So there you have it—either leave or get married."

This judgment did not disturb the puzzling crank in the slightest, and he answered:

"What does it matter? Marriage too is a good thing; it was established by God. If it's necessary, I'll get married."

"But make sure you don't aim too high."

"I won't aim too high."

"And pick one out in a hurry."

"Oh, I've already got her picked out; only, I'll have to go and see whether anybody else has already taken her."

The governor burst out laughing at him:

"Just look at you there, you sinner!" he said. "Talk about sin never getting near him—and there he's already turned up a wife for himself."

"Who said sin never got near?" answered Alexander Afanásyevich. "The vessel is full of abomination. Only, I haven't yet proposed to the girl, but I really have got her picked out, and I'd like to get your permission to go and take a look at her."

"And where is this girl of yours—not one of our local ones, surely? From somewhere else?"

"Well, it's like this: she's not from here and she's not from somewhere else. She lives down at the spring near the swamp."

The governor laughed still more, gave Ryzhóv leave, and then waited full of curiosity to see when the queer fellow would come back and what he would say.

CHAPTER SIX

Ryzhóv really didn't aim too high: a week later he brought his wife to town—a hefty, rosy blonde with good-natured brown eyes and submissiveness in every step and gesture. She was dressed in peasant fashion, and husband and wife walked one behind the other, carrying on their shoulders a yoke from which a painted trunklike basket of bast was suspended by a piece of linen cloth. The basket contained her dowry.

People experienced in trade recognized at once that this was the daughter of the old Kozlíkha woman, who lived in an isolated hut at the spring on the edge of the swamp and was reputed to be a wicked old witch. Everybody thought Ryzhóv had taken a witch's daughter as his housekeeper.

And this was partly true, except that before he took this housekeeper home, he got himself married up to her. His life as a married man didn't cost him a bit more than his life as a bachelor. On the contrary, it even became more profitable, because as soon as he brought his wife into the house, he dismissed the farm girl to whom for better or worse he had been paying a copper ruble a month. From that time on, the copper ruble stayed in his pocket and the work around the house went better. The healthy hands of his wife were never idle; she would spin and weave, and on top of that she turned out to be an expert at making felt stockings and doing the gardening. In a word, his wife was a simple, skillful peasant woman, faithful and submissive, with whom the Bible-reading eccentric could live Biblically, and there is nothing more to tell about her except what has already been told.

Alexander Afanásyevich's way of treating his wife was as simple as it could be, but peculiar: his manner of speaking to her was familiar, and hers showed that she looked up to him; he called her "my old woman," and she called him Alexander Afanásyevich; she waited on him, and he was her lord and master; when he spoke to her, she would answer, and when he was silent, she dared not ask him anything. At the table he would sit and she would serve him; but they held the bed in common, and probably this was the reason why their marriage was fruitful. Just one fruit appeared—an only son, which his "old woman" brought up, and he did not meddle in the upbringing.

Nothing in their relations ever gave any evidence whether his "old woman" loved her Biblical husband or whether she did not love him, but there was no doubt about the fact that she was faithful to her husband. Besides that, she was in awe of him as a person who was placed above her according to God's law, and who had a divine right to her. Her peaceful life was not disturbed by that. She could not read and write, and Alexander Afanásyevich would not fill this gap in her education. Needless to say, they lived a Spartan existence, in the strictest frugality, but they did not look on it as a misfortune. This was perhaps helped a lot by the fact that a good many others lived all around in no easier circumstances. They drank no tea and never kept any around, and they ate meat only on high holidays. During the rest of the time they ate bread and vegetables, either pickled or fresh from their garden, and especially mushrooms, which grew in abundance in their wooded part of the country. In the summer season the "old woman" would go through the woods and pick these mushrooms herself, and she herself would store them away, but to her misfortune the only way she could store them was by drying them. They had nothing to salt them with. The cost of salt in the necessary quantity for their whole supply did not enter into Ryzhóv's accounts, and once when his "old woman" salted a little tub of choice mushrooms that a tax-farmer had given her in a sack, Alexander Afanásyevich, upon finding out about it, patriarchally gave his "old woman" a beating and took her to the archpriest so that he could impose a penance upon her for disobeying her husband's precepts; and as for the mushrooms, he rolled the tub with his own hands up to the tax-farmer's yard and told him to "take it away, wherever he wanted," and then he gave the tax-farmer a tongue-lashing.

Such was this eccentric, about whom there is little to tell from all the years of his life; he stuck to his place, carried out his little task, which drew no particular sympathy from anyone, and he sought no particular sympathy from anyone. The rulers of the roost in Soligálich considered him to be "damaged by the Bible," and the simple people passed upon him their simple judgment that he was "a certain sort of regular whatcha-may-call-it."

For them this rather unclear description had a clear and comprehensible meaning.

Ryzhóv did not care in the slightest what people thought about him. He gave honest service to everybody and no special favors to anybody; but mentally he rendered an account to the only one in whom he believed with unshakable firmness, calling him the founder and master of all creation. Ryzhóv's pleasure consisted in fulfilling his duty, and he found his greatest spiritual comfort in philosophizing about the highest questions of the spiritual world, and about the way the laws of that world were reflected in the appearance and fate of individual persons and whole kingdoms and nations. It is not known whether Ryzhóv had the weakness common to many self-taught men of considering himself more intelligent than anybody else; but he was not arrogant, and he never tried to impose his beliefs and views on anybody, or even tell anybody what they were. He would only write them in big notebooks of blue paper that he sewed into one cover bearing the significant title "Singlethought."

What was written in all this enormous manuscript of the philosopher-policeman remained concealed, because Alexander Afanásyevich's "Singlethought" disappeared at the time of his death, and nobody could say much about it from memory. Only two or three passages from all the "Singlethought" were shown by Ryzhóv to one important person on one extraordinary occasion in his life, to which we are now drawing near. The remaining pages of the "Singlethought," the existence of which was known to almost everybody in Soligálich, were used up as wallpaper, or perhaps burned up in order to avoid trouble, since this work contained a great deal of the kind of foolish raving and religious fantasy for which at that time both authors and readers would get packed off to pray at the Solovétsky Monastery.[5]

The spirit of this manuscript, however, became known as a result of the following event, which is famous in the chronicles of Soligálich.

CHAPTER SEVEN

I cannot remember exactly, nor do I know where to find out, in just what year Sergéi Stepánovich Lanskói, later a count and the well-known Minister of Internal Affairs, was appointed to Kostromá as the provincial governor.[6] This dignitary, according to the apt remark of one of his contemporaries, "had a powerful mind and a haughty presence," and this brief description is correct and quite sufficient to give our reader an adequate idea of him.

One might add only that Lanskói respected honesty and justice in people and was good himself, and he also loved Russia and the Russians; but he had a nobleman's understanding of them, as an aristocrat with an alien view and a western standard of measurement for everything.

Lanskói's appointment to Kostromá as governor took place at the time of Alexander Afanásyevich Ryzhóv's eccentric service as the Soligálich policeman—and it took place under certain unusual circumstances.

On assuming his duties as governor, Sergéi Stepánovich followed the example of many public figures and "swept the province clean," that is, he threw out a large number of bureaucrats who were negligent and had misused their positions, including the governor of Soligálich under whom Ryzhóv was serving as policeman.

After turning these worthless persons out of office, the new governor showed no haste in replacing them with others, so that his choice should not fall upon the same kind, or perhaps even upon worse. In order to pick out worthy men he wanted to look around, or as they say nowadays in Russian, to "get oriented." For this purpose the duties of the persons who had been dismissed were handed over to temporary replacements drawn from the younger bureaucrats, and the governor soon set out on a tour of the whole province, which had started trembling a very strange tremble at the very rumor of his "haughty presence."

Alexander Afanásyevich performed the duties of the town governor. I don't know just what he did as a replacement that was different from the former, "regular" procedures, but it goes without saying that he took no bribes as governor, just as he had taken none as a policeman. Nor did Ryzhóv change his way of life, or his relations with other people. He did not even sit on the governor's seat with the three-sided mirror of authority standing before him,[7] but signed his name "on behalf of the governor," while sitting at the entrance behind his little ink-stained table. For this last bit of stubbornness Ryzhóv had an explanation that was connected with the grand finale of his life. After his many years of service, just as during the first days of his work as a policeman, Alexander Afanásyevich *never had a uniform,* and he governed "on behalf of the governor" in that same greasy patched and repatched quilted jacket. And for that reason, when the clerk suggested that he move over to his seat, he answered:

"I can't; my garment betrayeth that I am not of the wedding party."

All this was duly noted down in his own hand in his "Singlethought," with the addition that the clerk had invited him to "change seats in his quilted jacket but to take the eagle off the three-sided mirror," but Alexander Afanásyevich "shunned this indecency" and continued to sit in his former place wearing his quilted jacket.

This lack of uniformity did not get in the way of administering police justice in the town, but the question took on an entirely different cast when the news arrived about the coming of the "haughty presence." In his position as ruler of the town Alexander Afanásyevich was supposed to meet the governor, receive him, and report to him about the flourishing condition of Soligálich, and also answer any questions Lanskói might ask him, and acquaint him with all the sights of the town, from the cathedral to the jail, and including the waste land and the gulleys that nobody knew what to do with.

Ryzhóv really did have a problem. How could he go through all this in his quilted jacket? But he did not worry about this in the slightest. Everybody else, though, worried about it a great deal, because Ryzhóv and his disgraceful appearance might plunge the "haughty presence" into a fit of anger at the very first step. It never entered anybody's head that none other than Alexander Afanásyevich himself was destined to astonish and even *delight* the awe-inspiring "haughty presence," and even to prophesy a promotion for him.

The generally conscientious Alexander Afanásyevich was not embarrassed in the slightest about how he looked. He shared none of the general timidity of the bureaucrats, and this exposed him to condemnation and hatred and led him to fall in the opinion of his fellow citizens, but he fell only to rise afterwards higher than all the rest, and to leave behind a heroic and almost legendary memory.

CHAPTER EIGHT

It is not inappropriate to recall once more that in those recent but wholly departed days to which the story of Ryzhóv refers, governors were not at all what they are in the cunning times we now live in, when the majesty of those dignitaries has noticeably dropped—or, in the words of a certain ecclesiastical chronicler, "did most cruelly decline." At that time governors would make "awesome" tours and would be greeted with fear and trembling. Their movements were accomplished in the midst of grandiose bustle and bother, which was the work not only of all the junior administrative authorities but also of the common rabble and the four-legged brutes. In preparation for the arrival of the governor, towns would be anointed with whitewash, black paint, and yellow ocher. The barriers at the entrances to the towns were repainted in the governmental tricolor; the watchmen and crippled veterans were advised to "wax their hair and mustaches"; and the hospitals stepped up their number of discharges marked "cured." Everybody right up to the limits of the realm took part in the general excitement. Peasants, men and women, were rounded up in the villages for road work; and they wandered about for months, filling in marshy stretches, patching up log-paved roads, and repairing bridges. At the post stations there were delays even for madcap couriers and all the various lieutenants who were traveling in haste on innumerable official missions. Taking revenge upon that impatient crowd for the intolerable offenses they had committed, the stationmasters in unshakable firmness of spirit would make them plod along at that season on any kind of nags that happened to turn up, because the good horses were "getting their rest" in anticipation of the governor. In a word, nobody could pass through without becoming aware through one or another of his senses that something extraordinary was taking place in the nature of all things. Thanks to this, everybody, young and old, knew without any idle talk from a chattering press that the one man was coming than whom there was none higher in all the province; and about this occasion everybody expressed his various feelings as best he knew how to his neighbor. But the most exalted activity took place in the central nests of the district lords and masters—in the judicial offices, where the matter began with a tiresome and boring check of the registers and ended with the merry operation of sweeping the walls and scrubbing the floors. Floor-scrubbing was something in the nature of those classical orgies at the season of the grape harvest, when everybody strenuously rejoiced with only one thought in mind—to live gaily until the hour of death should come. A small convoy of bent old war veterans would bring out of the jail and into the offices some feminine prisoners who had all but perished from boredom and who, seizing upon this brief moment of happiness, made use here of the captivating rights of their sex in order to alleviate the sad lot of mortals. The low necks and short sleeves in which they set about their work had such a stimulating effect upon the young clerks on duty among their papers that the consequences of this, as was well known, would often appear in the jails in the form of so-called "floor-scrubbing babies," who were of unacknowledged but indubitably noble origin.

During those same days in the homes dress shoes were blackened, riding-breeches were whitened, and moth-eaten dress coats, stiff with storage, were put into shape for wearing. This also enlivened the town. The dress coats were first *hung out* in the sun on a hot day, spread out on ropes that were stretched across the courtyards, all of which attracted a crowd of curious persons to every gate; then the dress coats were spread out on pillows or thick felt and *beaten* with switches; after that they were *shaken;* still later they were *mended, pressed,* and finally *spread out* on an armshair in the hall or some other company room; and last of all, at the conclusion of everything, they were stealthily sprinkled with holy bottles of Twelfth Night water, which, as long as it is kept before the icon in a vessel sealed with wax, will not spoil from one Epiphany to the next and will lose none of the wonder-working power it received at the moment when the cross was plunged into it during the singing of "Save Thy people, O Lord, and bless Thy property."

When they left for their meeting with the important personage, the officials would wrap themselves in their duly sprinkled dress coats, and in their capacity as further property of God they would gain salvation. About this there were many reliable accounts, but in the face of our general skepticism at present and especially of the Offenbachian atmosphere that reigns in the world of officialdom, all this has been discredited in public opinion, and, along with many other things rendered sacred by time, is frivolously subjected to doubt. Unto our fathers, however, who had a firm and genuine belief, it was given according to their faith.

In those days waiting for the governor was long and painful. At that time there were no railways, and trains did not arrive at fixed hours according to a timetable, bringing the governor along with all the other mortals. Instead, a special road was prepared, and after that no one knew exactly the day or the hour when the dignitary would deign to make his appearance. For that reason the exhausting wait was lengthy and full of special and ceremonial anxiety, at the very height of which there stood the regular policeman on duty, who had the task of watching the road from the highest bell tower in town. He was obliged to keep wide awake and guard the town against an unexpected incursion; but naturally it occasionally happened that he would doze and even drop off to sleep, and then in such unfortunate cases there would be all sorts of trouble. Sometimes the negligent sentinel would let the governor get too close before he rang his little bell, so that there would not be enough time for all the officials to get into their dress coats and dash out, for the archpriest to put on his vestments and take his stand with the cross on the steps, or sometimes even for the town governor to ride out to the entrance gate, standing erect in his cart. In order to avoid this the sentinel was obliged to keep walking around the top of the bell tower and bow at every opening in the direction it faced.

This provided the sentinel with a diversion and society with assurance that he who kept his vigil over them neither slumbered nor slept. But even this precaution did not always help; it sometimes happened that the watchman possessed the ability of the albatross: he would sleep as he walked his rounds and made his bows, and in his sleep he would beat a false alarm, having mistaken a landowner's coach for the governor. Then a vain commotion would take place in the town, which would end with the officials taking off their dress coats again and the town governor unhitching his troika, and the imprudent sentinel being slightly, or not so slightly, thrashed.

Such difficulties were encountered often and were not easily overcome, and they bore down with all their weight chiefly upon the town governor, who would always gallop out in front of everybody to meet the governor of the province, and be the first to receive his gubernatorial glances and outbursts, and then would gallop back, still standing, ahead of the governor's coach to the cathedral, where the archpriest would be waiting at the door in all his vestments, with the cross and aspergillum in a chalice of holy water. Here the town governor would open up the step of the provincial governor's carriage, by all means with his own hands; and with this gesture he would, so to speak, let the newly arrived personage descend from his wandering ark onto the native soil. Now all this is no longer done this way. It has all been spoiled, and even through the actions of the provincial governors themselves, among whom there were some who took pleasure in selling themselves short. By now, perhaps, they repent, but what has passed away can never be brought back: nobody opens up the step for them except lackeys and gendarmes.

But the former town governor was not at all embarrassed about performing this duty, and he served for all as the prime touchstone; he was always the first to find out whether the governor had arrived rabid or benign. And if the truth must be known, a lot depended on the town governor: he could spoil matters at the outset, because with just one awkward step he could throw the provincial governor into a rage and cause him to rip and roar; and also, with one deft hop, turn, or other appropriate contortion, he could put His Excellency into a state of benevolent good humor.

Now every reader, even though he may not have known those patriarchal customs, can judge how natural the panic was among the upper crust of Soligálich officialdom when it had to be represented by such an awkward, peculiar, and hard-headed town governor as Ryzhóv, who in addition to all his inconvenient personal qualities had a wardrobe that consisted of one quilted jacket of striped mattress-ticking and one shaggy peasant cap.

That was bound to be the first thing that would come as a blow right between the eyes for the "haughty presence," about whom idle tongues had brought the most frightful news to Soligálich. How could anything good be expected to come from this?

CHAPTER NINE

Alexander Afanásyevich really could fill anybody you chose with despair. He let nothing disturb him, and while he was awaiting the governor he behaved as if the dreadful impending event did not concern him at all. He did not tear down a single fence before the house of a single inhabitant; he repainted nothing with whitewash or ocher, and in general he undertook no measures either to spruce up the town or even change his own absurd costume. Instead, he continued to go about his business in his quilted jacket. Whenever some project was suggested to him, he would answer:

"It won't do to make the people lose a lot of money on this. After all, is the governor coming to lay waste the land? Let him go through, but let the fence stand." As for the demands about a dress coat, Ryzhóv beat them off by saying that he had no income for that and, as he said, "What I've got I'll wear. When I appear before God, I'll be stark naked. It's not a matter of clothes but of common sense and conscience. 'Greet him according to his clothes, take leave according to what he knows.'"

Nobody had any hope of out-butting the bull-headedness of Ryzhóv; and yet this was important not so much for stubborn Ryzhóv, who might not care at all, from his Biblical point of view, if the second person in the realm banished him from sight in that quilted jacket. Rather, it was important for everybody else, because the governor would naturally fly into a rage when he saw such a sight as a town governor in a quilted jacket.

Setting great store by the first impression of the guest they were expecting, the Soligálich officials pressed for only two things: (1) that a new coat of paint should be put on the log barrier that was raised and lowered across the highway at the entrance to the town, where Alexander Afanásyevich was to meet the governor; and (2) that Alexander Afanásyevich himself should appear on this occasion in a uniform suited to his position rather than in his striped quilted jacket. But how could they manage it?

Opinions differed. Most people tended to favor taking up a collection both to paint the barrier and to dress the town governor. This was all right, of course, as far as the barrier was concerned, but as a way of getting Ryzhóv into a uniform it wouldn't work at all.

He said, "That's a gift, and I won't take gifts." Then there triumphed over them all the proposal that was brought forth by the reverend archpriest out of his ripe store of wisdom. He saw no need for any kind of collection, either to paint the barrier or to put the ruler of the town into uniform. Rather, he said, the whole thing ought to rest upon the one who was guiltiest in spirit, and in his opinion the one who was guiltiest in spirit was the tax-farmer.[8] Accordingly, everything ought to fall on him. He alone had the obligation to paint the barrier at his own expense, and not through any kind of compulsion but out of zeal, in return for which the archpriest promised to mention it in a few brief words upon meeting the governor and, in addition, to pray for the contributor in a special ecclesiastically worded prayer offered straight from the altar table. Besides that, the reverend archpriest opined that the tax-farmer should give the court assessor, over and above his regular payment in kind, a triple portion of rum, French cognac, and grape vodka, for which the assessor had a constant hankering. Then let the assessor turn himself in on the sick list and sit quietly at home, drinking this supplementary payment in kind and keeping off the street; and let him hand over his dress coat, which was identical with a policeman's uniform, to Ryzhóv, who would scarcely find grounds for refusing it. Then the sheep would be safe and the wolves would be sated.

What made this plan still more fortunate was that the indispensable assessor was fairly similar to Ryzhóv in size and shape; and in addition, having married a merchant's daughter not long before, he had a full uniform in excellent condition. Consequently there remained only the task of prevailing on him, in the interests of the general welfare, to go to bed under cover of a serious illness when the authorities arrived, and hand over his accouterments for this occasion to Ryzhóv, whom the reverend archpriest, counting on his spiritual authority, undertook to persuade— which he did. Seeing in this neither gifts nor rewards, honest Alexander Afanásyevich—to the great good fortune of everybody—agreed to put on the uniform. Ryzhóv and the assessor's uniform underwent measurements and fittings, and after all the hems and seams in the coat and trousers had been let out on all sides, the matter was brought to a satisfactory conclusion. Although Alexander Afanásyevich felt a great deal of uncomfortable constraint in the uniform, still he was able to move about, and now he was after all a passable representative of authority. The decision was made to cover the little white cornice remaining between the dress coat and the linen trousers with a patch of the same kind of linen, which successfully hid this cornice. In a word, Alexander Afanásyevich was fitted out so that the governor could turn him in all directions and admire him this way and that. But it pleased an evil fate to turn all this to mockery and to leave Alexander Afanásyevich with the appropriately impressive appearance only on one side, and to spoil it completely on the other, and in such an ambiguous fashion that it gave rise to the most arbitrary interpretations of his political outlook, which even before had been puzzling enough.

CHAPTER TEN

The barrier at the town gates was painted in the national colors, consisting of black and white stripes with red borders, and before it even had time to get covered with dust, the news blew in that the governor had left the neighboring town and was bearing down on Soligálich. At once and everywhere soldiers were posted as signalmen, and at the fence before Ryzhóv's humble hut three lively post horses gnawed at the earth, hitched troika-fashion to the cart into which Alexander Afanásyevich was to spring at the first signal and dash out to meet the "haughty presence."

In these arrangements there was an enormous lot of awkward complications that filled everybody with troubled anxiety, and the cool and collected Ryzhóv did not like this at all. He made up his mind "to be always in his own place": he drove the troika from his own fence down to the gates of the town; and there, in full uniform, wearing his dress coat and white trousers, with report in hand, he sat down on the painted beam of the barrier and settled back like a hermit on a pillar. Around him there gathered a crowd of the curious, whom he did not drive away, but on the contrary entered into conversation with them, and in the midst of this conversation it pleased him to note that a cloud of dust had gathered on the highway, out of which there began to come forth a pair of lead horses with a postilion, decorated with copper disks. That was the governor racing along.

Ryzhóv quickly jumped into the cart and was about to drive off when suddenly he was startled by a general groan and sigh from the crowd, which shouted at him:

"Master, take off your britches!"

"What's that?" Ryzhóv asked.

"Your britches, Master—take 'em off!" the people answered. "Just look at the place where you sat. The whole barrier's done got printed on the white part."

Ryzhóv looked over his shoulder and saw that all the stripes of the national colors on the freshly painted barrier had been printed on his trousers with amazing clarity.

He frowned a little, but immediately sighed and said: "Coming this way there's nothing for the authorities to see," and he started his troika off at a gallop to meet the "haughty presence."

The people only threw up their hands in despair:

"He's hopeless! What will become of him now?"

CHAPTER ELEVEN

The fleetest of foot in the crowd quickly succeeded in letting the clergy and the elders at the cathedral know about Ryzhóv's ambiguous aspect as he went to meet the governor, but now it was every man for himself.

The most terrified of all was the archpriest, because the officials had hidden inside the church, but he stood with his cross on the entrance steps. He was surrounded by a very small group of clerics, among whom two figures stood out: a thickset deacon with a big head and a long-legged sexton in his vestments with holy water in a silverplated chalice that was trembling in his terrified hands. But now their fearful trembling gave way to petrification: on the square there came into view the galloping troika that pulled the post wagon, in which the gigantic figure of Ryzhóv towered with remarkable dignity. He was wearing the hat, the dress coat with its red collar, and the white trousers with the linen cornice sewn onto the top, all of which from a distance was spoiled by nothing at all. On the contrary, he appeared to everybody like something sublime, and indeed that is just the way he was supposed to appear. Standing firm on the wagon as it rolled at full speed, with the coachman bounding up and down on the driver's seat, Alexander Afanásyevich wavered neither to the right nor to the left but sailed along with his heroic arms folded across his chest as if he were on a triumphal chariot, throwing a whole cloud of dust on the coach-and-six and the springless carriage that followed behind. This springless carriage contained the bureaucrats. Lanskói rode alone in the coach; and in spite of the solid air of importance that distinguished him, it was evident that he was greatly interested in Ryzhóv, who was racing along ahead of him, standing erect in his undersized dress coat, which was too tight to cover the pattern of the national colors printed on his white trousers. It is quite possible that a large share of the governor's attention had been attracted to just this curiosity, the meaning of which was not too easy to understand and explain.

Just at the right moment the wagon turned off to one side, and just at the right moment Alexander Afanásyevich jumped down and opened the door of the governor's carriage.

Lanskói stepped out, having, as always, his invariably "haughty presence," which contained, however, a rather good heart. Holding the cross over the governor's head, the archpriest said: "Blessed be He that cometh in the name of the Lord," and then sprinkled him a little with holy water.

The dignitary applied his lips to the cross, took a batiste handkerchief and wiped off the drops that had fallen on his haughty brow, and then walked into the church *first*. All this took place in full view of Alexander Afanásyevich and greatly displeased him—all this was "haughty." His unfavorable impression grew still stronger when the governor, having entered the house of God, did not cross himself or bow to anybody— neither the altar nor the people—and walked up to the altar platform straight as a stick without even nodding his head.

This was contrary to all of Ryzhóv's principles in regard to respect for God and the duty of those in high places to set an example for those who are lower. His pious spirit roused itself and rose to incredible heights.

Ryzhóv kept walking behind the governor, and as Lanskói drew closer and closer to the platform in front of the iconostasis, Ryzhóv kept shortening the distance that separated them. Suddenly he seized him by the arm and said in a loud voice:

"Sergéi, thou slave of God! Come humbly, not haughtily, into the temple of the Lord, and present thyself as the greatest of sinners—like this!"

With that he put his hand on the governor's back and gravely bent him over in a full bow, then let him go and stood at attention.

CHAPTER TWELVE

The eyewitness who passed on this anecdotal story about the Soligálich eccentric said nothing about the way it was received by the people and authorities who were standing in the church. We know only that nobody was bold enough to stand up for the bent-over governor and halt the intrepid arm of Ryzhóv. But the information about Lanskói is somewhat more detailed. Sergéi Stepánovich gave not the slightest cause for a continuation of the disorder, but on the contrary, "exchanged his haughty pride for sensible self-possession." He did not interrupt Alexander Afanásyevich, nor did he say even one word to him. Instead, he crossed himself, turned around and bowed to all the people, and then quickly went out and left for the apartment that had been prepared for him.

Here Lanskói received the officials, both appointed and elected; and those who appeared worthy of greater confidence he questioned at length about Ryzhóv, asking what kind of man he was and in what manner he was tolerated in society.

"That's our policeman Ryzhóv," answered one of the officials.

"What about him—no doubt a little off?"

"Oh, no, sir—he's just always *like that*."

"Then why keep a man *like that* in the service?"

"He's good in the service."

"He's insolent."

"He's the humblest of men: if his superior sits on his neck, he will reason: 'This is what I must bear,' and he will bear it. Only, he's read the Bible a lot and that has unsettled him."

"You are talking nonsense: the Bible is the book of God."

"Yes, sir, that's right; only, it's not suitable for everybody to read: among the monks it arouses the passions, and among the laymen it disturbs the mind."

"What twaddle!" Lanskói answered, and went on with his questions: "And how is he about bribes—moderate?"

"Oh, good heavens!" said the official. "He won't take any at all."

The governor became even more skeptical.

"That," he said, "I refuse to believe on any account."

"But he really won't."

"Then tell me," he said, "what does he live on?"

"He lives on his salary."

"You're talking nonsense—there is no such man in all of Russia."

"You'd think there wasn't," he said, "but such a man has turned up here."

"And what salary does he get?"

"Ten rubles a month."

"But you know very well," he said, "that's not enough to feed a sheep."

"That's right," he said, "it's not easy to live on it—only, he does."

"How is it that nobody else can and yet he does?"

"He's filled up on Bible-reading."

"It's all very well to be 'filled up on Bible-reading,' but what does he eat?"

"Bread and water."

And here the official told all about how Ryzhóv handled everything.

"Why, he's a perfectly amazing man!" Lanskói exclaimed, and he sent for Ryzhóv.

Alexander Afanásyevich came and stood at the threshold as a sign of his submission to authority.

"Where were you born?" Lanskói asked him.

"Here. I was born on Low Street," answered Ryzhóv.

"And where did you go to school?"

"I didn't go to school. I grew up at home with my mother, and my mother baked pies."

"Did you study anywhere?"

"With the sexton."

"What is your religion?"

"Christian."

"You behave very strangely."

"I haven't noticed it: everybody thinks anything is strange that he himself is not used to."

Lanskói thought this was a provocative, insolent remark and, looking sternly at Ryzhóv, he asked sharply:

"Do you not belong to some sort of sect?"

"There is no sect here. I go to the cathedral."

"Do you go to confession?"

"I confess to God in the presence of the priest."

"Have you a family?"

"A wife and son."

"Is your salary too small?"

The ever unsmiling Ryzhóv broke into a smile.

"I get ten rubles a month," he said, "and I don't know whether that is a lot or a little."

"It's not much."

"Report to the Emperor that for a servant of the devil that is too little."

"And for a faithful one?"

"It's enough."

"They tell me you use no special funds?"

Ryzhóv looked at him and said nothing.

"Tell me honestly: can that be so?"

"And why should it not be so?"

"You get very little money."

"If you use a lot of restraint, you can get along without a lot of money."

"But why don't you ask for some other position?"

"Then who would fill this one?"

"Somebody else."

"Do you really think he would do it better than I?"

Now it was Lanskói who smiled. His not entirely cold heart had begun to take a genuine interest in the policeman.

"Listen," he said, "you really are a queer fellow. Please sit down."

Ryzhóv sat down opposite the "haughty presence."

"They say you are a connoisseur of the Bible?"

"I read it as much as my time allows—and I advise you to."

"All right; but—can I convince you that you can talk to me completely frankly and impartially?"

"Lying is forbidden in the Ten Commandments—I'm not going to lie."

"Good. Do you have respect for the authorities?"

"No."

"Why not?"

"They are lazy, greedy, and hypocritical about the throne."

"Well, you are frank. Thank you. Do you also prophesy?"

"No, but I draw conclusions from the Bible about what clearly follows."

"Can you perhaps show me one of your conclusions?"

Ryzhóv answered that he could, and at once he brought a whole sheaf of papers with the inscription "Singlethought."

"What prophecies are there here about the past that came true?" asked Lanskói.

The policeman leafed through the familiar pages and read: "The Empress in her correspondence with Voltaire called him a second Chrysostom. For this foolish comparison the life of our ruler will not have a peaceful ending."

On the lined margin opposite this passage there was the notation: "Fulfilled with the grievous marriage of Paul Petróvich."[9]

"Show me something else."

Ryzhóv again started turning through the pages and pointed out a new passage, which consisted of the following: "A new decree has been issued about the felling of trees. Henceforth the cold will be worse in the huts of the poor. We may expect a special punishment." And once again there was a note in the margin: "Fulfilled; see page so-and-so," and on that page there was a note about the death of the young daughter of Emperor Alexander the First, with the notation: "This was the consequence of the tax that was placed on forests."[10]

"But wait a moment," said Lanskói. "Aren't the forests property?"

"Yes, but warming the air of a house is a necessity."

"Are you against property?"

"No; I am only for keeping everybody warm in freezing weather. There is no reason to give the forests to those who are warm without them."

"And what do you think about head taxes? Should people be taxed?"

"We must have taxes, and we ought to have extra ones on every kind of luxury, so that the rich instead of the poor will pay the treasury."

"Hm, hm! You didn't pick up this doctrine anywhere, did you?"

"From the Scriptures and my conscience."

"You're not guided in this matter by any sources from modern times?"

"All other sources are impure and full of vanity."

"Now, finally, tell me this: how is it that you have no fear of what you write or of what you did to me in the church?"

"What I write, I write for myself; and what I did in the house of God, I had to do in order to defend the authority of the Tsar."

"Why of the Tsar?"

"So that everybody should see that his servants respect the national religion."

"But you know, I could handle you in an entirely different way from the way I am handling you."

Ryzhov looked at him in pity and answered:

"And what kind of evil can be done to somebody who knows how to support his family on ten rubles a month?"

"I could have you arrested."

"They eat better in jail."

"You could be deported for this insolence."

"Where could I be deported where things would be worse for me, and where my God would abandon me? He is with me everywhere, and there is nobody to fear except Him."

The haughty head nodded, and Lanskói's left hand reached out to Ryzhóv.

"Your character is estimable," he said, and ordered him to depart.

But evidently he still did not completely trust this Biblical socialist, and he himself personally questioned several persons among the common people.

They twirled their hands in the air and answered in unison: "He's our sort of regular whatcha-may-call-it."

Nobody got anything more positive about him out of them.

When he said farewell, Lanskói told Ryzhóv:

"I will not forget you, and I will follow your advice—I'll read the Bible."

"Yes, but that's not enough," Ryzhóv added. "You learn too how to live on ten rubles a month."

But Lanskói did not promise to follow this advice. He only laughed, gave him his hand again, and said:

"You're a queer one, all right."

Sergéi Stepánovich rode off, and Ryzhóv carried his "Singlethought" back home and went on writing in it whatever his powers of observation and his prophetic inspiration brought forth.

CHAPTER THIRTEEN

A good deal of time had passed after Lanskói's journey, and the events that took place during that trip through Soligálich had already been largely forgotten and erased by the hurly-burly of everyday life, when suddenly, like a bolt out of the blue, and to the astonishment not only of Soligálich but of all enlightened Russia as well, the town that had just undergone its inspection received news that was not only completely incredible but even impossible in a well-ordered system of government. The policeman Ryzhóv received the Cross of St. Vladímir, carrying with it hereditary nobility—the first Cross of St. Vladímir ever awarded to a policeman.

The decoration itself arrived along with instructions to put it on and wear it according to regulations. Both the cross and the official document were presented to Alexander Afanásyevich with the announcement that he had been granted said honor and said award upon the recommendation of Sergéi Stepánovich Lanskói.

Ryzhóv took the decoration, looked at it, and muttered aloud:

"So I'm a queer one!" And in his "Singlethought" he noted opposite the name of Lanskói: "He will become a count"—which, as everybody knows, was fulfilled. But as for wearing the decoration—Ryzhóv had nothing to wear it on!

Ryzhóv the bearer of the Cross of St. Vladímir lived to be almost ninety years old, neatly and characteristically noting down everything in his "Singlethought," which has probably been all used up for the papering of walls in various restorations around the district. He died after fulfilling all the Christian rites as established by the Orthodox Church, although his Orthodoxy was generally acknowledged to be "open to question." Even in religion Ryzhóv was a "certain sort of regular whatcha-may-call-it," but for all that it seems to me that there was something to be seen in him besides nonsense—and may he be remembered for it at the very beginning of the search for "three righteous men."

NOTES FOR "SINGLETHOUGHT"

[1] A quotation from N. A. Nekrásov's poem "Moróz, krásny nos."

[2] An allusion to a traditional folk manner of paying a teacher, which Leskóv described in detail in "Gorshók káshi stáromu uchítelju" ("A Pot of Porridge for the Old Teacher"), an article published in *Sélskoe chténie*, Nos. 3, 6, 7 (1878), suggesting a way of providing old-age assistance to retired teachers who receive no government pensions.

[3] Freely quoted, with omissions and changes, from the first chapters of Isaiah, principally 1:3–23.

[4] An allusion to the words of the town governor in Gógol's comedy *The Inspector General (Revizór)*, Act I, Scene 1: "It was established by God Himself, and the Voltaireans won't get anywhere talking against it."

[5] A remote monastery in northern Russia used by the Orthodox Church authorities as a place of exile.

[6] S. S. Lanskói (1787–1862) was governor of Kostromá Province from 1831 to 1834 and Minister of the Interior from 1855 to 1861, when he played an active role in preparing for the Emancipation of the Russian serfs.

[7] The emblem of governmental authority that stood on the desk of Tsarist Russian officials. Its three sides bore three decrees issued by Peter the Great, and on top of it rested the two-headed Russian eagle.

[8] Tax-farmers held the government monopoly on the sale of alcoholic drinks.

[9] In 1773 Prince Paul (later Emperor Paul I) married the Hessen-Darmstadt Princess Wilhelmina, who died three years later.

[10] The first daughter of Alexander I, Maria, lived only from 1799 to 1800; and the second, Elizabeth, was born in 1806 and died in 1808.

NOTE TO "A JOURNEY WITH A NIHILIST"

Human societies that are not at peace with themselves seem to have a dia-
bolical need for a devil-word, into which they can pour all their shapeless
fears and hatreds and give them tangible form. Once in medieval Europe
the devil-word was "infidel"; later it was "deist." In America during the
First World War it was "Hun"; during the Second, it was "Jap." In the
North Carolina countryside in the early 1920's, after the hard-pressed
tobacco farmers had been stampeded in their efforts to defend their economic interests by organizing a co-operative, the little boy who later became the editor of this book used to hear mothers threaten their children
by saying, "The co-ops'll git you if you don't behave!"

In Russia during the last decades of the nineteenth century the devil-
word was "nihilism." When Turgénev gave the word currency in 1862
in his great novel *Fathers and Sons,* its meaning was precise: it stood for
the young revolutionaries who had suddenly appeared on the Russian scene
at the end of the 1850's. Leskóv used it in this sense in 1864 in his novel
Nowhere to Go (Nékuda), but the nihilists themselves never forgave him
for the fact that, along with attractive portraits of its two nihilist heroes,
the novel also contained lampoons of a number of nihilist types who in
their various ways fell considerably short of the heroic.

By 1882, when Leskóv wrote "A Journey With a Nihilist," the term had
acquired the necessary emotional heat and semantic vagueness to make it
serve as a devil-word. The story is based upon an actual incident that was
related to Leskóv in 1879 by a girlhood friend of his daughter. She told
about a crusty old gentleman whose refusal to remove a suitcase from the
seat beside him led his irate fellow passengers to make a formal complaint.
The old gentleman's reason for his refusal, and also his identity, turned
out to be the same as in Leskóv's story. Leskóv's addition of the nihilist

theme to the incident reflected the general state of anxiety in Russia that had followed upon the assassination of Tsar Alexander II in the previous year by revolutionary terrorists. Leskóv returned to this theme in 1894 shortly before his death in "The March Hare" ("Záyachi remíz"), a sparkling satire about the misadventures of an ignorant, ambitious provincial policeman who set out to win fame and fortune by catching nihilists.

"A Journey With a Nihilist" was first published in a leading Petersburg newspaper on Christmas Day, and it bears some of the earmarks of the genre that Leskóv called the "Christmas story." A typically Leskóvian *skaz* element is found in the deacon, whose preposterous ideas, symbolized by his preposterous language, set the plot in motion.

The two meanings combined in Leskóv's puns and malapropisms can almost never be translated literally into a punning equivalent in another language. What is important is to create a play on Leskóv's basic word that will reproduce the *effect* of the original. Readers who compare the deacon's Russian malapropisms with the equivalents in the present version will be able to judge for themselves whether this translator has succeeded in putting this principle into practice. One pun, *Nakhalkikánots*, forced him to surrender abjectly in a footnote. On the other hand, in the reference to escaping from prison by going out along with the candle he restores an old German pun on *ausgehen*, "to go out" in an anecdote that Leskóv had very likely picked up from his acquaintances in the Petersburg German colony but could not convey adequately in Russian. In 1864 Leskóv had used the same punning anecdote (less successfully) in Book II, Chapter 20, of his novel *Nowhere to Go (Nékuda)*. In the present story he uses the very pointlessness of the deacon's account to make a point about the deacon. This translator, however, cannot help feeling that Leskóv would not have missed the chance to keep the pun if the Russian language had made it possible. Fortunately, English does.

A JOURNEY
WITH A NIHILIST

Who gallops, who flies in mysterious haze?[1]
Goethe

CHAPTER ONE

I once happened to spend Christmas Eve on the train, and it was not
without its adventures.

It all took place on one of the small branch railway lines, quite isolated
from "high society," as you might say. The line was not yet completed,
trains ran irregularly, and passengers were stuffed in helter-skelter. No
matter what class you might choose, it all amounted to the same thing:
everybody turned out to be together.

There were no buffets yet; and many people, chilled by the cold, would
warm themselves out of pocket flasks.

These warming drinks stimulated sociability and conversation. The talk
turned more than anything else on the railroad, and people spoke of it
indulgently, which is a rare thing in our country.

"Yes, they do a bad job of carrying us," said some military man, "but
still we can be thankful to them—it's better than horses. With horses you
wouldn't get there in a whole day and a night, but now we'll be there
tomorrow morning and we can come back tomorrow night. For people
in government work it's a convenience to be able to see your family
tomorrow and then be back at your post the next day."

"Now, I think so too," chimed in a tall skinny cleric who had stood up
and was holding on to the back of the seat. "Their deacon there in town
his voice is ruint. When he sings out the amens he sounds like a rooster.
They offered me a ten-spot to go and sing the high mass for them. I'll
bellow my way through the service and get back to my village in one
night."

The only advantage they found in horses was that you could travel in a party of your own and stop wherever you wanted.

"But after all, in here you've got this company not for eternity, but only for a time," said a merchant.

"Still, if you get stuck with some people even for a time, you may remember it all your life," the deacon answered.

"How's that?"

"Well, suppose he's a nihilist, for example, and in his full vestments, with a sick-shooter and everything."

"That's something for the police to handle."

"It affects us all, because—don't you know?—all it takes is just a little shake and—boom! It's all over."

"Oh, come on, drop it. What got you started on that just as night is falling? We haven't got that kind of people yet."

"They can turn up anywhere."

"Let's get some sleep instead."

We all obeyed the merchant and went to sleep, and I can't tell you how long we had slept when suddenly we were jolted so violently that we all woke up, and right there with us in the railway car was a nihilist.

CHAPTER TWO

Where did he come from? Nobody had noticed where this unpleasant guest could have sprung from, but there could be no doubt about it: here was a genuine, purebred nihilist, and as a result everybody lost all thought of sleep at once. It was impossible to see him clearly, because he sat in the shadows in a corner by the window, but then we didn't need to get a good look at him—you could feel it in the air.

The deacon made an attempt to carry out an examination of his external features. He strolled over to the door of the car, right past the nihilist, and when he came back he announced in a whisper that he had very clearly distinguished "farthingale sleeves," in which there was unquestionably hidden a sick-shooter or nitroblistering.

The deacon appeared to be a very lively man and, considering his rural vocation, very enlightened and full of curiosity, and full of ingenuity as well. He at once began to stir up the officer and persuade him to take out a cigarette and go up to the nihilist and ask him for a light from his cigar.

"You are not a civilian," he said. "You've got spurs. You can stamp on him so hard that he'll roll out like a billiard ball. An army man can always be bolder."

We couldn't get in touch with the conductor, because he had locked us in and disappeared.

The army officer agreed. He got up, stood first at one window and then at the other, and finally went up to the nihilist and asked for a light from his cigar.

We vigilantly observed this maneuver and saw how cunningly the nihilist wiggled out: he did not give him a light from his cigar but struck a match and silently handed it to the officer.

He did all this coldly, quickly, skillfully but impersonally, and in complete silence. He thrust the lighted match into his hands and turned away.

Nevertheless, this one illuminated moment while the match flamed was all we needed in our state of strained attention. We saw that this was a thoroughly suspicious man, a man even of uncertain age, just like a carp from the River Don that you can never be sure about—whether it is this year's or last year's. A lot was suspicious—his round "Von Graefe" spectacles, his disloyal cap, not an Orthodox pancake type but one with a heretical neck covering, and over his shoulders a typical plaid robe that served as a kind of uniform for the nihilist profession. But what we disliked most of all was his face. It was not shaggy and administrative, like those of the orthodox nihilists of the 1860's, but a contemporary face, reminding you of a pike fish, a kind of falsified face that represented a preposterous hybrid of a nihilist girl and a gendarme. In general, it was the very likeness of a heraldic mountain goat.

I didn't say heraldic *lion* but precisely a heraldic *mountain goat.* Remember how they are usually represented along the sides of aristocratic coats-of-arms: in the middle there is an empty helmet and visor, and a lion and a mountain goat gnash their teeth at it. The goat's whole figure is tense and restless, as if "he did not seek happiness, nor did he flee it." [2] Moreover, the colors in which our unpleasant traveling companion was displayed promised nothing good: his hair was tobacco-colored, his face was greenish, and his eyes were gray and darted back and forth like a metronome set at a fast "allegro escapato." (There's no such tempo in music, of course, but there is in nihilist jargon.)

The devil knows whether somebody else was after him or he was after somebody else—you couldn't make heads or tails of it.

CHAPTER THREE

When the officer came back to his seat, he said that in his opinion the nihilist was rather neatly dressed, and was wearing gloves, and on the seat in front of him there was a laundry basket.

The deacon, though, at once proved that all this didn't mean a thing, and as supporting evidence he told several curious stories he had got from his brother, who worked somewhere in a custom house.

"They once had one of them come through there," he said, "not just in plain gloves but in real *fil de pomme,* and as soon as they started searching him he turned out to be a cardsharp. They thought he was a quiet kind and put him in an underwater prison, but he got out from under the water."

Everybody wanted to know how the cardsharp had got out from under the water.

"Why, it was very simple," the deacon explained. "He began to claim they had put him away for nothing, and he started asking for a candle. 'I am greatly bored in the dark,' he says. 'I request permission for a candle. I want to write a proclamation to Count Lorís-Mélikov[3] in the Arrestigating Commission and tell him who I am and in what anguistipation I comply for a pardon and a good job.' But the prison commander was an old muzzle-loading type; he knew all their tricks and he wouldn't allow it. 'Once we've nabbed a man,' he says, 'he can't comply for anything.' And so he kept him languishing in darkness. But when he died and a new one was put in charge, the cardsharp saw that he was green, and he started weeping and wailing and asking for at least a tiny piece of a tallow candle and some kind of religious book, 'Because,' he says, 'I want to read pious thoughts and come to repentance.' The new commander gave him a piece of candle and the religious journal *Orthodox Slurvey* and the man got away."

"How did he get away?"

"He and the candle just went out."

The officer looked at the deacon and said:

"You're telling some kind of nonsense!"

"It's no nonsense at all. There was an investigation."

"And what was the meaning of the candle?"

"The devil knows what it meant! Only they looked all over the cell afterwards, and there wasn't a hole or a crack or anything, and the candle wasn't there, and the only thing that was left of the pages from the *Orthodox Slurvey* was the spellbinding."

"Now what in the devil are you talking about?" the officer said impatiently.

"It's no nonsense at all. I'm telling you there was an investigation, and they found out afterwards who he was, but then it was too late."

"And who *was* he?"

"A Nakhalkikánets from the other side of Tashként.[4] General Chernyáev[5] sent him on horseback to take five hundred rubles from Kókorev[6] to the Bulgarians, but he lost all the money at cards in the theaters and at the balls, and ran away. He rubbed himself with candle tallow and he and the light went out."

The officer threw up his hands and turned away.

But the rest of the passengers were not bored at all by the talkative deacon; they listened in rapture as he made his way from the crafty Nakhalkikánets with his spellbinding to our own situation at present with our suspicious nihilist. The deacon said:

"I'm not taken in by his neatness, and since we're coming right now to the first station—there's an old woman watchman there that sells vodka out of a kerosene jug—I'll drink butterschaft with the conductor, and we'll give him a shake, and we'll see what's in the laundry basket—what kind of equipment he's got there."

"Only we've got to be careful."

"Don't worry—we'll do it with a prayer. InthenameoftheFatherandofthe SonandoftheHolyGhostforeverandeveramen."

Suddenly we felt a jolt and something started squealing. Many people shuddered and crossed themselves.

"That's it!" shouted the deacon. "We've hit the station."

He went out and started running, and in his place the conductor came in.

CHAPTER FOUR

The conductor took his stand right in front of the nihilist and politely said:

"Wouldn't you like to check that nice little basket, sir, in the baggage car?"

Then for the first time we heard the voice of our odious traveling companion. He insolently answered:

"No."

The conductor set forth the reasons why "it was not permitted to carry such big articles into the passenger car."

He answered through his teeth:

"And that's excellent that it's not permitted."

"Then don't you want me to check your nice little basket in the baggage car?"

"No."

"But how is that? You yourself agree that it's not permitted, and yet you won't check it?"

"No."

The deacon, who had come back in at that point, could not contain himself, and he shouted: "Well, can you beat that!" But when he heard the conductor threatening to get his chief and swear out a warrant, he calmed down and agreed to wait till the next station.

"That's a big town," he explained to us. "There they'll put the screws on him."

And indeed what a stubborn man that was: you couldn't get a thing out of him except that *"No."*

Could it be that those spellbindings really were mixed up in this?

It had become very interesting, and we waited impatiently for the next station.

The deacon announced that he had a gendarme there who was even a baptizing buddy of his, an old muzzle-loading kind of a man.

"He'll give him such a double-barreled poke in the ribs," he said, "that all that hired education will pop right out of him."

The chief appeared in the aisle of the car and said:

"As soon as we get into the station, kindly take away that basket."

But the nihilist answered him in the same tone:

"No."

"But read the rules!"

"No."

"Then I must ask you to come with me to the station master and explain yourself. Here is the stop now."

CHAPTER FIVE

We had arrived.

This station was bigger than the others, and had more trimmings. We could see lights and a samovar on the platform, and behind glass doors a lunchroom and gendarmes—in a word, all the essentials. And just imagine: our nihilist, who had put up such a flagrant resistance all the way, suddenly revealed his intention to make the move that is known among them by the name of *allegro escapato*. He picked up his little traveling bag and started for the door, but the deacon noticed it and adroitly barred his way. At that very moment the chief conductor appeared with the station master and a gendarme.

"Is that your basket?" asked the station master.

"No," answered the nihilist.

"What do you mean—no?!"

"No."

"Just the same, come along with me."

"You won't get away this time, brother!" said the deacon.

The nihilist and all the rest of us as witnesses were taken into the station master's office, and the basket was brought in there too.

"What kind of articles are in there?" the station master asked sternly.

"I don't know," answered the nihilist.

But they refused to stand on ceremony with him any longer: they instantly opened the basket and saw a brand-new light blue dress. Then at that very moment a Jew burst into the office with a desperate wail and shouted that that was his basket, and the dress in it was one he was delivering to a lady in high society, and the basket had really been put on the seat by him and no one else, and he called on the nihilist as his witness.

The nihilist confirmed that they had got in together and the Jew really had carried in the basket and put it on the seat, and he himself had lain down under the bench.

"But what about your ticket?" the Jew was asked.

"Well, about the ticket—" he answered. "I didn't know where to get a ticket . . ."

The Jew was ordered held, and the nihilist was ordered to show his identification papers. He silently handed them over. The station master took one look, abruptly changed his tone, and invited him into his private office, adding:

"They are waiting for your excellency in here."

And when the man had disappeared beyond the door, the station master put his hands to his mouth like a trumpet and announced to us very distinctly:

"That's *the prosecuting attorney of the court!*"

We all suddenly felt a sense of complete satisfaction, and we bore up under it in silence. Only the officer alone shouted out:

"And all this is the work of that loud-mouthed deacon! Now then—where is he? Where did he make off to?"

But we all looked around in vain to see "where he had made off to"— the deacon was gone. He had gone out like the Nakhalkikánets, and even without a candle. For that matter, it wasn't necessary, because the sky was already growing light and the church bells were ringing in town for Christmas matins.

NOTES FOR "A JOURNEY WITH A NIHILIST"

[1] The first line of Goethe's poem "Der Erlkönig," which Leskóv quoted in the Russian translation by V. A. Zhukóvsky.

[2] A quotation from Lérmontov's poem "Párus" ("A Sail").

[3] Count Mikhaíl Tariélovich Lorís-Mélikov (1825–88) was a prominent liberal who in 1880 was placed in charge of a "Supreme Commission for the Maintenance of State Order and the Social Tranquility."

[4] A fictitious geographical name with a Central Asian sound about it which is a pun on *nakhál*, "rascal."

[5] General Mikhaíl Grigóryevich Chernyáev (1828–98) in 1865 commanded the Russian troops that captured Tashként in Central Asia and in 1876 commanded the Serbian army in its war against Turkey.

[6] Vasíly Alexándrovich Kókorev (1817–89) was a wealthy Russian industrialist and supporter of Russian Pan-Slavism.

NOTE TO "DECEPTION"

Leskóv's pessimism over his native Russia in the 1880's led him to such despair that he once wrote to an old friend, "I cannot forgive myself for never having acquired the French language to the point where I could work in it like my native tongue. I would leave Russia at once and forever."[1]

It was fortunate for Russian literature that Leskóv's French was not very good; for he stayed at home, fumed and fretted, and transmuted his moral indignation into a series of little satirical masterpieces.

One of them is "Deception," which was first published in November 1883 and grew out of Leskóv's lifelong interest in the Jews and his concern over anti-Semitism in Russia. His manner of dealing with this inflammatory issue in "Deception" is so subtle that his less astute readers are constantly in danger of losing their footing on the slippery precipice of his irony. Instead of attacking anti-Semitism head on, he lures the reader into his trap with an opening scene in which a group of highly "respectable" Russians are voicing highly conventional opinions about the need to "finish off the Jews." Then within this setting he makes his defense of the Jews through the mouth of a self-centered, self-confident retired army officer whom no one could possibly suspect of harboring radical ideas. The officer's defense of the Jews consists, not in attempting to refute the respectable Russians' assumption that the Jews are rascals, but rather in telling a story designed to show that they are far surpassed in rascality by the Rumanians. The reader can see that the officer has merely replaced anti-Semitism with anti-Rumanianism, but Leskóv does not stop there. In the very act of telling his anti-Rumanian story the officer unconsciously reveals a whole host of negative traits in himself and his fellow Russians.

"Deception" is one of two stories in the present collection that were not included in the eleven-volume edition of Leskóv's works published in

the Soviet Union in 1956–1958. One of its editors, the late Borís Eikhen-
baum, told the present writer in 1955 that "Deception" would be omitted
from the eleven-volume edition because of misgivings in some quarters
lest the Rumanians should be offended. The present editor has no such
misgivings. Indeed, the only thing that in his opinion could justifiably
offend the Rumanians would be the assumption that they were unable to
appreciate Leskóv's irony.

It is highly possible that Leskóv's literary treatment of anti-Semitism
in "Deception" grew out of his work during 1883 on a powerful essay in
defense of equal rights for Jews entitled *The Jew in Russia: A Few Remarks on the Jewish Question,*[2] which was published anonymously and in
only fifty copies in early 1884 for circulation within the Russian government. The book created a sensation in highly placed circles in Petersburg.
When the editor of a prominent Jewish periodical got hold of a copy, he
devoted half a dozen editorials to an extensive summary of it, adding the
comment that the work was evidently written by some highly placed
government official, and expressing regret that the author of such a well-
written document was not a professional writer.[3] Leskóv wrote the book
as part of a joint effort by several prominent Russians, including the critic
M. A. Antonóvich, to furnish documents in support of equal civil rights
for Jews to the high commission created in 1883, under the leadership of
Count Pálen, to review the legal position of Jews in Russia.

DECEPTION

*A fig tree casteth her
untimely figs, when she is shaken
of a mighty wind.*
Rev. 6: 13

CHAPTER ONE

Just before Christmas we were traveling south, and sitting in the railway car we deliberated over those contemporary questions which provide a lot of material for conversation and at the same time require prompt solutions. We talked about the weakness of the Russian character, about the lack of firmness in certain agencies of the government, about classical education, and about the Jews. Above all else we devoted our solicitude to strengthening the government and finishing off the Jews, if it was impossible to reform them and bring them at least up to the well-known height of our own moral standards. The matter did not look very promising, however: none of us saw any way of taking charge of the government or of arranging for everybody born in Jewry to go back into the womb and get born again with an entirely different nature.

"And really now, how can it be done?"

"You just can't do it."

And we dismally hung our heads.

We were in good company: the people were modest and undoubtedly substantial.

In all fairness one would have to admit that the most remarkable person among the passengers was a certain retired army officer. He was an old man of athletic build. His rank was unknown, because the only part of all his martial ammunition that had survived was his cap; all the rest had been replaced by civilian productions. The old man was white-haired as Nestor and muscular as Samson—before he got shorn by Delilah. In the strong features of his swarthy face there predominated a firm expression of an unmistakable decisiveness. Without any doubt this was a positive character and a staunchly practical man. Such men are not to be sneezed at in our time, nor are they to be sneezed at in any other time either.

The old gentleman did everything intelligently, crisply, and according to plan. He had got into the railway car before anybody else and as a result had picked out the best seat for himself, to which he skillfully annexed the two neighboring seats and firmly reserved them for himself through a masterful arrangement of his equipment for the journey, obviously worked out in advance. He had with him three pillows of enormous proportions. These pillows constituted in themselves a sizable amount of baggage for one person, but they were so well garnished that each of them seemed to belong to a separate passenger: one of the pillows was done in dark blue chintz with yellow forget-me-nots—the kind that is found most often among travelers of the village priesthood; the second one was done in red calico, which is widely used in the merchant class; and the third, in a thick striped ticking—the unmistakable mark of a junior captain. Obviously the passenger did not aim at an ensemble but aimed rather at something more essential, namely, at adaptability to far more serious and substantial purposes.

The three unmatched pillows could have deceived anybody at all into assuming that the three seats they occupied belonged to three different persons, and this was just what that farsighted traveler required.

Besides that, the masterfully planted pillows by no means had only that one simple name which might be bestowed upon them at first glance. The pillow in the striped ticking was actually a suitcase and traveling larder for food and drink; and on these grounds it enjoyed preferential attention from its owner in comparison to the others. He placed it directly opposite him, and as soon as the train began moving away from the platform, he at once loosened and lightened it, unfastening for that purpose the white bone buttons of its pillow-case. From the ample aperture thus created he began to take out neatly and adroitly rolled-up packages of various calibers which turned out to contain cheese, caviar, sausage, rolls, tangy winter apples, and fruit tarts. What looked out at the world more merrily than anything else was a crystal flask that contained a fluid of a wonderfully pleasant color and bore an ancient and well-known inscription: "Monks also do partake of this." The rich amethyst color of the liquid was excellent, and the taste very likely corresponded to the purity and pleasantness of the color. Connoisseurs in such matters assure us that one never clashes with the other.

During all the time in which the rest of the passengers were arguing about the Jews, about the fatherland, about the lowering of moral standards, about the way we ourselves had been our own worst enemies, and in general concerning themselves with "rebuilding the foundations," the white-haired old warrior remained majestically calm. He behaved like a man who knew just when the time would come for him to say his word, and meanwhile he simply ate the provisions he had spread out on his striped pillow and drank three or four little glasses of the appetizing liquid "of which monks also do partake." During all that time he did not utter a sound. But when all that important operation had been completed according to plan, and when he had carefully put away the whole canteen once again, he snapped his folding knife shut and lit up with his own match an unbelievably thick cigarette he had rolled himself and then suddenly started talking. At once he seized control of everybody's attention.

He spoke loudly, impressively, and boldly, so that no one thought of talking back to him or contradicting him; but the important thing was that he introduced into our conversation a lively and universally interesting love element, to which politics and the censorship of morals was added only very lightly and left-handedly, without being tiresome and without spoiling the lively adventures of days long past.

CHAPTER TWO

He began his speech very delicately, with an extremely pleasant and in a certain sense even beautiful reference to the "society" now gathered here, and then he turned at once to the subject of our long-existing—and nowadays so widespread—discussion.

"You see," he said, "I am not only familiar with all this you've been talking about—I actually know it very well. As you can see, I am not a young man—I have lived a lot, and I can say too that I have seen a lot. Everything you say about the Jews and the Poles is all true, but it all comes from our own stupid Russian delicacy: we want to be more delicate than anybody else. We let foreigners walk all over us, and then we tramp on our own people. Unfortunately, that is very well known to me, and even more than well known: I have been through it myself. But you are wrong if you think all this has just come about recently: it got started a long time ago, and it reminds me of a fateful story. Even though I don't belong to the fair sex, which included Scheherazade, still I too could keep a sultan occupied with something more than frivolous tales. I know the Jews very well, because I live in this part of the country and I see them all the time; and in the old days, when I was still in active military service, and when I happened through a quirk of fate to be a town governor, I had a lot to do with them. I had occasion to borrow money from them, I also had occasion to pull them by their side-locks, chuck them out on their ears, all sorts of things—especially when a Jew would come for his interest and I hadn't the money to pay. But there were times too when I was good friends with them and would go to their weddings, and eat their matzo and kugel and homentashen; and even now I would rather have their caraway-seed rolls with my tea than our half-baked Russian bread—but as for what people want to do with the Jews now, that I don't understand. Nowadays they are talking about them everywhere, and even writing about them in the newspapers . . . What's it for? Among us in the old days you'd just swat him one on the back with your long-stemmed pipe, or if he was very insolent, shoot a few cranberries at him—and he'd light out. And the Jew is worth no more than that—but he shouldn't be finished off completely, because the Jew on occasion can be a useful man.

"As for the low-down tricks that are laid at the door of the Jews, I can tell you that's nothing at all beside the Moldavians, and especially the Wallachians; and what I would propose for my part is not to put the Jews back in the womb, because that is not possible, but to remember that there are people worse than the Jews."

"Who, for instance?"

"Why, for instance, the Rumanians!"

"Yes, they do say they are pretty bad," responded a solid passenger with a snuffbox in his hands.

"Oh-h-h, let me tell you!" our old man exclaimed, coming to life all over. "Believe me, they are the very worst people on earth. You have only heard about them, but other people's words are like a stairway—they can lead you the devil knows where. I have been through all that myself, and as an Orthodox Christian I will testify that even though they do belong to our same Orthodox faith, so that we may have to go off and fight for them too some time, still they are rascals such as the world has never seen before."

And he told us about a few rascally tricks that were current or had at one time been current in the parts of Moldavia that he had visited during his military campaigns. But it turned out to be nothing new and not very spectacular, so that one of his listeners, an elderly, bald-headed merchant, actually yawned and said:

"We've heard that tune before!"

This comment offended the hero, and frowning slightly he said:

"Well, it goes without saying that a rascal is nothing new to a Russian tradesman."

But then the storyteller turned to those who appeared to him to be more enlightened and said:

"Since it's gone this far, gentlemen, I will tell you a little anecdote about their privileged class; I'll tell you about the morals and manners of their landowners. Here there will be appropriate references to that clouded vision we have of everything, and that reticence by which we injure only our own people and ourselves."

Naturally we begged him and he started off, explaining that this constituted one of the most important events in the whole of his military life.

CHAPTER THREE

(This is the way the storyteller began:)

A man, you know, shows his real nature best of all in money, at cards, and in love. They say this also happens in time of danger at sea, but I don't believe it: in danger any coward may bluster and a daredevil may turn tail. Cards and love . . . Love may be even more important than cards, because it is in fashion always and everywhere. The poet expresses this very correctly: "Love holds sway in every heart." Even among savage tribes they don't live without love, and in it we military men "live and move and have our being." We may assume that that was said in reference to another kind of love, but still, no matter what the priests may concoct, every kind of love is an "attraction to the object." That's what Kurgánov said.[1] But then there are objects and objects—that's true. For that matter, in youth—and for some people even up to old age—the object in most general use for love is, after all, a woman. No preachers can abolish that, because God outranks them all, and since He said, "It is not good that man should live alone," that's how it is.

In our time women didn't have these daydreams they have today about independence—which I don't condemn, mind you, because some husbands are completely impossible, so that you can even say it's a sin to be true to them. In those days there weren't any of these common-law marriages such as have been introduced nowadays. At that time bachelors were more careful on that score, and they valued their freedom. Marriages then were only the regular kind, real ones, celebrated in church, and along with them there was ordinarily nothing against free love for the military. Just as in Lérmontov's novels, there really was a great deal of that sin, only it was all carried on after the manner of the Schismatics, that is, "without any proofs." And especially among the military: we're a wandering tribe who never take root—today we're here, and tomorrow we blow our trumpets and off we go to some other place. Consequently, hidden from sight—forgot overnight. We were free as the wind. On the other hand, they loved us and waited for us. Wherever we went, whatever little town our regiment might enter, it was like guests at a banquet—at once the place would start simmering all over with giggle-wriggle. No sooner would the officers get cleaned up and dressed up and start out for a walk than in all the enchanting little houses the young ladies' windows would fly open and out would float the sound of pianos and singing. Their favorite song was

> *Just look at him, O mama mine,*
> *How handsome is our lodger fine!*
> *His gold-trimmed uniform—like lace!*
> *His ardent eyes light up his face!*

> *Oh, heavens!*
> *Oh, heavens!*
> *If only he were mine!*

Well, as you can imagine, at whatever window you heard that singing you'd just cast a glance—and it would never be in vain. Toward evening of that very day little notes would start flying in the hands of the orderlies, and then the maids would flutter off to the officer gentlemen . . . Not today's kind of soubrettes, but serf-girls, and they were the most unselfish of creatures. And as you might guess, we often were unable to pay them with anything except kisses. In that way successes in love would often begin with a go-between and end with the sender. The actor Grigóryev even sang a couplet about that in the vaudeville at the theater:

> *To win a fair lady's heart*
> *First court her wench.*

In the time of serfdom they were never called maids—just wenches.

Well, you can understand how devilishly spoiled we officers were with all that flattering attention from the women! We went from Great Russia to the Ukraine and found the same thing; we went on to Poland and found even more of such good things. Our commandant told us: "Be careful, gentlemen," and indeed God saved us all—there was not a single marriage. One of us was so much in love that he ran off to make a proposal, but he found his future mother-in-law alone and was so taken by her that he never proposed to the daughter. And it was not surprising that there should be successes—we were a young tribe, and everywhere we met with a blaze of passion. Today's way of life didn't exist then among the educated classes . . . Oh, down below, of course, they would squeal their little protests, but among educated people the amorous itch was simply all-powerful; and in that connection outward appearances meant a great deal. The maidens and the married ladies confessed that the very sight of a military uniform filled them, so to speak, with an uncontrollable kind of sinking feeling . . . Well, we knew that the drake was given a mirror in his wings so that the duck would want to see her own reflection. We didn't keep them from admiring themselves.

Among the military very few were married, because the pay was poor and it was boring. Get married and you'd have to drag yourself along behind a horse, with your wife behind the cow, your children behind the calves, and the servants behind your dogs. And to what purpose, when bachelors, by the grace of God, never experienced the slightest loneliness in their bachelorhood? And as for those who were a little more attractive than the average, or knew how to sing or draw or speak French—well, quite often they simply didn't know where to hide from the horn of plenty.

It would even happen that along with amorous favors they would receive expensive knickknacks, and in such a way, you understand, that they couldn't get rid of them. There were even cases where after just one incident the poor soul would open up completely, like a treasure out of nowhere; and then you had by all means to take everything she offered. Otherwise she would start by begging you on her knees and end by taking offense and bursting into tears. I've got one of those sacred gewgaws here that's stuck to my hand to this very day.

(The storyteller showed us his hand, and on one thick, stiff finger there came into view a gold enameled ring containing a rather large diamond. Then he continued his story:)

But the kind of vileness all around today, getting profit out of men—in our day there was not a trace of that. And after all, where would it have gone, and to what purpose? Then, you know, there was income from the estates; and besides, life was simple. None of these clubs and bouquets you have nowadays that you have to pay money for and then throw away. They dressed with taste, charmingly but simply; either a nice marceline silk or a colored muslin; and very often they didn't scorn even a nice little calico or even some kind of nice little inexpensive colored linen. Many young ladies for the sake of economy wore little pinafores with all kinds of those little fringes and rickrack braid on the shoulder straps, and often it was very pretty and smart-looking and becoming for many of them. And the walks they took and their roundy-views were not at all like the ones today. And nobody would ever invite ladies to any of those taverns outside of town where they skin you alive for everything and then peep through the cracks in the wall. God forbid! At that time a girl or a lady would have burned up with shame at the very thought, and wouldn't for anything in the world have gone to such places, where just walking past the servants was the same as running the gantlet! And you lead your lady by the hand, and you see how those rascals leer behind your back, because in their loutish eyes an honorable girl or lady swept away by the passion of love or just any madame from Amsterdam—there's no difference. Even if the honorable woman behaves more modestly, they will esteem her even less.

"There won't be much profit here," they would say. "If you look at the dame you can measure the gain."

Nowadays they pay no attention to it, but at that time a lady would take offense if anybody offered her even the most pleasant seclusion in such a place.

At that time people had taste, and everybody tried to give tone to all that, and to give it tone not through any kind of braggadocio but precisely through elegant simplicity—so that nothing at all should offer any reminder of filthy lucre. The lovers most often would go for a walk, for example, beyond the edge of town, picking cornflowers from the fields in bloom, or catching fish under the vines along the little stream, or in general doing something else just as innocent and artless. She would come with her serf-girl, and you would sit on a boundary marker and wait for her. Naturally, you would leave the girl somewhere along the boundary, and you and the young lady would plunge into the pure ripening rye . . . Those ears of grain, the sky, the various insects climbing along the stalks and on the ground . . . And beside you a young creature, often still with her boarding-school innocence, who doesn't know what to say to a military man and asks you as if you were a teacher of natural science: "What do you think—is that a bugger or a buggess?" Well, what is the use of thinking about whether it is a bugger or a buggess when such a pure and lively angel is alone with you and leaning on your arm? Heads start spinning, and it seems that nobody is to blame, and nobody can answer for anything, because your legs don't carry you, but the whole field floats off into the forest, where there are, oh! such oaks and maples, and in their shade the dryads are so pensive . . . ! There is nothing, nothing in the world, that is comparable to such a state of bliss! Such holy and serene happiness . . . !

(The storyteller was so carried away by his memories of those lofty moments that for a moment he fell silent. But during that time somebody softly remarked that for the dryads it would begin all right but it always ended in trouble.)

Oh yes (the narrator answered). Afterwards, naturally—well, what can you expect? But I am talking only about us, their partners: we were accustomed to accept this feminine attention and these sacrifices for ourselves in all simplicity, without any arguments, as an appropriate gift from Venus to Mars, and we neither demanded anything more prolonged for ourselves nor ourselves made any promises. We came and took and that was the last they ever saw of us. But all of a sudden our fortunes changed abruptly. Suddenly we received a completely unexpected assignment from Poland to Moldavia. The Polish men hugely praised that Rumanian territory to us: "There," they said, "the cucoonas,[2] that is, the Moldavian ladies, are such beauties, such perfections of nature, as don't exist anywhere else in the world. And it doesn't cost anything to get their love, it seems, because they are terribly ardent."

To be sure, we looked forward to such a treasure.

Our boys spruced themselves up. Before we left, every last one of them did his best to buy up all kinds of gloves, pomades, and perfumes in Warsaw and came with this supply so that the cucoonas would understand at once that we were no hillbillies, wearing bast shoes for gloves.

The trumpets sounded, the harness bells started jingling, and we started off with a merry song:

Our mistresses we leave behind,
Our friends we leave as well,
For swords' clash and bullets' whine
And a fate none can foretell.

We were expecting no one knew what blessings, but matters turned out in a way that nobody could possibly have imagined.

CHAPTER FOUR

We entered their land with all our Russian cordiality, because the Moldavians were all Orthodox, but from the very first we got an unpleasant impression of their country: the lowlands, the corn, the watermelons, and the Jerusalem artichokes were excellent, but the climate was unhealthy. A great many of us became ill even on the march, and in addition we found no friendliness or thankfulness anywhere.

We had to hand over money for everything, no matter what we might need; and if we took anything at all from a Moldavian, even a trifle, without paying for it, the dirty lout would set up such a wail you'd think he'd been robbed of his own child. Hand it back to him—"Here, take your trash, only don't howl so"—and he'd hide it and run off so that you couldn't find the ragged devil high or low. Another time you might want somebody to guide you or show you the way, and there would be nobody in sight—they would all run away. They're the greatest cowards in the world, and in their lower class we didn't come across a single beautiful woman. Nothing but dirty wenches and the ugliest kind of old hags.

Well, we thought to ourselves, maybe they are like this only on the farms along the road—there the people are always a little worse. Now once we came into a town it would be different. The Poles couldn't possibly have given us such assurances about the beautiful cucoonas if there weren't some basis for it. Where were they, these cucoonas? We would take a look.

We came into the town, but here too it turned out the same way: for absolutely everything it was "Kindly pay for it."

With reference to feminine beauty the Poles had told the truth. The cucoonas and the cucoonettes pleased us a lot: they were so languid and willowy that they even surpassed the Polish girls; and as you know, the Polish girls are famous—although for my taste they are a little on the big-mouthed side, and they have a character full of caprices. You'll have to bow and scrape a long time before you get her to the point where you can tell her, in the words of Mickiewicz, "Oh, my darling, what need have we of words?"[3] But in Moldavia it was entirely different—there the Jew was busy in everything. Yes sir, just the ordinary Jew, without him you'd find no poetry at all. The Jew would turn up in the inn and ask you:

"Aren't you oppressed by your solitude, and haven't you picked up the scent of any cucoona?"

You would tell him you had no need of his services, because your heart had been enthralled by, let us say, such-and-such a lady, whom you caught sight of, let's say, in such-and-such a house under a silken awning on the balcony. And the Jew would answer you: "That can be arrenched."

You would cry out in spite of yourself:

"What do you mean—'arrenched'?"

He would answer that it was possible to have the company of this lady, and on the spot he would suggest where to go outside of town, to which coffee house—where she too would go and drink coffee with you. At first you'd think this was poppycock, but no sir, it's not poppycock. Well, from your masculine point of view you naturally would see no obstacles; we'd all looked around and sniffed out something or other, and we were all ready to go out to the edge of town and drink coffee together with some cucoona.

I also told the Jew about a cucoona I had seen on a balcony. A very beautiful one. He said she was wealthy and had been married only a year.

Somehow, you know, this seemed very good, almost too good to believe. I asked him over again, and again I heard the same thing: Wealthy, married a year, and it was possible to drink coffee with her.

"You're not lying?" I asked the Jew.

"Why should I lie?" he answered. "I will handle everything honestly: you just sit at home this evening, and as soon as it gets dark her old nurse will come to you."

"What the devil do I need her nurse for?"

"You can't do it any other way. That's the custom here."

"Well, if that's the custom, there's nothing to do about it. You don't take your own rules into another monastery. Good—tell her nurse that I'll sit at home and wait for her."

"And don't light any lamps at your house," he said.

"Why not?"

"So people will think you're not at home."

I shrugged my shoulders and agreed to this too.

"All right," I said. "I'll have no lights."

In conclusion the Jew demanded a chervonets[4] for his services.

"What!" I said. "A chervonets! A chervonets already, before I've seen anything! That's going too far."

But he, rascal that he was, must have burnt his fingers before.

He smiled and said:

"No, after you've seen her it will be too late to get it. They say you can't be sure then about the military . . ."

"Look here," I said, "you just shut up about the military—that's none of your business—or else I'll crack your skull."

Still, I gave him the chervonets and damned his guts and called in my faithful slave.

I gave the orderly twenty kopecks and said to him:

"Go wherever you want and get as drunk as a lord, just so you stay away from the house this evening."

Notice how the expense kept piling up. It was not at all like picking cornflowers. And for all I knew I might have to gild the nurse as well.

Evening came on. My comrades went their various ways to the coffee houses. There were girls serving there too, and some rather interesting ones; but I lied to my comrades and pretended I had a toothache, and claimed I had to go to the infirmary and get some toothache drops from the medical assistant, or maybe even let them yank the tooth out. I ran all the way around our block and then darted unnoticed into my apartment. I opened the door and sat down in the dark next to the window. I sat there like a bump on a log and waited. My pulse pounded till I could hear it in my ears. Then a tiny doubt crept into me, and I wondered whether the Jew had not deceived me. Had he told me all that rot about the nurse just to get hold of a chervonets? And now he was boasting to other Jews somewhere about how he had taken in an officer, and they were all dying with laughter. And after all, what was the point here of the nurse, and what was she to do at my apartment? It was a stupid situation, and I decided I would wait until I had counted to a hundred, and then I would leave and join my comrades.

CHAPTER FIVE

But I had not yet counted to fifty when suddenly I heard a quiet knock at the door, something crept in, and there was a rustling noise. At that time they wore long coats of Châlons worsted, and the Châlons rustled.

Without any candles it was so dark in my room that you couldn't make out at all clearly just what sort of a tomato she was.

From the light of the street lamp I could just barely see that my guest must be an old girl well up in years. And yet even this had to be said with reservations, because her face was covered with a veil.

She came in and whispered:

"Is that you?"

I answered:

"Don't be afraid, speak up, there's nobody here. I'm waiting, the way it was agreed. Tell me, when will your cucoona go and drink coffee?"

"That," she said, "depends on you."

And still in a whisper.

"Well, I am always ready," I said.

"Good. Then what do you order me to tell her?"

"Tell her I said I was smitten, in love, and suffering; and whenever it suits her I will be there—even, for example, tomorrow evening."

"All right, tomorrow she will be able to come."

After that you would think she'd have to leave, wouldn't you? But she kept standing there!

"Well?"

Evidently I had to bid farewell to another chervonets. I could have made good use of it myself, but there was nothing to do about it; I was about to hand her the chervonets when she suddenly asked "whether I agreed to send the cucoona *three hundred chervontsy* by her at once?"

"Wha-a-a-t?"

Imperturbably she repeated: "Three hundred chervontsy," and began whispering to me that even though her cucoona's husband was very wealthy, he was unfaithful to her and spent a lot of money on an Italian countess, and the cucoona was left entirely alone, and even had to order her entire wardrobe from Paris at her own expense, since she did not want to be worse-looking than the rest . . .

And so, you understand me, the devil knows what that was! Three hundred chervontsy—no more, no less! Why, that was the same as a thousand rubles in paper! A major's salary for a whole year! A million rounds of shot! How could such a thing be uttered, such a demand be made to an officer? Nevertheless, I was quick to answer. I didn't think I had that much money on me, but I was bound to uphold my honor.

"Money for us Russians," I said, "is a trifle. We don't talk about money. But who will guarantee to me that you will hand the money over to her, and won't take three hundred chervontsy for yourself?"

"Of course I'll give them to her," she said.

"No," I said, "the money is not an important matter, but I don't want to let you make a fool of me. Let me get together with her, and I will perhaps give even more than that to her in person."

But the tomato took offense and started reading me a lecture.

"Just what do you mean?" she said. "The cucoona wouldn't think of accepting it herself."

"I don't believe you."

"Well, it's this way or not at all," she said.

"Then not at all."

She filled me with such impressions that I actually felt a physical fatigue, and I was very glad when the devil took her away from me.

I went to the coffee house and joined my comrades, drank my fill of wine, and spent my time like the rest of them—gallantly. The next day I took a walk past the house where my chosen cucoona lived; and I saw her sitting at the window, pretty as a picture, in a green velvet jacket, with a bright double rose on her breast. Her collar was cut low; her bare arms were in broad, loose-flowing sleeves, embroidered in gold, and her body—that wonderfully rosy-hued body—peeped out of the green velvet just like a watermelon out of its rind.

I couldn't bear it, and I ran up to the window and started off:

"You have tormented me as no woman with a heart should ever do; I have languished and awaited the minute of happiness when I could see you somewhere, but instead of you there came to me some greedy and suspicious old woman, about whom i, as an honorable man, consider it my duty to warn you: she is besmirching your good name."

The cucoona did not get angry; I blurted out to her that the old woman had asked for money—and even at this she only smiled. And oh! the devil take it—when she revealed those little teeth they were just like pearls in the midst of coral. Everything was fascinating; and yet somehow there was just a hint about her of the simpleton.

"All right," she said, "I will send the nurse back."

"Who? That same old woman?"

"Yes. She will go back this evening."

"Oh, please!" I said. "You surely don't know that that greedy old woman makes you out to be some sort of person unworthy of respect!"

But the cucoona suddenly dropped her handkerchief out the window, and when I stooped down to pick it up, she leaned over slightly so that that confounded low-cut bodice loomed up before me like a ship under full sail, and she whispered:

"I'll tell her . . . She'll be kinder . . ." And with that the window snapped shut.

"I will send her back this evening . . . I will tell her to be kinder . . ." You could see that there was something more here than stupidity—there was also a bold, businesslike efficiency. And all this in such a sweet little pretty young woman!

I wondered just who could fail to be interested in this. Only a child, and yet she unquestionably knew everything and ran it all herself, and she herself had sent that she-devil to me and would send her back again.

I bolstered up my patience and thought to myself that there was nothing to do about it—I would wait again and see how it ended.

I waited till dusk and again concealed myself and waited in the dark. In once again walked that same tall bundle wrapped in Châlons worsted with a veil around the top.

"What do you say?" I asked.

"The cucoona is in love with you and has sent you this rose from her bosom."

"I thank her very much and I treasure it," I said, and I took the rose and kissed it.

"She doesn't need three hundred chervontsy from you, but only a hundred and fifty."

The compassion is fine . . . The discount is sizable—but just the same, a hundred and fifty chervontsi, please! That's no simple matter. Not a single one of us had that kind of money then, because we had left Poland with utterly wrong ideas about what to hope for. We had bought up everything we needed and didn't need, and had ordered new clothes tailored for ourselves, so that we should look our best here—but we didn't even think about what the customs might be here.

"Thank your cucoona," I said, "but I won't be going to have a meeting with her."

"Why not?"

"Now, there you go again—'why not?' I just won't, that's all."

"Can it be that you are poor? You're all rich, you know. Or is the cucoona not a beauty?"

"I am not poor either," I said. "There are no poor men among us, and your cucoona is a great beauty, but we are not used to this kind of treatment."

"And what kind are you used to?"

"That's none of your business," I said.

"No, tell me," she said. "What are you used to? Maybe we can arrange that too."

Then I stood up, assumed a dignified air, and said:

"This is what we are used to: that the drake has a mirror in his wings so that the duck will run after him to see herself."

She burst out laughing.

"There's nothing funny about it," I said.

"Yes, yes, yes!" she said. "It *is* funny!"

And she ran out so fast she fairly flew.

I was out of sorts again, and I went to the coffee house and again drank my fill.

Their Moldavian wine is cheap. It is a little sour but very drinkable.

CHAPTER SIX

The next morning, gentlemen, I was still in bed when that same Jew came to me who had gotten me into all this stupid mess, and now he suddenly came to ask me for another chervonets.

I said: "Just why, my good man, are you worth another chervonets?"

"You promised it to me yourself," he said.

I remembered that I really did promise him another one, but not until after I had a meeting with the cucoona.

That is what I told him. But he answered:

"You've already seen her twice."

"Yes," I said, "at the window. But that's not enough."

"No," he answered. "She was in your apartment twice."

"Some sort of old she-devil was at my place, not the cucoona."

"No," he said, "the cucoona was at your place."

"Don't lie to me, Jew—the likes of you get beatings for that!"

"No, I'm not lying," he said. "She herself was the one who went to see you, and no old woman. She made you a gift of her rose, and the old woman—she hasn't got any old woman with her at all."

I preserved my dignity, but this really scalded me. I was so angry and distressed that I grabbed hold of the Jew and gave him a frightful beating, and then I went and drank myself under the table on Moldavian wine. But even in that position I could not forget that the cucoona had been in my room and I hadn't recognized her and had let her slip out of my hands like a raven. It was not for nothing that that walking bundle of Châlons worsted looked suspicious . . . In a word, I was so pained and vexed and ashamed that I felt like sinking into the earth. The treasure had been in my hands and I hadn't known how to take it—what a fool!

But to my great consolation, at that very same time a story of the very same sort had taken place with some of my military comrades; and in our vexation we all simply drank, and ate watermelons with the coffee-house girls, and decided to punish the real cucoonas with our disdain.

Our cornflower period of innocent conquests had ended. It was boring in the company of no one but the coffee-house girls, without any woman of respected educated circles; but the fatherly old captains cheered us up.

"Do you really think," they said, "that just because you found no apples in one orchard there won't be any harvest at all? Cheer up, boys! It's the prize that makes the race."

We were cheered up by the fact that we were soon to be withdrawn from the town and sent out to be billeted on farms. There the landowners' daughters and society in general were bound to be different from life in town, and it could not be that we would find the same niggardliness there as here. That is what we thought, and we didn't imagine that what awaited us there was still worse and far more vexatious. For that matter, it was impossible to foresee what they would favor us with in their rural simplicity. The longed-for day arrived, and we started sounding our trumpets and jingling the harness bells. We began singing "The Black Daw" and marched out into the open country.

"Out here, no doubt," we said to ourselves, "the blue cornflowers will brighten our lives again."

CHAPTER SEVEN

Our assignments about where to stay turned out to be most variously bivouackish, because in Moldavia, according to the foreign manner, there are no large villages such as we have—there is nothing but separate farms. The officers struggled to get as close as possible to the Holuyan farm, because that was where the *boier,* or landowner, himself lived, who was also known as Holuyan. He was married, and his wife—so they said—was a beauty; and people said of him that he was a great one for business. You could get anything from him, including meals and wine—but only for money. Other units of our army had been stationed around there before us, and on the way we met the quartermaster, who had obtained receipts from Holuyan. We bombarded him with questions about how it was and what it was like, but he was one of those regimental versifiers who loved to answer in rime.

"It's not bad," he said. "It's a good farm. When you get there, you'll see:

> *Between the mountains and the pits—*
> *That's where that Holuyan bird sits."*

It's stupid, that way of talking about serious affairs in rime. You can never get anything sensible out of such people.

"And are there any cucoonas?" we asked.

"Why, of course," he answered. "You'll find many a cucoona—just as reachable as the moona."

"And are they good? That is, beautiful?"

"Yes," he said. "Beautiful and not very dutiful."

We asked whether their officers had been well received there.

"Why, of course," he answered. "On the tuna, on the tree, there our lives their end did see."

"The devil knows what sort of language that is—he talks in nothing but riddles."

We realized that this rascal was sly and would not reveal anything to us.

But just the same, now, believe in premonitions if you want to, and don't believe in them if you don't . . . Nowadays, of course, unbelief is in fashion, but I believe in premonitions, because in my stormy life I have had many proofs of them. But while we were on our way to that farm I became so despondent, so miserable, that I felt as if I were going to my execution.

Well, time and the road kept getting shorter, of course, and while I was walking along in my position, buried in thought, and dragging my boots through the mud, somebody up in front caught sight of it and shouted:

"Holuyan!"

This rippled through the ranks, and for some reason I suddenly shivered, but I crossed myself and began to look intently for that devilish Holuyan. However, even the sign of the cross did not drive away my depression.

In my heart I felt the same languor that was described in young Jonathan on his campaign when he caught sight of sweet honey in the field. Better had it not been there: then the poor youth would not have had to say: "I did but taste a little honey, and lo, I must die."[5]

The Holuyan farm really was right in front of us, and indeed it did stand between mountains and pits, that is, between some puny little hills and some shabby little ponds.

The first impression it made on me was extremely disgusting.

There were also some genuine pits, like empty graves. The devil knows when and by what evil spirits and for whom they had been dug, but they were very deep. Some said that clay had once been extracted from them, but others said they contained medicinal mud, which the ancient Romans had smeared on themselves. In any case, the spot was extraordinarily gloomy and strange.

Patches of woods could be seen here and there, but they looked like little graveyards. The soil was swampy and, we were bound to assume, was steeped in unhealthy dampness. It was a genuine hotbed of that wicked Moldavian fever, from which people die in a Moldavian sweat.

In the evening, when we drew near, the sky glowed with a powerful kind of red, and just above the green earth it was blue, as if a piece of dark-blue tulle had been spread out. That was the fog. There were no flowers, no cornflowers. Nothing could be seen but some kind of down-covered stems with heavy yellow cup-shaped flowers on top, like water-lilies, but most poisonous: you no sooner sniff them than your nose starts swelling up. And what astonished us even more was the great number of herons, as if they had been gathered from all over the world, some of them flying and some standing on one leg in the water. I can't endure it wherever that bird of Pharaoh multiplies: it has something about it that reminds me of all the Egyptian plagues. The Holuyan farm was rather large, but the devil knows whether it ought to be called a worthless one or a good one. There were a lot of farm buildings of all sorts, but everything seemed to be deliberately spread out "between the mountains and the pits."[6] You could scarcely distinguish anything from anything else—something in a pit here, something else in a pit there, and little mounds in between. It was just as if they had in mind something clandestine which was to be carried on here in great secrecy. More than likely, no doubt, they were counterfeiting our Russian money. The landowner's house was squat and very ugly . . . It was weather-beaten, had a tall chimney, and looked small outside but was roomy, so they said—there were supposed to be sixteen rooms in it. From the outside it looked just like those post houses built by the late Kleinmichel along the Moscow highway.[7] Buffets, offices, travelers coming and going, the stationmaster and his family, everybody packed in, the devil knows how—and still there was room. It was built without any trace of style, like a factory. It had an entrance porch in the middle, a buffet in the front hall, a billiard table right there in the hall; and the living rooms were specially hidden away somewhere as if they didn't exist. In a word, everything just as if in a post house or a highway tavern. And to complete this resemblance let me remind you that the buffet was set up right in the front hall. This was no doubt good "for the convenience of the officer gentlemen," but it looked strange just the same; and the organization of this buffet was also arranged in an underhanded, niggardly fashion, so as to provide the likes of us with nothing free of charge. Instead, it worked like this: "We place everything we have at your disposition, only, be so kind as to accept it for cash." Credit, we learned, could readily be arranged; but everything we received, whether vodka or their local wine, was noted down by a special knave in a dark-blue "zhupan" embroidered in red wool, who entered every last trifle in his Book of Life.[8] They even took money for food. For a long time we couldn't get used to paying money in a land-owner's home. It was most curious. At home in Russia or in Poland shame alone would have been enough to keep our hospitable landowners from starting up such a business operation. On our very first day that zhupan turned up and made the round of the officers, asking them whether they wouldn't like to dine with the landowner.

Our boys, of course, were simple and good-hearted, and they thanked him kindly:

"That's very fine," they said. "We'll be glad to."

"And where will you order the table to be set," the zhupan went on, "in the hall or on the veranda? We have a large hall," he said, "and we also have a large veranda."

"It doesn't matter to us, old boy," we said. "Just wherever you like."

"No," he insisted. "The master ordered me to ask you and to set the table by all means just where you want it."

"Just look at all this kindness," we thought. "Set it wherever it's better."

"It's better," he answered, "on the veranda."

"The air is fresher out there, no doubt."

"Yes, and there's a clay floor out there."

"What's the advantage in that?"

"Why, if any red wine is spilled, or anything else, it's easier to clean it up and the spot won't show."

"That's right, that's right!"

We could see they were making plans to drown us in drink.

We took for granted that their wine was cheap. It was true it did have an after-taste, but that didn't matter—they had some very respectable kinds.

Dinner time came. We appeared and sat down at the table, all in proper fashion, and our host there with us: Holuyan himself, a thin, swarthy man with a face of burnt clay, sinewy and ceramic, you might say; and he spoke in gasps, as if he were ill.

"Here, gentlemen," he said, "my wines of such-and-such year are of a very good vintage. Wouldn't you like to try them?"

"We'd be glad to."

He shouted at once to the servant:

"Bring the lieutenant such-and-such wine."

The servant would invariably bring an unopened bottle, and just before the last course the zhupan suddenly appeared with an empty plate and went around to everybody.

"What's this?!" we said.

"Money for the meal and the wine."

We were thrown into confusion, especially those who happened to have no money on them. They began stealthily reaching back and forth to each other under the table.

So that's the kind of swarthy rascal he was!

But what Holuyan used to bring us to bitter grief was not this, of course; it was a cucoonette, for the sake of whom all our lives were worn out on the tuna, on the tree; and I can say that I lost forever what I held to be dearer, more precious, you might even say more sacred, than everything else.

CHAPTER EIGHT

The family of our hosts consisted of Ban Holuyan himself, whom I have already sketched for you briefly: thin, sinewy, with little feet of clay, not yet old, and yet he always leaned on a cane and never let it out of his hands for a moment. When he sat down, the cane would rest on his knees. They said he was once wounded in a duel, but I suspect he tried to hold up a post wagon somewhere and the postman took a shot at him. Later this was explained in an entirely different way and then it became clear— but too late. But at first it appeared that he was an educated man of society—he had long white fingernails and always had a cambric hand-kerchief in his hands. Apart from his education he could not have held the slightest promise of any interest for a lady, because he had the appearance of a frightfully cold man. But his cucoonette was nothing less than a fairy-tale princess: she was not over twenty-two or twenty-three years old, at the very height of her beauty; thin, black eyebrows, a delicate frame; and her first plumpness had formed little dimples on her shoulders. She always wore clothes that were marvelously becoming, usually pale yellow or white with embroidered designs; and her little feet were shod in colored slippers trimmed in gold.

Needless to say, there began a general perturbation of hearts. Among us was an officer we called Faublas because of the remarkable speed with which he could cast a spell on women—he would walk past a house where some pretty little townswoman sat, say no more than three words to her, such as "angelic little eyes," and the acquaintance was formed on the spot. I myself was also madly devoted to beauty. Toward the end of dinner I saw that his mouth was watering and his eyes were boring holes.

I brought him up short:

"You're indecent," I said.

"I can't help it," he answered. "And don't interfere—I'm undressing her in my imagination."

I told him: "Don't be stupid!" But suddenly I myself began to daydream about the same thing, and suddenly I noticed that all the others' mouths were watering and their eyes were boring holes.

So there it is, I said to myself—so this is the first symptom of that confounded Moldavian fever!

After dinner Holuyan proposed a game of bank. Everybody agreed except Faublas. He stayed by the cucoona and kept talking with her right up to nightfall.

That evening we asked him:

"Well, how is she—interesting?"

He burst out laughing.

"In my opinion," he answered, "either her father or her mother must have been a little cracked, and she took after them. She's got very little strength of will: she never gets away from home. The question is: Who keeps watch over her, and who is she afraid of? Women are often lacking in will power and resourcefulness. You have to do their thinking for them."

In regard to the surveillance, our suspicions were aroused not so much on the score of Holuyan himself as his brother, whose name was Anthony.

He was completely unlike his brother: a sturdily built, peasantlike fellow, but with comically thin little legs. We nicknamed him "spindle-legged Anthony." His face also was entirely unlike his brother's. It was a simple sort of face—neither trimmed nor planed, but rather slapped together and discarded; but it seemed to us that in spite of his sheeplike simplicity he also had a tuft of gray wolf fur . . . A surprise was in store for us, however, which proved that all our suspicions were unfounded: it turned out that nobody at all was keeping watch over the cucoona.

The Holuyans' daily routine at home was most amazing—just as if it had been especially set up so as to play into our hands.

Right up to dinner time it was completely impossible to find the thin Leonardo Holuyan anywhere. The devil alone knew where he hid himself! It was said that he constantly sat in his remote private rooms and did something—occupied himself, they said, with some kind of literature. And spindle-legged Anthony as soon as he got up would go off to the fields somewhere with his little flat-bellied dog and stay out of sight the whole day, walking around the farm. In other words, we couldn't have wished for a better set-up.

All that remained was to win the cucoona's favorable attention with conversation and other devices. It was generally thought that this wouldn't take long and that Faublas would bring it off, but quite unexpectedly we noticed that our Faublas was having trouble. He looked like a man who had a wolf by the ears: he couldn't turn him round and he couldn't turn him loose, and meanwhile it was evident that his hands were swelling and would fall off any moment . . .

Clearly the poor fellow was terribly disconcerted, because he was not accustomed to failures, and he was unable to explain it not only to us but even to himself.

"Just what is the matter?"

"*Parole d'honneur*," he said, "I don't understand anything except that she is very strange."

"Oh well, a rich woman who is spoiled will have her whims—it's perfectly natural."

Our cucoona's daily routine was such that she could not help getting bored. From morning till dinner you could see her almost constantly, wandering around completely alone, or else fussing about with the stupidest bird in all the world—a chicken. It was a strange occupation for a young, elegant, wealthy lady; but what can you do if she takes such a notion? It was clear that she had absolutely nothing to do. She would come out dressed all in white or in a pale yellow negligee and sit down on the broad flagstones at the end of the veranda under the green hop vines. In her black hair she would have a tulip or a double poppy, and you felt like gazing at her all day long. Her whole occupation consisted in feeding grains of corn on her lap to her favorite little chicken with wattles hanging from its throat. The case was clear: She must have had very little education and didn't know what to do with her leisure. If she spent her time fussing over a chicken, that meant she was very bored; and when a woman is bored, it is a young man's duty to entertain her. But nothing came of it. It was hard even to carry on a conversation with her, because all you would hear from her was "shti, eshti, moldovaneshti, kerneshti"— you couldn't understand one word in ten. And to expressions of passion in sign-language she was terribly dense. Faublas threw up his hands in despair and was only filled with confusion when we laughed at him for being unable to compete with a chicken. We all went and danced around the cucoona to see who would be favored the most by fortune, but not a single one of us had any luck. You would confess your love to her, and she would look at you with her big black calf-eyes, or start something like "shti, eshti, moldovaneshti," and that was all.

It was sickening for all of us to see ourselves in such a stupid situation, and quarrels actually arose, and envy and jealousy toward one another. We would find fault with everything, and make biting remarks. In a word, we were all in a most uneasy state of mind—either daydreaming about her or secretly watching each other because of her. And she just sat there with her chicken and that was that. So we would look all day and sigh all night, and time passed and hatched up another misfortune for us. I told you that on the very first day, just as soon as dinner was over, Holuyan had suggested setting up a game of bank. From that time on we played every day: we would gamble from dinner till midnight, and whether it was because we became absent-minded or because the cards were stacked, in any case many of us succeeded in getting stripped right down to our last kopeck. And Holuyan kept cleaning us out every day, just as if he were shearing sheep.

We were ruined; we had grown impoverished in both intelligence and peace of mind; and there's no telling what might have become of us if a new person hadn't suddenly turned up in our midst. He created perhaps even greater uneasiness for us, but still he did give us the push that brought things to a head.

The man who came was a well-heeled bureaucrat in the department of military equipment. He was of Polish origin and middle-aged, but a terrible rogue—two-faced as the jack of spades—and he found out from everybody all about how we were living and sighing. He too went with us to dine with Holuyan and then stayed to play cards—but the rascal didn't even look at the cucoona. Well, sir, the next day he suddenly said: "I'm sick." The Moldavian fever, you see, had gotten him. And what do you suppose he thought up? Instead of calling the doctor he called the priest— to come and hold a prayer service for his recovery. The priest got there— a true cockroach type, all in black—and started chanting like something you can't imagine, worse than the Armenians. Even among the Armenians you can understand two words—"Grigorios Armenios"—but with this fellow you couldn't make out what he was mumbling.

But the rogue of a Pole knew a little of their talk, and he stirred up such a constitution with the priest that they became friends, and both of them were satisfied with each other. The priest was glad because the equipper had paid him well, and the equipper got well immediately after the prayer service and pulled off such a trick that it left us with our mouths hanging open.

In the evening, when all of us had already sat down by candle light to our game of bank, our equipper came in and did not start playing, but said: "I'm still sick," and went straight out to the veranda where the cucoona was sitting on the flagstones in the blissful twilight. Suddenly they both disappeared behind the thick hop vines and vanished in the darkness. Faublas couldn't stand it and he darted out, but they were already floating most advantageously on a little raft across the inlet toward a little island . . . Right before his eyes they landed and disappeared . . .

And Holuyan, the rascal, didn't even blink! He just kept shuffling the cards and checking the figures on those who had already lost everything in debts.

<h2 style="text-align:center">CHAPTER NINE</h2>

But I must tell you what kind of little island that was where they had landed.

When I told you about the farm, I forgot to say that the best thing about the estate was just that little island in front of the veranda. Right beyond the veranda was a flower garden, and immediately beyond the flower garden was the inlet, and beyond it the island—a little one, just about the size of the grounds in front of the landowner's house. It was all overgrown with honeysuckle and various flowering shrubs, in which there were a lot of nightingales. Their nightingales are very fine singers—not as loud as those around Kursk, but more along the lines of those in Berdíchev. The space on the island was entirely filled with little mounds or hillocks, and on one little hillock there stood a little summer house, and below it was a grotto paved with flagstones, where it was always very cool. Here there was an old-fashioned sofa where you could rest, and a big gilded harp on which the cucoona would accompany herself while she sang. Little paths were cleared all over the island, and in one spot on the other side there was a seat made of turf, which offered a broad view of the meadows. Communication with the island across the inlet was handled by means of an excellent little raft. The railing and all that on the raft was painted in an Oriental manner, and in the middle of it was a gilded seat. The cucoona would sit down there and take a double-bladed oar and sail across. The other person had to stand behind her seat.

This island and the grotto we called "Calypso's Grotto," but we ourselves never went over there, because the cucoona's raft was kept locked on a chain. The equipper found the keys to this chain . . .

To tell the truth, we simply wanted to beat him up; but he was a bold one, the scoundrel, and he calmed down all of us.

"Gentlemen!" he said, "what have we got to quarrel about? I will show you the way. The priest told me all about it. I asked him: 'How is the cucoona?' And he said: 'She's very good—she looks after the poor.' I took fifty chervontsy and silently gave them to her for her poor; and she, also in silence, gave me her hand and took me with her to the island. I'll stake my life on it: just put a stack of chervontsy in her hands and without saying a word you will be able to enjoy this same good fortune. The view by moonlight is splendid and the harp has a beautiful tone. But I can't enjoy all that any more, because my duty calls me: tomorrow I will leave you, and you will stay here."

So that was the solution!

He left, and we looked at one another, wondering how many of us could contribute fifty chervontsy apiece to help the poor in the local parish. A few of the others put on a brave front. One said, "I'm expecting some from home any day," and another one too was expecting some from home. But evidently poor people had turned up right there at home, in their own parishes, because somehow nobody received any money.

Then suddenly in the midst of all this there occurred a most unexpected event: Faublas broke the chain to which the raft was fastened, sailed over there alone, went to the grotto, and shot himself.

The devil knows what sort of thing that was! We felt sorry for our comrade, and at the same time we somehow felt it was stupid, completely stupid—and yet the sad fact had taken place and one of our brave men was no more.

Faublas had shot himself, of course, through love, and his love flamed up through wounded self-esteem, since he had always been successful with the women in his own country. We buried him with full honors, including a military band; and we all got together in the room of one of us and drank to the peace of his soul, and started telling each other that it was impossible to leave matters like this—here with our customary simplicity we would perish. But the major of our battalion, who was married and a reliable man, said to us:

"Now, don't get upset; I've already reported to headquarters that I couldn't guarantee there would not be reason to withdraw you from this farm, and I expect to get new orders by tomorrow. Let the devil stay here with that Holuyan! Confound the farm, and confound the owner!"

And we all felt the same and were glad to have a chance to get away, but all the officers were annoyed over having to leave without punishing the rascals.

We thought over various tricks we might use to get even with Holuyan. We thought of giving him a beating, or of shaving his head in some ridiculous fashion; but the major said:

"God forbid, gentlemen! I beg you: Let there be nothing resembling the slightest kind of violence; and for those of you who owe him money, please borrow it wherever you like and settle your accounts. But if you think up something nice and innocent to avenge your honor, that will be all right."

At last the major said he had been holding out on us; actually he had our orders to pull out in his pocket right then, and tomorrow would be the last day brightened by our Venus, and the day after tomorrow we would leave at dawn for other localities.

Right then some mare kicked a bright idea into my head.

"If we leave the day after tomorrow," I said, "so that tomorrow will be our last evening here, then please give me a free hand. Holuyan will learn a good lesson and boast to nobody that he ever got the better of Russian officers."

Some of them praised me and said, "Good for you!" but others laughed skeptically: "What do you think you can do? Better not meddle with him."

But I said:

"Gentlemen, that's my affair. I will take care of everything myself."

"But what are you going to do?"

"That is my secret."

"But will Holuyan be punished?"

"Frightfully!"

"And our honor will be avenged?"

"Absolutely."

"Swear to it!"

I swore by the shade of our unfortunate friend Faublas, which had condemned itself to wander in solitude about this accursed place, and I smashed my wineglass on the floor.

All my comrades supported me, gave their approval, kissed me heartily, and drank to our oath. But the major held us back from smashing all our glasses.

"That," he said, "is a theatrical farce and nothing more."

We separated in excellent spirits. I was firmly convinced that my plan was a very good one. We had to make a complete fool of Holuyan in the midst of his trickery.

CHAPTER TEN

Tomorrow dawned—the last day brightened by our Venus. We received our salary, paid in full whatever we owed to Holuyan, and had the kind of money left that didn't even require a purse. I had a little over a hundred rubles, that is, according to their rates at that time, a little over ten chervontsy. But according to the plan for my scheme I needed at least forty more chervontsy. Where could I get them? My comrades had none, and besides, I didn't want to borrow from them, because I had another plan too. And so I put it into execution.

We arrived for the last supper with Holuyan. He was short of breath as usual, and he invited me to play.

"I'd be glad to play," I said, "but I have no toys."

He begged me not to stand on ceremony and offered me a loan from his bank.

"Very well," I said, "please let me have fifty chervontsy."

"With pleasure," he said, and pushed a stack toward me.

I took them and put them in my pocket.

The rascal gave us credit as if we were all Sheremétevs.[9]

"If you'll allow me," I said, "I won't make a bet just now. I'll walk around for a moment in the fresh air." And I went out on the veranda.

Two of my comrades ran out after me and said, "What's that you're doing—how are you going to pay him back?"

"That's not your affair," I answered. "Don't worry."

"But you know it's impossible," they insisted. "We're leaving tomorrow—you by all means have to pay it back."

"And I will."

"But suppose you lose?"

"I'll pay it back in any case."

And I lied to them and claimed I had government money in my pocket.

They left off, and I flew straight up to the cucoona, bowed and scraped, and gave her a handful of chervontsy.

"Please accept this from me," I said, "for the poor in your parish."

I don't know how she comprehended that, but she stood up at once and gave me her hand. We walked around the flower bed, down to the raft, and sailed away.

CHAPTER ELEVEN

As far as her playing on the harp is concerned, there's nothing very remarkable to tell: we went into the grotto; she sat down and started playing some sort of écossaise. In those days there weren't yet any of those inflammatory songs like "O My Little Tiger," or "Tiger Me to Death," but only écossaises, nothing but simple écossaises, to which you could dance only one step, and then there was no telling what you might be ready to do in time to that music. And so it was in this case: first an écossaise, and then "hootchie-cootchie, tootsie-wootsie, eshti, moldavaneshti"—the rest is clear . . . And we both sailed back in very satisfactory fashion.

CHAPTER TWELVE

To tell the truth, I won't deny that I was in a very dreamy mood, which did not correspond at all to the plan I had hatched up. But you know, I was getting on toward thirty, and that is always the age when the first notes of prudence appear. Everything came back to me—how that "life of the heart" had begun, all those modest cornflowers in the rye in my distant homeland, then those little Ukrainian and Polish girls in their modest little cottages, and suddenly—devil take it!—Calypso's Grotto, and this goddess in person . . . Say what you will, that really is something to remember. And suddenly I became so melancholy that I left the cucoona to fasten the chain to her raft all by herself, and I went single-handed into the hall I had left while they were playing bank. Now instead of the game I found a quarrel—and what a quarrel! Holuyan was seated, and our officers had all stood up and some of them had even purposely put on their caps, and the whole crowd was arguing noisily about the fairness of his game. He had cleaned them out once again.

The officers said, "We will pay you, but in all fairness we don't owe you a thing."

I came in just at these words, and I said, "And I don't owe you anything either. Those fifty chervontsy I borrowed from you—I've just turned them over to your wife."

This embarrassed the officers terribly, and he turned white as a sheet in vexation over the way I had outsmarted him. He grabbed the cards in his hand, shook them, and shouted:

"You're lying! You're a cad!"

And the rascal threw the cards in my face. But I did not lose my composure and I said:

"Oh no, brother, I'm higher than a cad by more than a head," and smack!—I gave him a slap . . . Then he shook his cane and a Toledo swordblade slipped out of it, and he—the scoundrel—attacked an unarmed man with it!

My comrades threw themselves on him and held him back. Some of them held him by the arms and others, me. And he shouted:

"You're a scoundrel! Not one of you has ever seen my wife!"

"Well, old boy," we said, "just leave off trying to prove it to us. We've seen her very well!"

"Where? How?"

"Leave off," we said. "In that matter there's nothing to argue about. Of course we know your wife."

But in answer to that he burst out laughing like the devil himself, then spat, disappeared through the door, and locked it after him.

CHAPTER THIRTEEN

And what do you think? He really was right!

You can't even imagine what kind of trick had been played on us. What sort of cunning on top of cunning, and baseness on top of baseness! Just consider: it really did turn out that we had never even once laid eyes on his wife! He somehow considered us, you might say, too unworthy of that honor for him to make us acquainted with his real family, and during the whole time of our stay he kept them hidden away in those remote rooms that we never visited. And that cucoona over whom we all lost our heads and took it as a great good fortune to kiss her little hands and feet, and one man even died for her—she was the devil knows what—simply a harp-player from a coffee house, who could be hired for one chervonets by anybody to dance in the costume of Eve . . . In anticipation of our arrival she had been taken out of a coffee house for the sake of profit, and he got an income from her . . . And this Holuyan himself with whom we played was not Holuyan at all, but a hired card-sharp; and the real Holuyan was only spindle-legged Anthony, who was always off hunting with his flat-bellied little dog . . . He was the one who organized all this business! There are real scoundrels for you! And now just judge how we officers felt, what a foolish position we were in—and through whose kindness? Through the kindness, you might say, of the most contemptible trash!

And I was the one who found out about all this before anybody else, but it was still too late, after my whole military career had been ruined by that dirty trick, thanks to the stupidity of my comrades. Our officer gentlemen actually took offense at my action and claimed that I had behaved dishonorably—I had betrayed a lady's secret, if you please, to her husband . . . That's the kind of stupidity, you see! Still, they demanded that I leave the regiment. There was nothing to do about it, and I left. But when I passed that way a year later the Jew revealed the whole thing to me.

"But tell me," I said, "why did their priest say about his cucoona that you could give her money under the pretense that it was for the poor?"

"Oh, that is right," he said. "But the priest was talking about the real cucoona, who was sitting in the back rooms, and not about that swine you mistook for a beaver."

In a word, we had swallowed everything—hook, line, and sinker. I am a man with a strong constitution, but I was so shaken by this that I even came down with the Moldavian fever. I barely managed to drag myself back to our simple hearts in the homeland, and I was glad to be able to get myself a job as governor of a little Jewish town . . . I won't deny it— I quarreled with them a good deal, and I'll have to admit I taught them a few lessons with my fists, but, thank the Lord, I've lived my life and I've got my crust of bread, even with a little butter. But just the memory of that Moldavian fever brings back cold chills.

And that unpleasant sensation led the narrator to unpack his capacious pillow once again, pour out a glass of the amethyst-colored liquid with the inscription, "Monks also do partake of this," and say:

"Let us drink, gentlemen, to the Jews, and to the ruin of those wicked rascals the Rumanians."

"Why not? That will be most original."

"Yes," said another member of our company. "But wouldn't it be still better on this anniversary night when the 'friend of sinners' was born, if we wished 'good to all and evil to none'?"

"Excellent, excellent!"

And the warrior agreed, said "Abgemacht!" and drained his glass.

NOTES FOR "DECEPTION"
Introduction

[1] Letter of August 17, 1883, to S. N. Shubínsky, printed in N. S. Leskóv, *Sobránie sochinénii* (Moscow, 1965–68), XI.

[2] *Evréi v Rossíi. Néskolko zamechánii po evréiskomu voprósu* (Petersburg, 1884). Reprinted in Petrograd, 1919.

[3] *Nedélnaya khrónika voskhóda*, Nos. 5 ff. (Petersburg, 1884).

Text

[1] Nikolái Gavrílovich Kurgánov (1726–96) was the compiler of a famous collection of reading material, commonly known as the *Pismóvnik (Letterwriter)*, which went through at least eighteen editions and provided a kind of one-volume general education for generations of Russian readers.

[2] A distortion in English—as in the original Russian—of the Rumanian word *cucoana* "lady."

[3] "Kochanko moja, na co nam rozmowa?"—the first line of a poem by Mickiewicz, and also the title of one of Leskóv's earliest literary efforts, published in a Petersburg newspaper in 1863.

[4] Chervónets (plural: chervóntsy)—an old Russian monetary unit, a gold ruble.

[5] A reference to the Old Testament story told in I Samuel 14.

[6] The generally suspicious air of this scene is enhanced by the fact that in the slang of that time the Russian word for *Pharaoh* was used for "police" and the Russian word *yáma*, "pit" was used for "prison."

[7] Count Peter Andréevich Kleinmichel (1793–1869), served under Nicholas I from 1842 to 1855 as administrator of highways and public buildings.

[8] Zhupán—an old kind of short overcoat common in Poland and the Ukraine. In Polish the word is also used for a kind of official. In his use of the Biblical phrase "Book of Life" Leskóv exploits the pun inherent in the word *zhivót*, which means "life" in Biblical language and "belly" in everyday Russian.

[9] The Sheremétevs (also spelled Sheremétyevs) were a family of wealthy Russian nobles.

NOTE TO "CHOICE GRAIN"

"Choice Grain" is permeated from beginning to end with the spirit of Gógol. Its plot is a deliberate echo of the plot of *Dead Souls,* and its characters are as consistently negative as the characters in *The Inspector General.* What distinguishes Leskóv here from Gógol, however, is his ironical justification of rascality as a way of life through his enunciation of the principle of "sociable-ism." The Russian word, *sotsiabelnost,* like its English translation, is a symbolic distortion of "socialism." "Sociable-ism," Leskóv implies, is the adaptation of a foreign ideology to the peculiar genius of native Russian traditions, which make it possible for all classes of society—landowners, merchants, and peasants—to contribute to the general welfare through their individual rascality. By his choice and identification of his characters Leskóv gives epic proportions to his unheroic satire. A nameless bureaucrat tells the story, which deals with an equally nameless landowner and merchant and two peasants whose names have the same generic significance as "John Smith" in English.

"Choice Grain" was published in early 1884, less than two months after "Deception." In both stories the gloomy state of mind that weighed upon Leskóv during the early 1880's was somehow distilled into a kind of social satire that sparkles with deceptively innocent-looking irony.

Some literary scholars in the Soviet Union have questioned this translator's reference to "Choice Grain" as a parody on Gógol. Their question evidently arises from the fact that the Russian word for "parody" implies disparagement, whereas the English word may even imply a flattering recognition of excellence. "Choice Grain" is an unmistakable parody on Gógol, but a parody in the positive English sense of the word—a tribute to the writer whose works were possibly the most important single influence on Leskóv's literary formation.

CHOICE GRAIN

A Short Trilogy in a Doze

*But while men slept, his enemy
came and sowed tares among the wheat.
Matt. 13, 25.*

I was in a hurry to pay a visit to some dear friends, and having no free time, I was forced to make the journey right in the midst of the holidays. Thanks to this I had to spend New Year's Eve in a railway car. I felt in a sad and depressed state of mind.

According to the religious counselors, we ought to examine our consciences every evening. I don't follow that practice myself, but at the end of each year the pious advice of these teachers comes to mind and I begin to examine myself. I do this all at one time for the whole year, but I regularly end in all-round dissatisfaction with myself.

On this occasion my customary dissatisfaction was complicated by vexation with others—especially with Prince Bismarck for his disrespectful comments about my fellow countrymen and his unkind predictions about our future. His cast-iron rudeness had permitted him to come out bluntly and say he thought the only thing left for Russia was to "perish." How could that be! Why should it perish? I began thinking and trying to figure it out—was there really any reason why, or was there no reason why?

All around me everybody was asleep. The five or six passengers whom fate had sent me as traveling companions had all turned their backs upon one another and were giving forth snores full of sound and fury.

I became ashamed of my despair and my idle thoughts. Why could I not sleep when everyone else was asleep? Why should it make any difference to me what Bismarck had said about us, and why did I have to believe his predictions? Better pay no attention to all this, conform instead and go to sleep like unto other men; and then matters would move along more cheerfully and interestingly.

That is just what I did. I turned away from all the others who had already turned their backs on me and I began to make zealous efforts to fall asleep, but I slept fitfully and with constant interruptions, until finally fate sent me an unexpected diversion which for a while drove all sleep away and at the same time armed me against unfavorable conclusions about our native disorder.

When the train pulled up to the platform of one little town two men got on—one of them walking with a light tread, evidently a young man, and the other somewhat heavier and older. I could not get a good look at them, because the lamps in the car had been covered with dark blue cloth and did not let through enough light for me to examine the strangers' faces. Nevertheless, I immediately got the impression that these new passengers were not only well-to-do, but also well-educated. They came in without any noise or loud talk and in general tried as far as possible to keep their arrival from disturbing anyone, and they settled down quietly and unassumingly in the empty seats they found. By chance these happened to be very close to the dark corner where I was curled up for my nap. Willy-nilly I was bound to hear every word they might say, even though it was spoken in a half-whisper. This was just what happened, and I must say I have no complaint to make, for the quiet conversation that started up between my new neighbors proved so interesting that I wrote it down at once as soon as I got home, and now I have decided to offer it to you readers.

The first words of our new passengers made it clear that they had already been discussing some very interesting subject while they were waiting at the station for their train, and now they were simply giving further illustrations for the points they had already made.

One of the two passengers spoke in an old, well-worn baritone—a voice that might have befitted an important stockholder, or a privy councilor at the very least—obviously a man who in one way or other was exploiting the natural resources of the country. The other man merely listened and only at rare intervals put in a word or asked for some clarification. He spoke in a rather clear falsetto, such as may be found most often among up-and-coming young bureaucrats who have a weakness for literature.

The baritone began, and what he said went like this:

"I will give you a concrete illustration right now of this sociable-ism of ours and how it was manifested not long ago in an affair that in my opinion was most interesting. This case may show you that our original Russian genius, which you refuse to acknowledge, is not by any means nonsense. People may say if they like that we are *Rashians* and there is nothing but disorder all over our native land, but the fact is that anyone who can observe things dispassionately is bound to discover in this disorder something extraordinarily mutual, or as *you* might put it, something 'sociable-istic.' Bismarck once said somewhere that nothing was left for

Russia but to 'perish,' and all the newspaper gossips picked that up and chattered about it no end. But don't you listen to their chatter; just take a good look at matters as they really are, and then you will see that we have a genius like nobody else for getting ourselves out of trouble. In fact, we can't be frightened by situations such as perhaps have never even entered the head of Mr. Bismarck himself, and might simply overwhelm other people who lack our sturdy temper."

"You pose the question most interestingly, and I am eager to hear what you have to say," remarked the falsetto.

The baritone continued:

"If I were to publish the three little stories I want to tell you on the subject of our sociable-ism, I would probably call them a trilogy about how thief robbed thief and everything ended happily for all. For that matter, since nowadays every nincompoop, as you might say, poses as a literary man, I too will try to make my story literary. And so I will divide up my story for you into sections, like a trilogy; and in the first one I will bring in an intellectual, that is, a landowner, who according to some people is supposed to have 'lost contact with the soil' more than anybody else. But you will see at once how silly all that is, and that in our country, as the proverb goes, 'Every pine tree rustles to its own forest.'"

CHAPTER ONE

THE LANDOWNER

One summer I set out on a journey and I came to an exposition. I walked about and looked over all the sections, trying to find some native product I could admire; but, as you might expect, I soon saw that nothing would come of it—there wasn't anything worth admiring. The only thing that caught my fancy—and I must admit it really did seem remarkable—was somebody's wheat that was on display in a certain showcase.

In all my life I had never seen such big, clean, well-filled grains. You might have said it wasn't wheat at all but choice almonds such as I used to see at home in my childhood, when my mother used them to decorate Easter cakes.

I looked at the inscription and was even more astonished. There I read that this marvelous, luxuriant grain had been gathered from fields in my own native district, on an estate that belonged to a neighbor of my relatives, a prominent landowner whose name I will not mention. I will say only that he was a well-known promoter of Slavic causes, and was active in the Red Cross, and so on, and so on.

I had known this gentleman in high school, but I must admit that I didn't feel very friendly toward him. This all went back to certain child-hood memories: at first he used to steal all the penknives in the class and sell them, and then later he began to paint his eyebrows and engage in certain affairs of a much worse nature.

Now I thought to myself, no doubt this too is a fraud! He probably bought a bag of good wheat somewhere from German colonists and is exhibiting it as if it came from his own fields.

I reasoned this way because our fields are rye-fields and if they produce wheat it is a very poor grade. But in order not to condemn my neighbor too harshly I thought I had better go to the lunch room and drink a drop of our good Russian wine and eat a piece of meat pie. A critical spirit can't survive a full stomach.

Hardly had I taken a seat in the restaurant, though, when I noticed a gentleman sitting quite near me whose looks appeared vaguely familiar. I glanced at him and turned my eyes away, but I felt that he was staring at me, and suddenly he bowed to me and said:

"Excuse me, if I am not mistaken you are So-and-so, aren't you?"

I answered:

"You are not mistaken; that is indeed who I am."

"And I am So-and-so," he said, introducing himself.

I suppose you can guess that this was that very same schoolmate of former years who had stolen penknives and painted his eyebrows in high school and was now cultivating and exhibiting this most extraordinary wheat.

But after all, that's all right. Mountain may never meet mountain, but it's easy enough for man to meet man. We flung a few questions back and forth—who, where from, and what for. I said I was just traveling, like Chíchikov,[1] for my own pleasure; and he jokingly prompted me with: "Surveying the situation, no doubt."

"I am not surveying anything," I said. "I simply want to look around for my own pleasure."

He said he was an exhibitor and told me that he had placed wheat on display.

I answered that I had already noticed his wheat and was curious to know what kind of seed it had come from and in just what place it had grown. He explained the whole thing eloquently, going into all the details. I was astonished once more when I learned that the seed had come from our district and the fields that had produced such wonderful grain were right next to the fields of my cousin.

I was astonished, I repeat, because our district had never produced very good wheat in the past. But he answered:

"Oh well, that was in the past, but now things are entirely different in our part of the country. Especially on my farm. You can't compare it with the old days. There's a great difference, brother, a very great difference; everything has changed since the time you left our province to get rank and honors and easy money with your bold maneuvers on the stock market. But we sit on the ground, brother, like Ilyás of Múrom;[2] and we've sat and we've sat till we've hatched something up. Now our day, the day of the landowners, is coming in again, and your day, the day of the bureaucrats, is on the way out. People have remembered our grandfathers' saying: 'A ruble from the land is narrow but long, while a ruble from trade is wide but short.' We landowners have gone back to the plow and we look neither to right nor left; we know it is not Petersburg but the plow that will save us."

"Yes," I said, "all that is well and good; but just the same, my cousin lives over there in your district and I have visited him, but I've never heard about any such wonderful grain as this growing there."

"But what does that prove? Visiting is not the same as managing the place. Take me, for example: in one of my villages there's a young priest, and when he's away I go over and visit his wife, but I can't say that I manage his place; the master of the house is still the priest. And about your cousin, I must say—if you'll forgive me—he's hidebound in his ways."

"Yes," I said, "my cousin is not much of a man to take risks."

"Not he! Oh no! There aren't many men like me so far, but we have already made real progress in our farming and here you see the results; this is my wheat. Maybe you haven't yet read about it, but I've already won a gold medal here for my wheat. That means as much to me as setting our Slavic principalities in order—which the Berlin Treaty kept us from doing.[3] But we can't be blamed for what we're not guilty of. And at least nobody can dictate to us about how we are to run our agriculture. Let's go back over to my showcase."

I was very glad to do so, if only to finish with the "principalities," because I know precious little about that question. We walked over to the showcase. He picked up a little silver scoop and began to dip in and let the grain run out before my eyes.

"I'm amazed," I said. "I see it but I can't believe it. How could such enormous, wonderful grain have grown on our own little old lands!"

"Well, just read here," and he pointed to the sign on the showcase. "You see, here's my name. And besides, brother, there can't be any trickery here. They've got all the documents in the exposition office— affidavits, certificates, and everything. All the proofs are there to show that this really is grain from my harvest. Now the next time you go to see your cousin, do come over and pay me a visit. All our peasants will also tell you this grain comes from my fields. Method, brother, method—there's the whole secret."

"I can't believe it," I thought to myself, "but still, the Lord be praised!"

"And what sort of price," I asked, "have you put on such unusual grain?"

"Oh, it's a good price. These wormy Frenchmen and Englishmen won't leave me alone; they keep pestering me, and they're offering me exactly twice as much as the top price. But naturally I won't sell to those rascals."

"Why not?"

"Sell to foreigners? Oh, no, brother, no—I won't do it! No, brother, even as it is we have enough of this miserable conflict between words and deeds. Why fool around with them, after all? What are these foreigners to us? If we are true Russians, then we've got to support our own true Russian traders, and not foreign ones. Let our true Russian merchant buy from me; I will sell to him and sell gladly. For our own Orthodox man I'll even knock a little off the price the foreigners offer—just so a true Russian profits by it."

And at that very moment, while we were talking, I really did see two foreigners suddenly rush up to him. I had the impression that they were Jews but they both spoke excellent French, and they began urging him to sell them his wheat.

"You see how they keep wheedling," he said to me in Russian. "And then look over there—that red-headed devil's examining that Smolénsk flax. It's nothing but a stall. He hasn't got any use for flax. That's an Englishman, and he's after me too."

After all, I thought, maybe that really was true. At that time foreign agents were mixing among us, and among our own prominent men there were not a few who were ready to crush the decadent West under their heel. Very likely this was one of them too.

Two or three days went by after that meeting, and I had almost forgotten about the gentleman. Then I happened to meet him again and got better acquainted with him. It took place in one of the best hotels during dinner; I had sat down to dine and I saw the model agriculturist sitting not far away with a serious-looking man who was unquestionably Russian in build and even unquestionably a merchant. Both were dining well and drinking still better.

He noticed me, too, and at once sent his waiter over with his card and a glass of champagne on a silver tray.

It would have been awkward not to accept. I took the goblet and sent him a long-distance bow.

On the card was written in pencil: "Congratulate me! I have sold my grain to this fortunate Russian and we are drinking cream de tea. When you have finished your meal, come over."

Well, I thought, that's the last thing I expect to do. But he seemed to have read my thoughts and came over himself.

"I've finished it, brother," he said. "I've let it go, sold it—but to our own kind, to a Russian. That merchant has bought up my whole crop, and right off he gave me five thousand as a down payment for my wheat. It's not a trifling deal—about forty thousand in all. To tell the truth, I sold it too cheap at that, but at least it's going to our own kind, a Russian. The Frenchmen and the Englishmen are in a rage, they're foaming at the mouth, and I'm tickled. The devil take them, now let them quit spreading nonsense and saying we have no patriotism. Let me take you over and introduce you to my customer. He's an odd sort in his own way; he comes from real, simple, true Russian people and has worked his way up to the merchant class. Now he's rolling in money, and he's all the time giving it away for new churches, but when the chance comes his way he doesn't mind having a little fling too. As a matter of fact, he's in just such a mood right now. Don't you want to come along with us? We'll all go together to some place 'where there's a cozy little corner for the man who's feeling low.' "[4]

"No," I said. "Why should I go on a spree?"

"Why not? Nobody here stands on rank and title; we're all simple people, and every man of us plays the fool in his own way."

"The trouble is," I said, "that I can no longer drink at all."

"Well, I see there's nothing to be done with you. Have it your own way and stay behind. But meanwhile take a look here at our contract and admire the way we've got everything spelled out. I won't do business, you know, except in the proper way, with notarized papers. Yes, *sir*—with our good Russian types you've got to be firm about everything; there's nothing to do but bind him fast with legal papers, and then you can go out and drink cream de tea with him. You see here, I've got everything put down in black and white—five thousand as a binder, he picks up the grain on my estate, 'the whole crop, threshed and stored in barns in the village of Cheritáeva, and the money to be paid at once, before the sacks are loaded on the barges.' What do you think about that? Have I overlooked anything? It seems to me it's all worked out pretty carefully."

"That is my opinion too," I said.

"Yes," he answered, "I know him a little. He has given money for Slavic causes, but you've got to watch your step with him."

The landowner was in genuine high spirits, and so was the merchant.

That evening I saw them at the theater in a box with an all too beautiful and flashily dressed woman who could scarcely have been either the wife or a relative of either of them, and who appeared to have made their acquaintance only a very short time before.

During the intermission the merchant appeared in the buffet and ordered "cream de tea."

At once the waiter followed them out with peaches and other fruits and a bottle of *crème de thé*. When I left the theater my old schoolmate caught up with me and urged me to join them for supper, informing me that their lady was a product of "the very highest school."

"Genuine *haute école!*"

"Well, so much the better for you," I said, "but as for me, at my age, et cetera, et cetera"—in a word, I declined this alluring invitation, which would have been especially awkward for me because I intended to leave that gay town early the next morning and continue my journey. My fellow countryman let me go but in return made me promise to call on him without fail the next time I visited my relatives, and take a look at his model farm and especially his wonderful wheat.

I gave him my word, though with some reluctance. I can't tell you just why—whether I was disturbed by memories of penknives at school and worse things on the order of *haute école* or whether it was his genuine Nozdryóvianism[5] that repelled me; but anyhow I couldn't get rid of the feeling that once he had me in his home he would palm off a greyhound or a barrel-organ on me.[6]

Some two months later, after loafing about here and there and taking a few treatments at the mineral baths, I really did get back to my native haunts, and after resting there a while I asked my cousin:

"Tell me, where is So-and-so, and what sort of man is he? I've got to pay him a visit."

My cousin looked at me and said:

"How's that? Do you know him?"

I told him that we had been in school together and later had renewed our acquaintance at the exposition.

"I can't congratulate you on that acquaintance."

"Why not?"

"Why, because he's the most illustrious of liars and a genuine, copyrighted scoundrel."

"To tell the truth," I said, "I thought as much myself."

Thereupon I told him how we had met at the exposition, how we had reminisced about our schooldays, and how he had told me all about his farm and his activities on behalf of our Slavic brethren.

My cousin burst out laughing.

"What's funny about that?"

"Everything about it is funny, except for a few parts that are disgusting. Incidentally, I hope you weren't too outspoken with him about politics."

"Why?"

"Well, he has one very peculiar habit: he constantly steers the conversation in a certain direction and then suddenly he will recall that he's a 'nobleman' and start protesting and threatening. Occasionally that has earned him a beating, but even more often he has been simply dosed with champagne until his memory was befuddled."

"No," I said, "I didn't get off into politics with him, and even if I had nothing would have come of it, because all my politics consists in disgust for politics."

"But that doesn't mean a thing," he said.

"Why not?"

"He'll lie and slander you and say you were silently scornful . . ."

"So you really mean there's no way to escape him?"

"No way at all, unless you are bold enough to drive him off."

That sounded a little too strong to me.

"I'm surprised," I said. "How is it that everybody is so mistaken about him?"

"Who, for example?"

"Well, now, he came up to Petersburg from you people during the Slavic War," I said, "and up there they wrote about him in the papers and important people entertained him."

My cousin laughed and said nobody had sent that gentleman off or authorized him to act on behalf of the Slavs; rather, he himself had seen this as a good way to patch up his bad financial plight and his even worse reputation.

"And if you people in the capital made a fuss over him and entertained him, it's only your love of following the fashion that is to blame. It's always like that among you people up there; as soon as you get in a dither over some movement or other you'll take up with anybody at all, no matter who he is."

"But look here now," I said, "do you think *we* are to blame? There is no pleasing you. First Petersburg seemed cold and stand-offish to you, and now you're ready to tell us it's some sort of simpleton that any of your rascals can lead around by the nose."

"And you know, that really is true."

"I beg your pardon!"

"It's true, I can assure you. The whole trick lies in listening to whatever may be rattling around in your Petersburg heads at a given moment and whatever foolishness may be holding forth up there. Whether you are discovering your Slavic brethren or dazzling your trans-Atlantic friends with your wit, or getting together to start ringing peasant shoes instead of bells—it's never hard to catch on to what your latest fad is; and then a man has only to tune his second fiddle to your first fiddle and after that everything is simple. You people send up a howl about 'our provinces—our fresh, unused power. They see things in a different light from us worthless, disgusting, pitiful, unnatural weaklings, dragging out our weary existence in the swamps of Ingermanland.' You Petersburgers beat yourselves black and blue with the cooperation of some literary liar, and our provincials read it and think, 'There, brothers, we've gone up in the world!' And then when the more rascally ones among us have read about how down-and-out you feel in the capital and how you expect us provincials to bring new life to you, they deck themselves out and go to Petersburg to give you some of our businesslike spirit and our 'strong, healthy national ideas.' Good, peaceful people naturally look on all this in amazement, but meanwhile the smart rascals make a good thing of it. These liars bring you just what you want to get from the provinces—they too are brothers to the Slavs and friends to the trans-Atlantickers; they are ready to move forward, and they are equally glad to move backwards. In a word, they will turn into whatever you want. And you think, 'This is the *land*, the provinces!' But we stay-at-homes know that is neither the land nor the provinces but simply our native liars. And the man you are getting ready to visit right now is just that sort. You people up in the capital stuffed him full of honors, but the way we look at it he doesn't even deserve the name of human being, and down here among us nobody for heaven knows how long has been willing to have anything to do with him."

"But still, he *is* a good farmer."

"By no means."

"But he's got money—that's a rare thing nowadays."

"Yes, since he went to Petersburg to teach you people national ideas he's had a little money clinking in his purse; but we know what he bought up there—and whom he sold."

"Well, in that case," I said, "I am better informed than all of you; I myself saw how he sold that splendid wheat of his."

"He hasn't got any splendid wheat."

"What do you mean—hasn't got any?"

"He just hasn't, that's all. He hasn't now and never has had."

"Just a minute now—excuse me, but I saw it myself."

"In the showcase?"

"Yes, in the showcase."

"Well, that's not surprising. Our peasant women picked it out for him by hand."

"What!" I said. "They *couldn't* have picked all that out by hand!"

"Why not by hand? Of course they could. The women and girls sat around on spring days in the shade of the barns, singing about how 'Anthony leads the goat' and sorted out handfuls of wheat grain by grain. That's not at all impossible."

"Nonsense!" I said.

"It's not nonsense at all. A skinflint like my neighbor would not pay good money for nonsense, and he paid forty peasant women five kopecks a day for a whole month. It's true that he did pick a good time for it, because in the spring you can get our peasant women to work for almost nothing."

"But how does it happen," I asked, "that there were affidavits at the exposition that this wheat came from his fields?"

"That's true, it did. After all, these choice grains grew in his fields too."

"Yes, but—that means this is an outrageous, bare-faced swindle."

"And not the first or the last—don't forget that."

"But how can he? And that merchant he caught with his ironclad contract—surely he must have sued this landowner, didn't he? Or did he go bankrupt?"

"Yes, he undoubtedly did sue, only in a very special court."

"Where was that?"

"Before a peasant. According to the way you people think nowadays, there can be no higher appeal than that."

"Come on now," I said, "I've had enough of your joking and your talking in circles. Just tell me straight out, the way you ought to, what happened in this private enterprise of yours."

"Give me a chance," he answered, "and I will tell you."

Then, brother, he told me a tale that really does surpass all hidebound foreign notions about how to stimulate the business life of the country. I don't know how it will strike you, but to my mind it is original and cannot help rejoicing the heart of any real self-made man.

At this point the falsetto interrupted the storyteller and started begging him to go on with the rest of his trilogy, that is, to tell how the merchant settled accounts with the rascally landowner and how they were both reconciled and rescued by the peasant, to whom everybody seems to look nowadays for answers to whatever problems life turns up.

The baritone agreed to go on and said:

"It's a rather curious case. Just imagine, bold and resourceful as the landowner was whom I have just described to you—and God grant that nobody should ever get mixed up with him in business affairs—still the merchant he swindled and entangled so unmercifully turned out in the end to be even more bold and resourceful. Any rattle-brained foreigner would have seen only two ways out of all this: either to go to court or else—devil take it—settle the whole thing with blood. But our simple, clear-sighted Russian intelligence found still another dimension and another way out, which led neither to court nor to a quarrel nor even to any loss for anybody. On the contrary, everybody preserved his innocence and everybody made money out of the deal."

"How interesting!"

"Why, sure! Out of this scandalous, perfidious, and thoroughly revolting affair, which would have been enough to make any Western European lose the shirt off his back, our paunchy Orthodox merchant came forth with flying colors and even made a handsome profit—and most important of all, my good sir, he benefited society with it. He gave support to a lot of truly unfortunate people, he put their finances in order, and, one might say, brought many of them real prosperity."

"How interesting!" the falsetto put in once more.

"Now just listen. I'll guarantee that the merchant who will now appear before you is more than a match for the landowner."

CHAPTER TWO

THE MERCHANT

It goes without saying that the merchant to whom the choice grain had been sold was cheated unmercifully. All those Frenchmen who looked like Jews and all those Englishmen, as well as the *haute école* lady, were only what you might call the landowner's window-dressing, his agents, who played a part like that of the well-known Comforter in Gogol's *Gamblers*.[7] Such choice grain as this could not possibly have been sold to foreigners because, first of all, they would have found no way to cope with such a purchase and would have raised a scandal in court; and in the second place, they all have consuls and ambassadors hanging around who refuse to observe our own diplomats' rules of nonintervention and will interfere on behalf of their own people at the slightest provocation. With foreigners the matter might have led to a nasty mess; and the landowner, who had both feet on the ground, understood that an invention of Russian origin could be overcome only by that same Russian national genius. Therefore the choice grain was sold to a fellow believer.

The merchant sent his assistant to the landowner to get the wheat. The assistant went into the barns, took a look at the wheat in the bins, stirred it a little with a shovel, and of course saw that his boss had been fearfully swindled. But meanwhile the merchant had already used the samples to sell all the wheat abroad. The perplexed assistant's first thought was that he had better refuse the whole thing and get the down payment back; but the contract was so worded that there was no way out: everything was set forth in black and white—the crop, the years, and the barns —and the down payment was not to be returned under any circumstances. There is a saying among us that "money down is money gone." The assistant went around to see various lawyers, and they all told him there was nothing to do but take the wheat just as it was and pay the rest of the money. A lawsuit could be started, of course, but there was no telling how it might turn out, and meanwhile the ten thousand the merchant himself had received in down payment would melt away and the foreign purchasers would be in no mood for joking. He would have to deliver what they had bought.

The assistant sent a telegram to his boss urging him to come at once.

The merchant came, listened to the assistant's story, took a look at the wheat, and then said to the fellow:

"You are a fool, brother, and you've managed the whole thing stupidly. The wheat is good and there is no need for any sort of quarrel or publicity. Trade loves secrecy: we must take the goods and pay the money."

But with the landowner he had quite a different sort of talk.

He went in, crossed himself before the icon, and said:

"God send you good health, sir!"

And the landowner answered:

"May God send you the same!"

"And now, sir," said the merchant, "you are a scoundrel. You know you have rooked me royally."

"But what's to be done, friend? Really now, do you merchants ever show mercy to anybody? Do you ever swindle people like us? It works both ways."

"That's how it is, all right," answered the merchant. "It really does work both ways. But now the question is, how to straighten it out."

The landowner agreed about this, but he said:

"I'd like to know just what you mean by 'straightening it out.' "

"Why, I just mean that since you swindled me when your turn came, now it's your Christian duty to lend me a helping hand, and I will pay you all the money I owe you and may even add a little to boot."

The landowner said he would be glad to lend him all kinds of helping hands under those conditions. "Only tell me straight out, though," he said, "what kind of new job is required for the sake of your honor?"

The merchant answered briefly:

"I don't need very much from you. Only act toward me as the prudent steward acted in the Gospel story."

The landowner said:

"I always get to church after they've read the Gospels; I don't know what it says there."

The merchant informed him from memory:

" 'And having called every one of his lord's debtors unto him, he saith, "How much owest thou? Take thy bill and write a second one." And the lord commended the unjust steward.' "[8]

The landowner listened to him and said:

"I understand. You very likely want to buy still more of such rare wheat from me."

"Yes," answered the merchant. "Now we must continue, for in no other way is it possible for us to save ourselves. And besides, we must not think only of ourselves; we must allow our poor fellow countrymen to earn a little something."

The landowner just let that remark about the poor fellow countrymen go in one ear and out the other, and he asked:

"How much more wheat do you want to buy from me?"

"Why, I'll buy a lot more. I need enough to fill one whole barge with nothing but this fine wheat."

"Hm! I see. Very likely you want to take extra good care of it?"

"That's exactly right."

"Aha! I understand. I'm very glad, very glad that I can be of service to you."

"I need documentary evidence that I have loaded the whole barge with wheat."

"Of course, of course. Can anything be done in our country without documents?"

"And what will the price be? How much will you charge for this extra purchase?"

"I will charge no more than I would for dead souls."[9]

The merchant didn't understand what this meant, and hastily crossed himself.

"What put that into your head? Their fate is to rot but ours is not. We are talking about the living. Tell me, how much will you charge just for selling me something nonexistent?"

"In just one word?"

"In just one word."

"Two rubles a bag."

"Oh, come on, now!"

"That's cheap."

"No, now be a good Christian, let me have it for half a ruble."

The landowner put on an expression of astonishment.

"What do you mean? Half a ruble for a bag of *wheat?*"

But the merchant tried to make him see reason:

"After all, what kind of wheat is that!"

"Now, we won't argue about whether it's one kind of wheat or another; the point is that you're trying to do me out of real money for it."

"That will be as God grants it."

"Well, God will be sure to grant it to you, all right. I don't know why, but God is frightfully kind to you merchants. Honest to God, it's enough to make a man envious."

"Now, don't be envious; envy is a sin."

"Yes, but why must all money flow into your hands? You people are rolling in money."

"It's because we always fall on our knees and pray—and you should pray too. God gives plenty to the man who prays."

"Maybe so. At least, you've got plenty. You give a lot for churches."

"Yes, I do."

"Now, I'll tell you what! You raise your price a little and then I'll give something too."

The merchant burst out laughing.

"You're a rogue," he said.

And the landowner answered:

"What about you yourself?"

"All right, I'll tell you what I'll do. Since I see that you know the Scriptures and want to abide by the faith yourself, I'll give you ten kopecks a bag more than I had intended. Let me have them for sixty kopecks a bag, and we'll say nothing to anybody about it."

But the landowner answered:

"All right, but it'll be still better if you give me a ruble a bag, and then you can tell anybody you please."

The merchant looked at him and they both together burst into laughter.

"Well," said the merchant, "I'll tell you, sir, they don't often come more rascally than you, even in the very lowest classes."

Without batting an eyelash the landowner answered:

"It can't be otherwise in our times, brother; nowadays we have an aristocracy, but we haven't got the peasants to look after our aristocracy; and besides, it's the fashion nowadays to imitate the Russian common people."

The merchant didn't try to bargain any further.

"It's plain there is no use talking with you any more. Cross yourself before the icon and let's shake on the deal."

The landowner agreed to cross himself but he wanted his money in advance, and he pointed to a spot on the table before him where he would like to have the money laid.

The merchant put the money down on that very spot.

"All right," he said. "Only, be quick and give the order to have the new bags filled with whatever is handy. I want all the loading to be done and the caravan to sail off while I am here."

The barge was loaded with bags filled with the devil knows what to make them look like bags of costly wheat. The merchant insured it all for the highest possible amount. Then they had a prayer service and the blessing of the waters; they fed their humble Orthodox brethren with meat pies made of livers and lights, and then the ship got under way. The barges floated off down the river, and the merchant lost no time in settling his accounts with the landowner in Godly fashion. Then grabbing his papers he sped off to Petersburg and straight to the English Wharf, where he found the big Englishman to whom he had previously sold his wheat with the use of the marvelous sample that had been on display at the exposition.

"The wheat is on its way," he said, "and here are the documents and the insurance policy. Now please give me the rest of the money you owe me."

The Englishman looked at the documents and turned them in at the office, and then took the money out of a fireproof safe and handed it over.

The merchant wrapped it up in a handkerchief and left.

Here the falsetto interrupted the storyteller and said:

"You are just telling a yarn."

"I'm telling you just what actually happened."

"And so, then, once the merchant had gotten his money from the Englishman, I suppose he left the country with it, did he?"

"He didn't run away at all. Why should a true Russian leave the country? That is contrary to his principles, and besides he doesn't know any other language than Russian. No, he didn't run off anywhere."

"Then why wasn't he afraid of the English consul or ambassador? Why should the landowner have been afraid of them when the merchant was not?"

"Very likely because the merchant was more experienced and better acquainted with our national resources."

"Oh, enough of that! What kind of national resources can you use against the English? Those international hucksters can take in anybody they please."

"But who told you he wanted to swindle the English? He knew it didn't pay to fool around with them, and he had worked out a new program for the successful continuation of his affairs in the future, and in this new program he had already foreseen that he would have a useful agent, in whose hands would be all the means necessary to keep his business within the proper framework. He would give everything the sort of turn that neither a Rothschild nor a Thomson Boner[9] nor any other genius of commerce would ever have thought up."

"And who was this great businessman—a lawyer, or a broker?"

"Neither. A peasant."

"A peasant!"

"Yes indeed. He managed the whole affair—he, our simple, our resourceful and intelligent peasant! Besides, I don't see why you should be surprised at that. Surely you've read in Shchedrín how a peasant fed three generals, haven't you?"[10]

"Of course."

"Then why do you think it is strange that a peasant should have been able to break up a swindle?"

"Have it your own way; for the time being I will hide my astonishment."

"And I will finish by telling you about the peasant, who incidentally did not feed three generals but a whole village, and all by himself."

CHAPTER THREE
THE PEASANT

The peasant to whom the merchant turned for help was, like every Russian peasant, "drab in appearance but keen in wit." He was born near the good broad Mother Vólga; and his name, we'll say, was Iván Petróv. This slave of God Iván had once been young, but now he had reached a venerable old age. Nevertheless, he did not lie on the stove and eat his bread for nothing, but he served as a pilot on the Tolmachóv rapids, at Hensford. As you probably know, the pilot's task is to steer ships through dangerous passages in the river. The pilot receives a certain sum of money in payment for his work, and this money goes to his pilots' co-operative and is distributed afterwards among all the pilots in his neighborhood.

Any master can steer his own ship through on his own responsibility, without a pilot; but in that case, if anything happens to the vessel, the pilots' co-operative is not responsible. For that reason, if the ship's cargo is insured, the terms of the insurance require the presence of a pilot. This was of course taken over from foreign practice, without due regard for our unparalleled originality and directness. Foreign gentlemen introduced the custom of insuring cargoes among us and thought that their Rhine or Danube was just like our Svir or Vólga, and that their pilots and ours were all the same. But oh, brothers, how wrong you were!

Our river pilots are simple people; they are no scholars; they guide their ships and they themselves are guided by God alone. To be sure, they have a certain kind of experience and skill. It is said that after flood-time they examine and check up on the river bed, but we may assume that this belongs rather to the realm of soothing Russian illusions. Still, in their own way the pilots are great businessmen and at times they earn sizable sums. And all this is carried on in simplicity and humility, fearing God and not offending the world—in other words, not forgetting their own people.

The peasant Iván Petróv was well-to-do. He not only ate meat in his cabbage soup but he would also put a spoonful of sour cream in his rich, greasy porridge—not so much for the taste as for the sake of his social position, so that it would run down his beard. And along with all this, for the sake of his digestion he would drink a glass or two of our good simple Russian vodka, from which nobody ever got the gout. On Saturdays he would go to the bath, and on Sundays he would pray diligently and politely, that is, he never dared ask for anything directly in his own name, but he would seek the intercession of illustrious saints, and he would not even approach them empty-handed but would take gifts and offerings into the temple with him—shrouds, chasubles, candles, and incense. In a word, he was a Christian of the most genuine Moscow stamp.

The merchant whom the landowner had offended with his choice grain knew the pious peasant Iván Petróv through trustworthy rumors about the very sort of activities for which he himself needed the peasant now. For he was just the man who could mend the whole matter in such a way that there should be loss for no one and *profit for all.*

"He saved others, and he's got to save me too," the merchant reasoned. He called to his office that same assistant who alone knew what the insured bags on the barge were filled with and said:

"You take charge of the caravan, and I will meet you at the proper place."

And he himself set out with little luggage as an ordinary pilgrim straight toward the Tíkhvinskaya Shrine, but arrived instead at the Tolmachóv rapids near Hensford. "Where thy treasure is, there will thy heart be also." [11] Our merchant stopped there at the inn and then went off to learn where the great man Iván Petróv was to be found and how one could arrange to meet him.

The merchant walked along the river bank and wondered how he ought to handle the matter. Handling it in straightforward fashion was out of the question because of the thievish nature of the deal.

To his good fortune the merchant caught sight of a hale and hearty white-haired old man who was sitting at the river's edge on an upturned boat. He was wearing a wadded velveteen cap, he had a beard of a gray-green hue, and from his neck was suspended a copper Kórsun cross that lay on the front of his peasant shirt.

The respectable appearance of the old man pleased the merchant.

He walked past the old man once, and twice, and then the old man asked him:

"What seek you here, master, and what do you wish to find—that which you never had, or that which you have lost?"

The merchant replied that he was merely "taking a stroll," but the old man was no fool. He smiled and answered:

"What sort of a stroll is that! Going for a stroll is for fine gentlemen: it is not a Christian occupation. A prudent man walks for business and keeps his eye out for business. He does not flee his business, he feeds his business. Is it possible that you at your age are passing your time in vain?"

The merchant saw that he had discovered a man of great understanding and insight, and at once he revealed that he was indeed feeding his business and not fleeing from it.

"Referring to what place?"

"Referring to this very place."

"And consisting in what?"

"Consisting in the fact that I have been wronged by a most unrighteous man."

"I see. Nowadays, friend, few there are who live by righteousness rather than by wrongdoing. And whom seek you upon our shores?"

"I seek a benefactory man."

"I see. And by virtue of what power?"

"By virtue of the greatest of all powers—the power to take away sin and offense."

"Ah, brother! How can all sins be washed away? In the Scriptures, where they speak of the Apostles, it is written: 'The whole world is plunged into sin.'[12] It cannot be all washed away—it can only perhaps be washed away in part."

"Then at least in part."

"That is just it: the Lord washed away all sins with a flood, but they came back again."

"But instruct me, grandfather; where can I find here the useful man whom I need?"

"And what name was he given of God?"

"His name is John."

" 'There was a man sent from God, whose name was John,' " murmured the old man. "And how was he called according to the name of his father?"

"Petróvich."

"Well, I who stand before you am that very man—Iván Petróvich. Tell me wherein lies your need."

The merchant told him the story, limiting himself, incidentally, to only the first half—that is, to the part about what a scoundrel the landowner was who had sold him the choice grain. He kept silent about his own scoundrelly part of the story, and indeed there was no need to tell it, for the wise old man understood everything through the silence, and delicately formulated his answering speech:

"So the cargo is insured?"

"Yes."

"And already contracted for?"

"Already contracted for."

"By foreigners?"

"By Englishmen."

"Oh! Those slick-talking rascals!"

The old man yawned, made the sign of the cross before his mouth, and then stood up and added:

"Come unto me, sorrowful man, at my house. We must talk about this matter after I have given it thought."

Some time later the "sorrowful merchant" came as they had agreed to Iván Petróv, who took him out to the garden, sat down with him on the steps of the bath house, and said:

"I have considered your matter carefully. It is indeed necessary to help you out of your obligations, for it would be a sin to let our own fellow Russian fall into furrin hands; and the means of saving you does lie within our power, only there is a certain rule of our community that does not permit it in this case."

The merchant began begging him.

"Be gracious unto me," he said. "I am willing to go into the thousands, and I will put down the money right now in advance for an icon—either a Saint Nicholas or a Redeemer, just as you wish."

"Yes, I know, but it is impossible."

"Why?"

"It's very dangerous."

"And just when did you start fearing danger?"

The old man looked at him and remarked with solid dignity that he had always feared danger.

"Still, you have helped others."

"To be sure, I have helped others when it was done according to principle and the whole community would stand behind me."

"But you mean the community would stand against you now?"

"I think so."

"Why?"

"Because an insured vessel went down here at Hensford last year and all our villagers earned plenty from the salvaging work; but if we should have that happen again here this year, the people down at Hogsford would get angry and report us. They've had a fire down there this year and pretty near the whole village burned to the ground. They need help to rebuild their houses and repair their church. It's not right to send blessings only to our own people, they need to get some down there, too. Now you go to Hogsford tonight and call at the third house in the village for a man named Peter Ivanóv. He is your man and he will do everything unto your salvation. And don't spare the money—they need to rebuild their houses."

"I won't."

That very night the merchant made the journey for which Grandfather Iván had given him his blessing. He had no difficulty in finding the helpful

Peter' in the third house in the village, and they quickly came to terms.
He paid rather dear, perhaps, but everything worked out so neatly and
honorably that it brought him nothing but comfort and joy.

"What do you mean—comfort and joy?" asked the falsetto.

"Why, such comfort and joy that when the merchants' caravan arrived
with the barge that carried rubbish instead of costly wheat, everybody
gathered on the bank in front of the chapel and sent up prayers, and then
Peter Ivanóv the pilot got on the tug-boat and took the helm and steered
everything through safely until all at once he gave the tiniest turn to the
wheel, and managed it so well that all the other vessels passed through
and only that one barge got caught and turned over flat on its back, like
a frog, and sank.

"A crowd of people had gathered on both banks, and they all saw what
happened and shouted: 'Say, look at that! What d'ya know about that!' In
a word, 'there was an accident,' and nobody knew how come. The men
pulled at the oars with all their might, and Uncle Peter struggled and
sweated at the helm, and the merchant, white as a sheet, stood on the
bank and prayed, but it was all in vain. The barge went down, and the
owner won over everybody with his spirit of resignation. He crossed himself and sighed, and said:

" 'The Lord giveth and the Lord taketh away; His Holy Will be done.'

"The peasants were more straightforward and more lively than anybody
else. They at once began to crowd around the merchant and besieged him
with entreaties: 'Don't think ill of us now! God has sent this to us poor
orphans.' And then the cheerful work began: on the one hand they went
through the rites of filling out the forms and making the legal affidavits
so that the merchant could get his insurance payment for the rubbish
that had been lost in the guise of valuable wheat; and on the other hand
all the peasants fairly bubbled over with excitement and set about rebuilding the whole village."

"How did that happen?"

"It was all very simple. The Germans do everything according to their
foreign brand of rules; an insurance agent came and started hiring people
to work at recovering the sunken cargo. They were anxious not to lose
everything. That was no small job and it lasted a long time. The peasant
victims of the fire knew how to take advantage of the circumstances; the
men were hired for a ruble and a half a day and the women for a ruble
a day. They didn't try to rush through the job, and with God's help they
managed to work all summer long. Meanwhile on the bank there was a
regular festival. The fire victims dried their tears, everybody started singing songs and dancing a jig, and up on the hill the axes of the carpenters
they had hired beat out a merry tune, and nice little huts sprang up like

mushrooms out of the ashes of the village. And in this way, sir, they rebuilt their whole village, they got rid of their misery and want, they ate their fill, and they restored God's temple. Everybody prospered, everybody led a life full of praise and thanks unto the Lord, and nobody—not a single person—was left with any loss or bitterness. Nobody had suffered by it!"

"What do you mean—nobody?"

"Well, who did suffer? The landowner, the merchant, the peasants— everybody got nothing but profit."

"And what about the insurance company?"

"The insurance company?"

"Yes."

"Good Lord, brother, what are you talking about?"

"Well, didn't they have to pay?"

"Why, of course they had to pay. Why shouldn't they have paid?"

"And in your opinion that is not vileness but—*sociable-ism*?"

"Why of course it's sociable-ism! So many Russians put back on their feet, and a whole village fed for a year, and fine new buildings put up— and then you want to call that 'vileness'!"

"But about the insurance company—you don't call that a sociable-istic enterprise?"

"Of course not."

"Then what is it?"

"A scheme the Germans cooked up."

"But it has Russian stockholders too."

"Yes—the sort that associate with Germans and kowtow to everything foreign and go around praising Bismarck."

"So you don't praise him then?"

"Heaven forbid! He's even started preaching about how we Russians 'have begun to carry our misuse of our stupidity too far.' So let him find out how stupid we are. I won't have anything to do with him."

"Well, the devil himself knows what all that means!"

"What what means?"

"Why, just what you've been telling me."

The falsetto burst out in laughter and added:

"No, I utterly fail to understand you."

"Imagine that! And I don't understand you either."

"If some third person who didn't know us had been listening to all this, he would be quite justified in thinking we were either rascals or fools."

"Perhaps so, but that would merely prove his own shallowness, because we are neither rascals nor fools."

"Well, if that is so, then I dare say we ourselves don't know who we are."

"Why shouldn't we know? As for me, I know perfectly well that we are simply two happy Russians returning homeward from the marshes of Ingermanland to our own warm beds, our cabbage soup, and our wives fortunate . . . And by the way, here is our stop."

The train began to slacken its speed, we heard the whistle and the shriek of the brakes, and the two men got off.

I half raised up to get a look at them, but the shadows were so thick that I did not succeed. I could only tell that both men were tall and well filled out.

NOTES FOR "CHOICE GRAIN"

[1] The rascally hero of Gógol's famous novel *Dead Souls*. He attempted to acquire a fortune by traveling over the Russian countryside and persuading the landowners to sell him the title to their dead serfs, or "souls," who in the eyes of the tax office continued to live until the next official census. Chíchikov planned to use this paper property as collateral for a bank loan big enough to enable him to buy a genuine estate.

[2] A legendary hero of Russian folklore who sat on the ground unable to walk for thirty years and then through the aid of holy pilgrims was cured and acquired enormous strength.

[3] The treaty of 1878 that the Western powers forced on Russia and that represented a crushing defeat for Russian foreign policy.

[4] A quotation from A. S. Griboédov's comedy *Woe from Wit (Gore ot uma)*, Act IV, Scene 14.

[5] Nozdryóv was a rascally landowner in Gógol's novel with whom Chíchikov bargained in a vain effort to get the title to Nozdryóv's "Dead Souls."

[6] In Chapter 4 of Part I Nozdryóv tries to sell Chíchikov a greyhound and a barrel-organ.

[7] The leader of a gang of cardsharps in Gógol's comedy *The Gamblers (Igrokí)*.

[8] A reference to the parable in Luke 16:1-8.

[9] The name Rothschild is too well known to need identifying, and the name Thomson Boner is apparently Leskóv's mistake for Hans Boner (born before 1463—died in 1523), a wealthy German-Polish merchant who financed Polish kings and was a generous patron of the arts.

[10] A reference to M. E. Saltykóv-Shchedrín's fable in prose, "The Story of How One Peasant Fed Two Generals" (1869).

[11] A quotation from Matthew 6:21.

[12] A quotation from 1 John 5:19.

[13] A quotation from John 1:6.

NOTE TO "NOTES FROM AN UNKNOWN HAND"

Among the second-hand booksellers in Moscow during a short visit in October 1883 Leskóv came across a manuscript called "Astonishing Stories About Seven Wise Men," which was written in 1702 by a priest in the town of Velíkie Lúki. "These *superb* stories taken from God knows what Latin original," Leskóv wrote to his friend S. N. Shubínsky, "are all stories dealing with love and are truly 'astonishing.' They have never been printed anywhere, and I believe my copy is *unique*. I am confirmed in this by Gattsúk, who is a real connoisseur of old literature. . . . The stories are all short . . . and they will be read with laughter and interest. There is bawdiness in them, but it is a simple, guileless kind, as in the *Arabian Nights*." [1]

The editor of this letter maintains that Leskóv never made any use of the material in this manuscript in his own literary works. There can be no doubt, however, that we see here the source of Leskóv's inspiration for his "Notes from an Unknown Hand," which he began publishing scarcely two months later in the *Gazette of A. Gattsúk*. His letter makes it clear that the device of presenting the little stories in "Notes from an Unknown Hand" as if they were taken from an old manuscript had its basis in fact. The illusion that they were written by some artless, unknown priest in the provinces is reinforced by the old-fashioned and comically awkward style that Leskóv adopted in these tales. For all their ingenuous air, however, the satire lurking just beneath the surface of these stories did not escape the vengeful eye of E. M. Feoktistov, the head of the Russian censorship, who had never forgiven Leskóv for transparently lampooning him two decades earlier in his novel *Nowhere to Go (Nékuda)*. Feoktistov issued both a First and Second Warning to the editor of the journal on account of Leskóv's little tales, and they were halted in April 1884, after nineteen of them had been published. (A Third Warning would have automatically closed the journal.)

Contemporary critics tended to dismiss these little stories as mere anecdotes. The same charge might be leveled at some of the stories in the *Decameron* or some of the *Canterbury Tales*. In the artistry of his awkward style, the serious implications of his humor, and the unifying elements running through his variegated mosaic of provincial life, Leskóv's "mere anecdotes" deserve much closer critical attention than they have been given in the past. The six stories selected for translation here should give the reader an opportunity to test this statement for himself.

NOTES FROM
AN UNKNOWN HAND

During my last stay in Moscow a second-hand bookseller I know from the Sukharyóv Tower delivered a few old manuscripts for my examination, among which was the one that I now offer to the reader. It was in an old-fashioned binding with blue paper pasted around the edges, and it had neither a signature nor a title. It also lacked many pages at the beginning and end. Still, what has remained intact seems to me to offer considerable interest as an artless portrayal of events that once interested a certain social class which was evidently very much respected, very original, and very serious in its outlook.

Herewith I offer in the original these notes of an unknown chronicler, in the same order and with the same individual titles under which they were set down in this half-destroyed manuscript.

A CLEVER RESPONDENT

A secretary, reproached for much acquisition, had a weakness for the building of new houses and country cottages, and during the extensive period of his government service he provided himself with them in such quantity that this was pointed out by his foes to his newly arrived department head. The department head replied:

"Very well, I shall test him, and if he does not convince me about how he got hold of all this over and above his government position, then I will deal with him as required."

But he sternly instructed the informer himself, and all those who stood (or sat) in attendance upon him, that they should in no wise let that secretary know, by even the remotest hint, about the keen question which was being made ready for him. And when the secretary, knowing nothing about what was premeditated, presented himself at the usual time to report on requests, having finished his report, he was interrogated thus:

"Is it true that you extort bribes from petitioners and even coerce them through extortion into bringing gifts of money to you, and refuse to examine their cases otherwise?"

The secretary, blinking not even one eye, made answer that all this was pure slander, and he supported his statement with a mighty oath in the name of God.

"All right," answered the department head, "but in the first place it is unseemly of you to swear such oaths, and in the second place I will believe your words only when you explain to me how, in your position, you got hold of five houses and six country cottages."

And the secretary, upon hearing this, replied that all those houses and country cottages and all that was found therein belonged not to him but to his wife.

"But your wife did not bring you all that as a dowry, because it is well known to me that she is the daughter of poor people."

"Yes, sir," answered the secretary.

"In that case, where did she get hold of such property?"

"I don't know," answered the secretary.

"What do you mean, you don't know?"

The secretary revealed within himself great confusion, and shrugging his shoulders he answered again:

"Have it any way you please, but I really can't explain it even to myself."

"Well, you might at least come right out and ask her!"

"I *have* asked her, many times."

"And what did she say in answer?"

"She answered nothing."

"What do you mean, 'nothing'?"

"It's like this: I would ask her, 'Darling, where do you get that money?' And she would only blush, but she wouldn't say anything."

The department head looked at this resourceful secretary and added:

"I see that you really are a clever respondent."

After that the secretary kept his position, and nobody could prove that he had no source of funds.

HOW IT IS NOT GOOD TO CONDEMN WEAKNESSES

Father Ioánn, a good priest, beloved of his parishioners and an experienced church administrator, had conducted himself from his youth onward in remarkable sobriety and lived a life of the most exemplary behavior; but when he was close to sixty-seven years of age, he lost his wife and fell victim to other misfortunes, each one of which would have been enough by itself to unnerve the most stouthearted soul. His son-in-law lost his mind, and his daughter came and took shelter under her father's roof with a sizable family; and his son gave himself up to wicked passions and became an actor. And Father Ioánn suffered still further grief and loss from a burdensome increase in the price of silver that was announced by the treasury, through which Father Ioánn's property suddenly declined in value, since he had kept all his savings at home in the form of paper money. And then in consequence of all this Father Ioánn began to seek forgetfulness of his woes in strong drink, which he had previously never used in all his life. At first this innovation remained hidden within the walls of his home; but afterward, since there was nobody to take constant care of the unfortunate old man, outsiders began to notice his weakness, and finally there was an awkward incident in God's temple when he, having given the call to worship, fell asleep and was slow to awaken. His parishioners, who loved him very much, tried to cover it up, but through the zeal of Father Irodión, who coveted the head priest's position for himself, it became known to the archbishop. His Eminence was stern and would not let this go unnoticed, and having called Father Iván unto himself, he said that for the benefit of his soul, in view of his declining years, he was relieving him of his duties as head priest, and he advised him to spend his time reading the *Hours of Devotion;*[1] and for the benefit of the service he appointed Father Irodión in his place.

This blow so cruelly influenced Father Iván's self-esteem that instead of reading the *Hours of Devotion* he became even more reckless; and when his daughter allowed him no further spirits at home, he began to drop in at taverns through the back door; and he went especially often to one of his parishioners, a tavern keeper and his spiritual son, who had long held him in reverence. This tavern keeper gave him a carafe of his own homemade trefoil bitters, and Father Iván made use of it with relish, and said: "This bitterness brings consolation to me, for it prefigures the bitterness of my life." And his spiritual son the tavern keeper sheltered him against the eyes of the public and offered it all to him not in the tavern itself but in his own living quarters, and not in the form of tavern business but of hospitality in his own home. And when Father Iván was unable to move under his own power, he would lie down and rest right there on the tavern keeper's sofa, having covered his face with a handkerchief, and the family would even take the canaries out of that room so that they should not awaken him too soon with their squeaky singing. Having thus taken his rest, the priest would then leave without any public notice of his condition. But once, when the tavern keeper and his family had been distracted by some incident and had not taken out the canaries, Father Iván awoke before he had got all the sleep he required, and he went out reeling. Considering himself still able to get home, he went further, but when he started off, his powers failed him, and his old legs started walking uncertainly through the slippery autumn mud, and he slipped and fell at the street corner and was not in a condition to stand up again.

It happened by chance that the new head priest, Father Irodión, was returning just at that moment with the old psalm-reader Ilkó from the house

of some parishioners, having performed the baptism of a baby; and seeing
Father Iván in his unfortunate position, he spitefully smiled and said:

"What an unworthy spectacle! Take a look at that and be prepared to
tell what you see."

But the psalm-reader Ilkó, having a good heart and being an old schoolmate of Father Iván as well, made answer:

"Excuse me, Reverend Father, but I don't know what you see."

"I see a disorderly wretch who has denied the blessing of his office."

"And I see an unfortunate man full of sorrow, and I dare not deny the
blessing within him because it is inherent," answered Ilkó. And with these
words he lifted up Father Iván, stood him against the wall, and said:
"Give me thy blessing, Father!"

And Father Iván opened his eyes and blessed him; and then, growing
weak, he lay down again. But Ilkó went to his house, and having called
one of the servants, they carried him home and cleaned him up.

Shortly afterward Father Iván died, having given his blessing to everybody, and also even to Father Irodión, who had taken blessedness away
from him, and for a long time the good parishioners held memorial services
at his graveside, and they did not love Irodión.

SUPERFLUOUS MOTHER LOVE

The widow of a collegiate assessor, remaining with her young son in good
circumstances, devoted all her attention to his upbringing, preserving him
from all colds and illnesses and also from every kind of incompatible conversations and words, from which his childish mind could be corrupted
and learn about vice. For this purpose nobody entered her house, not a
single man except the delivery boy and the baker, and then her confessor,
Father Paul, who came on the first of every month for prayer and edification. He was tall in size, sharp in understanding, and frequently humorous
in conversation. He would enter into the circumstances of this his com-
municant, and remaining with her after prayers for tea and refreshments,
he would regularly praise the modesty and circumspection of the assessor's
widow, but he disapproved of her keeping Ignásha thus behind closed
doors in the presence only of herself and the domestic women servants,
to such a point that he had nothing in his character akin to the masculine
sex and had come to resemble a girl, or rather, he had no relation to one
group or the other.

And Ignásha was then in his sixteenth year and had not yet studied
anywhere.

The assessor's widow, while recognizing Father Paul's authority in
everything, would not listen to his useful counsel in this matter and would
bring up examples from her past life in argument against his various
proofs. Most often she would recall that during her married life with the

assessor she had put up with a great deal from him, for he had such a custom that, whenever he went banqueting with some petitioner, he would not return home for several days, but would go off to various places and sing and gamble and perform various dancing steps to the music of a hand organ.

This dancing caused so much sorrow in the existence of the assessor's wife that it was understandable why she feared lest her son should follow in the footsteps of his sire.

But Father Paul, being sound in judgment, said: "Madam, you can keep no fruit beyond its time, and if you do, you will have to throw it out." And he pointed out to her that such an unforeseen occasion could turn up when something unusual in life would be suddenly revealed unto the youth, and then he would fail even worse to recognize how he should conduct himself and could suffer still more. But the doubting widow insisted on her own way and would not believe Father Paul, and thus successfully did she preserve Ignásha until the age of twenty and accustomed him to housework, taking him with her around the orchard and the outbuildings so that he should not remain alone for one minute. And meanwhile the occasion that she had refused to admit crept up in the greatest inexpectation and very soon was revealed.

The assessor's widow had a brother, a retired brigadier and a marshal of the nobility, whom she saw very seldom because he lived a little too gallantly on his own estate nearly a hundred and fifty miles away and would not hear of any visits from his female relatives, and twice a year he would send them holiday gifts of linen and other cloth, according to the choice of the countrybines living in his household. But since everything in this world finally comes to an end, in the seventy-third year of his life the brigadier's turn came to die, and on the threshold of death he remembered his sister, the assessor's widow, and sent a messenger to tell her that he was dying and wanted to bid farewell to her and his nephew.

The possibility about which Father Paul had hinted more than once to the assessor's widow was now imminent. The occasion arose from the fact that just before this time, while she was hanging up smoked chicken meat in the top of the shed, she had slipped and fallen off the ladder and so badly sprained her ankle that she was in bed and could not move, and for that reason she could not under any circumstances go to see her dying brother. Meanwhile, however, she was home-minded and property-loving and knew that in addition to her brother's real estate, which she firmly expected to inherit, he also had many things of great value—watches and tobacco-cases with portraits, covered with precious stones and awarded to him for his bravery from the Cabinet of His Imperial Majesty. And the assessor's widow feared lest he in his weakness should make a gift of these things to some of those feminine members of his entourage who had been deemed worthy of his favors in the course of his free life, or else that they themselves, in case her brother should die before she got there, might in their greed make off with all that and afterwards claim that "there wasn't anything," or "he gave them to us."

Thinking upon these things with an aching heart, she spent a sleepless night, and toward morning she resolved to send Ignásha to the dying man without her, dispatching along with him the faithful corporal's widow who lived with her, so that he should go and live with his uncle up to the very end and win his favor as diligently as possible.

In the morning she gave orders to hitch up the buggy and told Ignásha and the corporal's widow to get ready, and she sent word to Father Paul asking him to come straight from mass to lead the special prayer service "for him who setteth out on a journey" and to give Ignásha his blessing for the trip.

Father Paul came in answer to the invitation of the assessor's widow and chanted the prayer service in her room, so that she too could take part in it from her bed; and afterwards, when a breakfast of calf liver in sour cream and meat pastries was served there on the table for the departing traveler, Father Paul, while eating with Ignáty, counseled him at the request of his mother on how to conduct himself at his uncle's.

"Do not act like a child," he said. "Do not await your mother's advice at every step, because she will not be with you; instead, be guided by your own intelligence in doing what is useful for you. Show your affection for your uncle: kiss his hand and smooth out his bed covers and pour out his medicine for him at the proper times and give it to him in his spoon; and look around everywhere to see where fine and valuable things are and praise them and express your approval, so that he may understand how much you like them. And whenever he tells you about anything, 'That is for you,' kiss his hand at once and take the thing off to your room and lock it up from his servants and countrybines. And a little later, when he is in his right mind again, you just praise his service and his bravery, for which he received gifts of great value, and here again, hold those things up before him and keep praising them until he says, 'Take that too for yourself.' And keep in his good graces with this kind of affectionate behavior right up to his last breath. And when you are alone with him, talk against the others so that he will not trust anybody else. But if you can't manage to be alone, then get up and pretend to straighten his pillows and whisper in his ear. In this way you may receive everything—even with a little left over for me if you want to show that you value my counsel."

And having given Ignásha this edifying advice, he blessed him, and Ignásha and the corporal's widow set out; but when he came to the town gates, he put the corporal's widow out of the buggy and sent her back, and he worked up enough self-confidence to go on alone.

And after the death of his uncle he came back in flourishing condition and with a considerable number of gifts in goods and in a part of the estate; but he complained of two unforeseen events: first, his departed uncle had not allowed him to show tender affection toward him a single time and had not taken medicine from his hand; and second, his mother noticed that he did not sleep well now—he would tumble and toss in bed and smack his lips. And as for the second of these two events, he did not reveal to his mother how it had happened to him.

The assessor's widow, with whom her son had formerly been frank and open in everything, begged him with tears in her eyes to reveal to her why this restless sleep and smacking had come over him, but he mumbled something indistinct and revealed nothing. His mother began to wonder whether he had caught something from the deceased, or whether something had happened to him through the shock of seeing a death, or through vexation because the crude man could not value his affection even when he was dying, and then in accord with her unswerving faith in Father Paul, the assessor's widow sent for him in this case too for prayers, and then over refreshments she told him all about Ignásha, saying: "There has been a great change in him since that trip all alone to his uncle. By day he is sad and thoughtful, and by night he doesn't get to sleep till very late, and he turns and twists in his bed and keeps smacking his lips.

"I know," the assessor's widow went on, "that nowadays even the clergy has stopped believing in witchcraft. Still, the witch called forth Samuel himself from the grave and showed Saul the prophet's ghost, and it's not for nothing that the church books have prayers in them against evil spells and for driving out spirits; and so, one way or another, I beg you—and I've even made a new under-cassock for you with my own hands out of my marceline dress as a surprise—do take Ignásha in hand and get the whole truth out of him, and help him."

Father Paul said, "All right," and taking the package with the marceline under-cassock in one hand and young Master Ignásha in the other, he went out with him into the orchard, as if to inspect this year's harvest of cherries. And there, stopping under a heavy-laden tree, he began to show how much fruit the sparrows ruined, and from this he suddenly passed on with a sigh to another kind of ruin—how morals are corrupted.

"It will swoop down like a bird, you don't know where from, and it'll peck away at those good little plants. Did something like that, maybe, happen to you too?"

Ignásha was deeply and pleasantly moved, and was confused only because the question was so unexpected.

"That's right, Father Paul," he said. "A bad deed did happen to me, and—maybe—some of it is still there, and I am suffering for my sin."

And Father Paul shook his head and said:

"Now here's what we'll do: you go and pick me a good burdock leaf full of cherries, the very ripest ones, and especially the ones the sparrows have pecked—they are the sweetest of all—and bring them to me."

Ignásha performed it all quick as a flash—he picked the best cherries and the ones the sparrows had pecked and handed them over to Father Paul on a big burdock leaf, as if it were a big plate. And Father Paul sat down on the grass under an apple tree and opened up his cassock and put the leaf full of cherries on his knees and said:

"All right, friend Ignáty Iványch, now look; since there are just the two of us here—you and me—and nobody else, and above us is Almighty God, from whom nothing remaineth hidden or concealed, now let's you and me just talk frankly as if we were in paradise, and you tell me everything just like at confession—what it was that happened to you, and why it is you're so downhearted that you even make your mother downhearted too, because she sees how you are gloomy in the daytime and you toss in your sleep and keep smacking your lips at night. I'll sit here in the grass and eat the cherries you have picked, and you just confess all your secrets to me, and then you'll feel better."

Ignásha answered:

"That is just what I myself want to do very much, Father, only I don't want Mama to find out about it."

"She will never find out. I give you my word about that, and the law believes the word of the clergy without an oath. I've already told you I will accept what you say just like confession, and we are not permitted to reveal what we hear at confession to anybody except the political authorities."

"Well if that's the way it is, and Mama won't know about it, I will reveal my sin to you."

"Start revealing."

"I went to my uncle's so as to get into his favor before he died and get his things and an inheritance . . ."

"Well, what about it? That was your duty as a relative. There's no sin in that."

"Yes, sir. I received a lot of things, and got a hundred souls and the estate as an inheritance . . ."

"Well, why do you hesitate? You received a hundred souls and the estate—and that's not bad. I don't see any sin here either. If it had come to me, I'd have been glad to get such an inheritance."

"You couldn't," said Ignásha. "The clergy can't keep peasants in bondage—only the nobles can do that."

"Well, that doesn't matter. I'd sell the peasants cheap within six months to some nobleman for resettlement in the empty steppes, and I'd live on the estate myself. There is no sin in all that—but look, I'm soon going to be done eating all these cherries and you've been telling me nothing but trifles I know all about already, and you're still holding back on the sin."

Then Ignáty, seeing that he would have to bring their talk to an end, said he had found at his uncle's a great crowd of ladies dwelling there who were permanent guests, unrelated to him, but the brigadier drew them closer to him than he did his own relatives, and took his medicine from their hands and let no one but them sit close to him on the bed, and made his nephew get away, and even made fun of him. These same ladies had relatives of their own with them, young girls and old women. One of them was a young midwife, or dutchwife,[2] who had come from Moscow, gay in temper and full of laughter, round-faced, with heavy eyebrows and her hair parted on the side—exactly as if she were a good-looking boy. This young dutchwife did not like to languish at the sick man's bedside, and would keep running off to the orchard and taking Ignásha out there with her, and there she would get him to push her in the swing, and blow on the hot coal in her pipe so that she could have a smoke.

And when the brigadier had died and Ignásha started home, he could not get horses at the second post station, because they had all been taken, and he had to stay overnight at that station. And he had barely fallen asleep for his first nap when he heard a noise, and into the room where he was sleeping, besides which there was no other, there came that same dutchwife, who was also on her way home and also had to stop there till morning because she could not get horses. Then she, having taken off her cloak and her outer garments, lay down on the other bed in nothing but her white bodice and started smoking her pipe. Ignáty turned away from her toward the wall and diligently dozed very quickly through his second nap and turned back quietly toward her to see whether she was asleep. But she was not asleep. And having looked at him, she burst out laughing and puckered up her lips at him in a kiss. And he quickly turned back toward the wall and diligently sought to go to sleep as quickly as possible for his third nap, but he could not do this, for he kept hearing how she, giggling, would smack her lips in the form of a kiss right up to daybreak. And when he awoke the next morning in order to travel onward, she was no longer there, and he smacked his lips just as she had, and that habit remained with him from that time onwards.

Having heard this whole story, Father Paul asked whether he had not dreamed it all. But Ignáty expressed his firm conviction that it had all happened to him in reality. Then Father Paul, having eaten up his last cherries, shook off the spat-out cherry seeds that had stuck to the burdock leaf and placed the burdock leaf upon Ignáty's head, and slapping him on the back, he said:

"Good for you! I commend you. This time also you have come through pure and sinless. And now you just hold this leaf firmly on your head and walk around with it, take a stroll along the garden path until you get rid of the last of those notions, and I will go back to your mother. I will not reveal your secret to her, but I will put her mind at rest and tell her how she can save you, so that you may sleep sound, just as you used to, during your first nap as well as your second and third."

And, having sent Ignásha down the garden path to walk around under his burdock leaf, Father Paul went in to the assessor's widow and said:

"Have no worry for yourself and your son, whom you have brought up at your side. I have examined his conscience and found no fault whatever within him."

The assessor's widow crossed herself and wanted to ask questions, but Father Paul would not reveal anything to her.

"I gave my promise to Ignáty," he said, "and according to my priestly service I cannot, because what is revealed to us in confidence must remain forever a secret from everybody, with the sole exception of the political authorities. But I can assist you in setting your maternal feelings at rest, and I will give you some useful counsel."

"Do be so kind, Father," said the assessor's widow. "I will make you a worsted sash embroidered with flowers for the Feast of the Holy Virgin's Intercession."

"Good," he said. "But you listen now and carry out everything exactly."

"I am listening, Father. I am listening, and I will be sure to carry it out."

"Get up tomorrow morning at early dawn, when the dew has not yet dried on the grass."

"I will, Father Paul," she said. "I will even get up before dawn."

"Yes, and take a new sickle with you—one nobody has yet used for harvesting."

"I've got two new sickles in the tool shed."

"And take it and go out to the orchard, and seek out the leafiest apple tree of all, and make sure it has rosy fruit all over it."

"I've got one like that, I've got one."

"And with your pure motherly hands cut the grass all around it, and dry thirty pounds of hay in the sun."

"I will do it all just like that."

"And have him eat those thirty pounds of hay."

"Who?"

"Why, your son Ignáty, of course."

The assessor's widow was astonished.

"But how can that be?" she said. "He's not my horse, is he?"

And Father Paul answered:

"Your horse? Oh no, he's not a horse at all, but he's a most remarkable ass."

FEMALE ASPIRATIONS TOWARD UNDERSTANDING LEAD TO VAIN DISTRESS

A police colonel's wife who was not yet elderly but was very pious loved to make confession in great detail, and was so greatly concerned over her soul that she fasted during each of the four yearly fasts and repented at confession before Father Ioánn, about whom it has already been written how he was exposed to weakness and suffered on the occasion of being awakened by the singing of canaries. This good priest was able to endure everything, but he was so fatigued by the colonel's wife that he would say, shaking his head:

"May the Lord save me from her—she is talkative beyond all sense and nature."

And when Father Ioánn departed for a better world, the colonel's wife spent a whole year in uncertainty over which member of the priesthood she should honor with her choice as father confessor, and for that reason she tested many of them one by one with her fasting and repenting, and in this way she finally got around to Father Paul, about whom it has already been reported in the history of the son of the assessor's widow.

Father Paul was always impatient, but during the fasts he was often even worse because of his potato diet and his beets and cucumbers, and then he would confess people sharply and in irritation, and that woman liked to tell everything in detail, and in the manner of a school girl she would keep exclaiming *"Oh là là!"* No matter what she was asked, and no matter what she herself took it into her head to tell about, she would always begin with her favorite word, *"Oh là là!"* For example, *"Oh là là,* I'm a terrible sinner!" or *"Oh là là,* how unhappy I am!" and so on, which became very tiresome.

And Father Paul, seeing that she had come and bowed down to him, asked first of all why she did not pick out one priest instead of changing over and over. And she answered:

"Oh là là, I am so unhappy . . . I'm terribly nervous, and I can't get used to one . . ."

Father Paul said:

"That is perfectly understandable. As long as you keep changing, you will never get used to one."

And she started off again:

"Oh là là, I can't!"

"Why not?"

"Oh là là! It's so hard."

"It is hard because you keep oh-là-là-ing. Stop oh-là-là-ing and just go ahead without any oh-là-là's."

"Oh là là, I can't! I'm very sensitive. *Oh là là!"*

"There you go again with your *oh là là!"*

"Oh là là, I just can't help it!"

"Just try."

"Oh là là, I did try once, and I felt so—*oh là là! Oh là là!"*

Father Paul interrupted her.

"Once," he said, "is nothing. It is all right to *oh-là-là* just once, but there is no point in keeping it up."

The colonel's wife angrily left him and went to the archbishop and made a complaint against Father Paul, weeping and saying that he had offended her.

His Eminence gave her a drink of water to halt her tears, but in regard to the offense she claimed Father Paul had committed, "That," he said, "I do not understand."

And the colonel's wife said:

"Oh là là, O gracious God—but I understand it."

"Then you tell me."

"Oh là là! I can't talk about it."

"Then what can be done?"

"Oh là là! I've just had an idea."

"If your idea is a good one, carry it out; but if it is a bad one, abandon it."

"Oh là là! It's not a bad one at all. I will write down for you on a piece of paper what I think he meant, and you go into the other room and read it."

And having received permission for this, she wrote down her interpretation of it in French, and he returned the piece of paper to her with the inscription: "I do not understand."

When all this became known among the people in the town, they too did not understand why His Eminence had not understood—whether it was the French dialect, or what had been written in it. And on account of this a great deal happened about which the colonel's wife took offense and told her husband, but for Father Paul it all passed without serious consequence.

ON THE HARM THAT EXISTS FOR MANY
OF READING WORLDLY BOOKS

A rector did maintain in his seminary his own nephew, whom he truly loved; and having no other living relations who bore the family name, he singled him out among all others for special marks of his favor: he decked him in fine linen and clean clothes, and he intended to leave him as the heir and support of his name and all his property—which he set down in his will, and having had it signed and sealed by witnesses he laid it away to remain until he should depart this life. This same nephew was fair of face, quick of wit, and pleasing in heart, and he passed through all the rhetorical and philosophical sciences and reached the theological class, and since everyone knew of the rector's love for him, in keeping with the proposal of them all he was made the librarian. And for this position a salary was arranged for him of seven rubles a month. This was wondrously pleasing to the nephew-cherishing heart of the rector, and it opened up before his young relative numerous and seemly comforts and conveniences for one of his years, such as colored neckties for the Sabbath day, in contrast to the situation of the others, or scents and pomades for those times when he should go out for a stroll. But he began to spend the money thus granted unto him in a manner that was not at all expected from one of his youth: he bought neither gloves, nor false shirtfronts, nor neckties; neither did he buy for himself scents or pomades or anything else of similar innocence or appropriateness for one of his years. Rather did he give himself up to the reading of books by alien writers, most often by the English writer Dickens, through which his mind, hitherto inaccessible to any kind of fantasies, was now attacked by weaknesses that prepared the way for the temptation from which he was to perish, having inherited neither the glory nor the riches nor the goodness of his uncle, and having left behind unto others nothing except a frightful example for their edification.

Not far from the seminary, in a little hut on the bank of a stream, there lived in great poverty and misfortune the widow of a certain teacher of drawing, and at last there was given unto her a daughter, who, having reached her sixteenth year, began to assist her in the sewing of shirts for the seminary students. Thereupon they both began to receive from this their meager earnings, and therewith they patiently and honorably supported themselves for two whole years. But no less than the enemy of the human race, who everywhere succeeds in sowing calamity, did these two women, who appeared so honorable, become the perpetrators of a great misfortune for the worthy youth who had been destined for happiness, and who had every right to be under the protection of personages of the highest distinction.

It was the custom for the mother and her daughter to do sewing for the seminary students, and when the time came, the steward would send two servants with a basket, and the mother and daughter would place the garments they had sewn in this basket, and the servants, having passed a long pole through the handles of the basket, and having placed its ends upon their shoulders, would carry it together, and the widow would quietly follow after them, her daughter remaining behind in their hut. Upon receiving this linen the seminary steward would examine it with great care and verify its worth, and only then would he accept it; but all this took place without strife, for all things brought unto him from them were always in good order. Then the steward would draw up an account, and the widow would receive the money upon her signature, and not a single seamstress would agree to work more cheaply than they, for they alone could work so cheaply because they lived in their own little house. Although this little house was mean and small, still they paid nothing just the same for living quarters, and the reverend steward, who had given up the merchant class in Túla to become a monk, took this into consideration and lowered the price they received. But there was no joy in what followed from this, which was, so to speak, of the most romantic sort.

There once arose such a circumstance that the widow herself took sick with a dangerous illness of the legs from a chill and could not go to the accounts on Saturday in order to receive the money, and so she sent her daughter, having said unto her: "You see that I am unwell, and you are no longer a little girl: go in my place and receive the money for our use."

Her daughter went to the reverend steward, and since she was very skinny in appearance, the reverend steward did not keep her standing before him on her feet very long, but said: "Sit down," and seeing how inexperienced she was there before him, he began to discount more severely for the sake of economy, and he did economize somewhat from her pay, but in return, seeing that she had made no objection, before sending her homeward again he gave her to eat on the way a piece of Turkish delight, which had been prepared with attar of roses, so that its sweet and pleasant fragrance was as overwhelming as the hands of an archbishop, and pleasantly caressed the nostrils.

This same maiden, having accepted the sweetmeat, thanked him; and when she came again for the accounts on the following Saturday, she brought unto the steward as a gift in return for his Turkish delight a simple white handkerchief, but with a stork bird most skillfully embroidered in silk in the corner, and offering it she said that she begged him to accept it for his kindness to her sick mother, to whom she had taken the sweetmeat given her by the steward, and she was now bringing this embroidery that she had done with her own hand.

The steward accepted this ill-fated gift and chanced to show the intricate handkerchief to the rector, who said: "To what purpose is that for you? I too wish such a one for myself, and I have greater need of it when I have an occasion to take it out at some merchant's dinner. Only tell her that for me the bird should be another and more appropriate one, and not a stork." And the respectful little orphan quickly made two handkerchiefs and brought them unto the rector for his choice according to his taste, and in the corners of both handkerchiefs there were different birds worked in with silk: a heron was building its nest in the top of a tree, and a ring-tailed hawk was floating through the dark air and looking with red eyes into the darkness. All the embroidery was most artful, but the rector did not like it, because he expected soon to be made an archbishop, and he already dreamed of standing on the soaring eagles woven into the arch-bishop's carpet and of lifting up his spirit on high, but he did not wish to speak about this through the steward, lest there should be a tumult among the people. But the maiden, to whom all this understanding was alien, had embroidered two birds for him—a night bird and a swamp bird—which was as though in mockery of him. The rector invited her to come before him in person, and he said:

"Your embroidery is skillful, but the fantasy in your choice is inappropriate. Why did you vainly embroider for me, a man of the cloth, such a bird as the heron, which sits in the swamps or only walks about in the filth of muddy shores? That is out of place."

And she answered unto him that she had embroidered a heron in consideration of the fact that the heron was an ancient bird, from Egypt, and that it had swallowed serpents and foul reptiles and thus had helped to cleanse the land of suspicious crawling things. And she cited from her unexpectedly wide reading that large swamp birds were distant descendants of those whose work had freed the earth of the reptiles with which it had swarmed in its primitive state and had thus made it possible for better inhabitants to live upon it. And for this reason she had concluded that the heron would be very acceptable to a person of the cloth.

"In vain do you reason so much," answered the rector. "And even if it were so, still to what purpose is this other bird—this owl, or hawk, with its red eyes staring into the darkness?"

"Why, this," answered the maiden, "was intended to show that in the darkness encompassing him he carries light within himself and sees those who are injurious to life."

"Well now, I see that you are quite a freethinker and you reason very liberally . . . But tell me then, why did you give a stork to the steward, with his humble rank?"

"Storks love order and pass judgment with justice."

"Aha! That's the kind of Scheherazade you are! Just the same, I am not a sultan and I do not intend to listen long to you, but you reason very liberally. Now make two more handkerchiefs for me to choose from, but in such a way that they may be suitable for me. Indicate such a bird as is given to soaring in the uttermost heights and to looking down from there with great breadth of vision."

He said this unto her clearly indicating that the bird he had in mind was the eagle, upon which he wished to rest his feet, but he did not want to tell her outright, lest she should repeat it; rather he relied upon her taste and her reasonable conjecture. But even though she had a finely developed taste through her study of her trade, still through much reading of worldly books she had completely lost the ability to please important personages with respectful conjectures, and had spoiled her mind and the goodness of her sentiments. Led thus by her own devices, she brought back to the rector the two new orders, where on the one was skillfully embroidered a bird that was small in body and had extremely long wings, like sails in a full wind, and on the other was a swallow. Understandably, neither one pleased the rector, and he asked about the first:

"What sort of broom is that, and what does it mean?"

The maiden answered:

"That is an ocean bird, the 'man-o'-war bird' by name. It flies above the boundless waters for distances so great that not a single eagle would dare to attempt them."

But the rector replied:

"It is not your place to speak of eagles; it is upon the likeness of the eagle that the highest rank of the church takes his stand."

The maiden blushed and began to offer apologies, because she did not know about the eagles that were used in church services and had judged about eagles from the fact that they lived as birds of prey, destroying others and shedding the blood of life. For that reason she had thought that eagles were portrayed on heathen banners, and to her it had seemed that better than eagles for Christian tastes would be the quiet swallow, the pleasant little blue-gray bird that dwelt in the windows of peaceful houses, regularly flying away and coming back to us from everywhere.

The rector listened to her and looked at her and spake:

"Now, who has filled you with this raging spirit? Obey me and make a full confession."

And she obediently confessed and asked forgiveness, and answered that she had had no other instruction than through conversations with her own departed father, the teacher, from whom she had acquired the habit of reading many books, taking time for that from her sleep and repose.

"And what writer's books have you read the most?"

"Dickens's."

And to the question, what she liked most in Dickens, she answered that she found comfort in emulating the virtue and the principles of those modest persons whom this writer portrayed in the simplest everyday affairs, and that she drew strength for herself from the meek heights of their Christian spirit. In answer to the question whether she had a model of feminine virtue for herself which she took pleasure in following, she named "Little Dorrit," who with her father, in the bad company in which she lived, among the most corrupt people, still loved everybody and distinguished herself by her purity and gentleness. The rector ordered her rather to take as her example Ruth the Moabite; but she, looking modestly at him, answered that Ruth was not equally pleasing to her in all her actions, and as a Christian she could not follow her in everything.

Such an obstinate answer did lead the rector to order her to depart at once, and after that the handkerchiefs of her workmanship were sent back to her immediately by his nephew, without being purchased; and the sewing of linen was taken away from them and handed over to other seamstresses. And through this just punishment, which was merited by the impudence of this girl, she and her sick mother began to suffer great hardship, and she passed imperceptibly from one vice to another. For when the nephew was sent to her for the purpose of seeing the disorder of her thoughts, which had come from the reading which he also had selected, it turned out that he, having brought back her handkerchiefs and spoken a little with her, and also having seen their poverty, yielded to ardent youthful delusion and began to find in her soul something pathetic for him, and suddenly he began to praise her nobility, and he began to condemn his uncle, in whom he had such a benefactor and edifying teacher. Soon after that it was learned from a man who was devoted to the rector that the nephew had brought and handed over to the mother of that girl all his salary, seven rubles, which he had received for the month, and when the rector confronted him with this, he rudely answered that even if they were enemies, one must feed one's enemies, and that he could not bear their nobility in their poverty, and he considered the giving of aid to be a greater pleasure than the purchase for himself of gloves, neckties, and pomades. And a short time later he revealed to a sincere schoolmate his intention to give up his priestly calling, enter secular life, and marry that Dickens girl. This schoolmate, having a properly organized mind and valuing the opinion of the rector, as was fitting, betrayed this secret to him secretly for the salvation of his friend; and then other measures were taken, namely, then the rector requested the police to find out, by testing this heir of the teacher's doctrine, of what spirit she might be, and he announced unto his nephew that he now must choose one or the other: either to marry the daughter of the archpriest and receive a good position, or else be deprived of everything; and he gave him only three days for reflection.

The police tested the girl to find out of what spirit she was and sent her home with the report that nothing had been discovered against her, and the young man, after many tears and stupid wails and groans over the loss of his dreams, on the third day agreed to give up his passion on condition only that a little money at least be given to that girl, and that she should renounce and reject their compact of love, for he wanted to remain true to his gullible oath, but he also did not want to miss the chance of a position in a good parish.

Seeing this hesitation, the rector, moved by familial indulgence toward his nephew, fulfilled his insistent desire: he sent a clerk unto the girl with two hundred rubles, so that she should take the money and immediately write a refusal to the faint-hearted boy, but she revealed arrogance even here: she by no means accepted the money and would not even take it in her hands, but she haughtily and quickly wrote the required refusal. And since at this time the end of the school term approached simultaneously, the liberated nephew at once married the archpriest's daughter, was ordained as a priest, and was appointed to an enviable position. But for his disobedience, which he did not abandon even afterward, this disobedient man was not destined for lasting happiness by destiny. He was given material blessings and a thrifty wife, simple and not a day-dreamer, who in three years of wedlock presented him with no less than four excellent babies, so that he partook to the fullest of marital bliss, but still he could not dull the sting of sorrow, and in the midst of all these joys he wasted away in secret grief; and when in the fourth year of his marriage that self-willed girl to whom he had been engaged died of dread consumption, the sting of sinful love that had been hidden within him so long was laid bare to such an extent that he forgot everything about his holy orders, and went to the holy temple where her last rites were being performed, and, standing beside her bier, wept bitterly. And afterward, as if he took note of nothing, he began taking walks toward the town windmills that stood on the common town pasture behind the hut of the orphaned widow, and he was seen to go more than once unto the widow, and to comfort her with words, and to give her money, and he himself at her side wept tears unworthy of manhood. Thus he arrived at such melancholy that, upon coming to those windmills where the late departed liked often to sit, he himself spent long hours in grief, and even feared not when night would catch him unawares and darkness would cover him, and there was only the breathing of the wind and the noise of the briskly waving arms of the windmills, and occasionally the miller would look out of his door for a moment with his lantern, and a dog would yap under some cart that had brought wheat to the mill to be ground, and again everything would grow quiet. But he was not burdened by any of these impressions, and after one stormy night he was found killed by a windmill arm, which he had evidently run into while buried deep in his thoughts, and at first had been thrown high in the air, and then, hurled back by force, had been dashed against the ground, which at once deprived him of this life, so unbearable to him, and perhaps of the future life as well, for he himself had willfully cut short his days.

The rector, who by then had become an archbishop, himself conducted the funeral of this unfortunate madman; and, standing upon his eagle, truly showed everyone his firmness and composure; for, as befitted his position, he no longer gave a welcome in his heart to kith and kin, but took in whomsoever he was placed over as a shepherd.

And so the reading of romantic books destroyed so many souls that might have been able to have their lawful joys, and also—what is still more costly—it turned into nothing a man who was worthy of all family concern over kinship and sincerity. Such is Dickens.

ABOUT THE FOLLY OF A CERTAIN PRINCE

During the first centuries of Christianity and during certain later years before our present period of complete order only the bishops were "husbands of a single wife." The rest of the clerics, including the priests, in case they became widowers did not refrain from a second marriage, and would even commit a third one. By this means they were saved from temptation and suspicion, but at the same time they became like everybody else, without any special respect. Subsequently, however, when Christianity achieved its present state of perfection, which shall never pass away, the above-mentioned leniency in repeated marriages continued to infect only the Lutheran peoples, such as the Germans, the Swedes, and the English, whose clergy was deficient and lacking in grace. In our Eastern confession, however, which is glorious among all others in the fullness of its beneficent gifts and has all the clerical ranks, in order to fulfill it with even greater fullness, the abundant rules and regulations of later ages are encouraged still more by promotions. Thus the exalted rank of bishop is among us completely celibate, and the priests and deacons can enter the state of matrimony only once, before their consecration, and then not otherwise than with a maiden, and not with a widow. For a widow, however honorable and goodness-loving and virtuous she may be, is still unworthy of having a husband who is preparing himself to receive the blessing of priesthood from the hands of a bishop. Wherefore, even though such a rule is most necessary and useful for the propriety of the church, if the widows of priests are still young, they can in no wise marry a suitable man who is preparing for the priesthood, but if through the boredom of loneliness or the oppression of material circumstances they are led for the second time to seek a support in matrimony, they can marry within their own priestly profession only a psalm-reader or a bell-ringer, but within the civilian ranks anybody who turns up. But this happens only in such cases when the priestly widow has some property, and when she has been educated to some extent for worldly life in respect to conversation, dances, and so on, which in worldly life is not as it is among the priesthood. Otherwise, perpetual widowhood becomes for the young priest's wife her unavoidable lot, to which she must submit. But even in this kind-hearted and undefying class there will occasionally appear those who are willful, disobedient, and deficient in understanding, among whom the case of one such is presented here.

There were two priests, both of them academically learned, and such passionate lovers of card-playing that their names had actually been forgotten in town, and they were called, one of them, Father Whist, and the other, Father Preference, which they shall remain on this account.[3] It so happened that one of them, namely, Father Whist, quite unexpectedly died, and he left a sixteen-year-old daughter, most pleasant in appearance and possessed of a certain education. And Father Preference had a son at seminary in the theological class whom people preferred to call "the illogical ass."[4] He was at the bottom of the class and completed the course with great anguish and the help of his parents, for he had no memory, and he was afeared to the point of such stupidity that he himself did not know what he was afraid of, and right up till he was grown he would always ask somebody to accompany him wherever he went, or else he would not go. Through the intervention of his father this most wondrous coward was offered the place of the deceased Father Whist, with the obligation to take as his wife that most pleasant beauty, the young Whist daughter. And so this was all carried out just as the authorities upon due examination had pronounced to be suitable. The Preference son was married and ordained as a priest, and he served a whole year, but owing to the defect in his memory he could not learn the liturgy at all, and he would always be taken by the hand and led to the church by an old psalm-reader who knew the service well and would prompt him, and at home he would be managed by his wife or her mother. But they were both unhappy over their authority, and indeed, the mother often complained and wept because her daughter's husband was afraid of everything just like a stupid child, especially at night time or when he would remember dead people, whom he could not bear to get near or touch, and when he chanted their funeral service at a distance, he would keep shaking for a long time afterward. And in general through his fear he would never go to sleep otherwise than with candles burning and everybody sleeping in the same room with him—his wife and his mother and anybody else who was in the house—and he himself would always burrow under the bedclothes and press against the wall. But even though he was at all times constantly cautious and accompanied by someone, nevertheless, upon coming out onto the porch one evening for a certain purpose, he started hastening in the darkness and, having imagined something frightful, he piteously screamed and fell in terror, striking his head on the iron boot-scraper and damaging his temple. In consequence of this he lost all his remaining capacities and brains, and for two whole years he hid himself everywhere, and he would only bleat in hunger like a calf when the time came to give him his feed. And in the third year he died and was buried with honors, as befitted his ecclesiastical rank, in his robes, and with the holy Gospel, and with a cross, and his place was immediately given to another. And the young widow of this unfortunate man, who at that time was still only nineteen years old, remained free to do whatever she wished, without any kind of assistance. But she had a counsellor in her godfather, and he would not let matters remain thus, and he went to the archbishop and very boldly revealed unto him a certain secret of which he had knowledge: that the widow of the timid deceased was entitled to all the rights of a virgin and, upon marrying a second time, should provide happiness for herself and her husband, for her long patience with that deceased man demonstrated the excellence of her heart and character. For this reason he begged His Eminence to undertake action in her behalf so that the vacancy should be reserved for her as a maiden, but His Eminence answered: "Since such a case has never been anticipated previously, it is not worth while now, so that no rumors may spread among the populace." This curious incident, even though it was perhaps capable of repetition at some time or other, did not remain in complete confidentiality; instead, it crept into rumor. The widow, remaining in bitter need and in addition having her mother with her, refused to wait for marriage either to a psalm-reader or a shopkeeper or a peasant freeholder; and instead she joined a chorus of singing Gypsies who were then passing through Kursk for the festival of the wonder-working icon of the Most Holy Virgin of Kóren.[5] And the Gypsies, for the sake of the pleasant and pure voice of that woman, received her in their camp and took good care of her and her mother, but since the rumor about her was well known, the whole chorus nicknamed her "Mademoiselle Priest's-Wife," and she lived in Moscow in the Georgian Quarter, and was famous for her singing, and afterwards she married a wealthy prince, who would not have taken her as his wife for anything in the world if she had been a priest's widow instead of a free Gypsy.

Thus in their senseless scorn of the priestly race do men of the worldly professions punish themselves and lower their own race by uniting it rather with the Gypsies.

NOTES FOR "NOTES FROM AN UNKNOWN HAND"
Introduction

[1] Letter of October 20, 1883, in N. S. Leskóv, *Sobránie sochinénii,* XI (Moscow, 1958), 288.

Text

[1] *Hours of Devotion* was a translation of *Stunden der Andacht,* written by Johann Heinrich Daniel Zschokke (1771–1848). It is not without significance that when the old priest was removed from his office Leskóv's unknown chronicler shifted from the solemn ecclesiastical form of 'John'—*Ioánn*—to the ordinary form *Iván.*

[2] Leskóv's word is *bábka-galándka,* "trained midwife," from the Russian word *gollándka* "Dutch woman," which according to the lexicographer Dal very likely reflects the importation of Dutch midwives by Peter the Great.

[3] Preference—from the name of a French card game.

[4] This is the nearest the translator could come to conveying in English Leskóv's pun on *bogoslóv,* "theologian"—*bog oslóv,* "god of the asses." "Theologian" was the name given to a student in the final class in seminary. Cf. the American "senior" in college.

[5] According to Orthodox legend the Kursk Icon of the Virgin made its appearance in the thirteenth century; and every time it was carried off or destroyed, it would miraculously reappear unharmed.

NOTE TO "ABOUT THE ROOSTER
AND HIS CHILDREN"

When the official Second Warning from the censor on April 22, 1884, halted the publication of Leskóv's "Notes from an Unknown Hand" in the *Gazette of A. Gattsúk*, several completed stories in this series remained unpublished. Among them was "About the Rooster and His Children," one of the best in the whole series, which did not appear in print until the period between the first and second Russian revolutions of 1917, when there was no Russian censorship. This story is more than twice as long as any of the others Leskóv wrote for "Notes from an Unknown Hand," and it has often been republished separately, just as it is in this book.

ABOUT THE ROOSTER AND HIS CHILDREN

(A Matter of Heraldry)

Brigadier Alexander Petróvich was not big in the nature of his frame but was pot-bellied, and he always took great pains to have cooks that were good in the preparation of food, and for this purpose every three years he would hand over two young men to a club in Moscow for training in the art of cookery and in the various confectionery ways of executing various decorations. Through such domestic foresight the brigadier never lacked for cooks; on the contrary, he possessed them in abundance, and all noble gentlemen hankered after his victuals. But he, following his rule without intercession, at one time dispatched to Moscow two striplings, among whom one, being in appearance most fresh and healthy of face, could not endure the fiery heat of the cooking stove and shed blood through nosebleed, while the other, Petrúsha, although in appearance weak and peepsie, held up excellently under all the hard learning and turned out to be a cook so skillful that at the club the leading guests and even Count Gúryev himself would not allow him to leave on any account, and gave orders to purchase his freedom from the brigadier at their expense for a very large sum. But the brigadier, awaiting those same joys for himself, would not hear of any purchase by them of Peter's freedom. But without waiting to taste even once of the victuals prepared by him, the brigadier suddenly kicked the bucket. His widow, the brigadieress, Márya Mórevna, liked to keep the fasts; and, observing all the Sabbaths and new moons, she ate simply, and, remaining the guardian of her children, her son Luke Alexándrovich and her daughters Anna and Cleopatra, she had no delicate tastes, ate as before bread-and-onion soup on fast-days, and on meat-days something in the national line—rich, sugary, and buried in plenty of cream. And for that reason she even let all the former cooks go off and work on quit-rent, and she let Petrúsha remain at the club, collecting seven hundred paper rubles a year from him. Petrúsha himself received more than two thousand paper rubles, and for a long time had been called not Petrúsha but Peter Mikháilovich and had become so self-confident in his independence that he had married the niece of the chief French cook, who had fallen in love with him through her feminine lightmindedness, and being uninformed about the laws of the Russian Empire, had not perceived that through such a union with a man of the Russian condition of bondage she herself had lost her freedom, and her children would become serfs.

And the brigadieress Márya Mórevna, hearing that Petrúsha had without her knowledge married a French subject, at first wanted to deal with him harshly, but being accustomed to taking counsel upon all matters with her spiritual father, she decided otherwise, and she laid upon Peter a quit-rent twice as great as before, since Peter, according to the reasoning of her priest, having now become related to the chief French cook, could himself ask for an addition to his salary and his income column. Peter Teréntyev fulfilled this demand for many years, and it did not exhaust him, and on the contrary he acquired not a little of this world's goods, and when the Frenchwoman bore him a daughter, he brought her up like a fine lady, in short little dresses, slippers, and lace pantaloons, and he had her taught grammar and manners by a foreign *madame* in a *pension*. Thus he was confident that he would be able to buy his freedom, and he carefully hid his serf condition from his wife's relatives and friends, sent off his quit-rent punctually, and always went to the post office himself to get his passport. But inasmuch as there is nothing hidden that shall not be made manifest, there came unto him in Moscow his own sister, a comely maiden, fleeing from the chastisement of the estate manager, who allegedly kept seeking her out and for this purpose oppressed her. The voice of kinship cried out within Peter and led him to commit another rash deed—to hide that sister in his own home, although he gave strict instructions that she should reveal unto no one her misfortune, from which she had fled, and that she should not betray through this their rank as serfs. However, owing to the suspicion arising about her that there was nowhere for her to flee except to her brother in Moscow, she was discovered there and deported for punishment at the town gates by the police and for restoration to her estate. And since this took place at that season when the brigadier's daughters Anna and Cleopatra had completed their learning and come of age, therefore as a punishment for Peter he was himself required to return to the country and be punished for concealment of his sister, and afterwards to stay there and cook for the landowners.

Then Peter's whole secret, hidden so long by him from his wife, was revealed in all its appearance before all men, and it administered such a powerful defeat to the arrrogant French pride of his wife that she, forgetting the laws of marriage and all the duties of conjugality, resolved to abandon her husband and flee with her daughter to her native-born country. And there were some who reported that even Peter himself gave her assistance in that and agreed never to see them again, in order that they might be saved from bondage to the masters. But the estate manager, arriving in Moscow to convoy them, discovered all this just in time, and handed them over to the police for delivery, and thereupon Peter's wife died in a hospital while being convoyed on the road leading through a little town, and Peter and his daughter were delivered to the estate, and Peter, for his disobedience and for his sister, was punished with birch rods at the estate office, and his daughter, Pólenka, who was in her fourteenth year, and was left without any punishment at all, and was even forgiven and assigned to the young ladies, among whom the younger, Cleopatra Alexándrovna, took great pity on her and gave her a place to sleep in her room. And Peter began to cook in the kitchen and started ailing powerfully in his chest, and coughing, and shortly thereafter he died.

The brigadier's widow truly lamented the death of this master of baking and boiling, for death overtook him, as if on purpose, just at the moment when the older of the young ladies, Anna, was to become betrothed to a distinguished man, for which many guests had gathered at the house of the brigadier's widow to make merry, and for the sake of her reputation it was necessary to make a brilliant display of well-educated hospitality and show a superfluity of property and delicacy. Hereupon there also arrived the brigadier's son, Luke Alexándrovich, and brought with him two officer comrades for the dances.

One of these, who was also of a distinguished family, soon fell in love with the other young lady, Cleopatra; having learned of her handsome dowry, he conceived a strong desire to marry her. And so, following upon the first wedding, of the older sister, a second one was awaited, and for her dowry, in addition to all that she received in her allotment, she also was about to take Peter's daughter Pólenka, who at that time was sixteen years of age; but Luke Alexándrovich began strongly protesting against this, and going to his mother, he confessed that in spite of his own will he felt toward that serf-girl an unconquerable passion.

The brigadier's widow considered this to be a common occurrence in youthful years and, being reasonable in this matter, she not only did not reprove her son but she even fulfilled his wish and did not hand over the serf-girl to her daughter. And Luke Alexándrovich after the wedding of his second sister spent a whole year on leave at home in the country and gave himself over to pleasure, being often visited by his own two comrades from the regiment, who also remained in the neighborhood of that village, enjoying the air and comforts of domestic life. And Pólenka during all this time was not idle and, having received from her mother, as was evident, an inborn French coquetteration, she so captivated Luke Alexándrovich through her tenderness and endeariments that he reached a state of unexpected madness, and, allegedly finding in her all the delights of intellect and a gentle heart, he again confessed to his mother that in the course of his year of criminal correlation with that semi-French girl his passion not only had not been extinguished or put to shame, but that on the contrary he could not bear to leave her in that position, and he asked permission of his mother for an unequal marriage with her. His mother began presenting to him experienced arguments in order to hold him back from ruin, for the military authorities also would never agree to his marrying a serf-girl, but he revealed the most stubborn recalcitration and, being then in the twenty-fifth year of his life, he began to say that he was no longer a juvenile and was ready for the sake of his love even to give up his military service and to marry Pólenka quietly, without any noble society, like simple peasants, in broad daylight, after Mass. Thus he intended to make up by marriage for the sin on his conscience, and to live in the country and occupy himself with farming.

The brigadier's widow, seeing such inflexibility, and loving her son, and lamenting his imprudence, and having tried everything she could in a tone of severity, did apply to her spiritual father, according to her ancient custom, for his final counsel, and she entreated him to go straightway from Mass with communion bread to admonish the officer and warn him with the terrors of religion for his unsubmissiveness to parental will. That same priest of their church obeyed her orders and, coming unto the officer, spoke to him according to instructions, but it was in vain; and thereafter yet once and twice and thrice more did he come, but he received from him such a refusal that he durst not come back a fourth time, for it seemed to this lost sheep that he had ever before him his sin against that defenseless orphan and considered it his duty in all conscience to set it right. "But you," he said, "try to turn me away from honorable intentions and lead me into dishonor. I desire to be more obedient to God than to my neighbor."

The priest, having perceived that he was in no wise successful but was only stirring up much vain converse, did leave the quarrelsome young man, and coming unto his mother he said that, according to the stubbornness there revealed, he expected nothing from severe measures; on the contrary, being experienced in life, he feared lest he should foresee something beyond repair, such as that the unsubmissive son should communicate with the regimental officers then sojourning in the environs and somehow on some dark night whisk away the beloved maiden in a troika of swift horses to some remote village, there to enter with her into holy matrimony, so that it would end worse than it began.

With these unexpected words the judicious priest gave the brigadier's widow such a fright that she started running to and fro before him like a captive slave, and she vomited forth upon her son the curses of this world, and wished to cast her mother love out of her heart, and to take down his father's icon of the All-merciful Saviour and utter a curse upon her son; but the priest restrained her from such an abominable act of folly, and counseled her instead to follow this kind of policy. His moral teaching was that she should make a trial of something entirely different: act as if she had altered her prohibition, and make a show of agreeing to that unequal marriage (but only in order to forestall it) by writing out a certificate of freedom for the girl and enrolling her in the first guild of merchant women, so that he could then marry her as a girl from the merchant class.

Meanwhile, since the brigadier's widow could not take this in quickly, she became still more angry even at the priest himself, and the priest said unto her:

"Tarry a little, I pray you, with your wrath against me, nay, more than that, try to understand, for you have already seen very well that your wrath will do nothing to bring relief; listen rather to my further proposition and consider, for what I have said is not proposed without purpose. Send your son into town to look personally after getting her freedom and status in the merchants' class; he will gladly agree to all that, and in his joy he will hasten thither, and at that same instant when he absents himself beyond the bounds of our village, in accordance with your orders we will marry off that girl without delay to any serf ignoramus you may indicate, and this will put a natural end to all these anxieties." He asked only one condition of her, and that was that the brigadieress should provide him with every kind of protection against her son's vengeance.

The brigadieress, having understood his plan, exulted and accepted it, and said unto him:

"If only you will pull off this deal for me in the way that you have so wisely elaborated, I will conceal you afterwards. I will place you in the cellar under my room, and I will hide the key to my room until he leaves; I myself will bring food to you, and afterwards I will make you a gift of a horse to fill your vacancy in time for the next plowing."

The priest went home rejoicing, and unable to conceal his feelings, he said to his priestess:

"Well, Mother, rejoice! I'll sigh no more for the old gray mare that kicked the bucket, and even before that used to balk at the plow. Before the next plowing you and I will have a good horse from the Mistress's stables. Then you can go whenever you want to visit our boys at the seminary and see who Míshka is running around with and why Grísha doesn't like the vittles."

And the priestess got into a stew and started asking:

"What sort of favor did you do for the Mistress, and what are you getting a horse for?"

The priest made answer:

"Don't keep pestering me, and just save your breath—I'm not going to tell you. This thing is a great secret, and it's just between me and her."

But the priestess was more cunning than the priest, and instead of trying to worm it out of him directly, she started fawning over him:

"Come on and lie down, you're tired, lie down here on the floor on this nice little drugget, and get a good rest, and I'll sit down at your head and hunt lice in your hair."

The priest had a weakness for lice-hunting in his hair, and he lay down on the floor under the spell of her tales, and she sat down and put his head on her lap and started tenderly, gently picking at his hair with a spinning-comb, and she lovingly and softly stroked him under the chin with her wedding ring, and when these movements had made a feeling of drowsiness sweep over him, she said:

"Will you still not tell me now why they are giving us a horse?"

The priest answered:

"That's right—I really won't."

And she waited a little, scratched around a little more in his hair, stroked him some more with her ring under his chin, and said:

"Now will you still not tell me?"

And after pestering him like this over and over, she got him to the point where he said:

"Oh, please leave me alone and let me sleep," and he told her the whole story.

And she, having let him go to sleep, covered his face with her kerchief, and turned it up over his nose like a little tent, and she herself went out, locked the door behind her, and taking the key along, went to see the brigadieress, and being cleverer than her husband, she talked the briga-dieress into giving her the horse at once, saying, "My priest will do it all for you, but I need to go to visit my boys and see why they are not sat-isfied with their vittles." And she took the horse by the bridle and led it from the stable to the lot behind their house and put it on the chopped straw.

The priest, when he arose and caught sight of the horse, was aston-ished and said:

"Why did you stick your nose into other people's business and pester people at the wrong time?"

And she answered:

"Shut up, priest, don't grumble—when you take it, then it's sacred.

You may have got taught in the seminary and trimmed with willow switches, but you're still not very bright."

"How come?"

"Why, don't you see that the brigadieress is getting old and she'll soon be leaving this world, but her son is just getting into the prime of life? Just look at you—if you go and do something that don't suit him, you can't hide the rest of your life in the cellar, and just as soon as you climb out, you will catch it and so will all the rest of us. Don't you know that you have to wait for daybreak by facing the rising sun, and not the setting sun?"

The priest, having listened to her riddles, began to shiver with fear, and he asked her:

"I see where I slipped up," he says, "but what can I do about it?"

And she answered:

"You won't do anything; *I* am going to do it."

The priest became even more frightened.

"You haven't gone and thought up something, have you?"

And she answered:

"That's none of your business; you go ahead and do what you promised, and I will do what has to be done that's useful."

The priest strove seriously to find out what his wife had in mind, but he could figure out no way to do it and he found out nothing.

"Now look," he said, "I haven't got any of your Eve-ish tricks to find out things from you the way you wormed everything out of me, by tickling me under the chin; but still, do me the favor to remember that Eve's folly led Adam to fall."

But the priestess would listen to nothing, and she said that if the priest would let her know in advance when the son was to leave for town and when Pólenka was to be married off to the peasant, then she would not get mixed up in it, but if he kept it from her, then her curiosity would start plaguing her, and then she could not guarantee just what kind of harm she might cause through her impatience.

The priest gave in.

"All right, then," he said, "I'd better tell you the whole thing, but this is only for you—don't go telling anybody else around here. Luke Alexándrovich is out of his mind with joy: he has made up with his mother and sent for his fellow officers. They are all going into town together tomorrow, and as soon as they leave, Pólenka's ambition will be cut short. Before he even gets to town, we'll have her hitched up to the Rooster."

The Rooster was an unmarried peasant in the Mistress's poultry yard—unclean and half-witted, well over forty years old, who had a red nose and talked in a loud, high-pitched chatter like a rooster.

Hearing this, the priestess threw up her hands and said:

"Oh, you devil, a plague on both you and the brigadieress! You old scoundrels and sinners, what a foul deed you have hatched up! No, I can't stand to see it, and I won't stay here for anything. Since I've got my own horse now that I begged out of the Mistress, let the hired man hitch up the sleigh for me early tomorrow morning, at dawn; I'll take a basket of eggs and a little tub of cottage cheese and I'll go by myself to town to the seminary and see how well their landlady is feeding them, and I won't be back till three days from now."

The priest was very glad.

"Go ahead, Mother," he said, "only, don't do me no harm. Go and visit Grísha and Míshka and give them my fatherly blessing, and tell them not to run around indistinctly with just anybody, but to remember that they are the sons of a priest, and not of a sexton."

The mother took the keys from the priest, ran down to the bell tower for a basket, put the basket and the cottage cheese into the sleigh, and started off. And as soon as she got beyond the village, she started stinging the horse's flanks with a switch. She flew along to the first post station and stopped.

"I've got to wait for some fellow travelers from another village," she said, "so that we can hitch up our horses together."

And after she had waited for a time, a sleigh with a bright-colored sleigh-robe dashed up, and in it sat Luke Alexándrovich and his two companions. She took Luke aside and said:

"Don't drive any further and don't lose a minute, but hurry back as fast as you can." She went on and told him how it was. "So that's the secret they've cooked up against you," she said, "they're doing it all right now, while you were driving here and while you are waiting."

Luke Alexándrovich clutched his temples and wailed:

"Woe is me! O cruel fate! If that's true, then it's too late—they've already had time to marry her off!"

But the priestess quieted his grief.

"Everything I have revealed to you," she said, "is the truth, but it's still not too late."

"Why not?" cried Luke. "It took us more than an hour to get here, and now we have to go back: how much more time than that do they need to put the wedding crown on her head?" [1]

But the priestess grinned.

"Don't lose your nerve!" she said. "They won't put it on her! Quick, now, get into your sleigh and fly back, and go right up and knock on the church door, and put this basket of mine beside your feet and on your way back, take a look inside. It'll do you good."

They galloped off. They whipped and beat the horses as if they were trying to wear them out in one stretch between post stations, and meanwhile they looked into the basket; and there, covered with chaff, in the place of eggs they found the wedding crowns.

The officers saw that their affair had been well managed; since the crowns were here and there were no others in the church, there was no way to perform the crowning event in the wedding ceremony.

They dashed up to the church, jumped out of the sleigh, taking the basket with them, ran straight to the doors and gave them a push. But they discovered that they had not been forgotten but were stoutly locked and barred from the inside, and beyond the door they could hear a commotion and people scurrying about, and the faint sound of weeping and groaning, and the shouts of the priest.

Hearing all this, Luke Alexándrovich and his two companions burst out in anger, and pounding violently on the door they shouted:

"Open up at once! For we know that a forced marriage is taking place in the church, and we will not allow it. We are going to break the door down right now!"

And when no answer came from within the church, they and their orderly started beating on the door, and they broke it open and dashed into the church—taking the priestess's basket with them.

The reason for the commotion in the church had been that nobody could find the wedding crowns, which the priestess had stolen away on purpose, and in their argument over it they were all shouting. The priest was raking the sextons over the coals, saying they had probably carried them off and pawned them, and the sextons were talking back to him and saying: "We never took the crowns out of the chest." But the deacon was not berating anybody, but was silently writing the official statement in the church record about the groom and his bride: "United in their first marriage: the serfs Pelagéya Petróva and Afonásy Rooster, registered by their masters according to the last census," and as wedding witnesses in place of their relatives two men stood there in their illiteracy and held Pólenka by the elbows, and the Rooster had been stood upright in his everyday repulsiveness but with his hair smoothed down with oil, as though he himself were unhappy but not responsible.

And then Luke Alexándrovich and his fellow comrades started pounding at the door—all of them warriors of courageous temper, including a Circassian bombardier, a man of enormous strength, in such a state of excitement as might have come from getting drunk on the elixir of life, like improper madcaps who were estranged from all reasoning about rightness.

Then they all started bustling about wherever they were standing, especially when they heard Luke Alexándrovich's voice, and forgetting all about the wedding crowns they rushed to finish what had to be done the fastest: they signed the official statement and took their stand at the lectern; they called upon the name of God and started chanting without themselves knowing how it would end since the wedding crowns had disappeared, and the deacon in his discontent kept thinking suspiciously that it was not fitting for the priest alone to get a horse from the brigadieress, and that it would not have been out of place to bring along at least an untrained yearling for his Deaconly Holiness, and with these thoughts in his head he walked past the doors carrying the book with the official statement written in it, and as he went by he gave the lower latch a kick and knocked it loose. Then the doors gave way and burst open, and all the besiegers came in, displaying a passionate look and an independent manner. The two officers who had the wedding crowns in their hands started pushing and grabbing everybody, and Luke Alexándrovich seized the Rooster by the scruff of the neck as he stood there waiting to be married and pitched him off to one side and took his place; and at a word from them the bombardier, the man of enormous strength, started squeezing the priest with his fingers just under the gills, so that such a pain ran through him that the priest let out a howl in an uncanny voice, and the officers, having also aroused the sextons by the hair of their heads, shouted: "Chant and read!" and in terror they started intoning so nasally that they themselves could not make out what they were doing. But the deacon, having escaped all this claptrap, and considering the fact that he had already written up the official statement of Pelagéya's marriage to the Rooster, and that these disorderly intruders, being of the military vocation, stood revealed as unfathomable ignoramuses in the spirit of laws and sought only to satisfy their shameless desires, being meanwhile all of the boldest character and including among them the bombardier, a man of enormous strength, so did he arrive at the following conclusion: "Oh, what does that matter to us? In the world man must live so as to please everybody—then all is well." And having put on his tunic, he proclaimed, "Thous hast placed the crowns upon their heads," and everybody, reassured, nimbly followed after him like sheep after a billy goat, and they finished.

And as soon as the crowns were taken off, the officers wrapped up Pelagéya in an extra fur coat and drove back to the city in those same sleighs, and soon on the open road they overtook the Mother Priestess, and they did not even thank her or recognize her, but, accidentally catching the side of her sleigh under the frame, they turned it to one side and upset it in the snow, and her along with it, and the cottage cheese that she was taking to her discontented seminary students was trampled and made one with the snow.

But the Mother Priestess, having a sagacious and healthy mind, did not become angry even over this, but only called after them with a grin:

"Never mind, in time you shall pay me back for all that all at once."

And those madcaps, having galloped through the town, took unto themselves fresh horses and galloped off again, and so they sped away, whither no one knew. And the priestess, having ascertained for herself wherein lay the cause of her seminary students' dissatisfaction with the vittles, returned homeward and found there a state of general prevarication: everybody was telling lies about everybody else, each one was more guilty than the next, and they all concealed everything from the brigadieress, for they did fear the terror of her wrath, and they said unto her: "The wedding has been celebrated," but they did not reveal the unexpectedness of the details.

The brigadieress bestowed gifts upon all the clergy in the parish: a five-spot to the deacon and a ruble apiece to the sextons, and since she was filled with wrath against Pelagéya, she did not oblige her to appear in person but only inquired the next morning how she was now getting along with her husband, after her previous treatment. But the chambermaids likewise durst not tell her the truth, and they made answer that Pelagéya greatly wept.

The brigadieress was very well satisfied with this and said:

"Now she must indeed ever weep for her immodesty, for the blood of Ham cannot reach unto the blood of Japheth." [2]

And nobody knew how and when to put an end to all this enormous lying, because all who were in the right as well as the wrong were fearful of evil and mischief in time of wrath. But the deacon, being in no small measure the cause of all this, but by nature a more cunning machinator than the priest and priestess, undertook to help and said:

"If you will go to the Mistress's cellar and get me some Falerno wine and a crock of big sweet apples soaked in bran mash, I'll take and help you."

Then ran the priestess to the housekeeper and the steward and, getting from them the wine and the sweet apples soaked in bran mash, she gave them to the deacon, for she knew that he was a most artful thinker-up of tales and was often summoned to the house for the winding and repair of the big English clock, which ran uncertainly. He knew how to moderate its pace by lightening the weights or by lengthening the pendulum, or by cleaning away the dust and oiling the wheels. And so he fared forth to the house; and while he was stretching the cables of the weights around the drum of the clock spring, he put a termination to the whole matter by suddenly and resolutely concocting the story that the Rooster's wife Pelagéya had run out of their cold attic bedroom on their wedding night and fled from him into the forest, barefooted and heavy with child, and there she had encountered a bear, who had eaten her up, together with her womb and the fruit thereof.

The brigadieress was filled with horror and asked:

"Can that be true?"

And the deacon made answer:

"I am a servant of the Lord and cannot take an oath; rather must my words be believed without question, and here is the holy cross for you, to show that I am telling the truth." And he crossed himself.

"Then why did they tell me nothing at all about this?"

And the deacon answered:

"That's because they were filled with fear of Your Grace."

"By why?" she said. "They had no need to lie about it to me. I'll order them punished."

But the deacon began explaining to her:

"Oh, good mother! Hasten not to inflame thyself in thy wrath, for there are lies and lies: there is the barefaced lie that leadeth into deception, and there is the lie that leadeth unto salvation. Verily, we are all guilty of that, and so hath it ever been."

Then began he to tell her stories from the Holy Scriptures about how it came to pass that the courtiers did lie to the kings in the land of the Pharaohs, and all did lie to the Pharaoh about every matter, that they might turn his eyes away from the suffering of the people. And there was fierceness, and each did contend with the other, even those who were reputed to be honorable and pious, and even he who was second in rank after the king did not lift up his voice to speak truth, and none but Potiphar's prisoner, thrown into the dungeon through slander and ignorant of the customs of the court, spake the truth to Pharaoh and declared that there should be famine. And then the deacon passed over to her business and said:

"Thou, noble lady, dost thyself rule over the living souls in thy domain, which is a reflection of the higher law, and thou hast full sway over all the fortunes and lives of thy faithful servants, and for that reason all of them, fearing thee, do not tell thee much truth; but I, paltry sinner that I am and unworthy of notice, who do take apart and oil thy clock— last night I did think so much upon the fleeting hours of our life, which pass by and vanish so quickly, that I have made bold to speak forth the truth. And for this let not thy wrath arise either against me or against others, but rather, having spread over us the cover of thy customary benevolence, consider quietly and generously how harmful the effects of all that can be, for from us who have been oppressed by thee there may go forth a denunciation unto the authorities in the provincial government that this wedding was performed upon Pelagéya by force at thy command, and then all of us, humble and obedient as we are, will suffer on account of thee, and as for thee thyself—reflect upon it—how wouldst thou answer to God for the whole clerical staff of this church?"

The brigadieress began to tremble with terror, but the deacon kept piling it on, saying unto her:

"And even in this life a certain sword shall pass through thy soul, and thou shalt be set free from no small part of thy goods in favor of the scribes and judges, and it may come to pass that they will diminish the fullness of thy power over thy slaves. For the sake of all this be compassionate and condemn not others, lest evil should befall thee also, but rather think upon this, while I go out into the open air and check thy clock against the marks of the sun."

And the brigadieress, having thought upon it, did indeed perceive that the deacon had spoken to her with good and kindly reasoning, and when he came back in from the sunshine she gave him a silver ruble instead of an answer, so that the whole parish clergy should celebrate a mass for Pelagéya's eternal rest, and then a requiem for the same money, and she herself promised to come to the requiem bringing a funeral cake. But the deacon, seeing that her wrath was assuaged, put away the ruble and spoke unto her in this wise:

"No, there shall be no requiem singing and sobbing, for I will now tell you the whole real truth, which is much happier and merrier, for Pelagéya is alive and married, but through such a cunning arrangement that it cannot soon be understood."

And thereupon he revealed the above-described misfortune to the brigadieress, but again with certain omissions. He told her that her disobedient son Luke had stood under the marriage crown with Pelagéya while a Circassian had held the Rooster to one side by his elbows; but when the brigadieress started to faint from horror, he soothed her in good time by telling her that the whole wedding was of no profit to her son, for it was inscribed in the church book as required—Pelagéya and the Rooster. The brigadieress heaved a sigh and crossed herself, but the deacon told her not that in the midst of all the great tumult no mortal knew what got chanted instead of the wedding ceremony. He just brought her from the church that book wherein was written "Pelagéya and the Rooster," and said: "There it is in black and white: once the pen writes down the facts, they can't be cut out with an ax. Even though your son is a bold daredevil, still he is green and knoweth not the law. No matter where he took her off to, let him disport himself in his error, and it will never enter his head that she is not his wife."

The brigadieress became downright merry, and she even felt sorry that she had not taken counsel with him instead of the priest in the first place, and so that he should feel no offense toward the priest she told him to go down to the stable to pick out any steed his eye might fancy.

But the deacon showed that he was cleverer and was not led astray by flattery, and he did not rush off in haste to pick out a horse, that there might be no envy in his superior.

"I wish something more modest for myself from your barnyard," he said, "just a fresh milch cow and her calf, and let us arrange in secret, just between the two of us, for me to get twenty rubles from you at Assumption and Christmas for my son in the seminary, so that he can live better and won't complain like all the others about the feed. And I will collect this and keep your secret in the greatest confidentialism."

Hearing this, the brigadieress answered:

"Well, I must say you're no enemy to yourself, and your cunning is enough to make a body feel nervous."

But the deacon replied:

"Nobody is his own enemy, but you have nothing to fear from my cunning. I have prepared myself for you like unto a good steed against the day of battle, and I myself will receive help from the Lord through you."

And she fulfilled his wishes, but through all the remaining days of her life she had great fear of him. And in regard to the wedded couple, Luke and Pelagéya, more is set forth below.

A SIMPLE REMEDY

Just as the intercourse of small streams joined together produces rivers which flow onward until at last they become a great sea, the shores of which lie beyond the reach of the eye, thus it is with tricks of human cunning: when they increase, there is formed something beyond all explanation. Thus was it also with this marriage.

While the brigadieress shielded her son with cunning tricks, that daredevil and his assumed wife, about whom no man can say to whom she was awarded, arrived in the capital, and disclosed unto his sister the secret sacrament that had taken place, and received abundant sympathy from her for Pólenka, so that the baby born soon thereafter was taken from the baptismal font by their noble acquaintances and registered as the lawful son of Luke Alexándrovich and Pólenka, and an extract to this effect was handed over to them.° Afterwards there were born unto them other children as well, and they likewise were registered, and then in the third year after that the brigadieress departed this world for the next, and Luke and his sisters inherited the whole estate, and Luke Alexándrovich and Pólenka moved to the estate and built new houses for the clergy and lived blessfully until the season came to send their son off to military school and their daughter to the Imperial Institute for Girls. Now there arose a need for their birth certificates, and the archdiocese office could not give them out, because the marriage was registered according to the books not in the name of the landowner Luke Alexándrovich but of Rooster the serf. Thereupon, in boundless grief over such an unforeseen inexpectation after those many years, Luke Alexándrovich set out to plead his case in the capital, and he visited important persons and explained his event to them all, but among all those notables not a single one turned up who would help him, for what was written in the church register about the .marriage of Pólenka to Rooster the serf was done beyond question according to the rules of law. And he, after much expense and trouble, returned to his town and began to consider what he should do, for if he gave the Rooster his freedom, somebody might put the Rooster up to demanding his wife and children, but otherwise it was impossible to transfer serf children to the noble class. And again he was in confusion, because in his grief nobody had offered him any counsel.

But when one hope disappears completely, often another starts rising. Toward evening, when Luke was sitting alone in sorrowful despair, there came unto him from the archdiocese office a certain clerk, repulsive and niggardly in appearance and stinking of vodka, who said:

"Listen, good sir, I know thy sorrow and strivings, and I see that of all those whom thou hast asked none is able to help thee—but I can help."

Luke Alexándrovich said:

"My affair is such that no help is possible."

But the clerk answered:

"Not at all, good sir. Why should you despair? Despair is a mortal sin, and in Holy Russia there is no impossibility."

But Luke Alexándrovich, since he had already asked much counsel of genuine persons and received nothing useful from them, did not wish now to listen to that repulser, and he said to him:

"Go your way! Where can you help me when men of high rank have found no means?"

But the clerk made answer:

"No, good sir, do not neglect my counsel; great doctors do not know simple remedies, but simple people do, and I know a simple remedy to help thy grief."

Luke gave a laugh, but thought: "I'll try it and see what it is." And he asked:

"How much does your remedy cost?"

"Only two gold rubles."

Luke Alexándrovich thought to himself:

*This incredible incident is actually quite possible. At least, this is the thought that is prompted by Paragraph 42 of the *Instructions to the Priestly Administrator* in the edition of 1857, where mention is made of the need for "caution in giving evidence referring to persons as husband and wife who were not married here," and "who present no documents in proof of their marital status." Obviously this caution was called forth by something. *(Leskóv's note.)*

"I have already spent a lot, and this is no great amount." And he gave him the two gold rubles.

And on the next day that clerk came to him and said:

"Well, good sir, I have fixed up everything. Now hand in your request—and not to have them read the written certificate but to have them get the original church book."

Luke Alexándrovich said:

"You don't mean to say you forged my name there, you reckless devil! What is that you did? And I will fall under suspicion because of you!"

But the clerk made answer:

"Oh, good sir, good sir! How could that get into thy head! Brains are found not alone in big heads but also in little ones. Ask not what I have done, but ask for the book and thou shalt be right."

Luke Alexándrovich thought to himself that he had already tried a lot of remedies—why not try one more? And he requested that they get the original record book out of the archives and see how it was written. And when it was brought, it was discovered that the name "Rooster the peasant" was written there—but in a different ink in a spot that had been erased. And who had written this and when, and what had been in this spot before, was unknown.

Then an investigation was made, and everybody who was still alive was asked who had been married to Pelagéya, and everybody said Luke Alexándrovich, and the Rooster had stood to one side, and the marriage was confirmed, and the children hitherto presumed to be the Rooster's received the noble privileges of their birth. And the clerk had committed no falsification at all but had only written in the book the same thing he had erased. That was his "simple remedy."

NOTES FOR "ABOUT THE ROOSTER AND HIS CHILDREN"

[1] The culmination of the Orthodox wedding ceremony consists in the placing of wedding crowns on the bride and groom.

[2] A reference to the Biblical story (Genesis 9:18–27) about the curse of servitude that Noah laid on his son Ham, which is reflected in the tradition that the serfs were descendants of Ham. Hence the Russian *kham* and Polish *cham* "lout."

NOTE TO "FISH SOUP WITHOUT FISH"

"Fish Soup Without Fish" is linked thematically with "Choice Grain," which was very likely the work Leskóv had specifically in mind at the beginning of "Fish Soup Without Fish" when he referred to his newly published book of Christmas stories. Both works are examples of Leskóv's ironical variant on the traditional happy ending: in a society peopled exclusively by rogues the ultimate result of all their collective rascality is harm for none and prosperity for everybody. To the reader brought up on English literature, this sly commentary on the beneficent vices of society may recall Mandeville's *Fable of the Bees*.

Through its treatment of the Jewish question "Fish Soup Without Fish" is also linked up with "Deception." In both stories Leskóv attacks the ancient Russian plague of anti-Semitism in his own Leskovian manner. In "Deception," as we have already seen, he accomplished this first by shifting the focus of the Russians' prejudice from the Jews to the Rumanians and then by gently scoffing at the Russians themselves. In "Fish Soup Without Fish" the rascality of the Christians is repaid by their leading Jewish neighbor with a maneuver that brilliantly combines philanthropy and economic self-defense with poetic justice.

"Fish Soup Without Fish" was published at the beginning of 1886. Before the end of that same year Leskóv returned to his defense of the Jews with "The Tale of Theodore the Christian and his Friend Abraham the Jew," a simple, parable-like story resembling the manner of Leo Tolstóy's folk tales. The import of this story was very similar to the import of "Fish Soup Without Fish," but the tone of the two works is as different as the tone of Chaucer is from that of John Bunyan.

For all its excellence, Leskóv himself somehow failed to include "Fish Soup Without Fish" in the twelve-volume edition of his fiction that appeared during his own lifetime. It has evidently been reprinted in Russian only three times since it first appeared in *Virgin Soil (Nov)* in 1886. Its first publication in translation was in 1963, when Johannes von Guenther included it at the suggestion of the present writer in his three-volume collection of Leskóv's major works in German. The English version in the present book marks the second time this story has appeared in print in any language since 1902.

FISH SOUP
WITHOUT FISH

The New Year of 1886 began for me in pleasant company and with rather pleasant comments about my little collection of Christmas stories, which had just been published. The book had been praised in the newspapers, and it was favorably discussed in that hospitable home to which I had been invited for a glass of champagne at New Year's. People with an understanding of literature declared that I had been successful in my effort to observe the demands of the Christmas story without dragging in the demons and all the other mysterious and improbable elements that are commonplaces in such tales. But here, as everywhere and always, it turned out that not everyone held the same opinion. Somebody remarked that I had gone too far, and that my stories, for all the approval they had won, actually contained no really virtuous characters. Good, conciliatory impressions could be found in them, but somehow they lacked will and purpose.

"Everything is tastily cooked and flavored, but when you start examining what it's all made of, it turns out to be some sort of fish soup without fish."

There was a general outburst of laughter, and many persons thought the remark was clever. A few others said it was hard to distinguish between good and evil in my stories, and even that it was sometimes impossible to tell whose actions were harmful and whose were beneficial.

They attributed this to some sort of inborn craftiness in my nature.

I merely listened and learned, of course, and answered not a word. An out-of-town guest, however, who happened to be present took my part and remarked that "fish soup without fish" was by no means so absurd as it appeared. Figuratively speaking, he said, this kind of fish soup is cooked in real life, and often it is rich and appetizing, even though you can't discover what it is made of or how it was prepared.

"There's no lack of good people in this world," somebody remarked in a conciliatory tone.

"No, that's not it at all. Quite the contrary: 'fish soup without fish' to my way of thinking is like a play without any actors in the leading role. It has no particular men of good action, and yet good actions take place. And I tell you, in this our author is right."

I gratefully made a bow.

"Now for example," the guest went on in my defense, "I happen to know of just the kind of incident that would make real fish soup without fish if I told it."

"What is it?"

"A simple affair of the Christmas type, with good deeds ignored completely by the one who performed them."

"How was that—through a misunderstanding?"

"No."

"A miracle?"

"No."

"By accident?"

"On the contrary."

"Then what?"

"Why, through just the kind of 'fish soup without fish' that is cooked up by life."

"Well, tell us about it!"

"All right, if you wish."

The town near which I live on my little estate is very small and, to tell the truth, a miserable place. It is not outstanding in any way, but it has one peculiarity: year after year the largest part of its babies are regularly born right at Christmas. This fact is widely known and has been confirmed over many years by the parish birth register. You may be a little surprised at this, but there is really nothing at all about it that ought to be surprising, and still less that cannot be explained or is—heaven forbid!—supernatural. It doesn't depend in the slightest on spirits, or the climate, or the nature of the water and soil, or on the peculiar nature of our women, but rather on the economic conditions of our life. I must explain this to you so that there won't be anything hidden and secret between us.

Even if everything is clear and plain to everyone, mystery will still creep in somewhere, as you will see.

That's what Christmas is for!

o   o   o

The region around our town is extremely well suited to truck farming; wherever you look, you see nothing but fields of vegetables and melons. But our local inhabitants are well known for their laziness, and do what you will with them, they just won't take to working in the fields. A few did try, but they turned out to be incapable of growing anything worth while. In a word, they are both lazy and lacking in skill, and for that reason our large-scale truck farming is entirely in the hands of migratory farmers from Rostóv. These invading Varangian Russians[1] lease all the best flood-lands around our town and do their best to wear them out as rapidly as possible. But if they succeed in this it will be only in the future; so far the land is still holding its own and brings forth every seed a hundredfold.

The Varangian Russians themselves do not live a settled life here. They usually arrive when the rooks fly up from the south, in March or April, and as soon as they have made themselves comfortable in their roomy straw-covered barracks in the fields, they set to work. Their work begins with the hiring of a great many girls and old women. The Rostovians have a lot of women's work to get done: there is food to be cooked, clothes to be washed, fields to be hoed, plants to be set out, weeds to be pulled, seedlings to be watered, water to be carried—all of it women's work. In autumn these Northerners gather the fruits of other men's fields, turn them into money, and leave once more for Rostóv until the following year; and their summer supply of woman-power stays at home and doesn't finish reckoning up the summery caresses of the Varangians until about Christmas time.

If you will make a calculation, keeping in mind that the Rostóv Varangians reach our neighborhood in March or April, you will clearly see why our local statistics show the largest number of births in December, just at Christmas.

It's the most natural thing in the world, and there is nothing remarkable about it whatsoever.

Now I will go on.

o   o   o

In our town we have all the leaders and authorities that are ordained of God so that every town may live piously and honestly, according to the best principles and customs of divine and civil law. We have an energetic district governor, a justice-loving judge, a philanthropic physician, a learned archpriest (and besides him an ordinary priest as well), and then we have citizens, singers, warriors, guardsmen, and common people—in a word, everything that is mentioned in the most complicated advertisements. Our town's inhabitants, or common people, are all simple souls, but officially they are divided into "two communities": one is the "Christian community of the municipality" and the other is the "Jewish community of the municipality." The degree of scholarly education in both of these communities is almost equal, but on the Jewish side there is more literacy, of course. The religious smugness of both is just about equal: the Jews make everybody else aware that Jehovah took them unto Himself through special favor, having elected them above all other peoples of the universe; and the Christians answer them: "Understand and submit, since God is on our side."

Which of these two communities is the lazier, I couldn't say.

The Christians work half a year at one thing or another and then lie around the other half. The Jews never perform any genuine, sweat-of-their-brow work, but on the other hand they never stop running about and twitching and jabbering their gibberish. It goes without saying that all our traders are Jews. Whatever you fail to buy on Friday by the beginning of the Sabbath, you'll have no chance to get until Sunday. In this way the Jews get all the money that the lazy, sorry Christian population manages somehow to earn.

Among the Christians in our town there is positively not a single capitalist, while among the Jews there are several rather well-to-do persons, and among them one old man by the name of Solomon is actually considered wealthy. He alone among all the private individuals in the town lives in a stone building of his own, on the market square, and in this building the district chief has his headquarters and the district nobility hold their annual meetings.

Rabbi Solomon is a person of consequence; he knows everybody, and lives a respectable Old Testament life, but he shows charitable condescension toward the Christians, and with a view to demonstrating his tolerance he even used to play cards with the district governor and the archpriest, as a result of which his tone of voice became significantly more refined and his manners more decorous. For example, when he held out the pack of cards for the Reverend Archpriest to pick one, Solomon would always say with an air of respect:

"Your blessings upon them!"

Some people were of the opinion that Solomon's tolerance and impartiality went no further than this, but they were wrong: both his tolerance and his impartiality went much further.

o o o

Rabbi Solomon was intelligent and well read in Jewish literature, but above all he was devilishly well experienced in life. His fame even reached as far as Chernóbyl itself, and among his own people he had a reputation for extraordinary wisdom. Even today he probably still has the letter that the rabbi of Chernóbyl wrote to him about some question or other in his own hand, and for that reason, perhaps, many people look on him as a pillar of Judaism. And indeed he really was firm in the faith of his fathers; he observed all the rites and fulfilled all the obligations, and neither in his long Judaic cloak nor in his prayer shawl nor in his hisses and shushes was there anything lacking in all that God Himself had established. Solomon's character was strong, firm, and persistent. By temperament he was sensitive and passionate, but he was a master of self-control and he would quickly recover from the slightest disturbance of the equilibrium in his inner world. Solomon was proud but not proud through vanity; he was filled with self-respect because no one had ever duped him, whereas he himself had duped a great many people. Everybody knew that, and no one dared even attempt to use this to damage his reputation. All this gave Solomon an air of composure and majesty.

But suddenly something unusual happened to our sage. Solomon made a misstep . . .

And how did this come about?

How? Nobody could give an answer. But many people took note of the incident that led up to it.

o   o   o

Not long before Christmas, Rabbi Solomon, as a respected personage in our town, was in the best of company at the home of the district governor. He was playing cards there with very distinguished persons and even held five rubles in winnings. But the next morning he went home to his family looking down in the mouth over something, and from that time on his spirits were low. He took on an air of gloomy, pensive dejection. One eye somehow sank back in the hollow of his head. His brow was darkened with wrinkles. He wrapped himself up in scowling silence, or else wagged his skull-cap in even more scowling impatience and sent everybody to the devil. Often he would even give absentminded answers to questions, and finally right out in public he committed a deed so contradictory to his vocation as a Jew that it was bound to destroy at one blow his reputation as a pious Talmudist.

We shall see in a moment just what he did and how this plunged two communities into confusion—the "Christian" and the "Jewish." And then we shall see how all this was corrected *ad majorem Dei gloriam*, with benefit both to the Jews and the Christians.

o   o   o

Among the girls from the town who spent their summers weeding the fields of the migratory Varangians from Rostóv was one young wench by the name of Paláshka. Paláshka, of course, knew Rabbi Solomon, "that-there rich Jew," but Rabbi Solomon did not know Paláshka, because she was not worthy of his attention.

Paláshka was a girl without kith or kin, for she too had been planted by the Varangians in the fields. Now that Paláshka had grown to maturity,

God had given her, too, a lively baby at the Christmas season; but poor Paláshka had not the means to pay for a christening. Our christenings don't cost very much, the rate is only one ruble apiece, but this poor girl could not find a single volunteer to stand godfather to her child and pay the ruble for the baptism.

"There are too many of you!" good people would tell her. "God knows how and where you may commit all your sins, but 't ain't no business of ourn to pay out good rubles for other people's sins."

And that was right, but meanwhile the poor thing suffered terribly over it just the same.

o   o   o

Such fateful circumstances were not at all rare in our town, and a way had been devised to cope with them, and it worked rather well.

As soon as one of our girls became a mother and nature helped the poor creature to overcome her infirmity, she would wrap the baby in a few rags, go down and stand on the bridge, and beg the passers-by:

"Good people, help this-here baby get baptized in the Christian faith."

Whoever was full of lovingkindness would not refuse. If a hundred compassionate souls came by and each one gave a kopeck, there were a hundred kopecks for you. That made a ruble, and the baby was "baptized in the Christian faith" at once.

And inasmuch as the world is not without good people after all, some girls were lucky enough to stand on the bridge with their unbaptized babies only three or four days, and by the fifth they had already collected enough to buy a little cross and pay the baptizer.

But a special misfortune fell to the lot of poor Paláshka; she had to stand on the bridge not by herself but along with three other girls, who had happened to enter the equation at the same time and under the same denominator. The poor girls were all begging together for the same purpose, and the other three were more experienced than Paláshka: they all stood so that Paláshka would be last in line. A passer-by might give alms to the first one, sometimes to the second one, and occasionally even to the third; but when he got to the fourth he would just say: "God will take care of you." Three good deeds are enough for the salvation of anybody's soul; no one is expected to go further than that. Consequently, there is no reason to throw your money away for nothing.

o   o   o

And so Paláshka's three companions each collected their hundred alms and joyfully carried their babies off to be baptized in the Christian faith, but poor Paláshka was left standing there in the cold for eight days, weeping bitterly. And indeed she had good reason to weep, because she had nowhere to go and earn any money, and she was overcome by weakness and hunger and cold. But what was more terrible than anything else was her worry about the soul of her new-born child, because the last day before Christmas had already begun, and every baby born before Christmas day must by all means be baptized before Christmas. Otherwise, it will be an unlucky baby, deprived of its enviable lot in heaven. The matter concerns not only this short earthly life, which for every man with the proper views is of little significance and offers nothing permanent. Rather is it a question of all eternity—where will they find a place up there for a new-born soul?

This depends on taking the proper measures down here, which have the very greatest influence on all the future destiny of each human soul after it has left its body.

How can a mother be expected to bear this calmly when the baby she holds in her arms is still unbaptized?

° ° °

And so poor Paláshka wept and wept. She shook all over as she wiped away her tears with the same old rags that someone had thrown to her to wrap up her unbaptized baby. And her eyes grew so dim with her tears and woe that she seemed no longer even to see, or to make out which people she turned to for alms. Whoever came by, Christian or Jew, she would beg him to help her baptize her child in the faith. The Jew would go by without saying anything, and the Christian would say: "God will take care of you."

And so this is the way it happened that Paláshka, without seeing a thing in front of her, once called out, "Help me baptize my baby in the faith!" and someone spat in anger, jumped back from her, and instead of saying, "God will take care of you," invited her and her baby to go to the devil.

Paláshka wiped her eyes and saw that two Jews had just passed by, one in a heavy gray coat of squirrel fur and the other in a threadbare cloak of fox fur.

Paláshka saw that this was Solomon, and since she was a maiden courteous in manner she called after him:

"Pardon me, Mister Solomon, I didn't see who you was. I thought you was a Christian instead of a Jew."

Solomon stopped, looked at her, and said:

"Fool!"

"That's just it, Mister: I *am* a fool."

Solomon looked at her again and remarked:

"It is good that you're a fool."

"Of course. It's just the way God made me."

"Aha! All right, all right. Now what's this you're saying in your foolish way about a Jew?"

"Just that the Christians give a kopeck apiece to baptize my baby in the faith, but the Jews don't give nothing for that."

"They don't? . . . Hm! Yes, yes, you're stupid, but you do know what you need to know . . . They don't! Jews don't give anything when they don't have to, but when they have to, they do . . . Now look here, I am going to give you one whole ruble, and you can take it and do whatever you want to with your baby."

"I'll get it baptized in the faith, Mister. Your ruble will get his soul saved, Mister Solomon."

"That's all the same to me, young woman, never mind. Go ahead and take him into your faith. I'm only sorry that I haven't one ruble for you just at the moment."

"That sure is a pity, Mister. So I still can't get my baby into the Christian faith."

"Oh yes, you can! Why not? I haven't got *one* ruble with me, but I *have* got five. Now, I'll give you all five, and you get change and take out one for yourself and do whatever you want to with it, but bring the four rubles back to me at my home on the market square."

"All right, Mister."

"You'll bring them back?"

"Why, sure, Mister. How could I help a-doing that? You do so much for me and trust me with five rubles, and then me not bring back the change! So help me God, I'll bring 'em back."

"All right, then, go and do what you need to do, and bring me back my four rubles, and for the fifth one come and do my washing for a week."

"I'll wash everything for you, Mister."

Solomon pulled out an old billfold, took a five-ruble note out of it, and handed it to Paláshka. She bowed down to his feet and ran off to get her baby into the Christian faith, and Solomon caught up with his companion in the fox-fur cloak and made his way home.

Thereupon there took place between these two gentlemen an unexpected but rather sharp discussion. The old Jew in the fox-fur cloak indignantly demanded to know why Solomon should have given money to a heathen. But Solomon answered that that was his business and did not concern anybody else.

Such a reply was rude to the point of impropriety, because everything one Jew does invariably concerns all his fellow believers, and besides, the person to whom Solomon replied in this way was an important man in the community: he was Rabbi Leizer, a most scholarly rabbi, who knew the whole Talmud by heart and was the most faithful guardian of the inviolable precepts of Judaism. He really had the right to reproach Solomon for giving the money to the "heathen" that might have gone to the benefit of the Jews. But Solomon persisted in his strange behavior and said:

"No, Rabbi Leizer, it is better for this money to go to the Christians; they won't get rich off it."

"How is that?" shouted the gray-haired old rabbi.

"Well, they just won't . . . I won't tell you anything more about it now, but it had to be done the way I did it. I'm no fool, you know, Rabbi Leizer."

"But what will that heathen girl do with it?"

"What? . . . She'll christen her baby and bring me back the four rubles change, and she'll work off that fifth ruble three times over."

The rabbi struck his forehead with his hand and closed his eyes.

"How," he cried, "could you, a sturdy, faithful Jew, give money for them to carry out that offensive ceremony upon a child? O Solomon! Solomon!"

"That's right, I am Solomon."

"O miserable Solomon! Thy name shall perish among our people."

"No, Rabbi Leizer, it will not perish. It will be lifted up."

"A demon has seized thee, or else thou hast lost thy reason. In any event I wish to know thee no longer; my feet shall never again cross thy threshold, and I shall cause thee to be scorned among all and a stranger among thine own people."

But Solomon did indeed act as if a demon had taken hold of him: not only did he show no shame at the words of Rabbi Leizer, but he even laughed in his face, and said:

"Don't talk nonsense, Rabbi!"

"I am not talking nonsense. You have done an evil deed, and you will be despised for it by everybody."

"No—a thousand times no!" answered Solomon. "I commit no foolishness, and I have not done any bad deed whatever. On the contrary, I have done a very good deed. No, Rabbi Leizer, I shall not be despised. Rather shall I be respected both by our own people and by others, for the bank note I gave to that girl was counterfeit . . . I received it over there among their people; they gave it to me when I beat them at cards. I could not pass it on among our people and risk leading them into danger; so I returned it to them through that girl, who is stupid and will bring me back the change. Look! there she comes now, bringing my four rubles back, and in return for the fifth one she'll work three weeks for me."

And at that very moment Paláshka went up to Rabbi Solomon, handed him four rubles, and joyfully thanked him, because she already held in her arms a baptized baby.

"Now do you understand me?" Solomon asked Rabbi Leizer.

"Oh, I certainly do!" answered Leizer.

"And are you still going to tell everybody Solomon is unworthy of his name and has done an evil deed?"

"No, Solomon, no!" answered old Leizer, vigorously shaking his hand. "Now I shall tell everyone that you are worthy of your name, that you are truly a great and wise man, and that you have done a very fine deed, which must gladden the heart of everyone who hears about it."

o o o

And that is the way it really turned out: the deed that Solomon performed gladdened the hearts of all, and in this sense it must be recognized as a good deed, since it brought a share of joy and benefit to everybody. The Jews were pleased because they had in their midst such a wise man as Solomon; the Christians were touched by Solomon's goodness and praised him for the kindness and compassion he had shown to poor Paláshka. Paláshka considered him not only her own benefactor but the benefactor of her child, whose soul had received hope of eternal salvation thanks to Solomon, and Solomon himself had exchanged bad money for good, and had even made a little profit, since Paláshka gratefully worked for him in return for the ruble not a mere three weeks but the whole winter through. And so now, just consider how many good results came from this! And you must acknowledge that no direct benefactor in the real sense of the word is to be found anywhere. The fish soup was somehow cooked up without any fish, and still it is fish soup just the same; and any author who might tell this story would not be to blame, I hope, if this was the way the dish was prepared in his day and age.

NOTE FOR "FISH SOUP WITHOUT FISH"

[1] The word "Varangian" was an ancient Russian name for the Normans, whom the Russians themselves—according to legend—invited to come over from Scandinavia and rule them.

NOTE TO FIGÚRA

Toward the end of Leskóv's life a critic wrote a long review of his latest works under the title "A Sermon in Art" ("Khudózhestvennaya própoved"). "Figúra" provides a striking illustration of that title. From beginning to end it represents one of Leskóv's major efforts to embody in literary form the teachings of Leo Tolstóy about nonviolence.

Leskóv's interest in Tolstóy can be traced back almost to the beginning of his own literary career. Certain aspects of what was later to be known as Tolstoyism can be found in Leskóv's writings even before Tolstóy himself underwent his great inner religious revolution at the end of the 1870's. Throughout the first half of the 1880's Leskóv wrote of Tolstóy frequently in his newspaper articles, and in 1885, when the Tolstoyan publishing house "Intermediary" was founded to make good literature available at very low cost for the masses of Russian peasants, one of the first four books it published contained Leskóv's Tolstoyan story, "Christ as the Guest of a Peasant" ("Khristós v gostyákh u muzhiká").

For Leskóv the principal stumblingblock in Tolstóy's teachings was his doctrine of nonresistance to evil through violence. It was not until 1886, a year in which he wrote at least six articles on Tolstóy, that Leskóv finally worked out his own highly original explanation and defense of Tolstoyan nonresistance. In an article entitled "About Goads" ("O rozhné"), which was completely overlooked in all the literature on Leskóv's relations with Tolstóy until the middle of the twentieth century, Leskóv declared that Tolstóy by no means preached nonresistance to evil. On the contrary, he believed in resisting evil—but he recognized that any effort to overcome the evil in others before one had got rid of it within oneself was foredoomed to failure.

From 1886 until his death in 1895 Leskóv counted himself a humble and devoted (though not entirely uncritical) follower of Tolstóy. The extent of his reverence for Tolstóy was revealed in a comical incident that took place near the end of Tolstóy's life when somebody showed him a notebook Leskóv had left behind after his death. The wisdom embodied in the observations Leskóv had written down impressed Tolstóy so much that for days he read them to everyone who came to visit him. Finally his secretary, Valentín Bulgákov, asked to see the Leskóv notebook. "But Leo Nikoláevich," he exclaimed to Tolstóy, "these are simply quotations Leskóv copied down from your own writings!"

Shortly before the publication of "Figúra" in 1889, Leskóv sent a copy of it to Tolstóy, along with a letter telling him that the story dealt with the founder of Ukrainian Stundism. This was the Protestant movement that had spread to the Ukrainian peasants from their German neighbors in the early nineteenth century and has since become one branch of what is now the Russian Baptist Church. "Very little is made up here," Leskóv wrote about the story. "It is almost all fact." In regard to General Sacken, however, he begged for further details from Tolstóy, who had served under Sacken in the 1850's in the Crimean War. Tolstóy's reply has not been preserved, but Leskóv's next letter indicates that Tolstóy did supply some additional details on Sacken.

"Figúra" is a characteristically Leskovian frame story, told in the words of a former Russian officer who has taken up the life of a Ukrainian peasant. At the beginning and the end of Figúra's account, when the reader's attention is focused on the setting in which he tells his story, Figúra's speech is heavily colored with Ukrainianisms. This use of Ukrainianized Russian presents such a difficult problem in Leskóv's works that previous translators have simply ignored it. For example, the otherwise admirable translation we have in English of "The March Hare" ("Záyachi remíz"), provides no equivalent for the comical effects Leskóv achieves through his use there of Ukrainianized Russian. The present translator has worked according to the following principle: Ukrainian, for all its closeness to Russian, is an independent language with a beauty and expressiveness all its own, which was given a place of dignity among literary languages by the great poet Shevchénko. But Ukrainian words and phrases *as perceived by Russians,* particularly in the nineteenth century, sounded countrified and comical. This was the effect that Leskóv achieved in his frequent use of Ukrainianized Russian, and the present writer is convinced that this effect can best be reproduced in translation through the use of a countrified English.

FIGÚRA

CHAPTER ONE

When I was still getting educated in Kíev and had not the slightest idea of taking up writing, I happened to make the acquaintance of a poor but honorable family who lived in their own tiny house in the most remote corner of the town, near the abandoned St. Cyril Monastery. The family consisted of two elderly sisters, maiden ladies, and a third old lady, their aunt, who was also unmarried. They lived modestly, on a very small pension and the income from their cows and vegetable garden. Only three persons were in the habit of coming to see them: the well-known Russian abolitionist Dmítry Petróvich Zhurávsky,[1] me, and an unconventional man, completely like a peasant in appearance, whose name was Vigúra but whom everyone called "Figúra."

This memorial speech is going to tell about him.

CHAPTER TWO

Figúra—or as it was pronounced in the Ukrainian, "Khvegúra"—was about sixty years old at the time I knew him, but he still possessed considerable strength and never complained of ill health. He was enormous in stature and of athletic build; his hair was bushy and brown, with scarcely a trace of gray, but his moustache was salt-and-peppery. In his own words, he "had started turning gray at the muzzle, like a hound," that is, beginning with his whiskers rather than his hair, the way old dogs turn gray. His beard would also have been gray, but he kept it shaved. Figúra had big, gray, languishing eyes, red lips, and a swarthy, sunburnt face. His look carried with it an expression of fearlessness and intelligence along with just a suggestion of smoldering Ukrainian irony.

Figúra lived like a genuine, full-fledged peasant on the edge of town in the outlying settlement of Kurínevka, "under his own roof," that is, on his own little farm where he did his own work, with the help of a young and extraordinarily beautiful peasant girl named Christie. Figúra did all the farm work with his own hands and maintained everything in simple but impeccable order. He himself spaded up the garden, worked the

ground, and planted it with vegetables, and carried these vegetables to
the Rye Market in the Podól quarter of Kíev, where he would pull up
with his wagon in line with the other incoming peasants and sell his
cucumbers, pumpkins, melons, cabbages, beets, and turnips.

Figúra did better than the others, because his vegetables were always
outstanding for their quality. His soft, sweet pumpkins were particularly
famous and were of enormous size, occasionally weighing as much as
thirty-five or forty pounds.

It was the same with his cucumbers and beets and cabbages—everything
Figúra had was the biggest and the best.

The women who traded in produce at the Podól Rye Market knew that
"you won't find nothing better than Figúra's," but he did not like to sell
to speculators, because "they were highway robbers"; he sold direct to
"people," that is, to the consumers themselves.

Figúra had it in for the trader men and women, and he liked to expose
the tricks of that crowd and hold them up to ridicule. No matter how
well the speculators might disguise themselves, and no matter what secret
agent they might send to buy produce from Figúra's wagon, he would see
through them at once; and in reply to their question, "What'll you take
for five dozen?" he would answer:

"I'll take money—but unfortunately this ain't for Your Grace."

And if the secret agent tried to persuade him that he was just a plain
man, "a-buying for his self," Figúra, without even taking his pipe out of
his mouth, would tell him:

"All right, now, cut out the bluffing—you won't get away with it!"
And he would say no more.

Everybody at the market knew Figúra, and they knew it was said that
"he didn't come from country people, but only took up with country
people"; but what his real rank and title were and how he came to "take
up with country people"—that was something nobody knew or tried to
find out.

For a long time I did not know it either, and to this day I don't know
his real rank.

CHAPTER THREE

Figúra's house was an ordinary Ukrainian clay-walled cottage, divided into
one little room and a kitchen. The food he ate was always vegetable
and milk products, but of the very simplest peasant kind, which were
prepared by the Ukrainian girl Christie, whose remarkable beauty I have
already mentioned. Christie was a "covered girl," that is, a girl who was
obliged to wear a kerchief because she had had a baby. The child was a
beautiful little girl by the name of Katie. In the neighborhood people

thought she was "Khvegúra's kid," but Figúra at that would only make a face, dismiss it with a snort, and say:

"That's right—she sure is mine! It's true: since God has give me the chance to feed her, why, then I reckon she's mine now—and whoever brought her into this world to starve, well, I don't know that kind feller. But let people figure it any way they want to. If they think she's mine, then let her be mine—hit don't matter to me."

As far as Katie was concerned, people still had some doubt, but in regard to the beautiful Christie herself they had no doubt at all that she was Figúra's "mate."

Figúra remained indifferent to that too, and if anybody tried to get his goat about Christie, he simply answered:

"And what's a-troubling you—envy?"

On the other hand, both Figúra and Christie, as well as the entirely innocent Katie, had a penance laid upon them; none of the three ate any meat or fish—nothing, in a word, that contained any conscious life.

The Kurínevka women knew why this penance had been imposed on them.

But Figúra only grinned and said:

"Cabbageheads!"

CHAPTER FOUR

Christie's relations with Figúra were tender but were such that nobody could make them out very clearly.

Christie lived in the house not like a hired girl working for her mistress but as if she were a relative living with her kinsfolk. She "toted water" from the well, scrubbed the floors and daubed the clay walls of the hut and washed the clothes and sewed for herself, Katie, and Figúra, but she did not milk the cows, because the cows were "strong," and Figúra himself would do the milking with his appropriately strong hands. All three of them ate together at the same table meals which Christie would serve and clear away. Tea they did not drink at all because it was "a useless habit," but on holidays they would have a drink they made of dried cherries or raspberries—and again all together around the same table. The only guests they had were those elderly maiden laides, Zhurávsky, and me. When we were there, Christie would keep running around in such a dither that we could hardly sit her down for one minute, and when the guests got up to go, the irrepressible Christie would bounce out of her chair and hasten to bring everybody their overcoats and galoshes. The guests would try to resist her help, but she insisted, and Figúra would take her part. He would tell the guests:

"Do allow her to fulfill her vow."

Christie would calm down only when the guests allowed themselves to be "clothed and shod as is proper according to law." This was "her vow," her assignment as a servant, to which the simple-hearted beauty remained faithful and devoted.

In conversation with each other Figúra and Christie used different forms: Figúra spoke to her familiarly and called her "Christine" or "Christie," but she spoke to him in respectful terms and called him politely by his first name and patronymic. They both called little Katie "Daughter," and she called Figúra "Daddy" and Christie "Mama." Katie was nine years old and was the image of her mother—a beauty.

Neither Figúra nor Christie had ties with any relatives at all. Christie was a complete orphan. As for Figúra (or rather Vigúra), though he did have relatives, one of whom was even a professor at the university, still our Figúra from Kurínevka had nothing to do with those Vigúras, because, as he said, "they herded together with aristocrats," and in Figúra's opinion if that was not downright bad, at least it was not fittin' for him.

"Their church God knows what rank they are—Some-Kind-Of Assessors, maybe, or This-'n'-That-Kind-Of Councilors; and anybody can see from our snouts that we are just everyday swine."

But in his character and all his deeds the Figúra from Kurínevka was such an original personality that he takes away all the absurdity from the proverb that advises us to value a beaten man more than one who is unbeaten.

Here is one of his deeds that had importance for his whole life, which was in fact determined by this very deed. Scarcely a person knew about it or knows about it even yet, but I heard about it from Figúra himself, and I will pass it on just as I remember it.

CHAPTER SIX

In Kíev I lived in a very populous quarter between the two cathedrals of Michael and Sophia, and in addition two wooden churches stood there as well. On holidays there were so many church bells ringing that it was hard to hold up under it, and down below along all the streets that led to the Khreshchátik² there were taverns and beer halls, and on the square, show booths and swings. On such days I would escape from all that to Figúra. There it was calm and peaceful; the beautiful child played on the grass, kindly feminine eyes would sparkle, and the sensible and ever sober Figúra would quietly talk.

Once I started complaining to him about the uproar that had begun early that morning in my part of town, and he answered:

"Don't tell me! Ever since my childhood I haven't been able to put up with our Russian celebrations, and to this day I am always afraid some misfortune may happen. When we were cadets they used to take us up to the swings and say: 'Look! Real folk amusements!' But even then I would ask myself what good it was, even though it was a folk custom. In the prophet Isaiah we read: 'Your appointed feasts my soul hateth,' and it was not in vain that I had a foreboding that something bad would happen to me some time during all that revelry. And so it did, and the only good thing is that all the evil then was turned for me into benefit."

"And may I ask just what it was?"

"I think you may. You see, it took place when you were still in your grandmother's arms. At that time we had two armies: one was called the First and the other the Second. I was serving under Sacken—that same Eroféich who still keeps singing acathists.[3] He was a great one for praying, God be with him; he would always pray on his knees, or else he would lie down on the floor and keep lying there and lying there; and wherever he went and whatever he picked up, he would always cross himself. At that time many others in the army tried to imitate him in that and tried to make sure he would see them. Those who managed it got along well . . . And once it helped me too—so much that to this very day I receive a pension for it. This is the way it happened."

CHAPTER SEVEN

Our regiment was stationed in the south, in the same town where this Eroféich had his headquarters. And it fell to me to go to the powder magazines on watch, on the very night before Easter. I took over the watch on Easter Eve at twelve noon, and I was to be on duty till twelve o'clock on Sunday.

I had my army soldiers with me, forty-two men, and six Cossacks patrolling on horseback.

Night began to fall, and suddenly I began to feel very sad. I was a young man, and I was attached to my family. My parents were still alive, and my sister. But most important and dearest of all was my mother. Oh, my virtuous mother! I had a marvelous mother—wonderfully kind and pure, surrounded by goodness and wrapped up in goodness. She was so tender-hearted that she could not bear to bring grief to anyone, either man or beast; she would not even eat meat or fish out of compassion for animals. My father used to argue with her: "Now, please tell me, how fast do they multiply? There'll be nowhere to put them!" But she would answer: "Well, that will be some time later, but I raised these myself, and they are like members of the family. I can't eat my own relatives." And she would not eat any at the neighbors' either. "I saw these when they were alive," she would say. "I know them—I can't eat my own acquaintances." And then she even stopped eating strangers. "Just the same," she would say, "they were murdered." The priest would try to persuade her that "this is ordered of God," and in the prayerbook he would show her the prayer for consecrating meat, but she would not argue with him. "All right, then," she would answer, "you go ahead and eat the way you read it." The priest told my father that all this was done by some sort of "seductive women who penetrate our dwellings, ever studying and never making sense." But Mother told my father: "That won't hold water; I don't know any penetrating women. I just think it is repulsive to eat each other."

I can never think calmly about my mother—I always get upset. And that is what happened then. I longed to see my mother! I would walk back and forth, biting a straw in my teeth out of boredom, and thinking: now she is going along with everybody to the village for the all-night mass, from vespers to matins, and she will gather up the orphans, unkempt and in tatters, scrub them all in front of the stove, comb their hair, and put clean shirts on them. What joy to be around her! If I were not a nobleman, I would be living and working at home with her, and not standing watch. What are we standing watch over? It's all for killing in battle. But then why do I feel so sad? It's shameful! After all, I get a salary for my service, and I win promotions; but that soldier over there is a completely hopeless man, and in addition he is beaten unmercifully. He is far worse off by comparison, and yet he keeps alive, and puts up with it, and doesn't sulk . . . I've got to pull myself together—this will all pass. What, I wonder, is the best thing for a man to do if he himself feels low-spirited? First one thing, then another, and then still another would come into my head, and then at last the clearest thing of all came from my mother. She used to say: "When things go badly for you yourself, then hurry along to those who are still worse off." . . . Well, then, take those soldiers—they are worse off than I am . . . Let's see, I think to myself, how can I give those soldiers a bit of happiness? How about some refreshments? I'll give them some tea—I'll celebrate the end of the fast with them, and it will be on me!

I liked that.

CHAPTER EIGHT

I called my orderly, gave him some money from my purse, and sent him off to buy a quarter-pound of tea, and three pounds of sugar, and five dozen painted Easter eggs, and saffron bread with whatever money was left. I would have given him still more, but that was all I had.

The orderly dashed off and brought back everything, and I sat down at the table, broke up the sugar into pieces, and spread them out, and I busied myself with calculating how many pieces each man could get.

And even though it was a small task, now that I was occupied with it my melancholy disappeared, and I joyously sat there and counted out the sugar lumps and thought to myself that they were simple men, no one ever showed them any kindness, and they would be pleased with this inter-

est in them. As soon as I heard the church bells ringing for the end of
the service and the people leaving the church, I would call out greetings
and say: "Christ is risen, boys!" and I would offer them my refreshments.

We were standing watch outside the town, since powder magazines
are always kept far away from living quarters, and the entrance passage
into an empty vault, in which there was no powder, served as the guard-
room for our watch. The soldiers and I were there in the entrance room,
the sentries were standing outside, and the Cossacks had left—three of them
with the soldiers and three on mounted patrol.

From the town there came the sound of church bells, and lights flick-
ered here and there. And I saw by my watch that the time for the end
of the church service was certainly at hand. And so it would soon be
time for congratulations and refreshments. I got up to make the rounds
of the sentry posts, and suddenly I heard an uproar and scuffling. I started
toward it, and something flew under my feet, and at that very moment I
received a slap . . . Why are you looking at me like that? Yes, it was a real
slap, and *rip!*—there went an epaulette off my shoulder!

What was all that? Who struck me?

And the main thing was that it was pitch dark.

"Boys!" I shouted. "Brothers! What's going on here?"

The soldiers recognized my voice and answered:

"The Cossacks tanked up on vodka, Your Excellency, and got into a
fight."

"Who was it jumped on me?"

"That was a Cossack that socked you one too, Your Excellency. There
he is, lying at your feet—he's out cold. And they're tying up the other
two there in the cellar. They tried to fight it out with their swords."

CHAPTER NINE

Suddenly everything got mixed up in my head and started churning about.
It was an outrageous insult! Young and green as I was, I still looked upon
everything not through my own eyes but in the way I had been drilled
to, and my reasoning too was not my own but other people's, drilled into me
according to the custom. "*You* were struck—that is a disgrace; but if *you*
strike back in revenge, it will be all right—then it will be to your credit."
I must kill him, that Cossack! Cut him down on the spot! But I did not
cut him down. Now what am I good for? I am an officer who has been
slapped on the cheek. And so it's all up to me? I'll jump on him and
slaughter him! By all means, slaughter him! He's robbed me of my honor,
he has ruined my whole career. Kill him! Kill him for it at once! My
honor will be saved whether the court acquits me or not.

But down deep inside, someone said "Thou shalt not kill!" And I understood who it was—it was God speaking: I had evidence of that within

my own soul. Such strong, unquestionable evidence, you know, that there was no need to prove it, and no possibility of overturning it. God! After all, He outranked even Sacken himself. Sacken will serve out his command and then retire some time, decorated with a star, but God will remain in command of the whole universe throughout the centuries! And if He won't let me kill the man who struck me, then what shall I do with him? What can I do? Who can I go to for advice? Best of all to the one who himself submitted to that. Jesus Christ! They beat Thee too? They beat Thee and Thou forgavest . . . And what am I compared to Thee? A worm . . . abomination . . . a nobody! I want to be Thine: I have forgiven! I am *Thine* . . .

Now I felt only like weeping! I wept and wept . . .

My men thought I did it because of the offense, but—you understand— the offense no longer had anything to do with it.

The soldiers said:

"We'll kill him!"

"What are you saying? God save you! We must not kill any man!"

I asked the soldier in charge where they had put him.

"We tied up his hands and threw him in the cellar."

"Untie him at once and bring him here."

They went off to untie him, and then the cellar door was flung wide open, and the Cossack flew straight at me, as if through the air, and again fell at my feet like a bale of hay and wailed:

"Your Excellency . . . ! I'm a miserable man . . . !"

"Of course you're miserable," I said.

"What did they do to me!"

And he cried so sorrowfully that he fairly bellowed.

"Stand up!" I said.

"I can't stand up—I'm still out of my head . . ."

"How did you come to be out of your head?"

"I'm a non-drinker, and they got me drunk . . . I've got a wife and kids at home . . . And my father and mother are way up in years . . . Oh, what have I gone and done!"

"Who got you drunk?"

"My buddies, Your Excellency—they made me drink to the living and the dead during the bell-ringing . . . And I'm a non-drinker!"

And he told how they went into a tavern, and his comrades began forcing him to drink to the holy resurrection of Christ at the very first sound of the bells, so that all the living and the dead "would easily remember us"; one comrade offered him a glass, and then another, a second, and then he bought the third one himself and set up the whole crowd, and after that he did not remember how he took it into his head to jump on me and strike me and pull off my epaulette.

So there was the whole adventure for you! And now he was rolling about at my feet, crying like a baby, and all his drunkenness had gone. He kept groaning:

"O my children, my little doves . . . ! O my sorrowful father and mother . . . ! O my dear unhappy wife . . . !"

CHAPTER TEN

The poor fellow was in agony, and all the men looked at him and I could see that they were full of distress, and I was even more distressed than anybody. But as I started thinking about it, my heart began to slide back; again I began arguing to myself that if he had slapped me when we were alone I would not have hesitated one minute—I would have said: "Go in peace and do it no more." But all this happened right in front of my subordinates for whom I had to serve as the first example.

And suddenly again this word got a salutary hold upon me. What kind of "first example" had been given to us? I could not forget that, you know. I couldn't remember Jesus and at the same time go against him in the way I treated people.

"No," I thought to myself, "this is impossible; I had better put this aside now—at least for a while—and say only what is required by the regulations . . ."

I picked up an egg and started to say: "Christ is risen!"—but I felt at once that I had already begun to equivocate. Now I was no longer His— I had already become alien to Him. That was not what I wanted . . . I didn't want to get a discharge from Him. But why was I acting like those who were uncomfortable around Him, and who said, "Get Thee hence, Lord, for I am a sinful man"? Without Him, of course, it would be easier—without Him, I dare say, you can get along with everybody . . . win everybody's favor . . .

But I don't want that! I don't want it to be easier! I don't!

I remembered something else . . . I won't tell Him to go away, I will call Him to me . . . "Come here—nearer!" And I began to recite the prayer: "O Christ, Thou true Light, instruct and enlighten every man that cometh into the world . . ."

Suddenly the soldiers were all attention, and someone repeated:

"Every man indeed!"

"Yes," I said, "every man that cometh into the world"—and I interpreted this to mean that He would enlighten every one who came from enmity to *peace*.[4] And I called out in a still louder voice: "May the light of Thy countenance shine upon us sinners!"

"May it shine! May it shine indeed!" the soldiers breathed forth all together in one breath . . . All of them were shaking. All were sobbing . . .

All had seen the light that is beyond all understanding and had turned toward it.

"Brethren!" I said. "Let us keep silent!"

At once they all understood.

"Let our tongues dry up and fall out," they answered, "if we ever tell it."

"Well, then," I said, "Christ is risen!" And I first kissed the Cossack who had struck me and then started kissing all the others. "Christ is risen!"

"He is risen indeed!"

And in truth we joyfully embraced one another. And the Cossack kept weeping and said: "I'll go to Jerusalem and pray to God . . . I'll ask the priest to lay some pennants on me."

"Oh, Lord, no," I said. "You'd do better not to go to Jerusalem but just to stop drinking."

"No, Your Excellency," he wept, "I won't drink vodka, but I will go to see the priest . . ."

"Well, do as you like."

The next shift relieved us and we went back, and I reported that all was well, and all the soldiers kept silent, but it turned out just the same that our secret was discovered.

CHAPTER ELEVEN

On the third day of the Easter season the commandant summoned me, closed the door of his office, and said:

"What do you mean by reporting at the end of your last watch that all was well when such a terrible thing took place?"

I answered:

"That's right, Major, something bad did happen, but God brought us to our senses, sir, and so all was well in the end."

"A lower rank insults an officer and goes unpunished—and you call that 'all is well'? Now, what's the matter with you—have you really got no sense of either discipline or pride in your nobility?"

"The Cossack was a non-drinker, sir," I said, "and he lost his head because they got him drunk."

"Drunkenness is no excuse."

"I don't consider it an excuse," I said. "Drunkenness is a disaster, but I could not bring myself to report that a reckless man should be punished because of me. It is my fault, sir—I forgave him."

"You had no right to forgive him!"

"I know it very well, sir—I just couldn't help it."

"After that you cannot remain in the service."

"I am ready to leave."

"Yes. Hand in your resignation."

"Yes, sir."

"I am sorry for you, but your action was grossly improper. You have only yourself to blame, and whoever put such ideas into your head."

These words grieved me, and I asked his forgiveness and said I would not blame anybody, and especially not the one who had put these ideas into my head, because I had got these ideas from Christian doctrine.

This displeased the major terribly.

"Why are you coming to me with your Christianity?" he said. "I'm no rich merchant, and no fine lady either. I can't give money for church bells, and I don't know how to sew designs in tapestry; what I require of you is service. A military man must get his Christian principles from his oath of allegiance, and if you weren't able to make something agree with it you should have gone to get advice from the priest. And you ought to be very much ashamed that the Cossack who knocked you down knew better than you did what to do about it: he went to the priest and cleared his conscience. That alone saved him, and not your forgiveness. Dmítry Eroféich pardoned him not because of you but because of the priest, and all the soldiers who were with you on guard will be sent off to other units. That's what your Christianity has led to for them. And you yourself will go to Sacken; he will have a talk with you—just tell him all about your Christianity; after all, he knows the Church writings like the Military Code. And if you will excuse me for saying so, it's everybody's opinion that when you got that slap, you forgave it only so that the dishonor would not keep you from staying in the service. But that is impossible! Your comrades will not serve with you."

At that time, when I was still in my youth, that was brutal and insulting to me.

"Yes, sir," I said. "I shall go to Count Sacken and make a full report to him on how it all happened, and I shall explain what authority I was following—I will report everything in good conscience. Perhaps he will look at it differently."

The commandant dismissed me with a shrug.

"Say whatever you like, but I must tell you that nothing will help you. Sacken knows the church regulations, that's true, but just the same, so far he carries out only the military ones. He hasn't yet taken the vows as an archbishop."

At that time various absurd rumors were going the rounds among the military about Sacken. Some said he had visions and was told by an angel when to begin a battle; others told things that were even stranger, and a regimental paymaster who had a wide circle of acquaintances among the merchants claimed that the Moscow archbishop Filarét had told Count Protásov: "If I should die, then God help you, but don't make

Muravyóv the chief procurator of the Holy Synod, and don't make a Moscow metropolitan out of the rector of the Kíev Theological Academy (Innokénty Borísov). They only *look* good but they won't *do* good. Instead, put Sacken into your own job, and into mine put the very humblest monk. Otherwise I will come back in my dark splendor and haunt you."[5]

CHAPTER TWELVE

At that time I did not by any means want Sacken to assume that I had forgiven and concealed my slap so that I could stay in the service. What terrible stupidity! As if it should have mattered at all! Now it seems ridiculous, but at that time in my savage condition I really did feel that my honor depended a bit on the opinion of others . . . I could not sleep at night. One night I did not sleep on guard duty, and then for three nights I could not sleep from agitation . . . It was humiliating that my comrades should think badly of me, and that Sacken should think badly of me. It was necessary, you see, to act so that everybody should think well of us!

Once again because of that I could not sleep all night, and I got up early the next morning and reported at Sacken's reception room. So far only a military court clerk was there, but then others began to gather. They carried on a quiet buzz of conversation among themselves, but since I was acquainted with nobody, I kept silent, and I began to feel more and more sleepy—and at just the wrong time. I could hardly keep my eyes open. And for a long time I waited there with all the others for Sacken, who still did not come out, as if on purpose: he was still praying in his bedroom before his wonder-working icon. He was terribly pious: every day without fail he would recite morning and evening prayers and three acathists, and sometimes it would drag on forever. Occasionally he would get so tired of resting on his knees that he would actually fall and lie flat on the carpet, still praying. Disturbing him or in any way interrupting his prayer was considered—well, heaven help you! Nobody, it seems, would have dared attempt that even during an attack, because disturbing him was the same as waking a child before he has had his sleep out. He would begin to sulk and fret, and then you couldn't calm him down with anything. His adjutants knew this: some of them were also Godly-minded and others pretended to be. He made no distinction, and loved and encouraged them all.

As soon as he appeared, the staff officers could see at once whether he had had his fill of praying and was in a good disposition; then they would take all their papers in, because once he had filled up on prayer he was kind-hearted and would sign everything.

Just such good fortune fell to my lot: no sooner had Sacken come out into the reception room where we were waiting than one experienced old hand said to me:

"You're in luck: today he can be asked for anything—he's filled up on prayer."

I was curious: "How can you tell?"

The old hand answered: "Can't you see? His knees are white, and there are bright spots over his eyebrows, as if the light were shining. That means he'll be kind-hearted."

I couldn't make out any radiance above his eyebrows, but his trousers really had turned white at the knees.

He spoke to everyone in turn and dismissed them, and he left me to the very end and ordered me to follow him into his office.

"Well," I thought to myself, "this will settle it." And all my sleepiness left me.

CHAPTER THIRTEEN

In his office there was a big icon in an expensive mounting on a special raised platform, and a triple icon lamp with three flames burning.

First of all, Sacken went up to the icon, crossed himself, and bowed down to the ground, and then he turned to me and said:

"Your regimental commandant has interceded for you. He even praises you—he said you were a good officer. But I cannot allow you to remain in the service."

I answered that I was not requesting that.

"You're not requesting it? Why aren't you requesting it?"

"I know it's impossible, and I don't request the impossible."

"You are proud!"

"No, sir."

"Why do you talk that way—about the 'impossible'? That's the French spirit! Pride! With God all is possible. Pride!"

"There is no pride in me."

"Nonsense! I can see it. It's all that French illness. Self-will! You want to do everything in your own way! But I really cannot allow you to remain. There is a higher authority above me too. This freethinking notion of yours could get to the Emperor. What sort of fantasy was it that came over you?"

"A Cossack," I said, "followed a bad example and drank himself into a rage and struck me without knowing what he was doing."

"And you forgave him for that?"

"I could not help forgiving him."

"On what grounds?"

"I just couldn't—my heart led me to."

"Hm! Your heart! In the service your first duty is the service, and not your heart . . . At least, you've repented?"

"I could not have done otherwise."

"You mean you don't even repent?"

"No."

"And you're not sorry?"

"I'm sorry for him but not for myself."

"And I suppose you would forgive him a second time?"

"The second time, I think, would even be easier."

"Just look at that! Just look at what we've got here! A soldier strikes him on one cheek and he is ready to offer him the other one!"

I thought to myself: "Shhh! Don't you dare joke about that!" and I looked at him in silence with that kind of expression.

He seemed to become embarrassed, but then he got back on his high horse, general-fashion, and asked:

"But where is your pride?"

"I've just had the honor of telling you that I have no pride."

"Are you a nobleman?"

"I come from the nobility."

"And so then, you haven't got any of this—*noblesse oblige* . . . no pride in your nobility, either?"

"No, sir."

"A nobleman without any pride?"

I kept silent, and thought to myself:

"All right, all right: a nobleman and without any pride—so what are you going to do with me?"

But he kept on and said: "Why are you silent? I am asking you about that—about pride in your nobility?"

I kept silent again, but he repeated once more: "I am asking you about that pride in nobility which elevates a man. Sirakh says to 'take care of thy name.' "

Feeling by then as if I had already left the service and was consequently a free man, I answered that I had never run across anything in the Gospels about any kind of pride in nobility, but had read only about the pride of Satan, which was offensive unto God.

Sacken abruptly stepped back and said: "Cross yourself! Do you hear? I order you to cross yourself at once!"

I crossed myself.

"Once more!"

I crossed myself again.

"And still a third time!"

I crossed myself a third time.

Then he came up to me and himself made the sign of the cross on me and whispered: "You must not talk about Satan! You say you are Orthodox?"

"Yes, I am."

"Your godparents renounced Satan for you over the baptismal font, and his pride and all his works as well, and then they spat upon him. He is a rebel and the father of lies. Now spit at once."

I spat.

"Once more!"

I spat again.

"Good! Now spit a third time!"

I spat, and Sacken himself spat and wiped it out with his foot. We covered Satan over with spit.

"That's it! Now then, tell me . . . Let's see . . . What will you do with yourself when you've resigned?"

"I don't know yet."

"Have you got any property?"

"No."

"That's bad! Any relatives with connections?"

"None at all."

"That's wretched. Who do you count on then?"

"Neither on princes nor on the children of men: not a sparrow shall fall unless God wills it, and I won't either."

"Uh-oh! How you do know your Scriptures! Do you want to become a monk?"

"No, sir, I don't."

"Why not? I can write to Innokénty."

"I don't feel any calling to be a monk."

"But just what do you want?"

"I only want you not to think I kept quiet about the slap I received so as to stay in the service: I did that simply to—"

"To save your soul! I understand you! I understand! And that's just why I tell you: go and join the monks."

"No, I cannot become a monk, and I wasn't thinking about saving my soul: I just felt sorry for the other man and didn't want him to be beaten to death with rods."

"Punishment is often useful to a man. 'For whom the Lord loveth, he chasteneth.' You didn't read to the end. But still, I do feel sorry for you just the same. You have suffered! . . . Would you like a commission in the supply corps?"

"No, I thank you kindly."

"Why not?"

"I don't rightly know how to explain it to you . . . I'm just not competent for that."

"Well, what about going into food supplies?"

"I'm no good for that either."

"Well, then, ordnance! Honest people do turn up there occasionally."

He so overwhelmed me with all that talk of his that I became all but hypnotized and began to feel desperately sleepy.

And Sacken kept standing there before me, rhythmically wagging his head and bending down the fingers of one hand with the other as he counted:

"Well read in the Scriptures; has no pride in his nobility; slapped in the face; doesn't want the supply corps; doesn't want the food supplies; and doesn't want to be a monk! But I believe I understand why you don't want to become a monk—are you in love?"

I wanted only to go to sleep.

"No, sir," I said, "I'm not in love with anybody."

"You don't intend to get married?"

"No."

"Why not?"

"I've got a weak character."

"That's clear! You can see that at once. But why are you so shy? You're afraid of women, aren't you?"

"Some of them."

"And you're right to be! Women are vain, and . . . there are some who are very spiteful—but, you know, not all women are spiteful, and they won't all deceive you."

"I'm afraid of being deceptive myself."

"You mean—how? What for?"

"I have no hope of making a woman happy."

"Why? Afraid of differences in character?"

"Yes," I answered. "A woman may not approve of what I think is good, and vice versa."

"But you just prove it to her."

"Everything can be proved, but that only leads to quarrels, and a person becomes worse rather than better."

"And so you don't like quarrels either?"

"I can't stand them."

"Then get on your way, my boy, and join the monks! What else do you want? With your state of mind you'll make a first-rate monk!"

"I don't think so."

"Why not? Why don't you think so? Why?"

"I have no vocation for it."

"Now, there you're mistaken—forgiving offenses, a life without marriage: that's just what a monastic vocation is. And what kind of difficulties are left after that? Eating no meat! That's not what you're afraid of, is it? You know, they don't take that too seriously . . ."

"I never eat meat at all."

"But on the other hand, they have excellent fish."

"I don't eat fish either."

"What! You don't eat fish? Why not?"

"It's unpleasant for me."

"But how can it be unpleasant to eat fish?"

"I was probably born with it. My mother has never eaten any dead animals, and she's never eaten fish either."

"How strange! So all you eat is mushrooms and vegetables?"

"Yes, and milk and eggs. That leaves plenty to eat!"

"Well, it's clear you don't really know yourself: you're a natural-born monk—they'll even take you into the strictest order. I'm very glad! Very glad! I'll give you a letter right now to Innokénty!"

"But, Your Excellency, I won't become a monk!"

"Oh, yes you will. People who don't even eat fish are hard to find! You're as good as in the strictest order right now! I'll write at once."

"Please don't write, sir—I'm not going to live in a monastery. I want to eat my bread in the sweat of my brow."

CHAPTER FOURTEEN

Sacken frowned.

"You've been overreading the Bible," he said. "Now, you just leave off reading the Bible. It's all right for the English—they are heretical and unsound. The Bible is dangerous—it's a worldly book. A person with ascetic principles ought to stay away from it."

"Oh, good Lord!" I thought to myself. "What a tormentor!"

And I said to him: "Your Excellency, I've already told you I have no ascetic principles."

"Never mind—just go without any principles. Principles will come later. What's most important is that you've got it born in you. You don't even eat fish, to say nothing of meat. What more could you wish!"

I fell silent. I completely fell silent and could think of nothing except for wondering when he would dismiss me so that I could go to sleep.

But he laid his hands on my shoulders, looked me steadily in the eyes, and said: "Dear friend! You have already been called, but it still passeth your understanding!"

"Yes," I answered, "it passeth."

I felt that nothing mattered to me now—I was just about to fall asleep right there, standing up. And so, instinctively, I answered: "Yes, it passeth."

"And so," he said, "let us offer up our fervent prayers together before this holy image. This icon has been with me in France, in Persia, and on the Danube. Many a time have I thrown myself down before it in perplexity, and when I arose, everything would be clear. Get on your knees on the carpet and bow down to the ground. I will begin."

I got on my knees and bowed down, and he started reciting in an emotional voice: "Open to Thine eternal counsel . . ."

Beyond that I heard nothing. As soon as my forehead touched the carpet, I felt as if I had started tumbling down and down somewhere like a spike, deeper and deeper, into the center of the earth.

I felt that something was not quite as it should be: I ought to have been floating upwards somewhere, like a feather, but I was going down like a spike, down to where, in Goethe's words, "the elemental forms are boiling, the creative forces are bubbling." [7] And after that I remembered nothing.

I came back from the center to the surface very slowly, and I recognized nothing: the triple icon lamp was burning, the windows were dark, and on that same carpet in front of me some general, curled up in a ball, was asleep.

"What sort of place is this?" I had fallen asleep and forgotten everything.

Very quietly I raised myself up, sat upright, and thought to myself: "Where am I? What is that—is it really a general, or does it only seem to be one?" I touched it: nothing wrong—alive and warm. And I saw that he was beginning to wake up and stir. And he too sat up on the carpet and looked at me. Then he said:

"What do I see? Figúra!"

I answered: "Yes, sir."

He crossed himself and gave me the order: "Cross yourself!"

I crossed myself.

"Were you and I together?"

"Yes, sir."

"What do you know!"

I said nothing.

"What blessedness!"

I did not know what he meant, but fortunately he continued: "Did you ever see such a sanctuary!"

"Where?"

"In paradise!"

"In paradise? No," I said. "I wasn't in paradise, and I didn't see anything."

"What do you mean—didn't see anything? Why, we were flying together. Up yonder!"

I answered that I was flying all right, only it wasn't up yonder, but down below.

"Down below!"

"Yes, sir."

"Below?"

"Yes, sir."

"Hell is down below."

"I didn't see it."

"You didn't see hell?"

"No, I didn't."

"Well, what fool let you in here?"

"Count Osten-Sacken."

"Count Osten-Sacken—that's me."

"Now I see it is," I said.

"And you hadn't seen that till now?"

"I beg your pardon," I said, "but I seem to have been asleep."

"You were asleep!"

"Yes, sir."

"Well, get out of here!"

"Yes, sir," I said. "But it's dark in here—I can't find my way out."

Sacken got up, opened the door for himself, and said: *"Zum Teufel!"*

And so we took leave of each other, a little stiffly, I must say; but his kindness toward me did not come to an end with that.

CHAPTER FIFTEEN

I was completely at peace, because I knew that what I valued most of all was my freedom, the possibility of living by one code and not by several, without arguing, without betraying myself, and without trying to prove anything to anybody if it had not already appeared to him from above. And I knew where and how I could find that freedom. I wanted to enter no kind of service at all—neither the kind that required pride in nobility nor the kind where it was possible to get along without any pride. There was no kind of service in which a man could be himself; for he could not make promises in advance and then carry them out. And I saw that I was spoiled, I could not and dare not and must not promise anything, because the Sabbath was made for man and not man for the Sabbath . . . I was too tender-hearted, and I couldn't keep my promises: if I saw suffering, I could not hold out—I would betray the Sabbath! In the service you have to be firm in your oath, and know how to cast a spell on yourself, and I had no such talent. I needed something very, very simple . . . I thought and thought about what would be the very simplest thing, where I would have no need to cast a spell over myself, and I decided that the best thing of all was to cultivate the soil.

But an award awaited me even after my service.

Just before I left, the major informed me:

"It wasn't for nothing that you had your interview with Dmítry Ero-féich. He had just been filled to the brim that morning with prayer; and I understand that you prayed with him too, didn't you?"

"Why, yes," I said, "we prayed."

"And you sailed around together among the dwellings of the blest?"

"Well, now, how can I explain it to you—"

"Oh, you're a real politician! And do you know, you really did pull it off! He took a great liking to you. He gave orders to tell you that he's going to get you a pension through a special channel."

"But I haven't served long enough for a pension."

"Well, it's too late to do the calculations now; his recommendation has already gone in, and they won't turn him down."

I was granted a pension of thirty-six rubles a year, and I still receive it to this day as a result of that incident. And my soldiers gave me a kind farewell.

"Never mind, Your Excellency," they said. "We're satisfied with you and we're not complaining. It don't matter where we serve. But we'd like to ask you, Your Excellency, to come back to us as a priest and bless us for the battlefield."

What a thing to wish on anybody!

But instead of letting them wish it on me I went and bought this here farm. It ain't such a big farm, but it does right well. Maybe Katie and her husband will work it some day. Poor little Katie. I found her and her mother under the poplar trees in the park in Podól. Her mother was about to give her up to strangers and get a job herself as a wet-nurse for some lady. And I got my dander up and told her:

"Have you been that tetched all your life, or have you just gone batty here lately? What's got into you that could make you give up your own baby and feed your milk to some fine lady's brat? Let the lady that had the baby feed it too: that's what God commanded. And you just come over to my house and look after that little kid."

She got up, wrapped up Katie in her rags, and came along. She said: "What is to be, will be."

And so we've been a-living here, and we plow the fields and plant our crops, and we don't hanker after what we ain't got, because we are simple people. The mother is an orphan, the daughter is small, and I'm a beaten officer, and besides that, I haven't got any pride in nobility. Pshaw, what a no-account figure!

According to my information, Figúra died at the end of the 1850's or the very beginning of the 1860's. I have never run across any mention of him in print.

NOTES TO "FIGÚRA"

[1] Dmitry Petróvich Zhurávsky (1810–1856)—a pioneer in Russian statistical studies and a civic-minded citizen who devoted his life and a large part of his modest financial resources to buying the freedom of Russian serfs. Leskóv greatly admired him and made numerous efforts to preserve his memory.

[2] The main street of Kíev.

[3] Count Dmítry Eroféevich Osten-Sacken (1790–1881) took part in numerous Russian wars including the Crimean War, in which L. N. Tolstóy served under him, and was famous for his religious zeal.

[4] The Russian word *mir* means both 'world' and 'peace.'

[5] Filarét Drozdóv (1783–1867), the Metropolitan of Moscow, was the object of numerous satirical references by Leskóv, who once said that each day during Lent Metropolitan Filarét would eat one holy wafer and gobble up one priest. Count Nikolái Alexándrovich Protásov (1799–1855) was Chief Procurator of the Holy Synod, through which the Russian government controlled the Orthodox Church, from 1833 to 1855. Innokénty Borísov (1800–1857) whom Leskóv held in high regard, was rector of the Kíev Theological Academy from 1830 till his death. Andréi Nikoláevich Muravyóv (1806–1874) tried in vain for many years to have himself appointed Chief Procurator of the Holy Synod.

[6] From *Ecclesiasticus (The Wisdom of Jesus the Son of Sirach)*, 41:15, in the Apocrypha.

[7] A quotation from A. K. Tolstóy's poem "Ioánn Damaskín," which Leskóv mistakenly attributes to Goethe.

NOTE TO "NIGHT OWLS"

One of the many remarkable things deserving comment in this brilliant story is the fact that the character upon whom Leskóv trains the whole arsenal of his satire is not once mentioned by name. Leskóv's target is Archpriest John of Kronstadt (Ioánn Kronshtádtski, 1829–1908), who in the 1880's acquired an extraordinary following among the Orthodox Russians as a preacher and miracle-worker. In Leskóv's eyes John of Kronstadt, with his appeal to bigotry and superstition and his financially profitable exploitation of his followers, represented the kingdom of darkness in Russian religious life. At the opposite pole stood Leo Tolstóy, who in Leskóv's opinion represented a return to the true teachings of Jesus, uncorrupted by a church that had compromised itself through its alliance with secular power.

The central episode in "Night Owls" is a confrontation between the unnamed Archpriest and a young girl who is a follower of Tolstóy. The whole story is told in the words of a garrulous, meddlesome, inane, and utterly unscrupulous follower of John of Kronstadt named Márya Martýnovna, who deserves a very special place among the anti-heroes of Russian literature. As Márya Martýnovna's character takes shape in the course of her chatter, the reader comes to realize that he is expected to reverse all the plusses and minuses in her system of values, and in this way Leskóv achieves his satirical effect by exposing John of Kronstadt to the praise of Márya Martýnovna.

The climactic scene, in which the young Tolstoyan girl gets the better of John of Kronstadt in a discussion about religion, is brought to a sudden and hilarious conclusion with an episode strikingly reminiscent of the eavesdropping scene in Tolstóy's early story, "Childhood."

"Night Owls" and "The Steel Flea" are the two greatest examples of

Leskóv's verbal virtuosity. Márya Martýnovna's outrageous deformations of the Russian language reflect her equally outrageous deformations of moral and religious values. But there is a sheer exuberance in her mala-propisms that carries Leskóv beyond his primary satirical intent. For example, Márya Martýnovna's original pun on "drama" and "grammar" in her promise to tell the "grammatic" story of her life becomes the starting point for a series of puns on grammatical terminology that can be traced throughout the work. What is more, even though the whole story (apart from the frame) is told in her words, she does not limit herself to her own pet malapropisms. When she quotes other characters, we see their deformations of language, their pet phrases, sticking through the tattered texture of Márya Martýnovna's own phraseology.

When Leskóv published this story in 1891, it made a sensation. The critics, however, did not know what to make of Leskóv's deformations of language. Accustomed as they were to expecting serious literature to be written in serious literary Russian, they condemned Leskóv's style almost to a man. "I am taken to task for this 'mannered' language, especially in 'Night Owls,'" Leskóv was reported to have said. "But are there not a great many mannered people among us? All our quasi-learned writers produce their learned articles in this barbarous language. Just read the philosophical articles of our journalists and scholars. What is so astonishing if some lower-middle-class woman speaks it in my 'Night Owls'? In her mouth at least the language is merrier, funnier . . . And now others condemn me because they themselves do not know how to write this way. After all, for many years I have been collecting it—words, proverbs, and expressions caught in mid-air, in crowds, on barges, at recruiting stations, and in monasteries. Just work on this language as many years as I have . . . For many years I have attentively listened to the accent and pronunciation of Russians at various stages in their social situation. In my works they all speak *in their own way*, and not in the literary way. It is harder for a writer to acquire the language, the living speech, of the man in the street than to acquire bookish language. That is why we have very few artists of the spoken word, that is, artists who have full control of living rather than literary speech." [1]

Leskóv's language was always appreciated by ordinary Russian readers, whose minds were uncorrupted by the prescriptive standards of the critics; but it was not until the beginning of the twentieth century and the rise of the Formalist movement in Russian literature that Leskóv's style began to attract the attention of serious literary scholars.

It is possible to trace Leskóv's influence on such modern Russian writers as Zóshchenko, and it is possible to see parallels of a sort between Leskóv's treatment of language and the stylistic peculiarities of James Joyce. But a close examination of the artistic method underlying Leskóv's deformations of language will make it clear that there is nothing quite like his achievement in any other writer, either at home or abroad. This achievement has always been controversial and it probably always will be; for in the words of Hugh McLean in his article on "Night Owls," "The world has always been divided into punsters and antipunsters, and no amount of demonstration can ever prove the effectiveness of a joke."[2]

NIGHT OWLS

(Paysage and Genre)

The womanish babbling of the Parcae,
The trembling of the sleeping night,
The mouse-like scurrying of life.
Púshkin

CHAPTER ONE

. . . I had been feeling very gloomy and bored. It was still too early to leave town for the summer, but my friends had advised me to take a short excursion and see some new faces—the ones I saw every day seemed unbearably stale. Eventually I gave in to their urging and set off. I had no idea of the general lay of the land in the town where I was going and no knowledge of the customs of the people I would encounter there. Fortune, however, favored me from the very start. At the beginning of the journey I encountered some obliging and experienced persons who had taken the trip several times before, and they gave me instructions about where to stay and how to behave. I took their advice to heart and stayed where everyone stays whose calling brings him to this town. The institution in question is neither a hotel nor an inn, but a completely private house, adapted to the tastes and requirements of its guests. It is called the "Expectension."

I was given a small room. It was not customary for the guests to select their own quarters nor to make any complaints about their relative discomforts. This was something one learned even on the shortest visit. Everyone took the room assigned to him. Who was to be assigned to what room—this question was promptly decided by the penetrating eye of a very quick-witted woman known as the "leash-holder." In the absence of the "leash-holder" herself, the sorting of visitors was performed by her housekeeper and close subordinate. Both these women were apparently of noble birth; at any rate they were ladies who had seen a good deal of the world and had formed a pretty good notion of it. The respectable age attained by both these ladies ought to have insured them against any malicious gossip, and good sense and propriety were written large on their faces, though to be sure in rather different characters. The face of the "leash-holder" was in a dry, Byzantine style, while the housekeeper, with her arched eyebrows, belonged to the Italian school. Both these women were undoubtedly intelligent; they belonged to that species of which it is said: "They shall not be taken in." They smiled at each other like friends, but in their eyes there seemed to be a glimmer of other feelings quite incompatible with those of sincere friendship. A perceptive person might have concluded that it was fear of each other that bound them together.

Their extraordinary household was governed in systematic fashion. Whenever a throng or "raffle," as they called it, of customers arrived, the ladies would meet the guests and sort them out on the spot. Those they knew were taken straight to their regular rooms, but strangers were subjected to a preliminary scrutiny, after which each expectant in the "Expectension" ° received the quarters he deserved.

As a preliminary test all the expectants were hustled into a corner to pay their respects to the icon of the Blessed Virgin. There, in nervous expectancy, they would say a brief prayer before the huge image, and on the basis of this they were appraised and classified.

This rather large two-story house was entirely given over to lodgings for "expectants." Business was evidently done simply, but on a solid foundation. Great economic, executive, and police power was concentrated in the hands of the housekeeper, but the "leash-holder" kept the moral and political authority to herself. The domestic complement of the "Expectension" was rounded out by a number of female servants, kept continually on the run. Besides them the house boasted a "chefess." All these people belonged to a rather low class of servant types. However, the "chefess" possessed a long woolen cape, dating from her service with some "general." She was still very proud of it, and would wear it for her appearances before the public or "raffle."

There were two male employees: one stood at the door on the ground floor, while the other sat behind a small cabinet by the window at the end of the corridor. The former gave the impression of a rather dull-witted simpleton; the latter was a clever and foxy old retired soldier.

In layout the "Expectension" was well adapted to its function as a place of expectancy. A long corridor extended the entire length of both

---

°The word "Expectension" [Russian *azhidátsiya*, a contamination of *azhitátsiya*, "agitation" and *ozhidánie*, "expectation"] is used here in two senses: a) as the name of the institution where people "expect" [the favors of the religious personage domiciled in the town]; and b) as the act of "expectation" itself. In the former case it is written with a capital letter, and in the latter with a small letter. (*Leskóv's note.*)

floors, dividing them down the middle, with stalls along the sides. These were the "rooms for expectants." Here people were not called "new arrivals" or "visitors," but "expectants." This was felt to be more respectable and appropriate.

The corridors both upstairs and down were spacious and well-lighted, with a window at the end of each. The downstairs corridor was kept only moderately clean. It was impossible to maintain any very high standard of cleanliness, since people entered it directly from outdoors and used it as a place for taking off their wraps and wiping their shoes. There was a small stove there for heating samovars and an entrance into the kitchen, from which emerged a smell of fish and mushrooms. On one of the walls hung a large icon of the Blessed Virgin with a smaller icon alongside it; there was an icon lamp and a lectern in front of them. A well-worn prayer-rug lay on the floor, and on the opposite side stood a bench with a back, one of the so-called "hard sofas." In various places there were photographs and prints—all portraits of the same person in clerical garb.

On entering, all the expectants were expected to go and pray to the Mother of God, or, as they said, "fall before Her." Then they were all taken to their rooms.

Habitués had their favorite rooms, which seemed to be permanently reserved for them. Some of them would even omit the ceremony of praying in the corridor and go directly to "their" rooms after greeting the hostesses, whose only reply was "This way, please."

Of the others, those who were first in line and looked presentable on inspection were given vacant rooms on the first or second floor. They made up the aristocracy of this strange household. Their assignment was given them promptly; they were not obliged to wait until the others had been disposed of. All the rest were taken in hand by the housekeeper and shown into the public dormitory.

The retired soldier, armed with a very severe expression, was installed behind a little yellow cabinet by one of the windows in the lower corridor. A boy of about nine, bearing a remarkable resemblance to the ex-soldier, sat beside him on a small stool. In front of the boy there lay a heap of opened envelopes, from which he licked off the stamps and pasted them in an album. This operation he performed briskly and skillfully, with a striking and by no means childish air of solemnity which evidently fascinated the cook, who stood beside him in her woolen cape. She watched him for a long time; at last she gave a sigh and said, "Look at him go! His little hands scamper along like a mouse's paws!"

This diligent youngster's father evidently occupied a position of some importance. He sat solidly on a well-padded chair, under which a soft rug was spread. The ex-soldier kept glancing through some notes and making calculations on a small abacus, but this did not wholly engross him. He had eyes and ears for everything. No one could go by him without his looking up and following the passerby with his eyes and moustache.

His cabinet was covered with a soiled black oilcloth on which there were an inkstand with a quill pen and several sheets of cut paper. In the middle of the cabinet there were several unused remembrance books, oil for the icon lamps, wax candles and incense, and also a number of pamphlets and photographs of various sizes. This warrior was well along in years and undoubtedly a man of very firm character. The servants had nicknamed him "Fishback."

The rooms on the lower floor of the "Expectension" were all a bit on the dirty side and had a sourish smell, apparently an inseparable ingredient of all the meat pies with peas imported there from various places. All the "chambers" but two had a window each, with thin curtains, pricked full of holes in the middle where it was convenient to pin them. The furniture was rather scanty, but each stall had a bed, a clothes-rack, a small table, and chairs. In the two big rooms, which had two windows apiece, there was a wretched oilcloth sofa. One of these rooms was called the "dormitory," because it was used for those expectants who were unable or unwilling to take private rooms for themselves. There were icons and portraits in all the rooms; the dormitory had a much bigger icon than the other rooms, and an "ever-burning" lamp was kept burning before it. There was another "ever-burning" one before the Mother of God in the corridor.

There were also lamps for the icons in the private rooms, but these were lit only when the expectants entered—and even then it was assuredly at their expense, since there was an almscup alongside marked "For Oil." The lamps were lit by the warrior who maintained the trading post in front of the cabinet in the corridor.

Some of the expectants were not content with the light of the icon-lamps and in addition affixed wax candles in front of the icons in the private rooms. This practice was permitted and even encouraged, but only at times when the expectants were themselves in their rooms and were not asleep. On leaving their rooms or going to sleep they were obliged to put out the candles, but the icon lamps were allowed to burn all night.

There had been cases when people after praying and going to bed had left the lighted candles to burn out, but the "leash-holder" or her assistant invariably noticed this and would immediately knock at the door and ask them to put out the candles. They were very careful about this, and no one was allowed to violate this rule.

The upper story of the "Expectension" was much cleaner and nicer. The corridor was just as wide as the one below, but incomparably better lighted. It looked pleasant and even cheerful, and was used as a place for walking and conversation. In the windows at either end of the corridor were pots of the favorite flowers of the merchant class: geranium, impatiens, red burdock, and camphor wood, which was apparently powerless here against the enormous numbers of moths. In one window the flowers stood directly on the windowsill, while the other window had a cheap black wicker flower stand. Up above under the curtains there were two bird cages, one for a canary, the other for a siskin. The birds hopped about, tapped on their perches with their beaks and chirped at each other, and the siskin even sang. Here no commercial installations were in evidence. On the contrary, everything seemed designed to look respectable and proper. On the wall, in about the same place as in the lower corridor, there was another icon of the Blessed Virgin, also of great size and in a white frame with a gilded crown. It was mounted behind glass on hinges and lighted by a triple-flame lamp. On the floor in front of it there was a very clean rug with a rose pattern, and alongside stood a lectern with a cross and book on it. Both the cross and the book had a stole with a green lining draped over them.

The floor of the corridor was varnished, and shone. It had evidently been washed with soap and polished with wax. A jute runner with a flowery border stretched the entire length of the corridor.

Along the wall opposite the icon stood an armchair and several light Viennese chairs with woven cane seats. There were spittoons in the corners.

The rooms on the upper floor were much better furnished than below. Besides beds and chairs they contained dressers and washstands. Some of the rooms were divided in two by chintz draperies: one half became a bedroom and the other a sort of living room. Here there was a dressing mirror on the wardrobe and in the corner an icon, before which one could also light a lamp, or, if desired, a candle.

The candles, however, were more often used by the middling sort of "expectants" who, properly speaking, made up the "raffle," and lived in the lower rooms. The "upstairs customers" usually limited themselves to the icon lamps.

Here there was no odor of pea stuffing; only inside the drawers of the wardrobes did one notice an acrid smell of Volga caviar and salmon, which had left their traces in the form of large greasy stains.

Upstairs as well as down there was a dormitory room, situated next to the "leash-holder's" own quarters. This room, however, looked like a parlor. It was filled with overstuffed furniture and contained a large icon stand with numerous icons and in front of them a rug, a lectern with a cross and a book draped with a stole. The "dormitory" icon lamp was kept burning, and its light was beautifully refracted in a thick glass made of crystal finely etched with diamond facets. A sealed green alms cup for voluntary contributions was affixed to the icon stand.

People slept in this room only when there were more expectants than rooms. In such cases "extry expectants" of the same sex or a whole family were quartered there; at other times the room was considered a common meeting room and was open to all expectants who frequented the house.

After early vespers a prayer service was held there every day, at which anyone could pray and submit his requests for remembrance in the prayers of the clergy. Those who desired to arrange for private prayer services in their rooms in addition to the public ceremony had to make a special request to that effect. Such requests had to be submitted through the "leash-holder." The housekeeper would take no responsibility for this, and direct requests often did not reach their destination.

Candles, oil, and everything else needed for service were brought upstairs from below, and the warrior in charge of this business presented them in silence and with an air of triumphal solemnity.

General supervision of the institution was the province of the "leash-holder" herself, who lived, as stated, in a small room on the upper corridor next to the "meeting room." Downstairs the housekeeper looked after things, keeping an eye on the kitchen and on the petty officer in charge of candles.

The duties of the two ladies were distinct. The "leash-holder," as proprietress of the institution, reserved for herself the more intellectual sphere: she kept the helm of the ship. She alone knew the workings of her treasury and its devious sources of income. It was she who gave the proper tone to the whole undertaking and who had the power to obtain special spiritual consolations for those who were intelligent enough to seek her aid in procuring them.

Hers was, so to speak, the general sphere, while that of the housekeeper downstairs was more strictly confined to the narrow economic matters of transportation and petty affairs. The latter even occasionally ran into trouble, because she had to deal with the servants, who were chosen from among people of the lowest sort, and with expectants from that class of society which is called "undistinguished." The "undistinguished" character of this class is expressed not only by its station in life and relative poverty, but also by its coarse habits and not infrequent lack of honesty in monetary dealings. The "leash-holder" kept aloof from all conflicts of a pecuniary sort and had a reputation for "kindness"; but the servants called her a "big skinflint" and said it was "terrible" the way she kept after the housekeeper to protect her interests and income. The housekeeper had to resort to all sorts of tricks to get the bills paid.

"All power is in their hands"—such was the general consensus.

CHAPTER TWO

I arrived there without any recommendations. I might have obtained them, but this did not enter into my modest and unambitious plans. I only wanted relief from boredom and vexation of spirit, and therefore I presented myself as an ordinary "expectant." As an average sort of person, I was placed under the direct supervision of the ladies in a small room upstairs.

Not knowing how I was expected to act, I watched others and tried to imitate people of experience in everything I did. This was the only way I could fall in with the prevailing tone of the institution where I was accommodated, which was essential. I did not want to be the cause of any discord in the attitudes and feelings of this unusual group of people, whose faces showed that they had come with great and far-reaching hopes and sought to obtain what they needed at any cost. I knelt and prayed with them everywhere they did and observed all their customs as closely as I could, but this procedure soon became inexpressibly tiresome and indescribably tedious. Moreover, I had the feeling that all these people were peculiarly wary and frightened of one another, and I decided that my trip had evidently been in vain, since nothing of interest could possibly occur on this visit.

I was mistaken.

In the evening I took a short walk through the town alone, and that depressed me still more. There were a great number of pot-houses and taverns, groups of soldiers, emaciated shadows of ragged tramps, and a great many women of the well-known miserable profession roaming the streets.

I should have remembered that grace prevails where sin abounds, but I forgot that and returned dejected and thoroughly upset. I hastily drank my fill of tea in the meeting room and then went out to stand on the doorstep. I seemed to have disturbed the cook. Wearing her cape, she was talking to some personage in military uniform and kept repeating: "Well, what do I care! What's that to me?" So as not to annoy her, I went up to my room, intending to get a good sleep before morning, get up early, and return homeward the same morning without delay.

I was so tired and bored that bed looked very good to me. The bed, by the way, was quite tolerable, but just in case, I gave it a good sprinkling of insect powder.

My intention of getting a good sleep, however, was not to be realized. At first I was afraid of bedbugs—my nomadic life had brought me into many unpleasant encounters with them in Russian inns. Then I was overcome by a desire to determine what sort of company I had fallen among, what kind of people these were—good or bad, clever or stupid, simpletons or rogues. I could not arrive at any solution nor decide what names to call them and what category to assign them to. Meanwhile I no longer felt sleepy, and instead of getting a good rest, I was threatened by a long, vexing, tiresome night of insomnia. But fortunately, hardly had everything quieted down in the halls than I heard nocturnal noises coming from both sides of my room. Evidently I had loquacious neighbors. At first I was annoyed, but then I became engrossed and began to listen in earnest.

My neighbors on the right proved to be merely disagreeable and even, apparently, not quite upright in their behavior. From their voices they seemed to be an old man and his wife. They kept moving something around and grumbling. The old man said *sh* instead of *s* and kept drinking out of a "glash" and saying "on-core." They had evidently had some sort of family disturbance and had come to settle it and to threaten someone else, but at the same time they had much to be afraid of on their own account. Actually the old woman was the more upset; she was apparently a timid sort, while the man faced things with more courage.

"Never mind, mother," he said to the woman. "Never mind. Don't be shy like a timid fly. That's an old shaying of ours from the Caucashush. Wait and shee what he'll give ush—he's sure to give ush shomething. The very leasht he can give ush is twenty-five rubles. For lesh than that it wouldn't be worth coming!"

"Fine, if he only does!"

"He will, he hash to. I've already fixed her and the houshkeeper too. The head one got the whole point—how much I could hurt her or help her. I'll try to find out everything, and then she'll do her besht for ush."

"You're a lot of use to her!"

"Oh yes, mother, I am. She needs to know what ideas people come here with, and you know how I . . . I can find out what'sh inshide a man and tell her. I'll hang around with the newcomers, talk to everybody and find out all their past life. Then they'll be able to give them a surprise— they'll know everything already. I've thought it all out. They need me! Hey, gimme an on-core!"

"But how did you put it to her?"

"How? Just the way we decided. I told her we were gentry, from the Caucasian army, abandoned—a dishrespectful son—read too many fairy shtories . . . Gimme an on-core!"

"That he doesn't pray to God, did you tell her that?"

"Yesh, I told her. I told her he doesn't pray to God, doesn't want to go in the service and spends his time making boots . . . And he takes candles from the Jews after the Shabbath. I told her everything. I told her, and for that gimme an on-core and some shalmon!"

The old woman replied, "Take your salmon, but you don't need any on-core."

"What d'you mean I don't need one? An on-core is just what I do want."

"No, you don't need any on-core."

"What d'you mean! What d'you mean I don't need one? . . . I tell you, mother, pour me out a glash, a little one! I am smart, I thought it all up— now we're going to get along."

She poured him a glass, and he drank it down and gave a loud grunt. "Sh-h-h!" the woman warned him.

"What are you sho afraid of?"

"I'm afraid of everything."

"Don't be shcared, there's nothing to be shcared of. Don't be afraid of anything."

"It might get us in a mess."

"What mesh? What for?"

"And he can ask 'What for?' As if he didn't know!"

"Well, I don't."

"But we came with somebody else's recommendation."

"Well, what'sh wrong with that?"

"Maybe those neighbors of ours have already missed it, their recommendation."

"Maybe they have . . ."

"Well, they might turn up here."

"They won't do that."

"Why not?"

"Gimme an on-core and I'll tell you why."

"You're a drunk!"

"Hell no, I'm a smart man. Gimme an on-core."

"Why won't they come here?"

"Pour me an on-core and I'll tell you."

She poured him one; he drank it off and told her he had turned in a "suspicion" the day before against some neighbors of his, from whom this couple had apparently stolen some glowing recommendation.

The old woman quieted down; evidently she thought this an apt and ingenious scheme.

A moment later she asked him whether he had consulted anyone about some invented dream of his and what had been said. The old man replied that he had and at once lowered his voice and added, "She gave me a good leshon in how to talk about dreams."

"Well, how should you?"

"Watch how he listens to you, and if he puts his hand on his shide, then shtop talking right away. If he puts his hands on his shides like an offisher, that means he is getting mad. Why don't you give me an on-core? I can't get to shleep without it."

I covered my head with my pillow and lay like that for about twenty minutes. It became stuffy. I uncovered my head again and began listening. It was hard to tell whether the conversation was still going on or not;

finally the old couple seemed to have gone to sleep. It was true: I could hear the breathing of two people asleep. One of them seemed to be making a great effort to pronounce the word "on-core," while the other sent back a thin whistle, "fire-fire."

"Encore!"

"Fire!"

What were they doing in their sleep—hunting somebody, or even, perhaps, executing him, shooting him down?

God bless our home!

I got up quietly and, as quickly as I could, hung my coverlet over the door from behind which the sound of this enterprise had reached my ears.

The greedy tarantula and his viper, embracing on their marital couch, had passed out of my ken.

CHAPTER THREE

But just as the scene on the right quieted down, a quite different one began behind the wall on the left.

Two women were talking. The younger one called the older Márya Martýnovna; the other was named Aíchka. (Among the Moscow merchants Aíchka is used as a nickname for Raísa.) They were speaking softly and so calmly and circumstantially that I could grasp at once even how they were situated in their room and what their relationship was.

The older one, Márya Martýnovna, was speaking to the younger, Aíchka, in an insinuating, saccharine voice.

"So, my angel, I am glad you have lain down to rest by me in your little bed. This little room is outstandingly clean, and the beddie-bye is nice and soft. Snuggle tight, my little darling. You've got to have a nice good rest; otherwise it's unthinkable for you to go on. You don't need to get up for anything. I can see your azurey eyes perfectly by the light of the nice icon lamp, and whatever comes into your little head I'll notice it right away and bring it right to your little bed."

"No, I'll get up myself and turn down the icon lamp," answered Aíchka in a youthful voice with a Moscow drawl.

"No, no! You mustn't get up! Look, I've already shaded the lamp with a cute little book."

"I know you. You're not young, but you're quick on your feet."

"I can't be anything else. I've got a needle in my insides."

"A needle in your insides?"

"The very finest, Number 11."

"How did it get in?"

"I was doing a fast job of sewing and stuck it into my hand, and from there it went into my body. They tried to get a doctor but couldn't. They said, 'It will come out by itself,' but it's been going all around me for thirty years now and it doesn't come out . . . See, now the light won't hurt your azurey eyes, so I can rest easy. I'm going to sit here by your little footsies and stroke you ever so softly, and I'm going to tell you a story."

"Don't do that, don't stroke me, I don't like it! Sit over there in the chair and tell me a story from there," answered Aíchka.

"But I do so want to sit right here! That's what I love best of all—to be nice to a nice lady, to do what she likes, to sit at her footsies and dream with her about all sorts of things! I remember how when we were still young girls, before we were married, we used to whisper all our secrets to each other at night, and we used to play around until we went to sleep together in each other's arms."

"Well, I don't think it's much fun for a woman to embrace and caress another woman. There's nothing to dream about in that."

"Caresses, my angel, bring the dreams with them. That's why people who are friendly stay by themselves to dream. Of course, you can't have such a friendship with just anyone, but if a girl has a real, honest-to-goodness friend, 'what happiness, what torments' she will know! It's an experience you'll never forget!"

"I can't make it out at all."

"I'm surprised. *I* understand it very well. When I was a girl I had a bosomy friend like that—Shúra her name was. Oh, what a cute little thing she was, and how we loved each other! Mama used to get angry and say, 'Don't squander your innocent tenderness, you little fools. Save your caresses for your husbands.' But we didn't want to get married, for what more could marriage bring? The only bright spot in my life was before I got married, but then they made me a victim of those two Potiphars, and that was the end of the joy in my life."

"You mean you were married to two men? That's interesting."

"I buried one and married the other."

"Oh, that way! You married one after the other!"

"Well, what of it?"

"You said you were a 'victim' of two men."

"And you thought I married them both at once!"

Márya Martýnovna broke into a cracked laugh and said gaily, "Oh, you naughty, naughty girl! You thought I had one husband for the holidays and another for the weekdays?"

"Well, that happens too."

"It does, my dear, it does. What doesn't happen these days? But it wasn't like that with me."

"Some of them are cheaters. A married man doesn't tell about his first wife and marries again. He gets punished for it, but nothing happens to the second woman."

"Yes, if she pretends that she didn't know about it, then she isn't due for any especially outstanding punishment. But even so at the trial the defense lawyers will make fun of her, and the public prosecutor will cross examine her about shameful things."

"What harm is there in being questioned? When a woman tells things about herself, she becomes much more interesting for everyone afterwards. And anyway you can go on living with the same man they divorce you from."

"Yes, but then you're forced to live in sin."

"I beg your pardon, they don't perform real divorces at the altar any more, they don't remove the crowns in the church; they only read out a decree in the courtroom." [1]

"But then you have to register as a single person."

"That's of no importance!"

"Yes, according to the police regulations it's all the same, but the servants have less respect for you."

"Pay them more, and they'll give you plenty of respect."

"But anyway, it's impossible to live just the way the law says you should."

"But if you have money you can live as you please, and that's even better."

"Of course, with an outstanding capital like yours—for a young widow like you, twenty-four years old, all roads are open. You can do what you please. And I'll give you some advice: don't waste time, do it."

"Is that your advice?"

"From my whole heart. You've got to have something to remember your youth by. You suffered with your old husband for five whole years, and that's no joke."

"Don't remind me of him!"

"Forgive me, darling, forgive me! I didn't know you were afraid to remember the dead."

"I'm not afraid of him, but . . . I just hate to think of how he snored at night."

"Yes, men! If they snore, they're unspeakably nasty."

"I used to lie awake all night long, cover my head with a blanket, sit up in bed and cry. Even now if I dream of him snoring I wake right up and can't get back to sleep again."

"Yes, a man that snores ought not to get married, all the more so to a young girl like you with money and your outstanding beauty . . ."

"Now don't you flatter me about my beauty—I've looked at myself in the mirror . . . Of course, I'm all right, I'm no monster, but I'm on the coarse side."

"What makes you think you're not pretty?"

"It's not that I'm not pretty; I just don't like people to fawn on me and flatter me. It's not me they want, but my money."

"Well, my dear, I've been living with you for quite a while and you've never told me all about your money."

"I don't have to. I'll never tell anybody anything about my money. Money is a private affair."

"I'm not trying to pry. I was engaged to be your companion and help you with your housekeeping. That's my job, and I do what you want me to. If you want to walk in the garden, I take you there; if it's the theater, I go there with you. You wanted to come here, and I'm useful here, because I know my way around this place, but why you are so anxious to have a special prayer service held first thing tomorrow—that I don't know."

"And you'll never find out. What I want to pray for is my own business."

"Well, I'm not curious."

"Naturally! And if you stay that way you'll find it easier to get along with me. You leave my dreams alone—better tell me something about yourself."

"What, my angel?"

"Something 'outstanding.' "

"Oh, you naughty, how you do pick up my words!"

"I love the way you tell stories."

"You like it?"

"That's not quite it, but . . . Well, we used to have an old man in the house who told us stories about Gríshka Otrépyev . . .[2] Sometimes it was funny and sometimes sad."

"Yes, I do have a grammatic way of speaking. Lots of people have thought so. Nikolái Ivánovich Stépenev, the widow's brother-in-law, who manages all their affairs, would always ask me to stay and talk to him when he was feeling out of sorts after a spree."

"Didn't he have something else on his mind?"

"Nothing, my dear, except to make fun of himself and me. 'I'm a broozer,' he said. 'I like to hit the bottle; and you're a bare-tailer: you like to spread gossip. Play me a sinphony at somebody's expense.' "

"How she does tell it!"

"Good?"

"What do you keep asking me for? Just tell me a grammatic story of your life, that's all."

"In my life, my dear, there is nothing outstanding but sorrow."

"Well, then, tell me the whole sinphony: where you come from, what your family was like, and what you had to go through for nothing. I love to hear about people suffering for nothing."

"I had plenty of that. Don't forget, I come from a family of vodka distillers, and I was the goddaughter of Bernadákin, because Papa worked in his distillery. Papa got a big salary, but he used to say that it was terrible how much sin he had taken on himself on that account. Later he got scared of the Last Judgment, but he kept on drinking and finally died, leaving us nothing. Bernadákin had godchildren galore all around. He didn't provide for the education of all of them, only those whose parents had rendered outstanding service. They decided to send me to school, but I displayed a very strange capacity: I had a very big development for absolutely all ideas, but no memory for studies at all. I could remember and understand everything else very well, but not studies. No matter how hard I tried to beat the stultification table into my head, whenever they gave me a problem with the four rules of addition—plus-ing and minus-ing or figuring out in your head, for instance, what's the reminder when you take five from seven—I couldn't give the slightest answer. It was the same with Russian. I had a very good pronunciation for everything, flowery-like, but somehow the words kept coming out peculiar. And then when the bishop asked me a question at the public examination, 'Who wrote the Revelation of St. John the Divine?'—well, I didn't know."

"I shouldn't think so!" drawled Aíchka. "What's the use of that?"

"It's absolutely no use—they only mix you up. And then when I was sixteen, my little darling, I suddenly straightened up and got very pretty. I was a big girl, but I had a miniacute little face and a tiny beauty spot on my chin. I looked like a Frenchy. But then the vilest thing of all happened to me."

"Who was responsible for that?"

"It was all my relatives' doing."

"I might have known it."

"They caused me no end of grief. I was a Frenchy type, but they wanted to get me off their hands as soon as they could and marry me to a Russian. Right after that Mama started begging for help and trying to get them to hurry up and set aside five thousand for my dowry. Then they found me a suitor. What a looker he was—three yards around the waist! A real outstanding belly he had! Just imagine, he looked like a cucumber with a bay window!"

"The devil knows what it's all about!" said Aíchka excitedly.

"Yes, my dear, it's better not to think of him," replied Márya Martýnovna, and went on. "I was still afraid of everything then, but nobody asked my opinion. As soon as he arrived, he made an agreement with Mama and got away with three thousand of the dowry before the wedding. And at that the money was not my family's, but belonged to the office—it was Bernadákin's. Mama knocked off two thousand for herself. 'We,' she said, 'brought you up and fed you. Now we've got to think of your younger sister.' I didn't argue with her; I didn't know where my advantage lay. Mama discussed everything with my fiancé and tried to persuade him to respect my innocence of heart and not to nag at me. But then when he didn't get the other two thousand, he did nothing else but nag. He kept griping terribly all the time and sent me out to beg for the money and wouldn't sit home with me for anything. Sometimes he didn't even come home to dinner or to bed, and my miniacute French face and my figure and my beauty spot not only didn't attract him at all, but he got so he couldn't stand me. He started making the most insulting and cutting remarks to me for the very things that ought to have pleased him.

" 'What sort of pleasure is there with you?' he would say. 'What am I supposed to do, roll your bones? I adore ladies with well-padded figures.' "

"You just couldn't get his imagination to working," Aíchka put in.

"It was impossible."

"What nonsense!"

"No, it was impossible."

"Why, then?"

"He was as cold-blooded as a real snake. It was because I was scared of him that I stuck the needle into myself. He stepped on me, and I stuck the needle into myself instead of into the cushion. And then, when I was sick, if I felt the needle pricking me and asked him to send for a doctor and have the needle pulled out of me because I felt it, he would answer in the calmest way, 'What are you so impatient about? Wait a while; maybe the needle will come out of you somewhere by itself.' "

Aíchka burst out laughing and asked, "And how did it come out?"

"The way it all came out was that the needle never did come out. He found himself a well-padded lady and went on a spree. He had such luck that he kicked the bucket. Just to spite him I married a doctor's assistant right afterwards."

"Was he any better?"

"Worse yet."

"Don't tell me the other one was three yards around too!"

"No! Far from it! Just the opposite—this man was as thin as a rail, but a real outstanding viper. But Mama kept after me, 'Go on, marry him. You look like a Frenchy,' she says, 'and he is close to that breed.' The only French thing about him was that his name was Pomerántsev,[3] and the doctors used to call him 'Fleur d'orange.' It would have been better to call him Antichrist. I even had an omen not to marry him."

"Oh! I love omens! What was it?"

"I was just setting off from our gate to the church with him. On the front seat of the carriage there was a curly-headed servant boy sitting with the icon. We were obviously going to a wedding, but some passerby looked in at the gate and said, 'Look! They're taking somebody off to be punished.' "

"That's amazing! Well, how did he punish you?"

"I went through everything, my dear. First of all, he was a real sharpster and made out that he liked my miniacute face and wasn't interested in my money. When he came to ask for my hand, he was dressed up fit to thrill, like a real scion of society. He had a diamond ring on his finger and paid me compliments, saying that he was a man of taste and preferred thin, supple, graceful women. Then it turned out that was all a lie, and the ring belonged to the doctor, and he didn't like me at all. I asked him, 'In that case why did you lie and pretend to be in love?' And without the slightest shame he answered, 'Gold is the price; with that even you can look nice.' He turned out to be peeved because he had expected a lot of money from me. When he didn't get it, he too started despising me for being too thin, and he actually began to live like he wasn't my husband."

"For that you could have complained about him to the authorities."

"I did complain. The chief doctor called him in and said to him while I was there, 'Fleur d'orange! What is this?' And he started trying to talk his way out of it. 'Wait a minute, Your Excellency, this is unthinkable. She has a needle loose inside her.' And he too began to make complaints. The chief doctor was quite surprised; he ordered my husband to leave the room and said to me, 'What do you want me to do now? There is nothing I can do. If you have a needle inside you, then I can only advise you to pray to God that the needle may come out of you soon.'"

"My, what unhappy relations you have had with men, Martýnovna!"

"Yes, Aíchka, it's true. When I was little, people were nice to me because I was miniacute and slight, but for those very things I got nothing from my husbands but coldness and insults. Especially that doctor's assistant. He wouldn't call me anything but a 'humpbacked turkey,' and made up all sorts of lies about me. 'I can show by anatomy,' he said, 'that you have a stomach and then a back, and nothing else.' But the Lord God is truly merciful; He soon set me free from both of them. This same Fleur d'orange started drinking and going downhill, and once he drank himself to the point of going and renting a summer place and then hanging himself in the garden. I was left with nothing and went to live with respectable folk."

"That's hard to do."

"It's not bad. I have a good character, and everybody likes me."

"Now you're bragging."

"No, it's true."

"Well, you lived with the Stépenevs for a long time, but they finally kicked you out."

"Excuse me, Aíchka, no one ever kicked me out from anywhere."

"Well, they dismissed you. You can say that for the sake of politeness, but you were really kicked out."

"I wasn't even dismissed; I left of my own accord."

"What did you leave for? They had a good place—'outstanding,' as you would say."

"They had a very outstanding place, but for a certain reason it began going to the dogs. Besides, there was a mix-up with this place here."

"What place?"

"Right here, where we are staying in our present state of 'expectension.' "

"Well, you tell me about that right now. But please sit farther away from me, in the chair. I'm afraid of that needle of yours."

"What a suspicious person you are! But I, my dear, have taken on quite a bit of flesh. Feel it—it's as firm as a loaf of holy bread."

"I won't touch you; I am very suspicious. Besides, I think you had better bring me my purse with the money."

"I've shut it up tight in the dresser."

"No, give it here. I like to have my money under my pillow. And now tell me, why did you leave the Stépenevs'?"

CHAPTER FOUR

"The stock market clash had a lot to do with it."

"Did you really go in for playing the market?"

"I didn't, but the Stépenevs' brother-in-law did—Margaríta Mikháilovna's, that is. It isn't a big family. There's Margaríta herself, her daughter Klávdinka and her sister, Efrosínya Mikháilovna. Both of them are widows. Efrosínya is poor, but Margaríta's husband, Rodión Ivánovich, was a first-class factory owner. He was excessively strict with his workers, though. They called him 'Herod,' because he kept slapping fines on them. The other brother, Nikolái Ivánovich, was more easygoing with the people, but he was terrifically industriable. He was always in a terrible rush everywhere to put items on the gender. At first he built mind-layers and used to go off on terrific sprees with navy commandeers. Wherever he went there was a great hubbub and commotion, but when he came home he insisted on an absolutely impossible degree of silence. His wife was a raving beauty and very submissive. He had her so frightened that if she was sitting alone and knocked her spoon against her saucer, she would scold herself, make a threatening gesture with her finger, and say, 'You fool!' But he treated her awfully anyway and drove her into her grave. After she died he didn't want to marry again. He sent his son Pétya away to a German boarding school and started living with French girls and spent all the money from his mind-layers on them. We thought it was all over with our Nikolái Ivánovich the 'broozer.' But he came out of it again. He got together with some people and formed a company to put items on the gender; and they organized a deal-estate bank. Once again he was carrying around huge sums of money, and he went and spent most of it on a Polish lady, Krutílda Silvéstrovna. Her real name was Klotílda, but we called her Krutílda,[4] because she never did anything straight, but kept twisting around until she found some way of striking home where he'd feel it the most. Then if she wanted anything, she had only to lock herself up in the bedroom and not let him in, and he would agree to anything you please only to get in after her."

"That's the way to handle them!" remarked Aíchka.

"Yes, yes; you're right. For her sake he started studying French, but when his son finished school, he drove him out of the house. He was touchy because Pétya had made friends with Krutílda's niece; so he sent him off around the world with his navy commandeers. Krutílda chased her niece out too. She was young and miniacute, but she turned out to be pregnant, and Lord only knows what would have come of her. Nikolái Ivánovich didn't know what else to do for his Krutílda. He went around with his hair curled and combed, shaven, perfumed, and dressed up fit to thrill and went on studying French. He used to stand in front of the mirror, slap his thighs and sing *'Par derrière, ma garce.'* Then somebody made a mess of the accounts in their deal-estate bank. A fearful crowd of people— raffle they were—rushed in to get their money back, and he came home in such a state that he shouted, 'Quick! Close the scissors and bring me the gate!' And he was furious when they didn't understand him.

"We thought he had lost his mind, but he was afraid of the market clash and brought us coupons to clip. For that job of clipping he was brought to trial, but he was lucky enough to be declared an unfortunate bankrupt. Well, Krutílda, naturally, would have given him the gate, but his sister, Margaríta Mikháilovna, took him into her service and turned over all her affairs to him. He lasted through a couple of years very well, but then he ran into the commandeers again somewhere and got so drunk and crazy that no one could calm him down. He might lay off for a week or two, but then he would start in again and come home with terrible hallucinations. He would call one sister Blanche and the other Mimíshka— he didn't realize where he thought he was. And if you asked him to behave himself a little more properly, he would snap back, 'What's this? How dare you! How long ago did you graduate as a domestic-affairs lawyer? I had enough of such sinphonies in my childhood!' At such times he always quarreled with me, but then afterwards he would make up to me terribly and joke, 'Marmartýn, my Marmartýn, let me give you one altýn,'[5] and then he'd start a new quarrel."

"And why did you get into them?"

"For the sake of his sisters-in-law. They begged me to."

"That's no reason! Do you really think you can stand in a man's way?"

"Oh, my dear, how could I help doing it, when he was always in such a state that there was no telling what he would do? Suddenly he would feel like going off somewhere, but he didn't know where himself."

"He knew all right."

"No, he didn't. 'I'm tired,' he would say, 'of being in such a state. To get myself out of it I would go to the devil himself in hell.' His sisters-in-law were frightened and begged me, 'Talk him out of it.' So I said, 'No one knows the way there—stay home.' 'No, Marmartýn,' he said, 'no; you only need to catch the Antichrist's cabman, Number 666, and he knows the way to the devil.'

"And suddenly he started after me: 'Come on, Bare-tailer, let's sneak out of this house on the q.t. and find Number 666 and go to the devil! Why should we stay here with people any longer? Believe me, people are all rascals! I'm fed up with them!' And he kept begging me, even with tears in his eyes, till I felt sorry for him."

"Did you really go with him?" asked Aíchka.

"What else could I do, my dear? The women begged me to, and it happened," answered Márya Martýnovna. "I had come to feel like one of the family, and so when his sisters would ask me, 'See, this is an outstanding situation; go along with him out of town and look after him,' I went. So I had to be the victim of all his stupid jokes and wisecracks. Only the last time, when there was a real first-rate scandal, he took me along by force."

"How could he take you by force?"

"I was buying myself some boots in a shop and wasn't paying attention to anything else. The clerk was trying to cheat me, muttering, 'Wait a minute . . . First class . . . Bombé style, manufactured by Miller.' Then he came in, and suddenly a sinphony from his Moscow days came into his head.

" 'Hello, Sister Bare-tailer,' he said, 'I was riding along and saw you and remembered a very important piece of business. Pick me out right now six pairs of the very best bombé boots and let's go measure them on a certain lady.' 'You just go to heaven!' I said, but he threatened, 'Otherwise I'll turn in a suspicion on you right away.' "

"How he did keep after you!"

"Oh, he was terrible. Just like a leecher or a wet leaf in the bathhouse. He wouldn't let go. How could I bring him to his senses? In the first place he was a carouser and in the second place a debachelor, and what a debachelor! As soon as he got drunk he would forget about Krutílda and feel a new urge for feminine company—and never just for any women at all. They had to be outstanding, like questriennes from the circus, for instance, or other outstanding figures of their time. But he didn't know how to treat them generously. Wherever he was he would make a terrible disconfection, order everything in sight and yell, 'Come and get it! *Chaque à sa goût!'* Many of them would get offended and wouldn't want anything. They would call him a 'pig,' but he didn't mind. He would yell, 'Look, o infusoria! Look what I can do! I am not the U-neck Skopítsyn,[6] who cut himself off from all but his money. I live with all kinds of sinphonies!' And then he'd start off with the first of his usual sinphonies. He'd jerk the tablecloth and all the dishes onto the floor, and when they asked him to pay, he'd answer, 'Go to the devil.'

"I kept expecting someone to pull a knife on him.

"So I said to his sister, 'You know best, but I think he ought to be cured of his shamelessness by prayer.' Efrosínya was very much taken with that idea. But he wouldn't hear a word about prayers.

" 'So this is the item on the gender, is it?' he said. 'You think I'm a bad lot and you can pray me out of it? I know all about religious matters myself. I drank tea with Metropolitan Macarius[7] and ate Turkish delight with the patriarch in Constantinople, and after them even the prayers of Monomákh[8] himself couldn't satisfy me.' "

"Naturally, the most outstanding sacrifices were called for at once; but the widow Margaríta Mikháilovna Stépeneva, rich as she was, couldn't get herself out of her indefinitive mood. Of course I don't know anything at all about your money . . ."

"And you don't need to know," Aíchka broke in. "Go on with your story, and don't try to catch me unawares."

"Of course. I only said that by the way. I'm not curious, but it came out anyway. Margaríta Stépeneva, as I said, has a daughter, Klávdia. She is a young and beautiful girl, quite imposing. Her beauty is in the Anglican style, but she's a little cracked in the head . . . She got her education in a school for young ladies of the female sex, where she met a certain German girl. They became bosomy friends. This girl had a cousin, Dr. Versteht, and it was this Versteht who did her in."

"What did he do, seduce her?" asked Aíchka eagerly.

"No," answered Márya Martýnovna. "He couldn't seduce her, because she is a girl without any feelings, but he distilled a lot of senseless ideas in her."

"What about?"

"Well, for instance about the universal poverty of mankind. He himself was such an unheard-of sexcentric that he got along on nothing. People used to call him 'Doctor No-Bills.' He would treat anybody, and whatever he was paid, or even if he wasn't paid at all—he didn't care. He treated everybody just the same and even preferred going to poor people. He never refused a case, and if he was given money, he would stick it in his pocket without counting it, so as not to know how much anyone had given him. Well, this sort of indifferent behavior simply captivated her and reduced her to such a state of simplemindedness that she started thinking differently about the whole way of life of human beings. She began to wish for something special, something impossible which would cause everyone no end of grief."

"What, did she become disrespectful?"

"You couldn't make out whether she was respectful or disrespectful, but she began to like all sorts of amazing things. Her girlfriend's brother was studying at the uniworsety. When he graduated he refused to go into the government service. This disappointed everyone, but she was all in favor of it."

"Why wouldn't he go into the service?"

"He figured it out this way. 'In the service,' he said, 'you can be given various kinds of jobs which I wouldn't want to do. You have to waste a lot of time on trifles to please your superiors. You have to show respect to people who don't deserve it, and you are afraid that they might turn in a bad report on you. I don't want to get mixed up with anybody in any public affairs. It's better for me to serve people according to my own ideas.' So he was left without any rank, and spent the whole summer and winter in a light overcoat visiting the poor, until last year he caught a cold and died, leaving his family just like that with nothing at all. Luckily, at the funeral the Germans took up a collection and fixed things for the family. Klávdinka thought this was all just fine. Right after she met him she got very secretive with all her relatives. She started spending all her time reading the Gospels. She read and read and then threw away all her nice dresses and started worrying about the poor. She would just sit there, thinking. If you asked her, 'What are you thinking about all the time? What do you want?' she would answer, 'I have everything. I even have too much, more than I need, but why don't other people have even the barest necessities?' You would say to her, 'What's that to you? God ordained it in this way so that there would be people to serve the rich and the rich would have people to be charitable to.' She would shake her head and start thinking again and even bring herself to the point of crying."

"For the poor?" exclaimed Aíchka.

"Yes!"

"She liked them better than the rich, did she?"

"I used to tell her the same thing. What for? If you are sorry for them, go to church and give alms at the door. There is no reason to cry out of sympathy. But she would answer, 'I am not crying out of sympathy, but from vexation, because I am stupid and wicked and can't think of anything.' Well, she kept on thinking, and finally she did think of something."

Aíchka said, "That's interesting."

CHAPTER FIVE

"She began her new life by refusing to put on any expensive dresses or gold ornaments. 'What do I need them for?' she would say. 'They're quite unnecessary and not at all pleasant or gay. I feel ashamed even to have such things.' "

"What was she ashamed of?" asked Aíchka.

"Because she would be wearing expensive things when others didn't even have the simplest clothing."

"But this is done on purpose, so as to distinguish one person from another."

"Of course! How else could you tell the cat from the cook?[9] Her mother made her a cape out of Von Gora goat wool and covered it with plush the color of sea weed. But she wouldn't put it on."

"What was that for?"

" 'It's shameful,' she would say, 'to live in such luxury.' She liked a simple coat better. She sewed herself a black cashmere dress with white collars and cuffs and washed and ironed it herself. So she went around looking like an Englishwoman. In the summertime she wore a light chintz house dress. If her mother gave her money or silk stuffs, she would go right off and sell the silk and give away all the money—Heaven knows who to. At first her mother used to ask her in a joking way, 'What are you doing, Klávdinka?—giving it all to the church for prayers?'

" 'No, Mama dear,' she said. 'What do I want with hired prayers? That is something everyone must do for himself. I simply give it away to people who have a hard time earning as much as they need or can't pay for teaching when their children are excluded from school.'

"Her mother didn't contradict her. 'Well then,' she said, 'give it away if you want to. Let the poor pray for you.' But you couldn't get her to admit that.

" 'No, Mama,' she said. 'It's not for that at all. It's just that my poor heart can't bear it when I see how fortunate I am, and other people are living in poverty.'

" 'That's just why it's not good for you to go and look at all this misery. You look at it so long that you get yourself all upset.'

" 'I don't care about that, Mama,' she said. 'Even if I didn't look at them, I would still know they existed and they were suffering. So I ought to be doing something to ease their suffering.'

" 'Well, join a charitable society and ride about with nice ladies. I'll give you so much money that you can give away more than all the countesses and princesses.'

"She didn't want that. 'I know what I have to do,' she said.

" 'Then tell me. What is it?'

"She wouldn't answer.

" 'Why are you so sad and mournful? It hurts me to look at you! Why is it?'

" 'Mama, it's because I am still very wicked. I haven't yet broken myself down; I am still fighting.'

" 'Who are you fighting with, my angel?'

" 'With myself, Mama. Don't pay any attention to me. It will be easier for me if you don't. Somehow I'll get where I want to be, but I'm not there now, and I am disgusted with myself.'

"Her uncle Nikolái Ivánovich may have been a loudmouth, but he loved her. He said, 'Don't keep after her. She can't act any different. This all comes from her tactical education.[10] I know what ought to be done with her. You ought to give her a chance to have some gay sinphonies.'"

"He rushed off and bought her a box seat for a performance of the *Moor of Venus*.[11] They went for her sake, even though it was Lent. Then what did she do but burst into sobs right in the theater!"

"What was that for?"

" 'I told you,' she said, 'that I can't stand savagery and coarseness. What you think is amusing, I consider horrid and sad.'

" 'What is horrid? What is sad?'

" 'How could it be anything else? Such a huge, black man strangles a weak woman—and for what reason?'

"Nikolái Ivánovich said, 'That's something you don't understand yet. Out of jealousy even the most educated man will shed a woman's blood for love.'

" 'That's not true,' she said. 'What kind of education is that? It's stupid and bestial! It shouldn't be like that and it won't be. I don't want to see it!'

"So they left the theater. From then on there was no end to her interjections. Decent pleasures like the theater or concerts or the opera— she didn't like any of them. Instead she would bring ragamuffin street boys into her room, give them marmalade and nuts, play the piano for them, and sing them the song about how the frogs the path did run, stretch their legs and have their fun. She felt better with them, prancing and dancing. A beautiful girl like that playing leap-frog!

"When her mother saw that, she persuaded the parish priest at confession to have a talk with her. When he came with the cross at Easter time and was having a bite to eat afterwards he started arguing with Klávdinka. 'It is not well, Miss. You are in error.'

"She snapped right back at him, 'Yes, I thank you; I thank you. You are right. I also think we live in great error, but now I am a little happier.'

" 'How is that?'

" 'Because I am dissatisfied with myself. I am not what I want to be. I condemn myself, for I see the light.'

" 'Aren't you taking a good deal on yourself?' he said.

" 'I don't know,' she answered, stammering confusedly.

" 'That's just it!' said the priest. 'But we know that in this world there must be both rich and poor. It is so everywhere.'

" 'Unfortunately, that is true,' she replied.

" 'So it is useless to talk nonsense like that, demanding that everyone be equal.'

"She turned cold, and rubbing her temples, said in a whisper, 'People talk nonsense without meaning to.'

"And the priest said, 'Yes, without meaning to. But for raving like that, even if they don't mean anything by it, they can sometimes be sent far, far away. Do not go against religion.'

" 'I am not; I love religion.'

" 'Then why do you desire the opposite?'

" 'Is the desire for simplicity of life and the elimination of grinding poverty really against religion?'

" 'What do you think? Did Christ acknowledge the poor, or not?'

" 'He did."

" 'Well then, do you seek to oppose Him?'

" 'I am answering you, not Christ. Christ Himself lived like a beggar, but we do not all live as He lived.'

"The priest got up and said, 'So that's the way you are!' He turned to her mother and said, 'Margaríta Mikháilovna! I will tell you frankly, respecting you as a good parishioner, that I have talked to your learned daughter. However, out of respect for myself I must say, madam, that it is not worthwhile talking to her. You have only one recourse: pray that she may not perish utterly.'

"Margaríta Mikháilovna, all flushed and in tears, made excuses and begged his forgiveness for the mockery he had been exposed to. The priest was mollified and answered, 'As far as I am concerned, of course, may God be with her. Let her babble whatever she pleases. These stupid dreams are widespread in society now, and we have heard our share of them. But mark my words: this evil is new, but it is as bad as the old evil of annihilism. Your daughter is treading a wicked path, wicked, wicked!'

"Margaríta Mikháilovna gave him a ten-ruble note as quick as she could, but he was not to be bought over; he pressed the money under his thumb, but went on threatening her with his forefinger and repeating 'A wicked, wicked path!'

"Margaríta Mikháilovna got angry herself, and after he had gone shouted after him, 'What a sour one you've turned into!'

"Yet Klávdinka kept her temper, remarking, 'It is your own fault, Mama dear. Why do you bother them? He said what he had to say.'

" 'Then who can help me deal with you, what powers can I call on?'

" 'But really, Mama darling, why should you ask for help against me? How have I been disobedient to you?'

" 'You have been disobedient in a great many ways, the most important ones. It is true, you don't answer me roughly. But you don't dress as befits a girl in our financial position, to show people what we are worth. You don't live—you trail around with beggars. You are ashamed of the wealth your grandfather earned and for which your father committed so many sins and injustices.'

"At that Klávdinka seized her mother by the arm with one hand, and with the other covered her own prophetic eyes[12] and suddenly shrieked like a theatrical actress in a quavering voice, 'Mama darling! Mama! Dearest! Don't say that, don't! Let's not say anything about father. It's too terrible to remember!'

" 'No one denies—may the kingdom of heaven be his—that he was a viper. But I am the one who spoiled you, and I thought that your spiritual father, at any rate, might be able to teach you a lesson.'

" 'Mama! It is you who can teach me better than anyone else.'

" 'No, I can't, and I won't try to!'

" 'Why?'

" 'I am sorry for you!'

" 'There, I have been taught a lesson. You took pity on me, and by that you taught me! I love you, Mama, and I will not do anything that might grieve a Christian mother. And you are a Christian, aren't you, Mother?'

"And she looked into her eyes and played up to her, and so they made it up. Things went along quietly that way to the point where she could do anything she wanted with her mother. She not only refused to see a performance of the *Moor;* she also declined to hear the opera *The Huge Knots.*[13] 'I don't want to, Mama,' she said. 'Songs are good when people sing them out of feelings of sadness or joy, but to do it like that, for money, is nonsense. It's a shame to pay money to see such skeptacles. Let's give it to the poor children instead.' Her mother agreed with her right off and smiled, 'Well, give it to them. You must be an angel of God.' The girl answered her in raptures, 'Oh, if it were only true! If only I were really an angel of God!' And then she began laughing and joking again, singing and dancing. 'I am so glad,' she said, 'I'll put on a free performance for you.' And her mother was too happy for words. So it turned out that Klávdinka could do anything she wanted without even asking her mother's permission.

" 'I believe,' she would say, 'that she loves me and would never do anything to grieve me.'

"Klávdinka began going to artificial classes where various educational fads for both sexes are allowed, and she went and joined a class for modeling ugly faces out of clay and learned how to do that. She would take and model any appurtenance you can think of. Then she learned to paint on porcelain and filled the whole house with rubbish; you couldn't even get into her room. She wouldn't let you anyway; she didn't even let the servants in. She would mix a lot of green clay in a basin, pour it out on a board like dough, and then start working it with her fingers."

"That must have been hard," observed Aíchka.

"There's nothing hard about it," answered Márya Martýnovna impatiently.

"You mark off the nose and the mouth and then all the other appurtenances—and it's all done. She could draw on porcelain, but she still couldn't get along without the Russian peasant. She had to give it out to a peasant to have it baked. Then she took all these articles to the stores to sell them. Her mother and aunt were naturally horrified. As if she were in such need that she had to sell her handiwork! All the money they had, and such consequences! But if she was given money, she would take it off heaven knows where and give it to heaven knows who. And that was just the time, you know, when both the Arrestigating Commission[14] and a political conspuriousy were operating at the same time. Who was she taking the money to? If it was to the poor, then why shouldn't I, a poor woman who had lived with them so many years and received presents from both her mother and her aunt, why shouldn't I get a penny from her? Once I asked her myself, straight out, 'Klávdinka, why don't you give me any of your righteous works? For a joke you might at least have bought me a piece of chintz with empty patters on a background of nothing.' She couldn't even take a joke, but cut me off firmly, 'You don't need anything; you manage to worm things out of everybody.' Lord have mercy! Lord have mercy! What a heartless girl! I'm not proud, it's true. If I need something, I ask for it. But what business is that of hers? And she talked to her mother the same way. Just imagine, on her mother's name-day she picked a rose and brought it to her. 'Mama, my darling,' she said, 'you have no need of anything.' And imagine this: her mother agreed with her. 'I have everything,' she said. 'All I need is your happiness.' And she gave her a kiss for the rose. But Klávdinka went on, 'Mama dear! what is happiness? I live with you and I am happy, but there are a great many unhappy people in the world.'

"So she kept harping on her old idea, even on her mother's name-day! I couldn't stand any more and I said, 'Look, Klávdinka, on the name-day of your mother's guardian angel you might at least keep quiet about your gloomy ideas. There's nothing outstandingly pleasant in them at all.'

"But just imagine, her mother stood up for her and told me, 'Let her alone, Márya Martýnovna, and tell the servants to take the samovar away.' And when I had gone out, she presented Klávdinka with five hundred rubles. 'Give it to those poor wretches of yours,' she said. 'Lord, it is fearful to think what sort of people they are.' "

"But how could you see that?" asked Aíchka.

"I just looked through a crack. But Klávdinka didn't share any of this money with anybody in the house this time either."

"Why not?"

"Because she said, 'Everyone has enough to eat here.'"

"Well, she was right about that."

"How can you say that, my dear? You ought to be ashamed of yourself!"

"Not the least bit."

"No, you are teasing me. I know . . . As if all a person needs is to have enough to eat! And then no matter how many times I told her, 'All right, now, if you are only kind to people outside your own house, why are you so anxious that no one should know who you are helping out?' She would answer, 'The good man is he who cannot rest when others are not at peace. But I am not good. You do not have a proper notion of goodness.'

"'All right then, I don't know anything about goodness, but I do understand secretiveness. Why do you take such pains to hide where you take everything and who you give it to? No one can track you down. Is this really admissible or required by the rules of honor?'

"'Imagine,' she answered me with a smile, 'Yes, it is admissible and required by the rules of honor!'

"'Then kindly enlighten me, madam,' I said. 'Show me where these rules are, what holy book they are written in.'

"She went into her room and came back with a small volume of the Gospels."

"Always the Gospels!" interrupted Aíchka.

"Yes, yes! All the time! She was always reaching for her Gospel and dragging out some text I had never heard of in my life. Besides, she didn't understand them properly. She would always think up some quite simple and ordinary explanation that was not even interesting. Then she would give me the Gospel and say, 'Here's something you can do for yourself. Read this passage.' And she showed me the passage about how my right hand shouldn't know what my left hand is doing and that you shouldn't do favors just for your own circle of friends who can repay them . . . And so on.

"I knew I couldn't get the better of her in an argument, so I answered, 'The Gospel is a Church book, and its wisdom is sealed. Not everyone can understand it.'

"She objected right away, 'No, that's just the point: the Gospel can be understood by anyone.'

"'Well anyway,' I said, 'I had better leave the Gospel alone and ask the priest. Whatever he tells me I'll agree with, because they are the clergy.'

"And so I really did get the idea of arguing her out of it, and I went to the parish priest. The year before I had made him a present of a rose geranium plant. His mother was bothered by running wax in the ear, and the geranium leaf is a good cure for it: you just stick it in your ear. This time I went to the market and bought a titmouse. I took it out of its cage and tied it up in a handkerchief and brought it to him. He didn't like people to come to him without an offering.

"Once he had complained to me that there were an awful lot of bedbugs in his house and that they couldn't get rid of them. So I said, 'Father, here is a titmouse for you. It both sings and exterminates bedbugs. Only please don't feed it anything—out of hunger it will go all over the house and pick the bugs out of every crack and cranny.' "

"Is that really true?" asked Aíchka.

"What?"

"The titmouse, does it really pick out bedbugs?"

"Of course! It gets them all!"

"Amazing!"

"What do you mean? It's the most ordinary thing in the world. All our distillers and priests used to keep titmice for that. Anyway, the priest thanked me. 'I know it,' he said. ' 'Tis an ancient remedy. Put the titmouse back in its cage. When it has gotten its bearings, I'll let it fly around the room and catch bugs. The insect powder they sell nowadays is worthless; it has no effect at all. It's all adulterated.'

"I caught him up on that last remark, saying that it was impossible to tell what anything was like any more. And I told him about Klávdinka's antics with the Gospel. 'Is there really a law in the Gospel,' I asked, 'that says we should give up our acquaintance with important people and mingle only with the poor?'

"He answered, 'Hearken, O oaken grove, to what the forest saith:[15] these people interfere in what is not their affair. They can pick out texts, but they know not how to interpret them, and what they educe is vain and false.'

" 'And why,' I inquired, 'haven't you informed the authorities about these false texts of theirs?'

" 'We have,' he replied. 'We have, many times.'

" 'Then how can they dare to judge for themselves and base their ideas on the Gospel?"

" 'That is the way things are. The mistake is already made. These books have been printed in large quantities and sold to all and sundry for practically nothing.'[16]

" 'And why is that?'

" 'Well, it's a long story. People used to complain that the Scriptures were badly taught. Even then I used to say, "They are taught well—as much as each man needs. Cast not pearls before swine; they will trample them under their feet." And that is just what they are doing now—trampling them in the mire. And so this was the result: in the fields, failure of harvest, and among men, that incomprehensible disease called Beth-luenza.'

"So, to make a long story short, he spoke very well, but didn't give us any help. He even came to see them later, but when he was saying good-bye to her all he said was, 'You are oversalting it, Miss, you are oversalting it!' But soon after that she went him one better: she went off and disappeared altogether."

"Did she really disappear completely?" asked Aíchka.

"No, she sent her mother a dispatch, saying that a poor girl friend of hers had come down with the black smallpox; her mother was too old to do anything and nobody would look after her. Dr. Versteht had undertaken to treat her. Our Klávdinka had dropped in to see her and stayed on as a nurse, sending home this dispatch and asking her mother's pardon for not coming home—she was afraid of spreading the infection."

Aíchka sighed and said, "Believe me, she really had gone to the dogs!"

"Yes, maybe so; but if you talked to her, she still pretended that this too was according to the Gospel. She didn't care a fig for all the agonies her mother suffered, wondering whether she would come home pockmarked or blind. When she did come back—safe and sound—they had the priest talk to her again. And again he told her, 'You are oversalting it terribly!'

"But she had a joke ready for him. 'It's better that way, for if the salt shall lose his savor, wherewith shall it be salted? That's worse still.'

"But the priest caught her nicely on that one. 'It is not enough, Miss,' he said, 'to know texts. You must know more. The salt that loses its savor is not the salt that everyone uses now, but a weak Palestinian salt. Our salt is strong; it does not lose its savor. And so we have our own proverb about salt: "Undersalted—on the table; oversalted—on the back." It would do you good to know that. In other words, you can add salt to something that is undersalted, but for oversalting you are whipped.'

"But it didn't matter what you said to her; she wasn't afraid of anything.

"Then I said to her mother, 'It's obvious that no ordinary priest can put the fear of God in her. She needs something outstanding.' And I told her about the man from here.

"Her sister Efrosínya was simply bowled over with joy and started telling stories about things that had happened here.

"'Let's try it,' I said. 'We'll apply to him, and invite him here. Incidentally, it would also be a good thing for Nikolái Ivánovich, for his abstinence.'

"But Margaríta Mikháilovna looked somehow embarrassed. I saw that she was hiding something when she answered, incorrectly, 'In my sorrow no one can be of any help with her.'

" 'Why not?'

" 'Because she still orders her life according to the Gospels.'

" 'Please, enough of that,' I said. 'You have despair in your heart, and despair is a mortal sin. It would be another matter if it was the money you were worried about; he has no definite arrangement about how much you should give him. But whatever you give him, he doesn't keep anything at all for himself, not the least bit, but spends it all on good works. And Klávdia Rodiónovna herself worships good works.'

" 'It isn't the money I care about,' she said, 'but . . .'

" 'The trouble——is that it?'

" 'Not the trouble either. But what sort of faith will he find in us? That's what disturbs me. And it is not only Klávdinka. My brother-in-law Nikolái Ivánovich——he became an elder of the Church only for the sake of the decoration, and he certainly won't want to pray for his own abstinence.'

" 'Of course, my dear; but there is a remedy for that. We won't tell him that we are praying for him; we will pretend it's for Klávdinka.'

" 'And Klávdinka will be still more offended.'

" 'Well, we'll conceal it from her too: we'll tell her it is for her uncle.'

" 'And so we will start off by deceiving everybody. Is that a proper way to behave?'

" 'What's that? Yes, of course there will be a little deceit at the beginning, but they will profit by it in the end.'

"Margaríta was about to give in; I struck while the iron was hot and offered to go myself and arrange everything here. 'I'll find some outstanding people who know everything,' I said, 'and I'll go there and invite him, and then go meet him in a carriage. All you'll have to do is to give me the expense money.'

"She replied, 'That's not the point. But if he really does see right through into people's insides, I'm afraid of him, and I'm surprised you're not scared too. Or are you both free from sin?'

"Her sister Efrosínya Mikháilovna and I assured her that we were not free from sin, but that she didn't have to be afraid, because even if he could see right through you, he kept everything he saw to himself and didn't announce it to the world. Finally I asked her, 'What particular sins do you have on your conscience?'

" 'I have some,' she said.

" 'But what sort of sins are they?'

" 'Well,' she said, 'I don't really know myself. But whenever I start something against Klávdia, it comes out badly.'

" 'Well, that is temptation. And what else?'

" 'Besides that, my brother-in-law Nikolái Ivánovich has been living with Krutílda out of wedlock, and to please her he drove his own son Pétya out of the house. I am afraid of embarrassing him.'

" 'My dear lady,' I said, 'he did that to please a woman! Men in love always behave nastily to their children. These are all completely unoutstanding trifles!'

" 'No,' she said, 'it's no trifle to drive your own child out of the house. I have been on tender hooks for a long time, waiting for Klávdinka to make a violent scene with her uncle because of his injustice to Pétya.'

"I realized that she was just twisting about in her mind. What she was really afraid of was that he would discover something inside her beloved Klávdinka. But this time I didn't stand my ground; the hour for fulfilling the will of God had not yet struck.

"Once again she undertook to give Klávdia some diversion; she tried to get her to take seats for *The Huge Knots* and to hear Barebald,[17] but she lost patience with her and said to me, 'Dear friend, Márya Martýnovna. We consider you one of the family, and we always come to you for help eventually. Would you go out after her and see where she goes and who she gives her money to and why she doesn't want any pleasure in life?'

" 'Certainly, for you I'll do it,' I said.

"After that as soon as Klávdinka left the courtyard, I was after her like a police defective, but I kept my distance. If she walked, I walked; if she took the streetcar, I sat in the next car; if she took a cab, I did the same. I never let her out of my sight. Once, twice, three times I chased after her like that, and finally I tracked her down. The place she went to most often was a small white house, where she darted into one of the apartments with her packages. I went right to the janitor, gave him a tip and started questioning him. 'Who lives in that apartment?' 'A poor old woman occupies it,' he said. 'Who comes to see her?' 'A young girl and the woman's nephew.' 'Is the nephew young?' I asked. 'He certainly is!' 'And do they meet there?' 'Sometimes they come separately, sometimes together.'

"I had caught my little bird!"

"You may have caught her, but don't press on me. I told you, you may be as round as a loaf of holy bread, but I am still afraid of your needle," Aíchka interposed in a prolonged and sleepy drawl.

"Oh, you cute little thing! At least let me kiss your sugary little shoulder . . ."

"Not for anything in the world! My shoulders were not made for such kisses. Go on with your story."

CHAPTER SIX

"I went back home to the Stépenevs and told them everything as best I could."

"Well! I'm sure you did a good job of that!"

"Of course I did. A young fellow meets such an outstanding girl at an old woman's flat—do you need to guess what they do there? By the way, don't think I told her mother that. I only told her aunt, Efrosínya Mikháilovna. She recalled that their mother had been an Old Believer, and although she was extremely respectable in her behavior, she was still listed as a 'spinster' in her porter's records.[18] So she was sorry for Klávdia and gave me thirty rubles, saying 'Keep still about it, my dear Martýnovna. Don't tell anyone about this grandezvous, for that which is done in secret shall be judged in secret. If it has already happened, let her have her fun. She has a miniacute figure and *it* won't be noticeable; meanwhile we'll find her a husband. Then she won't be so capricious any more.'

"Aunt Efrosínya Mikháilovna started going to see matchmakers, trying to find a husband for Klávdinka, and she had considerable—you might even say outstanding—success. But just imagine, no matter who came and asked to marry her, she always gave the same answer: 'I don't know his way of thinking; it is essential for us to be of the same mind.'

"That's the way they do things—they don't choose a man for his family or his money, as they should, or like him for the exterior of his person. They choose people for their thoughts!

"Then she suddenly announced that she was of the same mind as a doctor relative of Versteht's. When her mother Margaríta, who is quite a portly woman, heard that, she plumped right down and sat on the floor. Klávdinka was about to help her up, but she ordered her, 'Let me alone. Kill me right here! Is he a German?'

" 'Yes, Mother.'

" 'And what is his faith?'

" 'He is a Reformist.'

" 'What do you mean, "Reformist?" What sort of a thing is that for us to be related to?'

"Uncle Nikolái Ivánovich was a little tipsy and said, 'I know what Reformists are. They're the people they hang.'

" 'Lord!' And Klávdinka half turned toward him and said, 'Uncle, stop getting Mother alarmed and making a fool of yourself. There is a Reformist Church.'"

"Nikolái Ivánovich said, 'That's another matter, but the item on the gender is that I, as the outstanding member of this household and a loyal putriot, desire you to marry an upright man of the true Orthodox faith.'

"She answered, 'What are you talking about, Uncle! When did you turn into a theologian? You talk like that, but you haven't the slightest idea what Orthodoxy is.'

" 'No, now you are lying! I was an elder and I even wangled a belly-band[19] for my priest.'

"At that Klávdinka gave him a gentle pat and said, 'That's all you do know, how to wangle belly-bands. You had better get up off that stool and have them clean you off. You are all smeared with clay.'

"Nikolái Ivánovich went out, and that ended it. But the next day he went in to see her again, drunk as a lord and seeing pink elephants with goats' feet all around. Again he said to her, 'Who would have expected a nice girl, the heiress of a merchant family, to mold such a monstrosity as this? What are these dummies for?'

"She wasn't at all angry and said, 'Order something else of me, and I will make you whatever you order.'

"Her uncle said, 'All right. I would like to order a statue from you, but it must be a religious one.'

" 'What shall it be?'

" 'Make me my patron saint Nicholas, showing how he slapped Arius in the face.[20] I'll take it and pay for it.'

" 'It would be better to show him caring for the poor or saving the condemned youths from execution.'

" 'No, I don't want that. I give to the poor myself, and I have seen people executed . . . That too is absolutely necessary . . . A priest accompanies them to the scaffold . . . But you show me how the saint smacked Arius on the cheek in the midst of the Council.'

"So a new argument broke out between them—about executions, and about the slap. At last Klávdinka said, 'I can't do that.'

" 'Why not? What do you care?'

" 'In the first place, I do care, because it is good to work on things you like, and I don't like that. And in the second place, thank God, it is now known that that fight never took place at all.'

"Nikolái Ivánovich was surprised at first, but then he started shouting, 'Don't you dare to say that to me! Because it did, yes, it did! He smacked him right in front of everybody!'

"Klávdia said, 'No, he didn't!'

"Her uncle said, 'You are only arguing with me to annoy me, because I revere him.'

"Klávdia answered, 'But it seems to me that I revere him more than you do, and I want you to know what you ought to revere him for.'

"To settle the argument Nikolái Ivánovich decided to go to midnight mass and after that to go see some professor and ask him whether the affair with Arius really happened. So he went off, and the next day he said, 'Imagine, yesterday I was playing pilliards with the professor. I took up the item on the gender with him about Arius, and he actually confirmed what our learned girl here said—the saint wasn't present at that Council after all. I was very sorry to hear it. I am likely to go through a terrible religious upheaval, because I liked that incident best of all. I flew into such a rage yesterday that I even let loose a pilliard ball at the professor's forehead. Now he is going to bring charges against me, and I will either have to suffer imprisonment for my faith, or else I will have to go and beg his pardon. That's the sort of calamity that Klávdia has brought on me!'

"He sat down and burst into tears. At that Efrosínya Mikháilovna stood up for him and said to her sister, 'You know best, Margarítenka, but what is this really, when everyone is crying on account of Klavdyúsha? Now even I feel frightened in your house; I'd like to run away.'

"Then Margaríta broke down and turned to me, 'Please, Martýnovna, go and invite *him* here.'

" 'It's high time,' I replied. 'This is now such an outstanding situation that all the ingredients can be mixed up in such a way that no one will be able to make out who we are doing it for. Nikolái Ivánovich will think it is for Klávdinka, and Klávdinka will think it is for Nikolái Ivánovich.'

"Both Margaríta and Efrosínya covered me with kisses.

" 'You are the clever one,' they said. 'Go off, darling, and do everything right and proper, so I won't have anything to do but pay out money.'

" 'All right, but write me a letter of introduction in your own name and in that of Nikolái Ivánovich, as the outstanding member of the family, so that I'll have something to invite him with. Without that it is unthinkable.'

"They agreed. The only difficulty was who would write the letter. The old women both wrote like hens scratching and were ashamed of their penmanship, and as for me, my n's and u's always look just alike, and sometimes you can't make any sense of it. Besides, we didn't know how to subscribe it: simply "To His Excellency" or "To His Super-Excellency"?

"We thought of appealing to Klávdinka; she had studied the catechism more than anyone else and ought to know all the forms for addressing the clergy. But when we asked her to come out of her room and write a letter for us, we had trouble with her again. She came out, sat down, and picked up the pen, but when she found out who we were writing to, she put it down again, wiped her hand, and stood up.

"Her mother asked her what she meant by that, and she apologized, 'Mama, I don't know how you ought to write to these gentlemen. Besides, if you will allow me to give you my opinion, I wonder why you summon a person from so far away when there are others of that calling nearby. Since they all do exactly the same thing, why offend your neighbors?'

"The old woman thought that over. I realized that a case of this singular aspect would lead to an infinitive discussion, so I broke in. 'Let it go,' I said, 'I will zip down to the fur shop on the Avenue. There are always people in expectension there, and they must know how to write him letters.' So off I zipped.

"They wrote it for me right away, and I went off to see Nikolái Ivánovich and have him sign it."

"You are a busybody," drawled Aíchka.

"Yes, I have a needle inside me . . . I have always been pert and lively like that. But just imagine . . . Tell me, do you believe in temptations, or don't you?"

"Well, sometimes I do and sometimes I don't."

"You believe in them once and for all. I have always believed in them, and they always come as though on purpose just when a person is drawing close to faith. So just imagine what happened . . . !

"I didn't find Nikolái Ivánovich in their store. The clerks said he was on a spree again and had gone off with some dry-goods Dutchman to the 'Pagánistan'[21] to have lunch and knock balls around. I went into the 'Pagánistan' and sent the porter up with the letter for Nikolái Ivánovich to sign. But he had already chased out all the Dutchmen and was sitting alone, drinking black coffee with cognac in it, and he asked me to come into his private room. I went in and saw that his face was the color of Burbondy. He still hadn't cooled off from the night before, and he added plenty of new zest to the old yeast. He tried to read the letter, but he couldn't make anything of it. He kept the paper in his hand and asked me, 'Why has this epistle to the Corindians been composed? I can't make it out at all.'

" 'That was what you wanted,' I said. 'To perform an outstanding act of piety and to give Klávdinka a useful bit of edifyance.'

" 'But now I don't care any more,' he said. 'If Arius didn't get a smack on the face, then no one needs any edifyance.'

" 'But we have already made a political conspuriousy,' I said, 'to take this learned girl of ours, turn her upside down, and give her a smack that will redden her cheeks. So look here! This is the person I want to bring to see her; all you have to do is sign this letter and go to meet him when he comes. It won't be hard for you to put on all your appurtenances for just an hour.'

" 'No,' he said, 'the way the item on the gender is now, I am upset to an outstanding degree. The most harmful sort of consequential affairs are being uncovered in my deal-estate bank, and if people find out on top of that that I am calling in some special Reverence, they are certain to think I am completely cleaned out, and that would be the worst thing that could happen to me. I don't want to have anything to do with your female political conspuriousy.'

"I saw what a regardless state he was in and asked him to come home with me, but he wouldn't hear of it.

" 'How long is it," he said, 'since you passed the exams for domestic affairs lawyers? I'll either give you a good domestic beating right here and now, or else I'll put an item on the gender and call in a political defective from the public room there and turn you in to be questioned for your conspuriousy. But if you want to escape all that, come along with me, we're going to a lying-in home.'

" 'Why a lying-in home of all places?'

" 'We're going there to pick up a certain staff midwife by the name of Márya Amourovna.'

" 'What has happened, have you gone completely to the devil? What do I want with a staff midwife?'

"But he was so indesistant that he stuck to me like a leecher or a leaf in the bathhouse. He had this midwife on the brain and started praising her to the skies, so high I couldn't even make out just what her situation was.

" 'Márya Amourovna,' he said, 'calls herself a midwife only for the appurtenances of the title, but she lives as she pleases. We'll go to the Hotel Angleterry[22] with her and we'll have a drink of Cluquot with her, *en trois,* in a nice and proper way. Then she will do a dance by herself.'

" 'Then why go *en trois?*' I said. 'I don't want to. You two go off by yourselves.'

" 'No,' he said, 'now there is a persecution of members of the female sex who take rides alone with men. Márya Amourovna might get in trouble. You'll be a sort of lady relative for us; we'll keep you behind a screen. For that I'll give you a cape made of caramel hair.'

"He kept after me until I gave in. We rode and rode *en trois,* and he kept hanging on to me like a leecher. I had to go with them and see all his infamies. They dilly-dallied there till morning, and I slept behind the screen. Finally the midwife started quarreling with him louder than before, and he fought back, and she went off alone. Then I managed to persuade him to come out and get into the carriage. But all the way he kept trying to go back, saying 'It's still early for me; I am a night owl.'

" 'What do you mean—night?' I said. 'Look at the clock on the watchtower: it's already morning!'

" 'That clock doesn't show its hand properly,' he replied. 'I can tell because I smell hic-scents; that means that the fuddle-drummers and saloon-players are still riding around in their night cabs. So it's still long before morning.'

"Then suddenly he got the notion that he had been given someone else's hat in the 'Angleterry.' I couldn't convince him that he had his own hat on his head, which he did.

" 'No,' he said, 'I remember very well. I had on a round bowler; then why should I have a flat topper on now? Maybe this is part of your political conspuriousy—they'll take a monumentary picture of me like this, and then I'll have to answer for you or some other dame and I'll be sent off to places so far away that the angels themselves don't know where they are . . . No, you won't catch me in any conspuriousy. I'll show you what a political trial is, and I'll shout, "Save, O Lord . . ." '

"And he started to call a policeman. To calm him down I said, 'The devil take you anyway! Go back to the "Angleterry"; I agree to all your prepositions.'

"He quieted down. 'Good,' he said. 'That's what I like to hear. Now we won't go back there; you and I are going to a dancing party. People criticize the hosts because honest women don't come to their parties; well, instead of an honest woman I'm bringing you. We can go on with the party there till late in the morning . . . But listen! Keep mum about this at home! Not a word!'

" 'Of course,' I said. 'Mum's the word. Why should I want to tell people about my shame and the places you have dragged poor little me into?'

"He started making up to me and said, 'If you want to be easy in your mind, don't get bad ideas. This is a public place; there are no crooks here—only people of various sorts, like Popular Councilors[23] and machinators. When we are together here we see each other's uncognitos and call each other "pal." There are three musket ears: Tupas, Tushas, and Tulas, and I am their commander. Tupas is a merry Dutchman; Tushas is believed to be a chemist in a factory, but he isn't that at all—he's really a great attorney-at-law; he'll turn you inside out—and Tulas is a machinator and ties everybody in knots. All you have to do is show him someone's card and he'll do the rest—make friends with him, tie him up, and deliver him into your hands.'

" 'Lord! What is that for?'

" 'For whatever you want or don't want,' he replied.

" 'Do you get a big salary?'

" 'The defective and the machinator do,' he said. 'But I entered this combination out of a noble desire for respectability, and now I can't get out of it.'

"The members of this gathering turned out to be mostly cocotties of all sizes. The big ones had on a random assortment of negligees, and the little ones were in silk undies, some of them in modest black ones, as if they were in mourning. They all went up to Nikolái Ivánovich like old friends and shouted 'Commander!' 'Commander!' I didn't embarrass them in the least; they shook hands and asked me politely, 'Met tay voo plass,' which means 'Take a seat.' But imagine this: as soon as he saw the defective and the machinator, he got that political conspuriousy on the brain again and whispered in my ear, 'You, if you please, will drink and not refuse anything, because this machinator is whirling before my eyes right now, and if I should get mad at you, I might tell him about the conspuriousy, and after that he might even mix me up in it.'

"I was more dead than alive. I thought I might let the cat out of the bag if I got drunk, but I was forced to drink anyway, and I didn't know how it would all end. The company was as awful as could be: this Dutchman looked like a watermelon from Komýshensk; the defective and the machinator were both small, but had terrific moustaches. There still weren't enough people for Nikolái Ivánovich, and he kept calling in people at random and introducing them to me. 'This man is an actor,' he would say, 'and I am very fond of him. He has grown old amusing people around the dinner table.' Then he would kiss him and say, 'Have a drink, old man! This man is a scribbler; he will write me a tender epitaph for my name-day. This one is an artist; he is going to draw me a plan for the statutory in the garden of Krutílda's summer place. This one is a basso rotundo in the opera; he sings better than Petróv.'[24] Then he would drop all the men for a while and try talking French to the cocotties in mourning. But he wasn't good at it; he kept putting in 'Come-on dear, come-on dear,' and they answered, 'tray share tea' and 'tray John tea.' He kept gurgling tur-tur-tur and 'pear met tay mwa sore tear' and stammering and jerking back. Then in Russian he would order something brought right away; they had to bring him everything—things they wanted and things nobody wanted. The Frenchies said nothing but 'passay' and 'passay back,' but they only pecked at the food, they didn't eat. The waiters kept bringing in more and taking away the stuff they had pecked at. Behind the buffet they kept adding everything in triple strength to the bill, but he went on ordering, 'Cluquot, Cornichons, Bradelaise, this kind of cigars and that kind!' They kept up their 'passay' and 'passay back' and finally got tired of eating. Then they only drank and clinked glasses and got into an argument about actors.

"The actor started counterdicting the basso rotundo and telling him he could never stand up to Petróv. They went on cursifying each other so awfully that all the cocotties left. The musket ears kept on slinging mud at each other at random and saying that nothing was any good. Someone even shouted that even Petróv was not worth talking about. The other would shout back, 'I like Timberlick[25] best of all.' Someone else said, 'I hear Calzonari[26] and Bosio'[27] . . . 'And I remember Barebald's appearance in *Il Drove Adore* and Lavróvskaya's[28] in *The Magic Marcher.*[29] Then someone said of Lavróvskaya, 'Why does she wink her eyes when she sings?' Nikolái Ivánovich stood up for her and shouted out that he admired Lavróvskaya most of all. He tried to imitate her, winking his eyes and singing in falsetto,

> *The bronze horse fell in the field*
> *And I ran up afoot!*[30]

"One of the military men didn't like this and said, 'Instead I'll sing you our regimental song from the Caucasus' and came out with:

> *Neath the Corkissus's crags*
> *With a shot in my insides*
> *I joyfully dropped off to sleep.*[31]

"The others divided up and took to singing along with one or the other of them. They made such a rumpus that it got quite impossible. Besides, Nikolái Ivánovich suddenly got into a fierce argument with the waiters about the cigars, and it looked like there was a threat of a real awful hand-to-hand grabble. He asked for something called 'Bueno-Gusto' and they lit it for him. Then when he asked for the box, the inscription turned out to be 'Gueno Busto' or something even worse. Nikolái Ivánovich took all the cigars, tore them to bits, threw them on the floor, and stamped on them. This was the sort of thing he usually did to start a grabble.

"At that point, to prevent matters from coming to blows, a German or Jew appeared from behind the buffet and began scolding him in French. But when money was concerned, he didn't want to be bothered with French; he thumbed his nose and asked in German, 'Habensi gelooked at that?'

" 'That is, you mean to say you won't pay?'

" 'No,' he said. 'Give me the bill.'

"When they handed him the bill, he wouldn't take it. 'This bill is padded,' he said.

"He started checking it. 'What's this written here, *"salade avec homards"*? I didn't order that . . . "Pickles capuchon"—we never had them.'

"The Jew said to him in Russian, 'Oh yes, you did, sir! That way you could say you didn't have any of it.'

" 'No,' he said. 'You can't talk to me like that! I'll pay for what I saw on the table. Here on the table I see a fish, and you can do with it whatever you wish, but I'll pay for it. As for the consummation, we didn't have it, but you put it on the bill and I won't pay for it.'

" 'What consummation . . . ? It's not on the bill at all.'

" 'Well, that doesn't matter, you added something else.'

"He got into such a fight that you couldn't do anything with him; he wouldn't pay a cent.

"So I told the boss, 'Be good enough to let him alone right now . . . He's in a state now, but tomorrow send him the bill at the storeroom. In general he is a very proper gentleman.'

"The Jew replied, 'We know that in general he is a very proper gentleman, but then why is he so bad about paying his bills?'

"But they let him go anyway. I thought that at last we would get him out in peace, but no, out in the porter's lodge he was about to give the porter a small tip when he got into another argument. 'These aren't my galoshes,' he said. 'Mine had high heels and carved tops!' He made a terrible racket and put all his change back in his pocket, didn't give the porter anything, and went off.

"Out in the air he started dozing off and kept crossing himself, half-asleep, repeating, 'Sane Pete, Sane Pete.' I gave him a few pokes to see if he was really dead, and he came to.

" 'I was afraid you were dead,' I said.

" 'I was afraid too,' he said. 'I seemed to have the ace and queen of splades and the king of drymonds.'

" 'Oho!' I thought. 'Now you've started to babble nonsense.''

" 'Nikolái Ivánovich,' I said, 'lean out the window. You need some fresh air.'

"He did so, took a deep breath and said, 'Yes, I feel better now . . . There's no more hic-scents in the air. The fuddle-drummers and saloon-players must have gone away. The little shops are already opening. Thank the Lord, it's morning! Here's the item on the gender now: you get out of the carriage and walk home; I am going alone outside the city gates and have some tea in a regular tavern.'

" 'Why don't you have your tea at home?' I said.

" 'No, no, no,' he answered. 'What kind of a domestic-affairs lawyer are you? I want to go outside the gates; I'm going to meet the professor there and take up an entirely different item on the gender with him with regard to Arius.'

" 'How about signing this letter?' I said.

"He told me to go to the devil. I even burst into tears. What was I to do? Everything I had endured that night had apparently gone up in smoke. I tried to wheedle him—I even kissed his hand, but what was that to him?

" 'Don't make me late,' he said. 'Here's a ruble for you. Go into that little shop and have the clerk sign for me. They do things like that.' And he kicked me right out of the carriage.

"I got out and went into the shop. The clerk crossed himself and said, 'You are the first customer, God bless you.' But he wouldn't sign for Nikolái Ivánovich. 'Of course,' he said, 'this is an unimportant matter, but right now we are afraid of the police and we don't even keep ink in the shop.'

"Fortunately for me, a palm-reader came rushing in at that point wanting to buy the sourest kvas they had, and he advised me to hop over to the church and see the sextant who signs the holy bread. He was sure to sign it. He did sign it, but the idiot added some unnecessary words: 'Nikolái Stépenev *and all his kin.*'[32]

"To make matters worse, I didn't look it over until later. I had had enough and was fagged out. I put the letter in my bosom and went home.

There I described all the antics of his majesty, beginning with Márya Amourovna, to his sisters, but I swore them to secrecy. Then I said, 'Figure out yourselves what to do with him.'

"Margaríta Mikháilovna, however, couldn't make up her mind yet; she was still in an indefinitive mood, thinking it would be enough if she took back the power of attorney she had given him. 'But by the way,' she added, 'if Klávdinka won't give up this life of simplicity of hers and still insists on marrying the Reformíst, then I'll agree; go and ask *him* to come.'

"They called Klávdinka.

"'Klávdia! Maybe you thought things over last night and won't insist any more that Versteht's brother is the man who suits your ideas. If you have, tell me, and we won't send Márya Martýnovna.'

"Klávdia answered in her usual caressing way, 'No, Mama dear. I cannot give up that idea. He is an honest and good man, and I love him because with him I could pursue in harmony the same aim in life.'

"'What is this aim of your life? Not to care for yourself, but only for others?'

"'Yes, Mama, to care not only for yourself, but for others as well.'

"'That is meddling where you're not wanted.'

"Then Margaríta Mikháilovna turned to me and said, 'In that case, Márya Martýnovna, go ahead.'

"At that for the first time in my life I saw Klávdinka cross herself up. She was a tight-lipped one all right, but she blushed and said, 'Mama! If you are sending off this strange expedition for my sake, then let me assure you it will come to nothing.'

"'Never mind, never mind. Let it go.'

"'But darling, nothing at all will come of it.'

"'Well, we'll see about that. Other people have benefited by it, and it will help us too. Go ahead, Márya Martýnovna.'

"Klávdinka pleaded with her some more to give it up, but her mother answered, 'Really, what business is it of yours? I only want to do some outstanding praying for myself! I trust I have the right to do that?'

"'All right, Mama, as you please!' replied Klávdinka, and went off to her room to mold some more forest sprites. I went off to do the will of him who sent me. I thought it would be simple to arrange everything here, just as you hope to now."

"Don't you bother yourself about me!" returned Aíchka. "I am a bold girl and I know why I can afford to be bold; I'm not afraid to spend money. If I want anyone, I make them come to me; if I want to go anywhere, I take a first-class ticket in a compartment."

"Well, I don't know how much you intend to spend, but even with money you sometimes have to eat crow."

"Oh no, with money you can tell anyone 'habenzi gelooked.' "

"No, when they get hold of you, you won't 'gelook' at any more of it."

"How are they going to get my own money away from me?"

"Yes, yes, yes! Anyway, I started off then, thinking everything would go very easily."

"What made it so hard?"

"There's not a single person on earth who can imagine everything that can happen at a big expectension."

"Don't keep beating around the bush and trying to show off how much you can do for me. Tell me what outstanding things happened to you."

" 'Habenzi'—you'll see."

"Now listen, don't you dare talk to me like that. I don't like it."

"Why not?"

"Because don't you repeat my jokes, but tell me how you came here and what started after that."

"Well, the Bassompierres started."

"Wait a minute. 'The Bassompierres started.' What on earth are Bassompierres? You look like you are mad at me. Well, don't sulk and also don't talk to me in an angry voice. With my money I'm not afraid of anything. I didn't insult you, and I don't like to spoil people who are my servants. Tell me now, what are Bassompierres?" [33]

"People called that."

"Well, tell me about them.

Poor Márya Martýnovna sighed, and swallowing half her sigh, continued her story.

CHAPTER SEVEN

"It was here my real troubles began," said Márya Martýnovna as she took up her story again. "Right from the beginning. I had no sooner got off the train and started walking than I ran into a real fine man, a cab-driver. He was an easygoing chap, but a great talker—he was really good at that. As soon as he saw I didn't know my way around here, he bowed to me and said, 'Having offered you my best wishes, may I make bold to inquire whether you intend going to hear the singer or to the Expectension?' "

"I didn't even understand him and said, 'Who is this singer? Why should I go hear him?'

" 'He does everything with a chord,' he replied.

"What the cabman said was undoubtedly very useful and fine, but I didn't understand what he meant by 'a chord'; so I said, 'I only want to know where the expectants gather.'

" 'Absolutely nothing will come of it. You'd better have the singer make you a chord, since he always accompanies *him* and is always at his elbow,' said the cabman quietly.

'Well,' I said, 'he must be some sort of sharper. I don't want to have anything to do with the likes of him, and I don't intend to take your advice.'

" 'Well, get in,' he said. 'For twenty kopecks I'll take you to the Expectension.'

"He brought me here honestly, but when I got here, the place seemed to have a peculiar air about it. I didn't find anybody downstairs but the boy who unsticks the stamps from envelopes. I asked him, 'Where does the audience take place?'

" 'Here,' he answered in a whisper.

" 'And where are the grown-ups?'

"He didn't know. No matter what I asked him, he didn't know. He had apparently been drilled not to say too much.

" 'And why,' I asked, 'are you collecting all those stamps? Can you answer that one?'

"He could. 'For that they give you a bottle of oil and a package of tea in Jerusalem,' he replied.

" 'A clever lad,' I thought, 'quite the business man.' But anyway, instead of listening to his childish conversation I would do better to go to church and see if the audience was being held there and incidentally say a prayer to the holy icon.

"I saw a crowd of people around the church who I took to be in a state of expectension too. Some other people kept going up to them and going away again and whispering. They looked exactly like plain-clothes defectives. That's what I took them for right off, and I thought perhaps that here too they were taking monumentary pictures of the passers-by, but later I found out that they were a local breed of Bassompierres. One of the ones walking around was a man of arthlectic build with a terribly outstanding knobby nose. He came up to me and asked in a pumpous tone, 'On whose recommendation are you here and where are you staying?'

" 'What kind of a cross-examination is this?' I replied. 'What business is it of yours?'

" 'Of course it's our business,' he answered. 'We are Moiséi Kartónych's men and we stay close to *him*.'

" 'Shoo! Now who on earth is Moiséi Kartónych and what does he count for?'

" 'Aha!' he said. 'So you don't know yet what he counts for! Then listen: he sits on heron eggs in a swamp and raises live cranes.'

"I told him I wasn't interested and asked if he knew where the leash-holder was. He nodded his head toward the church.

" 'Will vespers be over soon?' I asked.

" 'This isn't vespers for us; this is midnight mass.'

" 'That can't be,' I said. 'There is no outstanding holiday tomorrow.'

" 'There isn't for you, but there is for us.'

" 'What holiday is it for you?'

" 'To tell the truth,' he said, 'I don't know exactly. It's either the Seven Sleeping Maidens or the decrepitation of St. Cropius' head.' [34]

" 'Well,' I said, 'I see that even though you seem to be expecting something in front of a holy place, you are really crooks.'

" 'Yes, yes,' he replied, 'and now, with my best wishes, you beat it if you don't want to get thrashed.'

"I didn't say any more and went into the church. I stood through the service, but even there I kept noticing defectives whispering among themselves. I began to worry that when everyone crowded up to the holy image they would certainly grab my money. I went out, came back here, and took a room almost like this one, but much, much smaller, for two rubles. I saw all sorts of different people in the corridor and I began listening to what they said. There was an officer who had come from Tashként and brought his wife from there; she had suffered an unimaginable misfortune. They were riding on a camel cart in a terrible heat. The camel walked unevenly, jerking all the time, and she was feeding a baby at the breast, and on account of the rough ride the milk in her breasts fermented into koumiss! [35] The baby died of the koumiss, but she didn't want to bury it in the sand, and because of that a sort of craziness came over her. These people wanted to receive the very first blessing the next day and as much money as possible. I mean to say, naturally, the crazy woman wasn't trying to get it herself, but her husband was. To tell the truth, he was an unpleasant-looking man, with red eyes, and he kept playing up to everybody here, trying to get them to arrange a grant for him. He kept wheedling them, 'Try your best, and we'll go halves on what God grants.' But they would have nothing to do with him. Why go halves, when everybody would be glad to get it all for himself! Well, since I didn't intend to ask for any monetary blessings from him, I was puffed up with conceit and thought, 'What do I care? I don't need any help!' I hoped to take it all in with my female brain and so gain an outstanding end of my expectension. But who had the real power and what the most outstanding thing was—that I didn't understand."

"And what was the most outstanding thing?" inquired Aíchka curiously.

"Try and guess."

"I don't like guessing, but wouldn't it most likely be the blessing?"

"Exactly right: the blessing, but what sort of blessing? Anyone can say 'blessing,' but not everybody understands just what this blessing consists of. You must have studied sacred history, haven't you?"

"I did, but I've forgotten everything."

"How could you? It is unthinkable to forget everything."

"Well, that's what I did."

"Well, you remember Esau and Jacob. God discriminated between them when they were still in the womb: he loved Jacob and hated Esau."

Aíchka burst out laughing.

"What are you laughing at, darling?"

"What sort of tales are you spinning me?"

"Oh no, pardon me. Those are no tales."

"Do you think I don't understand? In his mother's womb a baby doesn't eat or drink anything; he only sweats. So what reason could there be for loving one and hating the other? The mother might hate them if she was ashamed of being pregnant, but what does God care about that?"

"Well, why God took a dislike for Esau—you ask the priests about that, not me. But the first blessing is always the most outstanding. Jacob put sheepskin stocking feet on his hands and grabbed the first blessing for himself, and Esau was left with the second. The second blessing can't be compared to the first. In this place here people have noticed that the most outstanding thing is to get hold of *him* as early as possible. Then you'll get your wish: money as well as a Bethluenza cure. But the later ones are all weaker. 'His power departeth and consulteth.' "

"Now I remember studying about that somewhere," Aíchka put in.

"Well, I may not have studied about it, but I took up my petition ahead of the others and put it down. But the leash-holder pushed me back and said, 'Please don't be forward.' However, *he* read my letter and said, 'Are you Stépeneva or not?'

" 'No, father,' I said. 'I am a simple woman.'

" 'They are all simple people,' he interrupted. 'But there are some Stúpins or Stúkins[35] besides.'

" 'No,' I answered, 'I'm not one of them. I come from the Stépenevs. It's an outstanding household.'

" 'Who is sick in their family?'

" 'No one is sick,' I replied. 'They are all in good health, thank God.'

" 'Then what is your request?'

" 'I was sent here,' I answered, 'to invite you to come and see them. They want to make a contribution to your good works.'

" 'All right,' he said. 'I will be there the day after tomorrow. You may expect me.'

"I received his blessing and took the first train back in great expectation. My heart was filled with the joy of victory: I hadn't bowed down to anyone and hadn't given anything to the singer or the wringer or the leash-holder and had managed everything just fine. I kept chattering like a magpie to the people going back with me, telling them he would visit us first two days later and that he had ordered me to meet him in a carriage. They asked me what fortunate family I belonged to. In my simplicity I didn't suspect anything and like a fool told them all frankly my own family was insignificant, but that the happy family was that of those outstanding merchants, the Stépenevs. Then an argument started about whether they were really an outstanding family or not.

"There was only one cook who stood up for them. 'I know some fruit-dealers named Stépenev,' he said, 'and they are outstanding: I lost my place at the general's on account of them—they passed off some fake cheese on me.'

"The other passengers pretended they had never heard of any Stépenevs. I foolishly went and gave them all the particulars, not having the slightest idea what lengths human nastiness could go to and what would come of it."

"What did come of it?" drawled Aíchka.

"Oh, there was a great hullaballoon. Suddenly the officer from Tashként rushed at me and started shouting, 'Shut up, you loud-mouthed imbecile! I can't stand listening to you, you irritate me! I don't believe that man is a saint at all. I spent twelve rubles coming to see him with my sick wife, and he only gave me ten rubles! What business! He takes in money like drinking from a trough, but when he gives it out he dribbles it through his fingers. And his henchmen keeping sounding their horns and printing rubbish. It's a bazaar!'

"At his yelling they all quieted down, because he had an awfully greedy look about him. He tossed two rolls to his wife like he was throwing them to a dog; he himself walked around and rolled his eyes in all directions.

" 'Don't answer him,' the others said quietly. 'He's a putriot who goes in for machicanery.'

"But there was a shopkeeper who recognized him and explained, 'He is no putriot; he's a swindler. That wretched woman he takes along as his wife is not his wife at all, but an idiot girl from a wayside inn.'

"And sure enough, as soon as we arrived and started getting out, two policemen came up to him and took him off to the station; the woman's relatives had been searching for her.

"We all let out a great sigh: Oh, oh, oh! What infamy! What treachery! And we were all amazed that *he* hadn't seen through him at all. Then we got scared. After all, how could you see through anyone in that hubbub? So we scattered, each to his own house.

"When I arrived home, I went straight to Margaríta Mikháilovna and said, 'Sign yourself with the cross and rejoice: God has been merciful. The day after tomorrow it will be our turn to celebrate and happiness will dawn upon you. I obtained his consent and in the morning I must go to meet him in expectension.'

"They were both delighted—Margaríta Mikháilovna and Efrosínya Mikháilovna—and they began to question me as to whether I had found out how they should receive him and present their request. I told them I had found out everything, but that nothing specially outstanding was needed, only tea with plain white rolls and grapes; if he should agree to stay for a meal, they could give him giblet soup.

" 'Maybe we ought to have some first-rate wine?'

" 'The only wine you can serve him,' I said, 'is first-class Madeira. But the most important thing for you to decide right now is who is to go meet him—you yourself or me or Nikolái Ivánovich, if he's in his right mind. In my opinion Nikolái Ivánovich would be the best, since he is a man and the outstanding member of the household. Only let's hope he isn't in one of his crazy moods right now.'

"They decided that Nikolái Ivánovich and I should go together; somehow we would manage to keep him under control until then. Nikolái Ivánovich was to ride back with him from there in the carriage, and I would come back in a cab.

"Fortunately for us Nikolái Ivánovich appeared that evening in a state of penitence and oblivion. He walked along waving his arms in front of him and muttering, 'A path, a path . . . goes the voice, crying prepare him a way in the wilderness . . . O Lord!'

"Then he plumped down in a corner and began searching through his pockets. I went up to him and said, 'What are you looking for—the day you wasted yesterday? Go up and take a rest right now.'

" 'Wait a minute,' he replied. 'I had a very important objective in my pocket, and it's not there now.'

" 'What objective?'

" 'Tverdamáskov made me an experimental portrait of Krutílda in undressabillé and I wanted to keep it so as not to show it to anybody, and now I have lost it. I don't like the idea of people looking it over. I am going out and hunt for it.'

" 'Now don't you do that,' I said. 'Now you're home, you hush up. You're not going out again.' So we locked him up for two days to make him come to his senses.

"The night after that I slept like I was in paradise, with ethereal angels flying all around me; you couldn't see their faces, but how they did flap their wings!"

"What did they look like?" Aíchka inquired with curiosity.

"They were like church singers with their investments and surpluses on. But when the dream was over and a new day began, my troubles started up again. Early in the morning we began bustling around, arranging everything for the next day. They were afraid to take a step without me. I had to go with Efrosínyushka to the fowlery and pick out the giblets for the soup—they had to be outstanding ones—and I helped keep an eye on Nikolái Ivánovich. The next day, when we were to meet him, I got up before it was light and ran to the coachman Mirón to have him do a good job of harnessing the carriage.

"He was a terrible rough one and an artful answerer and he couldn't stand taking orders from women. Whatever you said to him, he always had a cutting reply ready for you: 'I know it all figuratively myself.'

" 'Now don't you be coarse with me,' I told him. 'You do a good job with the harnessing—this is an outstanding event.'

" 'Nothing stands out any more. I don't care what you say; I'll put the harness on according to form, and that's all.'

"I was still more worried that Klávdinka might leave the house without me and make a skeptacle of herself, because we all knew she had no religion. I told Margaríta Mikháilovna, 'Take care, ma'am, that she doesn't pull off something outstanding on you.'

"So Margaríta Mikháilovna said to her, 'Klavdyúsha, please don't go anywhere today.'

" 'All right, Mother,' she replied. 'Why should I go anywhere if you don't want me to?'

" 'But you don't believe in anything, do you?'

" 'Who ever told you that kind of nonsense, Mama dear, and why did you believe it?' Margaríta Mikháilovna was overjoyed. 'Then you really do believe in something?'

" 'Of course I do, Mama.'

" 'What is it you believe in?'

" 'That there is a God and that Jesus Christ lived on this earth and that we should live as His Gospel teaches.'

" 'You believe that truly—you are not lying to me?'

" 'I never lie, Mama.'

" 'Swear it.'

" 'Mama, I never swear; the Gospel forbids us to swear.'

" 'Why shouldn't you swear for the sake of your mother's peace of mind?' I put in.

"She didn't so much as answer me a word, but her mother kissed her joyfully and said, 'She never lies and I believe her without any oath. You all want me not to believe her.'

" 'How can you say that?' I replied. 'I believe anything you want me to.'

"But I thought to myself, 'When *he* comes all this faith of hers will be put to the test. There is no point in splitting hairs with her now.' So I rushed off again to see to Mirón's harnessing. He had already harnessed the horses and brought up the carriage, but he was dressed in an ordinary peasant coat.

"'Why didn't you put on your best coat?' I stormed.

"'Sit down, sit down,' he replied. 'It's none of your affair. The best coat is only for winter.'

"I saw he was in a nasty mood.

"Nikolái Ivánovich meekly got into the carriage by me; the two ladies stayed home to get things ready for us. Meanwhile we had such outstanding adventures that they surpassed anything that happened to Esau and Jacob."

"What happened?" exclaimed Aíchka.

"The most outstanding first blessing was snatched away from us."

"In what manner?"

"That is where Moiséi Kartónych comes in!"

CHAPTER EIGHT

"So Nikolái Ivánovich and I rode up in the carriage. He had all his appurtenances on—his church-elder medal around his neck and a foreign order, the gift of the Shah. I was dressed as usual, modestly, as befits my station, nothing outstanding, but clean and neat. There was an impenetrable mob of people and several carriages standing in expectension. Some of them had ordinary horses and some of them had their manes clipped; there were grooms on the boxes with cracking-whips. Policemen were engaged in hand-to-hand grabble with everyone—they wanted to make them stand in line, but they couldn't.

"The assistant inspector was jumping up and down like a frightened sparrow and pleading with the crowd. 'Ladies and gentlemen! Don't be disorderly . . . ! You will all have a chance to see him. Why this lack of culture?'

"'Here's a man of education!' I thought. I went up to him and asked him to have our carriage put ahead of the others, because we had been assigned the first audience, but a lot of help he was! He didn't pay any attention to all my persuasive words, but ruffled up his sparrow feathers and said, 'What outcasts of Christianity! What swinish lack of culture!'

"Suddenly I noticed among the raffle that all my acquaintances of three days before had gathered there—the ones I came back on the train with—and especially the pious old woman whose whole family was down with Bethluenza. So I had a talk with her.

"'So you're here,' she said.

"'Naturally I'm here,' I replied. 'We were promised the first audience.'

"'You're from the Stépenevs, is that right?'

" 'Yes,' I replied. 'I'm from the Stépenevs, in their carriage. This is Mirón, our coachman.'

" 'Oh,' she said. 'Mirón the coachman . . .'

"Suddenly all the people gave a start and started making the sign of the cross and trampling on one another mercilessly, like a drove of wild horses trying to crush each other. There was such an uproar of groaning and squealing that, to tell the truth, it sounded like all the people had turned into beasts and were trying to strangle each other!

"The assistant inspector couldn't even yell any more, he only groaned, 'What outcasts of Christianity! What cattle without reason or pity!' The policemen were about to go into grabble again, but suddenly those bur-bondy faces crowded through from somewhere—the ones I had seen here, the Bassompierres who talked about the Sleeping Maidens. They scattered the whole mob at a stroke, policemen, expectants, and all! How they did scatter them! They grabbed hold of *him* and pushed him over toward some other carriages, yelling, 'This way! This way!' I even heard them mention the Stépenevs, but in the meantime they put him into somebody else's carriage and carried him off.

"I put up a shout, 'Wait a minute! this is unthinkable—that's not the Stépenevs' carriage . . . Our coachman is named Mirón!'

"By that time they had treacherously put him into the other carriage, with that very old woman, my pious fellow-traveler, whose family were all down with Bethluenza, and they took him off to her house.'

Aíchka intervened and said, "What is it? That's the way it should be."

"Why?"

"She had a sick family on her hands, and you didn't."

Martýnovna did not try to dispute this and went on with her story.

"I went up to the inspector and said, 'For heaven's sake, Colonel, how can you allow such disorder!'

" 'And what have they done to you?' he came back at me. 'You heathen! You did more shoving than anyone else. What happened, did somebody step on your favorite corn? There's an apothecary's, go in and get yourself a plaster.'

" 'The point is not the apothecary's,' I said, 'but that I was assigned the first audience, and she wasn't.'

" 'Why didn't you grab hold of it then, this audience of yours?'

" 'I would have, but the police didn't keep order. You saw it yourself, that it was unthinkable for me to get up to him; they grabbed away . . .'

" 'What did they grab from you?'

" 'They pushed me back . . .'

" 'But you had nothing stolen?'

" 'No, not stolen, but there was cheating with the audiences.'

"At that he waved his hand. 'That's of no importance!' he said. 'That often happens.' And he wouldn't pay any more attention to me.

" 'That's enough of you,' he said. 'Move along.'

"I went back to Nikolái Ivánovich, who had settled down in the carriage, and told him, 'What's the use of staying here? We've got to chase after them in a hurry and at least get the second audience.'

"He answered that he 'didn't care,' but Miróshka put up an argument right off.

" 'We can't chase after them,' he said.

" 'But you can still see them there on the bridge. Start after them and you'll catch up with them right away.'

" 'I can't chase after them.'

" 'And why not? You have always been a continual boor and an artful answerer.'

" 'That's just it,' he replied. 'I am an answerer. I'll have to answer for it. You'll be sitting in the carriage, but for that they'll formidably remove me from my box and put me behind bars in the police station. It's not allowed to chase after people at full speed.'

" 'Then why is that carriage there going after them in such a hurry?'

" 'Because those horses are different.'

" 'What's the matter with ours? How are they any worse?'

" 'They're not worse, but those are English racers and ours are Tambóv duffers, and there's a difference.'

" 'You may be an artful answerer, you've got an answer for everything, but the real reason is that their coachman is a better driver.'

" 'Why shouldn't he be a better driver, when their housekeeper in front of everyone gave him a whole bottle of cherry licker, and at home they don't even give me brown bread to drink with my tea.'

" 'You go as fast as he does and I'll give you a whole bottle of licker when we get home.'

" 'In that case,' he said, 'take your formidable seat as quickly as you can.'

"I got back in the carriage and we started off. Mirón kept up with them: wherever they went with their racers, we were after them with our duffers—we didn't lag behind. But whenever I looked out the window, it seemed to me that all the carriages going along with us were in expectension too. I counted seven carriages, and in the eighth I saw two ladies sitting and called to them, 'Keep back, if you please, this is my audience.'

"Suddenly Nikolái Ivánovich pulled me back with all his might, made me sit down, and hissed at me in a stifled nasty voice, 'Don't you dare yell like that! I'm ashamed to be with you.'

" 'For heaven's sake!' I said. 'What shame can there be with this shameless raffle?'

" 'That is no raffle,' he replied, 'that's a blonde I know; through a certain person she could put a very unpleasant item on the gender for me.'

"Then he gave me such a tug that my dress ripped. I got mad and smacked him on the hand and struck the door with my elbow. I hit the glass so hard that it shattered into smithereens.

"A policeman galloped up to us and said, 'Allow me to inquire what you mean by this scene of violence? What is that lady so noisy about?'

" 'Leave us,' he said. 'This lady is not in her right mind; I am taking her to the madhouse for a testimonial.'

"The policeman said, 'In that case go along!'

"So we chased off again, but just then we were cut off by a funeral procession. As if to spite us they were just taking some regimental corpse to be buried with a parade. There was a great lot of clergy, all walking by pairs in line, one after the other, with the archbishop behind. Then came the coffin. Then the soldiers shuffled by at great length, bringing up the rear with two cannons, as if they were going to make a fire on the crowd. After that there was no end to the carriages, most of them empty. Well, by the time all that had passed before our eyes, *he* had naturally gone and the racers were nowhere to be seen.

"We started off again, but we didn't know where to go. Luckily just then a man appeared from somewhere and said, 'Command me to get up on the box with the coachman; I am a co-pursuer, and I know where the first audience is.'

"We gave him a ruble, and he got up and we started off. I hadn't the slightest idea where we were going. The Stépenevs' house is in the Yamskáya village, but we had arrived at the grain wharves, where we really found a huge crowd of people gathered and standing in expectension . . . I was even scared to look, there were so many! We couldn't see *him* at all—he had got out of the carriage and, so they said, had been taken by force into the house to rescue him from the expectants. Now the doors had been closed behind him, and two policemen were stationed there and wouldn't let anyone in. If anyone got rough, they would grab him and take him away.

"Actually, however, all the expectants were behaving themselves very well, waiting and talking about his various miracles, mostly about winnings at cards and Bethluenza. Suddenly my master Nikolái Ivánovich flew into a rage.

" 'Why should I stand here with you bigots?' he said. 'I don't have the Bethluenza and besides, they might take me for a bankrupt! I don't want to fool around here with you any more waiting here. Stay here with the carriage and wait, and I'll take an ordinary cab and go off where I please.'

"I tried to argue him out of it. 'All are equal,' I said, 'in the eyes of

God. This is the expectension of God. If you wish to be deemed worthy of something outstanding, then you must wait patiently.'

"Somehow he agreed, reluctantly, to wait for one hour, and he marked off the time on his watch.

"During the hour we suffered through there I almost talked my tongue off trying to persuade Nikolái Ivánovich to stay. I was talking so hard I didn't notice that someone had come out of the entrance. That very second *he* was plunked into another carriage and rushed off to another audience. My God! Another sly trick! How could you stand it! We went after him again, and the third time we had the same success as before, because Nikolái Ivánovich with all his medals and appurtenances wouldn't come out where people could see him, but hid in the carriage. I looked too common, and they kept pushing me away.

"At long last Nikolái Ivánovich said, 'Now you keep quiet! I don't intend to be the last man in the suite any more. You can sit here and follow him, but I'm through with it.'

"With that he took off all his appurtenances and hid them in his pocket.

" 'Good Lord,' I said. 'How can I stay here alone? It is unthinkable!'

"But suddenly he got rambunctious and said, 'You stay and think about what is thinkable and what is unthinkable, and I'll go have some vodka and a bite of lamprey in the tavern.'

" 'Wait a while more,' I said. 'Pray to God with your fast unbroken and then eat. Everything is ready at home—not only lamprey, but all sorts of fish, and outstanding giblets and other appurtenances.'

"He actually told me to go to the devil. 'A lot I need that!' he said; 'I saw what your outstanding giblets are like!' But instead of going into the tavern, he took a cab and went off altogether.

"At that I actually burst out crying. I had taken a lot of baseness from people in my life, but how could I have imagined such outstanding vileness as that: they had dragged *him* off by force and by using someone else's name had lured him into the wrong carriage and carried him off.

"In my despair I told some others what had been done. They weren't surprised and said, 'Don't feel bad. They often do that with him.'

"As soon as he came out, I saw the same ones who had been so glib with their tongues rush at him like tigers, right before my eyes. For the fourth time they grabbed hold of him, pushed him into a carriage and carried him off.

"I simply dissolved in tears and shouted to Miróshka, 'Mirón, my boy, keep the love of God in your heart and drive those duffers of yours without pity. I've got to get to that fifth audience ahead of the others. Go at a gallop and don't let anyone pass you! I'll give you two bottles of licker!'

" 'All right!' answered Mirón. 'I'll give them a formidable rein!' And he whipped up the duffers with all his might so they ran faster than the racers. At one point we knocked an old woman off her feet and made a quick turn into a side alley. They caught up again and when the first carriage started making the turn, Mirón cut out in front of it and broke something off their vehicle. The two carriages hooked together, pulling theirs over on its side. Ours only creaked with the strain.

"The coachmen started swearing at each other. The policemen grabbed our horses by the bridles and started writing down Mirón's address.

"Just then *he* came out again, but this time I flung open the carriage doors and went right up to him. 'I beg your pardon,' I said, 'but did you not deign to promise to come to see us today? We are the Stépenevs, merchants . . . They are outstanding people and have been in general expectension since early morning.'

"He looked at me like a very tired or greatly surprised pigeon and said, 'What is the meaning of this? I have been at the Stépenevs' today.'

" 'When?' I said. 'Have mercy! No, you haven't been there yet.'

"He took out his notebook and looked in it to make sure.

" 'The Stépenevs?'

" 'Yes, sir.'

" 'Merchants?'

" 'Outstanding merchants.'

" 'Yes, here they are . . . outstanding . . . I have them crossed off . . . Their name is crossed off in my notebook. So I have been at the Stépenevs'.'

" 'No,' I said. 'I beg your pardon. This is unthinkable. I haven't left you for a minute since early morning.'

" 'But I went to the Stépenevs' the very first. I remember the family: an old woman in a dark dress took me there.'

"I guessed who that old woman was! It was the one I had talked to about the outstanding family of the Stépenevs.

" 'There has been treachery perpetuated,' I said. 'She didn't come from the Stépenevs' at all; the Stépenevs don't even live where you were.'

"He merely raised one shoulder and said, 'Well, what can we do about it? You wait here a little. I'll settle things here and go with you.'

"So I was left waiting again, this time for the sixth audience. I realized for the first time that there were people in the world like these Bassompierres! A whole guild of them had been collected; their master was the one who had made fun of me with the Seven Sleeping Maidens, the one with the arthlectic build and the outstanding nose. Vagabonds they were, guttersnipes, lazy idlers who wouldn't work. The only job they had was to keep watch and suddenly to crowd close together and not let anybody through. If you gave them something, they would stick him into your carriage, but if you didn't, they'd move back and . . ."

"Don't say it," joked Aíchka.

"I'm mum. Later on an old woman told me, 'Why do you follow him around like a fool? Can't you see who is running this show? Call over that man in the green blouse and give him something for his pains—he'll squeeze him right to you. That's their only bread and butter.'

"I beckoned to this industrial individual and gave him a ten-kopeck piece. But he was a sober lad, and not satisfied with my ten kopecks, asked for a ruble. I gave him a ruble; he cleared a pathway to our carriage, pushed and shoved, and finally squeezed him right up to the door, shouting, 'Good luck!'

"So I got him and took him off."

CHAPTER NINE

"I meant to ride separately from him, thinking myself unworthy to sit by him, but he was very unassuming and invited me in himself.

" 'Let's sit together,' he said. 'It's all right.'

"He is very simple and direct, even though he is an outstanding figure."

Márya Martýnovna's audience interrupted her and asked, "Where does his figure stand out?"

To tell the truth, I was also curious to hear that, but the narrator avoided answering it and said, "You'll see for yourself tomorrow." Then she went on:

"I sat on the front seat and looked at him. I saw that he was completely exhausted. The poor darling was yawning and kept taking letters out of his pocket. He had a tremendous lot of letters in his pocket, and he kept fishing them out and spreading them on his lap. He crumpled up the money as if it didn't mean anything to him and put it carelessly back in his pocket without counting it, because he never keeps any of it for himself."

"How do you know that?" drawled Aíchka.

"Oh, my dear, it's even a sin to doubt it; God will punish you for that."

"I don't doubt it, but I'm only curious . . . They say people steal from him—who knows?"

"I don't think so—I never heard about it."

"But I have."

"Oh well, he probably made up the difference out of his own money."

"That's just it."

"Oh well, that's clear. He's not interested in it . . . So he would open a letter, read it, put the money in his pocket and make a mark with his pencil. Then he would open another and in the meantime he kept joking with me just as friendly as you please."

"What did he joke about, for instance?"

"Well, for instance he asked me, 'What's the meaning of this? Is it true that I haven't been at the Stépenev's?"

" 'You certainly haven't,' I said.

"He shook his head, smiled and laughed, 'Maybe you are taking me there for the second time?'

" 'For mercy sakes,' I said. 'That would be unthinkable.'

" 'With you,' he replied, 'everything is thinkable.'

"Then he went on reading and reading and said again, 'But who was that then if it wasn't the Stépenevs? Because of this mix-up I don't know whom to cross off in my book.'

"I realized he was annoyed, but I didn't know what to say."

Aíchka interrupted, "How can he be a saint, when he doesn't see what is being done with him?"

"Well, you see, he supposed that the Stépenevs were the people where he had been taken first by treachery. They asked him to help their son, who is a terrible hell-raiser; he had made friends with a frivolous woman and wanted to get married. He wouldn't have anything to do with any other prospective brides of good family."

"Why was that?" asked Aíchka.

"You see, he felt a duty, an obligation to restrain her in a moderate life."

"More likely he just fell in love with her beauty."

"Of course . . . There was something outstanding . . . But I brought the conversation back to my own problems. I told him that the real Stépenevs didn't have an outstanding son . . .

" 'And what does the unoutstanding one do?'

"I replied that they didn't have an unoutstanding one either.

" 'In other words, they have no son.'

" 'None at all.'

" 'Then why do you mix things up with "outstanding" and "unoutstanding"?'

" 'Excuse me, that's just a saying of mine. The Stépenevs have a daughter, not a son, and the trouble is with her.'

"He shook his head in a tired way and asked, 'What is the trouble?'

" 'The trouble is that she is the heiress to a fortune and young and beautiful, but she doesn't want to live as she ought to.'

"Suddenly he caught on and remembered something. 'The Stépenevs, you say . . . Wait, isn't Stúpin a brother of theirs?'

"I didn't understand, and he was perplexed.

" 'We're going to the Stúpins' now, aren't we?'

" 'No, to the Stépenevs'. The Stúpins are one thing, and the Stépenevs are another. See, here is their house with a signal on the gate, 'Stépenev, merchants.'

"He looked sharply as if he had just remembered something he had forgotten and asked, 'What is the signal for?'

" 'It's the sign that marks the house.'

" 'Oh, a sign . . . Yes, I see it.'

"Suddenly he collected all the unopened envelopes, put them in his inside pocket and started getting out at the entrance.

"There was a tremendous crowd of people in expectension at our door. The raffle blocked off the entire street, and besides there were four more carriages waiting behind us for an audience.

We slammed the entrance door shut after him, but then an awfully annoying thing happened: an officer's wife who was trying forcibly to push her way into the house had two of her fingers crushed by some young lad and went into a kind of faint.

"We had just settled that when a policeman rang the bell to take Mirón to the station. They had to write a report on his running over the old woman and smashing someone's carriage. We hid Mirón in a hurry in the pantry room; I carried out my promise and gave him some licker. But inside the house there was something still more outstanding waiting for us.

CHAPTER TEN

"Naturally he made a marvelous entrance, like goodness personified, and said, 'Peace be with you all,' and blessed everybody—the mistress Margaríta Mikháilovna and Efrosínya Mikháilovna and the older servants. But when it was Nikolái Ivánovich's turn, we discovered that that most noble gentleman was not at home. Then Mama and Auntie rushed off to Klávdinka's room. Klávdinka was at home all right, but, if you please, she had no intention of coming out for the service.

" 'Where is your little daughter?' he asked.

"Poor Margaríta Mikháilovna, overcome with shame, answered, 'She is home; she'll be right here!'

" 'Right here' was a little strong when she wouldn't think of coming out.

"Before that she had been affectionate with her mother and had embraced her, not saying a word about not coming out. But now, when we had already arrived, her mother ran into her room beside herself, and said, 'He's coming! He's coming!'

"Klávdinka answered her in a very calm voice, 'Well, Mama, that's fine. I am glad this is going to be a pleasure for you.'

" 'Then come out and meet him and go up to him!'

"She only smiled that quiet smile of hers, but she wouldn't do it.

" 'So you want to make trouble for me?' her mother said.

" 'Not at all, Mama. I am very glad for you. You wanted to see him, and now your wish is being fulfilled.'

" 'I suppose for you it's not a pleasure?'

" 'Mama dear, it's all the same to me.'

" 'Then how could you say that you believed in God?'

" 'Of course I believe, Mama. I need no one besides Him.'

" 'But I suppose you don't need to observe any of the practices of the faith?'

" 'I do observe them, Mama dear.'

" 'What do you observe?'

" 'What is required of us all: to eat bread in the sweat of one's brow and not to do evil to anyone.'

" 'Ah, so that's what your beliefs are now! Then realize this: you are doing a great evil to me right now.'

" 'What evil? How can you say that, Mama? Well, forgive me.'

" 'No, no! You are disgracing me before all my family and before the whole town. What are you doing, getting ready to be a house painter or a laundress? What have you got all over yourself?'

"Klávdinka was kneading clay as she stood there.

" 'Put away your modeling right now!'

" 'Why do you want me to do that, Mama?'

" 'Put it away! Put it away right now! And take off that apron of yours and come out with me, or else I'll tear your apron off by force, throw all that clay-modeling antillery on the floor, and trample it with my feet!'

" 'Mama dear,' she replied, 'I'll do anything you please, but I can't come out.'

" 'Why not?'

" 'Because I believe that all this is improper.'

"At that her mother couldn't stand any more and—what had never happened with them—called her a bad name:

" 'You're a villain! A viper!'

"Her daughter answered her with an affectionate reproach, 'Mama dear! Mama! You will be sorry you said that later.'

" 'Come out right now!'

" 'I can't.'

" 'You can't?'

" 'I can't, Mama.'

"Then her mother slammed her clay figure down on the floor and began trampling on it with her heels. When her daughter was about to embrace her and try to calm her down, Margaríta Mikháilovna flew into a fury and slapped her right in the face."

"The statue?" asked Aíchka.

"No, my dear, Klávdinka herself.

" 'Don't be sassy with me!'

"Klávdinka gasped and clasped her face with both hands, rocking on her feet.

"She should have tied her hands!" remarked Aíchka.

"No, she didn't do that. Klávdinka merely begged, 'Mama dear! Have pity on yourself! This is terrible—why, you are a woman! You have never been like this!'

"Margaríta Mikháilovna, choking with rage, said, 'No, I have never been like this, but now it's come out. It's you who have reduced me to this! And from now on you are not my daughter. I curse you, and I shall send a request to the commission to have you placed in an incorrigible institution.'

"And so in such a situation, all upset and after such an exhibition, Margaríta Mikháilovna had to come out and meet *him!* You can imagine the outstanding lamentation!

"Apparently he didn't notice that there was anyone missing. He began saying prayers in front of the icons—he doesn't sing, but says it all from memory—but none of us prayed; we kept exchanging glances. The mother looked at her sister and made a sign for her to go and get Klávdinka. When Efrosínya came back she signaled that Klávdinka wouldn't come.

"Efrosínya went up for the second time, and the mother again kept watching the door after her. Again Efrosínya Mikháilovna came in alone and again made a sign that she wouldn't come.

"Her mother made a face, 'Why not?'

"Margaríta Mikháilovna signaled to me, 'Go and persuade her to come.'

"I indicated that it was unthinkable.

"But she said 'Please!' with her eyes and pointed to her dress, meaning, 'I'll give you a dress.'

"I went up. When I came in, Klávdinka was picking up the pieces of clay from the statute her mother had broken.

" 'Klávdia Rodiónovna,' I said. 'Give up making a skeptacle of yourself. Be nice to your mother and go down; please go.'

"She answered me in my own words, 'Please go!'

"I said, 'What a hard heart you have! You are sorry for outsiders, but here is a chance for you to be nice to your own mother, and you won't. You can at least do that even without any faith at all.' "

"Of course," confirmed Aíchka.

"Yes, naturally! Lord, no one believes everything the priests claim, but that doesn't make you hinder others from believing them.

"But as soon as I had finished giving her that bit of edifyance, she ordered me, 'Get out!' And what for? 'Because,' she said, 'you are falsehood incarnate and you teach me to lie and pretend. I can't endure you: what you say to me is vile.'

"I went back, and while I was explaining by signs all that had happened, I didn't notice that *he* had stopped reading and had gone over to the jardinary, broken off a stem from a flower and started sprinkling water with it. He thanked everyone, congratulated them, and didn't sing at all. Everything he did was somehow especially outstanding.

" 'I thank you,' he said, 'for saying a prayer with me. But where are the other members of your family?'

"So they had to lie again: they lied about Nikolái Ivánovich, saying that he had been called to the count's on a commission.

" 'And your daughter, where is she?'

"Well, at that Margaríta Mikháilovna couldn't stand it and burst out crying.

"Understanding, he caressed her like an angel and said, 'Grieve not! Grieve not! In youth there is much that is untoward, but later they see what is good for them and leave their evil ways.'

" 'God grant it! God grant it!' said the old woman.

"He soothed her, saying, 'Pray, believe, and hope, and she will be like all the others.'

" 'God grant it!' she said again.

" 'And God will grant it! It shall be unto you according to your faith. But if she does not care to come out and see us now, perhaps I could go in and see her?'

"When she heard that, Margaríta Mikháilovna actually fell at his feet from gratitude, but he lifted her up and said, 'What are you doing? What are you doing? It is meet to bow down to God alone, and I am a man.'

"That instant Efrosínya Mikháilovna and I rushed off to Klávdinka's room and said, 'Hurry! Hurry! You wouldn't come down to him, but he now desires to come and see you.'

" 'Well, what of it?' she replied calmly.

" 'He wants to know whether you are willing to receive him.'

" 'This is Mama's house,' replied Klávdinka. 'In her house everyone may go where he pleases.'

"I ran out and said, 'Come in, please.'

"He smiled sweetly at me in reply and said to Margaríta Mikháilovna, 'I say unto you, be not cast down! I work no miracles, but if a miracle is needed, there have always been miracles, there are and ever shall be. Take me to her and leave us for a moment. I must speak with her in nothing but the omnipresence of God.'

" 'Of course! Heavens! Don't we understand? Only help us, Lord!' "

"Well, I couldn't have stood it," said Aíchka. "I would have eavesdropped."

"You wait a minute. Don't get ahead of me."

CHAPTER ELEVEN

"We showed him to the door of Klávdinka's room and then ran around through the dining room, which had a window into her room over the door. Efrosínya and I climbed up on the table, but Margaríta Mikháilovna was too heavy and was afraid to climb onto the table; so she only stuck her ear up to the crack in the door and listened.

"As soon as he came in he put his hand on her head and said in priest style, 'Good afternoon, my daughter.'

"She calmly took his hand in hers, removed it from her head and simply shook it,[36] replying, 'Good afternoon.'

"He wasn't offended, but from then on he spoke to her coolly and formally.

" 'May I sit down and have a chat with you?'

" 'If you like, sit down,' she replied. 'But don't get dirty. Your clothes are of silk, and there is clay here.'

"He looked at the chair and sat down without noticing that he had accidentally knocked her little Gospel off it with his sleeve. Without any antecedent chit-chat he came out and asked her, 'You are engaged in clay-modeling?'

" 'Yes, I am,' she replied.

" 'Naturally, you do this out of desire rather than necessity?'

" 'Both from desire and from necessity.'

"He gave her an expressive look. 'What necessity?'

" 'Every person needs to work; that is his function and it is of benefit to him.'

" 'Yes, if it is not done to be fashionable, it is good.'

" 'Even if a person began to engage in labor in order to be fashionable and had not done so before, it would not be bad,' she answered.

"You understand, things had taken such a turn that it seemed as though it was she who would offer *him* edifyance. But he started questioning her more sternly.

" 'You seem weak and unhealthy to me.'

" 'No,' she said, 'I am quite healthy.'

" 'I am told you don't eat meat.'

" 'No, I don't.'

" 'Why not?'

" 'I don't like it.'

" 'You don't like the taste?'

" 'The taste, and I simply don't like to see corpses in front of me.'

"He was amazed. 'What corpses?' he asked.

" 'The corpses of birds and animals,' she replied. 'The food that is put on the table is all made of their corpses.'

" 'What! A roast or gravy is corpses! What simplemindedness! And you have taken an oath to observe this for your entire life?'

" 'I never take oaths.'

" 'Animals,' he said, 'are granted us to be used for food.'

" 'That's not my affair,' she answered.

" 'I suppose you wouldn't give meat to a sick person?' he said.

" 'Why not? If he needed it, I would.'

" 'Then what would happen?'

" 'Nothing.'

" 'And who taught you this?'

" 'No one.'

" 'But how did it come into your head?'

" 'Are you really interested?'

" 'Very much! Because this foolishness is widespread now, and we must know it.'

" 'In that case I will tell you where I got this foolishness.'

" 'Please do.'

" 'I was living in the country with my nurse. There was no one to slaughter the chickens, so we didn't slaughter them. We lived and the chickens lived and I fed them and I saw that it was possible to live without slaughtering anybody and I liked it.'

" 'And if at that time a sick man had come to you for whom a chicken needed to be killed?'

" 'I think that for a sick man I would have killed a chicken.'

" 'Yourself even!'

" 'Yes, myself.'

" 'With these tender little hands of yours?'

" 'Yes, with these hands of mine.'

"He elevated his shoulders and said, 'It is terrible how inconsistent you are!'

"She replied that to save a man you could even be inconsistent.

" 'It's simply obscurantism! Perhaps you don't want to own property either?'

" 'Under what circumstances?'

" 'It's all the same.'

" 'No, it's not; if I have two dresses and someone else has none at all, then I don't want two dresses as my property.'

" 'So that's it!'

" 'Yes, that is as it should be, according to the Scriptures.'

"And with that she was pleased to stretch out her dainty hand toward the place where her little Gospel always lay, but it wasn't there, because he had accidentally knocked it off. He stopped her himself, saying, 'It is vain for us to speak of this.'

" 'Why?'

" 'Because your only desire is to prove the straight crooked.'

" 'And it seems to me that your only desire is to prove the crooked straight!'

" 'That is all obscurantism in you,' he said. 'It is because you do not bear your familial responsibilities. Why are you still a maiden at your age?'

" 'Because I am not married.'

" 'And why not?'

"She glared at him. 'What do you mean, why not? Because I have no husband.'

" 'But perhaps you reject marriage?'

" 'No, I do not reject it.'

" 'You acknowledge that the most important mission of a woman is to live for her family?'

" 'No, I am of a different opinion,' she replied.

" 'What is your opinion?'

" 'I think that to marry a worthy man is very good, but to remain a virgin and live for the good of others is still better than being married.'

" 'Why is that?'

" 'Why do you ask me that? You must know the answer yourself: he who marries must take on cares in order to please his family, but a single person can have broader and higher cares than about his own family.'

" 'But those are mere words.'

" 'What do you mean, words?' she said. And again she moved her hand toward the table, but he stopped her and said, 'Do not try to prove it. I know where these things are said, but you must be able to understand them. The human race must multiply in order to carry out its mission.'

" 'Well, and then?'

" 'And children must be born.'

" 'And children are born.'

" 'And there must be someone to love and instruct them.'

" 'Yes! Yes! that is necessary.'

" 'And to love a child and care for its welfare is granted only to a mother's heart.'

" 'Not at all.'

" 'Then to whom?'

" 'To any heart in which there is love of God.'

" 'You are in error: for a child no stranger's heart can replace his mother's.'

" 'Not at all. It is very difficult, but it is possible.'

" 'But one can work for the general welfare in wedlock as well.'

" 'Yes, but that is still more difficult than remaining unmarried.'

" 'So for you there is no joy in life.'

" 'Oh yes, there is.'

" 'What is it?'

" 'To grow accustomed not to live for myself.'

" 'In that case it would be better for you to go into a convent.'

" 'Why should I do that?'

" 'Everything is arranged there so as not to live for oneself.'

" 'I don't by any means think everything is arranged in that way there.'

" 'What do you know about life in convents?'

" 'A good deal.'

" 'Where have you observed the monastic life?'

"But she cut him off, and said, 'Excuse me . . . Isn't it enough that I answer all your questions about myself? I am not accustomed to telling stories about anyone else.' And right in front of him she started kneading her clay again, just as if he wasn't there."

"Oo, what a smart one she was!" remarked Aíchka.

"How so, my dear?"

"Whatever you please—she could answer him like that and he couldn't trip her up."

"Oh no! He tripped her up all right, he really did!"

"How exactly?"

"He told her, 'Can you be so deceived that you think you understand about God better than anyone else?'

"She couldn't answer that and admitted, 'I have a very poor understanding of God and believe only in what I need to believe.'

" 'And what do you need to believe?'

" 'That God exists, that it is His will that we should do good and not think our real life is here, but should prepare ourselves for eternity. And so, if I remember only that one thing, I then know at each moment what God requires of me, and what I must do. But when I begin to consider what each man should believe, where God is and what He is like—then I get all mixed up. Permit me not to go on with this conversation. You and I will never agree.'

" 'No, we won't agree,' he said. 'And I tell you, it is fortunate for you that you are living in this time of weakness; otherwise you might smolder on a stake.'

" 'Perhaps you would conduct me there?' she answered.

"She smiled herself, and he smiled and said to her affectionately, 'Listen, my child: it grieves your mother so much that you are not settled, and it is the duty of children to pity their mothers.'

"At that something seemed to snap in her and her eyes filled with tears.

" 'Have mercy!' she said. 'Do you really think that after living with my mother for twenty years I have less understanding and pity for her than you, who have come to us just now on her invitation?'

" 'All right,' he replied, 'if you are such a good daughter, then choose yourself a worthy bridegroom.'

" 'I have already chosen him.'

" 'But your mother does not approve of this selection.'

" 'Mama doesn't want to find out what he is like.'

" 'What is there to find out, when he is an apostate?'

" 'He is a Christian!'

" 'Enough! Why should you not yield to your mother and select a husband from among your own people, people of circumstance and known to her and to your uncle?'

" 'Why isn't the one I have chosen a man of circumstance?'

" 'He is an apostate.'

" 'He is a Christian; he loves all men and does not distinguish among them by race and creed.'

" 'That is excellent. If he is indifferent, then have him adopt our faith.'

" 'What for?'

" 'So that you may be bound together more closely.'

" 'We are already closely bound.'

" 'Then why not make it closer?'

" 'Because nothing can unite us any closer than we are already united.'

"He looked at her attentively and said, 'And if you are mistaken?'

"Suddenly she answered sharply, 'Excuse me, I am of age and I feel and understand what I am. I know what I was until a short time ago and what I have become now. I know that a new life has been born in me, and I will not exchange my present state for my former one. I love and respect my mother, but . . . You must know that 'He who is within us is greater than all' and I belong to Him and shall not give Him up to anyone, even to my mother.'

"After saying that, she gasped for breath and blushed.

" 'Excuse me,' she said, 'I seem to have answered you rudely, but I have nothing more to add.' She moved the chair to get up.

"He also made a move and replied, 'Well then, if you are so closely united . . . You feel a new life . . .'

"She stood up, looked at him severely and said, 'Yes, we are united so closely that nothing can part us. It seems that we have nothing more to say!'

"He even swung away from her and said quietly, 'It seems to me that you are slandering yourself.'

"She answered him still more calmly, 'No! Everything I have said is true.'

"At that very moment Margaríta Mikháilovna gave a shriek and fell down in a faint on the floor. I, stupid sheep that I was, forgot I was standing on the edge of an ironing board and jumped down to help Margaríta. The ironing board flipped up and dropped Efrosínya Mikháilovna and smacked me below the belt with its other end.[37] We all fell in a heap and lay there. The racket could be heard through the whole house. *He* heard it and stood up, saying to Klávdinka in great dismay,

'What terrible disturbances! And all because of you!' She didn't say a word to that.

"Then he sighed and said, 'Well, I cannot waste any more time. I am leaving.'

"Klávdinka answered him quietly, 'Good-bye.'

" 'Good-bye—and is that all? When you say good-bye to me, haven't you a single word to say from the heart?'

"At that, just imagine, she perked up and gave him both her hands. He was pleased and took her hands, saying, 'Speak! Speak!'

"She answered him tenderly, 'Take no notice of us; we have more of everything than we need. Go at once to those who are in want.'

"With that she made him lose his temper. He seemed to choke when he replied, 'I thank you, ma'am; I thank you!' and asked her not to show him out."

CHAPTER TWELVE

"When he had made his appearance to the crowd outside the house, Klávdinka returned and came straight to the dark room where we were lying prostrate. She flung open the door and rushed to her mother. That Efrosínya and I were completely unable to get up—what did she care about that? Efrosínya Mikháilovna had dislocated her ninth rib, and I seemed to have broken my sacred Iliad. Besides that, we couldn't decide whether to be vexed or to laugh.

" 'She's a fine girl!' I thought. 'She told him everything . . . She herself doesn't hide . . .'

"So it all ended in this unheard-of and shameful disorder. We didn't see him get into his carriage: all the expectants were dispersed and again there was trickery and again he got into someone else's carriage and didn't notice, but started taking out letters. So they carried him off, and all our servants were terribly offended, because it had all come out differently from what they had expected. And then it turned out they had all heard Klávdinka herself, the mistress's daughter and heiress, beg him in front of everyone, 'Take no notice of us!' What more did they need! I don't think he had ever heard that from anyone before. People had only begged and implored him with tears to make them happy, to come and visit them, but she seemed to chase him away: 'Take no notice of us and go to those in want.' There were angry discussions universally. The coachman Mirón, who had always been a boor—and besides he had drunk two more lickers—brought his duffers out into the courtyard to sprinkle them with holy water. His duffers had just been fed and were snorting, jumping around, and fighting. Mirón tried to pacify them by talking to them, but he wouldn't take them back to the stable for anything.

" 'I,' he said, 'give glory to Thee, O Lord! I know formidably what the

Law and Religion require: first of all the holy water is sprinkled on the masters and then in the same manner on the beasts.'

"They took the horses away from him with some difficulty and took him off to bed, when suddenly Nikolái Ivánovich drove up in his most outstanding cups."

"A vile man!" observed Aíchka.

"A real scoundrel!" confirmed Márya Martýnovna and went on: "At that there was such an uproar that we were all completely worn out, and when twilight fell, everyone went to sleep on whatever couch he happened to be. But even in my sleep I dreamed how Klávdinka had distinguished herself with her shamelessness. Nikolái Ivánovich's snores could be heard through the whole house and Efrosínya was also sleeping face downward. But I couldn't even sleep—somebody seemed to be lifting me up, and it really was true. I pricked up my ears and heard that Margaríta Mikháilovna was not asleep either. She was walking around . . .

"I got so interested in this Margaríta of mine that I lay and made wheezing sounds as if I were asleep. But I had no mind to sleep; I kept the corner of my eye on her and listened to find out where she would go.

"She tiptoed through all the rooms, so quietly you could hardly hear her, and stopped by the jardinary. There she seemed to take some dry leaves in her hand; then she replaced the piece of sugar in the canary's cage, and picked up some little rag from the floor. She was listening herself, I noticed, to find out whether we were all sound asleep; then very quietly, tap-tap, she tiptoed out, like a thief.

"I sat right up on the couch and pricked up my ears. I heard her circling around through the hall and shuffling along toward Klávdinka's room. At that my heart gave a leap—what were they going to do?

"I rolled off the couch like a pea, tore off my slippers and put them under my arms, and running in my stocking feet made a different circle into the cloak room, from which there was a knot hole into Klávdinka's room over the door. Again I took my perch there very quietly, putting a chair on the table and standing on it. I looked in.

"It was half dark in the room. The lamp was burning, but the shade was pulled down so that the light came out only in one place, where she was modeling clay. She did that all herself—lit the lamp, put it out, and heated water in the samovar-top—all without the servants' help.

"And now, when the entire household was resting in peace, she, the zealous artisan, had already straightened up all her appurtenances as if nothing had happened.

"She was kneading and adding clay and modeling the devil knows what. I even looked at her figure to see whether there were any signs of what she had said about herself, but there was nothing yet, you couldn't see anything. She was still tall and slender.

"Her mother came in, but she didn't see her. My heart was pounding, thump-thump-thump. What would happen? Would the old woman give her a beating and would she take it submissively or, God have mercy, would she forget herself and raise her hand against her own mother? In that case I myself would be of use, because I would rush in and grab her arms and restrain her while her mother gave her a good lesson.

CHAPTER THIRTEEN

"I held my breath. Margaríta Mikháilovna was standing in the semi-darkness and moving closer and closer to her . . .

"Then Miss Klávdinka gave a start and dropped her clay.

" 'Mama dear!' she said. 'You're not asleep! How you frightened me!'

"Margaríta restrained herself and said, 'Since when has your mother become frightening to you?'

" 'Why do you talk like that, Mama? You're not at all frightening to me. I am glad to see you, but I was busy and didn't hear anything . . . Sit down with me, Mama darling!'

"Suddenly Margaríta clasped her in both arms with her palms on her head and burst out, 'Oh, Klávdinka, my own! My child, my little daughter, my treasure!'

" 'Mama! What is the matter? Calm yourself.'

"The old woman pressed her lips to Klávdinka's head; then suddenly she fell to her knees at Klávdinka's feet and wailed, 'Forgive me, my angel! My sweet! I have offended you!'

" 'This is a new twist!' I said to myself. I thought she had come to intimidate her with stern measures, and now she was asking her forgiveness.

"Klávdinka lifted her right up and put her in a chair and herself knelt in front of her and kissed her hands.

" 'Mama darling,' she said, 'I don't remember anything you said to me in anger. You have always loved me, and I have been happy with you all my life; you have permitted me to study . . .'

" 'Yes, yes, my darling, I was a fool. I let you study, and this is what has come of your studying!'

" 'Nothing bad has come of it, Mama dear.'

" 'What do you mean, "nothing"? What will people say about us now?'

" 'What do you mean, Mama . . . ? Anyway, let them say what they please . . . People seldom say anything intelligent, Mama; much more often what they say is stupid.'

" 'That's just it: "It's all stupid." No, if it has already happened, then I consent, so as to hide your sin as soon as we can. Marry him; I consent.'

"Klávdinka was amazed. 'Mama! Darling! Are *you* saying that?'

" 'Of course I am. Your happiness is dear to me; only don't leave my house—I would be lonely without you.'

" 'We will never leave you, Mama.'

" 'You won't leave me? He won't take you away from me?'

" 'Not for anything, Mama!'

"The old woman clucked, 'There, there! You've always been so good to me! And is he good?'

" 'He is much better than I am, Mama.'

" 'Why is that?'

" 'He is not afraid of death.'

" 'Well, why should he be? Let him live.'

" 'Do you feel for him?'

"Margaríta blinked and said through her tears, 'Yes!'

"They embraced again and both of them burst out crying. Will you believe it, even I was touched!"

Aíchka agreed: "Yes, it's very simple—they do touch you so!"

"Then Klávdinka calmly and without hurrying told her mother how his brother had had the kindest heart in the world and he did too: he would visit anyone, never quarreled with anyone, never asked anything for himself, forgave everyone everything, wasn't afraid of anyone, and didn't need anything.

" 'Except you?'

"She was embarrassed and replied, 'Mama! I worship him so. He has taught me how to live . . . He has taught me to feel everything that hurts people . . . He has taught me to love people and their Father . . . and so I . . . I . . . shall be happy forever and ever!'

" 'Well, go ahead, go ahead. Only . . . why . . . did you let yourself go so far?'

" 'What do you mean, Mama?'

" 'Let's not talk about it. Only let's have your wedding as soon as possible, and then I'll feel at ease . . . I am willing to forgive you everything . . . It's only other people that turn me against you. My sister, and that tale-bearing woman Martýnikha.' [38]

" 'Forget her, Mama: don't be angry at her—she is unhappy.'

" 'No, she is a vicious liar . . . She runs around everywhere and picks up gossip . . . I'll throw her out . . .'

" 'What are you saying, Mama! How can you throw anyone out? She is homeless. It would be better to give her some job so that she would have something to do and not to listen to the tales she bears about people. She doesn't understand how much harm she does.'

" 'Yes she does understand; she and my sister kept after me saying that you were queer. They wore me down to the point where even I began to think you were queer. What can be done if I am as weak as that? . . . I believed them and sent her to invite *him*, and from this general expectension I got still more upset myself.'

" 'It will all pass, Mama.'

" 'Oh, no, my dear . . . What has happened to you . . . That won't pass.'

"Klávdinka looked at her perplexedly. 'I don't understand you,' she said.

" 'Well, I'm not going to say anything if it's unpleasant for you. But I do think this: how can he be a seer if he can be tricked and put into someone else's carriage by treachery?'

" 'Oh, let's not argue about that, Mama.'

" 'I was going to give him five hundred rubles, but now on account of the unpleasantness I'm going to send him a thousand tomorrow.'

" 'Send more, Mama. I am sorry for him.'

" 'Why should we be sorry for *him*?'

" 'Of course we should, Mama . . . What a mission to take on oneself, what a part to play! People see him and lose their senses . . . They run around and crush one another like beasts and ask for money . . . Money!! Isn't it awful?'

" 'Well, it's all the same to me . . . The bad thing is that now there will be gossip; and I don't like to have people saying bad things about you. But I do respect Nikolái Ivánovich, no matter what he is—hell-raiser and debachelor—because he quarrels with you face to face, but he won't let anyone say anything about you behind your back. "For her," he says, "I'll give you a drubbing right now." '

" 'Uncle is a good man, and I am sorry for him—he is in darkness.'

" 'And why did they have to get up all this extraordinary business? All my life things have gone along in the ordinary way; our own priest would come and sing and have a bite to eat and play a game of cards and tell everyone "God will forgive you." '

" 'In all cases, Mama, the simplest thing is the best.'

" 'Yes, he baptized you; let him marry you too. And let's not have Martýnikha here any more, so she won't play any more of her outstanding tricks.'

"So that was all I would have got for all my troubles! But it was all decided differently, and quite unexpectedly."

"Who decided it?" asked Aíchka.

"The cat, and I too a little bit," continued Márya Martýnovna.

"But Klávdinka, to do her justice, finally stood up for me again and asked her mother to let me stay as a sort of outstanding servant in the house.

"The old woman replied, 'All right, even though I don't want to, I'll let her stay for your sake.'

"But my heart was all on fire. 'Oh no,' I thought. 'I can get along without you. I'm no great shakes, but I have my pride, like the haughtiest beast of them all, and I have a lot of friends besides you in this town. I'll never go into service as a lady's maid.'

"And I give you my word of honor that I meant to tiptoe right out of their house then and there, without saying good-bye to anyone, because heaven knows I am as proud as a beast. But imagine this: it didn't turn out that way.

"There was another incident that happened right on top of this one, and it held me back. While I was standing on the chair piled on top of the table, listening to their remarks, the fat cat got frisky, grabbed my felt slippers, which I had left on the floor, and the villain started knocking them all over the floor with his paw.

"Because of this trifle I was fairly gripped with terror. 'The wretch,' I thought, 'will knock a slipper against some light chair or stool and make a noise, and they will come right in here and how will I look to them on my watchtower? How can I look at them and what will I think of to say about how I happened to be clambered up here on the table?'

"I climbed down, terribly afraid of falling, and began crawling around on the floor looking for my slippers. I crawled and crawled; I covered the whole floor, but I didn't find the slippers. Meanwhile I was awfully afraid that mother and daughter would have already made it up and would come out and see that I was not on the couch where I had been sleeping. And then how would I go back while they were there—and through Nikolái Ivánovich's rooms at that? What would they think? So I ran back without my slippers and got safely back to my place. Nikolái Ivánovich was sleeping with his collar off, not snoring or tossing. I lay back on the couch in my stocking feet and just had time to pretend to be asleep when Margaríta Mikháilovna and her daughter really did come in."

CHAPTER FOURTEEN

"In a calm and collected voice Margaríta Mikháilovna ordered all the lamps to be lit and tea to be served, and she herself began waking everybody up for tea. When she came up to me, I said, 'I'll get up myself right away.' And I began looking for my slippers.

"And she, as if to spite me, asked, 'What are you looking for?'

" 'I am looking for my slippers.'

" 'Where did you put them?'

" 'I had them on my feet.'

" 'Where could they have gone off your feet?'

" 'I don't know myself.'

" 'Did your bridegroom come and take off your shoes? [39] But that only happens at Christmas time.'

" 'No,' I said. 'I don't have any bridegrooms coming to me, but maybe it's a joke.'

" 'Tell me another! Who would want to make fun of you? Please, everyone look for Martýnovna's slippers.'

"Where she got this irrepressible desire to look for my slippers—I don't yet understand. Just at that moment, to make matters worse, Nikolái Ivánovich came running out of his room in great excitement. He must not have had his sleep out or else he was frightened, because he was shouting, 'Oo ay la damn? Oo ay la damn?'

"His sisters-in-law answered him 'What are you saying, sir? What are you saying? Damn . . . ?'

"He was actually shaking with fury and replied, 'Damn means woman!'

"Margaríta Mikháilovna made the sign of the cross over him and said, 'What woman?'

" 'The one who has just done something vile to me.'

" 'What did she do? What was vile? Can't you tell us?'

"He tossed his head like a goat and in the most imperative mood said, 'I'll put this item on the gender for all of you: What bitch woke me up and left this slipper of hers on my bed?'

"And he showed them my slipper in his hand. Well, naturally, everyone thought it was funny.

"But I replied, 'That slipper is mine, but we must find out how it got there.'

"But he didn't listen to me. 'Everyone knows,' he said, 'how such things get there.'

"At that point the boy Egórka, the stove-tender, rushed in all pale and shouted, 'Someone is throwing something around behind the stove in our bathroom!'

"We went there, and there in the bathtub was my other slipper swimming around in the water, and that accursed cat was sitting on the edge of the stove.

" 'Good Lord!' I exclaimed. 'What is this? If everyone is trying to drive me out, I had better go myself.'

"And Nikolái Ivánovich hurried me on. 'Do us a favor, get out! We'll get along better without you!' And with that he turned my face to the mirror and said, 'Take a look at yourself and put this item on the gender: is it decent for you to go playing with your slippers?'

"The devil only knows what he meant by that in his drunken state of forgetfulness, and those foolish women told me they had drawn the interjection that I had been in his room and had followed him everywhere, even into the bathroom."

"And maybe you really did?" drawled Aíchka.

"Enough of that, please! As if I could fix it so that one foot was in his room and the other in the bathroom! It is unthinkable to tear yourself apart like that! But just imagine, that stupid old woman got offended and began whispering, 'I don't condemn anyone,' she said. 'But why should this happen just in my house, and just after a visitation . . .'

"I couldn't hold back and in return plunged a good fencing thrust into her chest: 'Don't say any more, please,' I said, 'about this being your house and just after a visitation! . . . Some people did such a job of showing the visitor out that they practically kicked him out.' And I told her how Klávdia had begged him to take no notice of everyone in the house and hurry off to people in want.

"But Nikolái Ivánovich thought that was as it should be. 'So he should,' he said. 'What was he doing here anyway? He ought to go off to the farms where the crops have failed and pray them in a big harvest for the multiplication of the loaves. He ought really to be ashamed of hanging around well-fed people like us.'

"'Why do you keep talking about shameful things to me?' I replied. 'It's not me that does the shameful things in your house . . . Look for it a little closer home . . .'

"As always, Nikolái Ivánovich liked to vent his malice on whoever came to hand, and he rushed at me like a hawk at a chicken and began to strangle me."

"Oh, my God!" said Aíchka sympathetically.

"Yes, yes, yes," Márya Martýnovna went on. "His sisters-in-law couldn't even get me away from him. He would have choked me to death, but Klávdia came in and said, 'Uncle, let go!' just like she was shouting at a poodle. So he let me go. Then Margaríta took five hundred rubles out of her bedroom and said to me, 'Here, Márya Martýnovna, are five hundred rubles as a reward from me to you. Now do as you please: either take this money for what you have suffered, or make a complaint against Nikolái Ivánovich and may God be with you. I am not angry with you, and if you would like to say good-bye to us nicely, I will give you still more, but please go.'

"'I don't make any complaint,' I said, 'because I am Orthodox.'

"But Nikolái Ivánovich bellowed, 'It's not because of that. You know that if you make a complaint, you'll get less.'

"'You can suppose what you please,' I said. 'But I don't want them to pronounce in court the sacred name of personality along with the maidenly secrets of Miss Klávdia.'

"At that he would have broken loose again, but Klávdia grabbed him and took him away and went out herself. Margaríta gave me three hundred rubles more and said, 'Dear friend, here, take this for yourself and go away. There's no use waiting here any more.'

"'I'm not going to wait,' I said."

"And you took the money?" asked Aíchka.

"You don't think I'd leave it to them!"

"Right! Or else Klávdinka would sneak off to her 'friends in need'!"

"Naturally!"

They were silent.

"Is that what you call saying good-bye 'nicely'?" asked Aíchka.

"Yes, I packed my things and by mistake instead of 'Good night' I told them 'May God rest your souls!' and went off."

"And you're not sorry that it turned out like that?"

"I'm not sorry; it's a sin to be sorry: they brought it all on themselves. God imperatively visited their sins upon them to make up for the way they behaved at the visit of His holy messenger. Their household had been outstanding in its magnificence, but now one calamitry has followed another and they have been reduced to the most ordinary position. And it all came from Klávdia Rodiónovna's tactical education, and if nobody puts a stop to it, she'll mix everybody up in her dilutions."

"Do you mean everybody started modeling appurtenances?" asked Aíchka.

"No, she did the modeling, and now they even give her orders for statutes, but she has brought still worse consequences on the members of her family."

"For instance, what has happened to them?"

"Well, for instance, this is what has happened: to begin with Nikolái Iványch. Once when he was coming back from his musket-earing he forgot what he had forgotten."

"My!"

"And it turned out later that he had forgotten he had in his pocket a dispatch from his son Petrúsha saying that he was returning the next day from his trip around the world. He did return and came one morning in a cab when no one expected him, and only then did his father remember the dispatch. He gave his son the worst possible reception and almost wouldn't even see him.

" 'I have no need of any trans-Atlantic idiot,' he said.

"But Klávdia was nice to this Petrúsha and only threatened her uncle with one finger of her left hand. Then she took charge of Pétinka and got him to the point where, though homeless himself, he asked his father's permission to marry that same niece of Krutílda, on whose account his father had exiled him. His father naturally wouldn't hear of it, and anyway it was unthinkable to allow it, because in the meantime she had committed still another transgression. None of us knew anything about it, but Klávdia Rodiónovna did, because it turned out that she had traced that individual, tracked her down in her misery, and had been supporting her at the old woman's place where I had followed her. There she had shielded her from all misfortunes and visited her, and finally convinced her cousin with this argument: 'You are to blame for her fall, since it was because you abandoned her that she fell again. You must smooth it over and take her and never reproach her with anything, because you yourself are responsible for all her misfortunes.' And she read the Gospel to him again to the effect that he daren't marry any other woman but that one and finally she won him over—Pétka agreed. Then she came and begged her uncle to let them marry and tried to convince him that the girl had a very kind heart and that her transgression resulted only from her being abandoned.

"The old man said, 'I suppose the item on the gender is: you think it's a good thing?'

" 'It is not good,' replied Klávdia, 'but it is the sort of thing you must forgive, because it all came about on account of you. He who abandons a helpless woman is himself responsible for her downfall.'

" 'Where is that written?'

"She was about to reach for her Gospel, but he took her hand. 'Let it go,' he said.

" 'No, I won't let it go, and if you are going to be cruel and demand that he abandon her for the second time, then it will be still worse for her.'

" 'How will it be worse?' he asked.

" 'You know better than I,' she said, 'what awaits those whom you lure away from the path of righteousness and then abandon. But you should know this: your son is no longer in your power.'

" 'Whose power is he in?'

" 'In the power of Him with Whom you will not dare to dispute: Pétya will hearken not to you, but to Him. The temptations of the world are not from Him.'

" 'So you are stirring him up against me?'

" 'No, I am not,' said Klávdia, 'but I say that they must not abandon each other! It leads to suffering and sin. After that Pétya would never be able to live with a clear conscience. I have convinced him and I shall continue to urge him to respect the will of his Heavenly Father more than that of his earthly father. And if you will not listen to what I tell you about eternal life, you will die an eternal death.'

"She talked and talked and browbeat him and wore him down until he was like a fish on a hook: his mouth was open and he didn't know what to say.

"And then Petrúsha started repeating the same thing after her, that his conscience had tormented him for three years in all sorts of places and still wouldn't give him any peace and that he had taken the guilt of this erring girl upon his own conscience and wanted to amend her life and his own.

"At that Nikolái Ivánovich began biting his lips and suddenly said, 'I suppose we must die and we really are all sinners. You look at a young mam'selle and right away you start thinking of ways to fix her so that the next day she won't be Mam'selle any more, but Gut Morgen. That is the viciousness of our whole sinphony; but Klávdia walks straight ahead!'

"And he gave his son his blessing to get married before the law and suddenly he even grew very fond of their little boy, his grandson, and even began introducing them to everyone, 'This is my son, Mr. Europe, and this is my grandson, Master Asia Minor.'

"But Krutílda had kept her pride and wouldn't stand for that. She went and married her Alconse and turned over Nikolái Ivánovich's I.O.U.'s so that he would be put in debtor's prison."

"She got him in a nice mess," remarked Aíchka, laughing.

"Yes. But Klávdinka wouldn't let her uncle go to prison; she begged a mint of money from her mother. 'This will be my dowry,' she said. And so her mother paid for him, and they sold their house and began living the whole year round at the factory. They are still living the year round in that hole, and Klávdinka likes it very much."

"And I suppose her beauty is fading there?" asked Aíchka.

"Naturally, everything is fading with that fool, but in spite of that the wretch is still very good-looking."

"And what about her Versteht?"

"With him things took a still purer turn."

"Did she marry him or not?"

"She didn't marry anybody!"

"He ducked out of it?"

"No, he didn't duck out, but they both started surpassing each other in one thing after another, and finally she packed him off to the next world."

"In what manner?"

"None!"

"But what happened then?"

"Nothing happened. 'We have found,' she said, 'that we don't need to take any obligations on ourselves and we also don't need to have a family.' They decided to remain friends according to their faith and that was all."

"What monsters!"

"Lunatics!"

"But how did she kill him off?"

"No one knew anything about it. Suddenly she came home very pale and didn't tell anyone anything, and later it turned out that he had died."

"Just like that!"

"Yes. Some poor child had gotten such an infection in its throat that no one would treat it at home. Following his brother's example, he went and for the sake of others wrote down everything about the disease, but he himself caught the infection and died."

"Was she very broken up?"

"I don't know how to say it—it was like she had turned to stone. Her mother said, 'Well, everyone knows about your sin; if you were not ashamed before God, it is not worth being ashamed before men. Go and say good-bye to him and kiss him in his coffin. You will feel better.' But she only burst into sobs and fell on her mother's shoulders, saying, 'Mama darling! I have already said good-bye to him.' "

"Did she confess?"

"Yes. 'When he started going there,' she said, 'I kissed him while he was alive; forgive me for that.' "

"You mean that was all there was to it, that she had kissed him once?"

"So she said."

"But what about . . . what she had confessed to before?"

"What was that?"

"Well, all you told me about . . ."

"Oh, about her conjugation in an indefinitive state?"

"Yes."

"Well, that remained in an indefinitive state."

"How did it come out?"

"Just that, nothing came out at all."

"You mean you had made up a pack of lies about her then?"

"I don't mean that at all; I mean only that I expected what would have followed according to the consummation of all the probabilities, but with them everything is turned around. It turned out that the 'new life' she had found in herself had been nothing but divine, as though Christ had united them only in their eternal thoughts. Just think how she could dare to think that up and claim such sanctity for herself!"

It took Aíchka some time to squeeze out an answer. "No, that's nothing. But where did they get the patience to live like that!"

"It's awful! Awful! There was absolutely no way you could upset them . . . No matter what you did to aggravate and insult them, they took it all, as if earthly grief didn't concern them in the least!"

"I think people didn't know how to pester them properly."

"Maybe so."

"No, definitely."

"What would you have done to them?"

"I'd put them barefoot on a hot frying pan and let them sizzle a bit."

"That's the way! That's the way! But they say that's cruelty."

Aíchka did not reply. She had either gone to sleep or perhaps had begun thinking of something "off the subject."

CHAPTER FIFTEEN

Márya Martýnovna stood up, went off somewhere, and then sat down in her place again. During that time Aíchka gave a sigh and said, without any apparent bearing on anything, "Sterile word-mongers!"

Márya Martýnovna understood what she meant and caught up her remark. "Yes, that's right! Some other girl might have a simple heart and live her life and do everything on the quiet and go to confession and repent of everything quietly. And no one would know anything. But these fools—wherever they step, they knock things about and then deprive themselves of any happiness. Later they shorten their lives by living for others, while they themselves remain in an indefinitive state . . . No, you just put this item on the gender for me: what's to be done with them to get them out of it?"

But Aíchka was silent again, and Márya Martýnovna resumed the conversation herself.

"Well, let's take your word for it, that people don't know what to do to them; I'll agree with you. But why are they so peculiar that they don't have any tears, never plead with anyone or complain, but accept everything that is done to them as if it had to be like that?"

"They are pretending."

"That's just what I think! For heaven's sake tell me this: such a disaster had just taken place—her fiancé had died. But the very day she buried him she sat down to work and even started a school to teach poor children for nothing. How did she get that way? But there's one good thing about it. Even though you say people don't know what to do with them, still they don't let them start up any little thing they please: her school was soon closed. But note this: again this time she wasn't at all bothered and didn't complain."

"They are incorrigible."

"That's just it! What can you do with them when they are so free from sorrow? They closed her school, but now she does services for everyone in whatever ways she can. She gives out books to children and sits down with them to read wherever she happens to be."

"That shouldn't be allowed either."

"There was a prohibition; on account of the books the district police officer came to make a general investigation of all her books. But when he looked through them, he left them all with her and even started apologizing.

" 'I have carried out my orders,' he said, 'and I am ashamed of myself.' "

"That's a good one for you!"

"That's not all! When she told him she was not offended and held out her hand to him, he even kissed her hand and said, 'Forgive me; you are a righteous woman.' "

"I suppose she won't get married now?"

"Her mother asked her whether she had taken a vow after the death of her first sweetheart not to marry anyone else. She replied that she didn't take vows. According to them it's not proper to take vows either. The old woman kept asking whether she hadn't perhaps promised the departed not to marry anyone. She said no to that too.

" 'Then perhaps you will gladden my heart and get married?'

"But she gave the same answer to that. 'I don't know, Mama, but I don't think so.'

" 'Why not?'

" 'It's very hard to live with me, Mama.'

"She admitted herself that it was hell living with her. And then on her mother's name-day she gave her mother a fine present by saying, 'Mama darling! I am yours! On this day, your name-day, I have made up my mind and have given myself up to serving you and the poor. I shall not marry.'

"That's the way things were left, and she is still living as an old maid. Instead of bearing her own children and surrounding them with love and tenderness and passing on to them the remnant of her capital, she has again collected a lot of ragged children and gives them clothes and sings to them about the frog on the path."

CHAPTER SIXTEEN

The conversation stopped. Márya Martýnovna was probably enjoying the pleasure of having brought her narrative to a conclusion in which her principal enemy, Klávdinka, had been put to shame. Aíchka made no response, perhaps because her mind was far away, thinking of something.

This conjecture was confirmed. After a rather prolonged interval she sighed and said, "Anyway, it really surprises me!"

"What's that?"

"Just imagine, I know an idiot just like that too."

"A man?"

"Yes, and a very interesting one, but this same foolishness has got hold of him too."

"Tell me, what kind of monstrosities does he commit?"

"Just like that girl: there's nothing he wants—good things to eat, nice clothes to wear—nothing in the world."

"And he doesn't need a woman's love either?"

"Imagine—he doesn't."

"That can never be! No matter what the situation, that doesn't go out of fashion."

"Oh yes, that's just it—it is going out!"

"I won't believe it for anything!"

"How can you help believing it, when I assure you it's true?"

"I just don't believe it, my dear one. A man can always be tempted by a woman's figure."

"And I am telling you, my cheap one, that he won't be tempted."

Márya Martýnovna seemed to choke on something, but she recovered herself and said, "Of course, my day is past."

"Even if your day weren't past, and even if you didn't have a needle inside you, you still couldn't convince me."

"Why is that?"

"Because they are completely inhuman. They don't worship beauty at all, but look for somebody who agrees with their ideas. So if you happen to fall in love with one of them, you get nothing but displeasure out of it."

"Do you like him very much?"

"How did you know?"

"Isn't it obvious? You ruin everything by showing your feelings to him like that."

"I'm not ruining anything; I just disgust him."

"The way a coin disgusts a beggar?"

"No, I disgust him completely."

"How can a rich young girl like you disgust anybody? What an outstanding idiot he must be!"

"He's not an idiot, but he's the same sort as that Klávdinka of yours. He keeps looking up things in the Gospel and trying to live simply and work and think about the poor—that's the sort of empty pleasure he gets out of life."

"Can't you attract him with all your capital?"

"Oh, what does he want with capital, when he doesn't need anything more than he has! You give him something nice to eat, and he answers, 'I don't need it; I've already had enough.' You ask him to drink your health and he says, 'Why should I drink? I'm not thirsty.'"

"Really, what kind of monster is that!"

"Yes; I won't live like that for anything."

"Naturally. Let him pick himself a wife that suits their style."

But when she heard that, Aíchka shrieked, "Wha-a-at?" and added sharply that she would never permit that.

"I'd rather see him on the table under a shroud than with another woman!"

"Well, that's a possibility," Martýnikha soothed her in a tranquil tone.

Aíchka lowered her voice. "That is—what? Can you really do that?"

"Put him under a shroud?"

"Yes . . . After all, a person might have to answer for that."

"You only have to wash out his shirt for him and put it on him for the night . . . That's all."

"Oo, what a vicious one you are!"

"But it's for your sake I would do it!" Martýnikha cut her off in some confusion.

"No, how could you dare to think of that for my sake! To wash out a shirt!"

"Well, let it drop, please. I suppose you can see I was joking!"

"You were joking! No, you thought you had found a foolish girl in love, and I would give you such a commission, and then I'd be in your power. I'm no fool!"

"And who told you you were a fool, my dear one!"

"That's just it, my cheap one!"

"O, Lord save us!"

"Yes, yes, yes."

"But how would you like to live?"

"To have him be my husband and live the way I want him to. That's all."

"Then maybe it would be better to explain it to him straight off: 'I love you; let's get married.' "

"There, can you imagine it? I have already been brought to that level of baseness. I did explain it to him."

"What did he do—get on his high horse?"

"Not in the least. He only pressed my hand and said, "Raísa Ignátyevna, you are mistaken on that score.' I even had a fit of hysterical weeping and I said, 'No, I love you and I'll give you all my capital.' But he . . ."

Aíchka suddenly burst into tears and sobbed and sobbed.

"There, there, my sweet, don't make yourself miserable," Márya Martýnovna begged her.

"Don't stroke me, I don't like it!" Aíchka said capriciously.

"Well, all right, all right, I won't. What did he say to you?"

"He didn't believe me, the fool."

Again tears were audible.

"Well, in that case he lacks either feelings or understanding," Márya Martýnovna decided.

"No, he has feelings, and he really understands very well. But he said, 'You are mistaken in your feelings—it is my despicable flesh that you love and you want to herd swine with me, but you don't love me for myself, and you can't love me in that way, because you and I disagree in our ideas and we work for different masters. I want to work for my own master and I don't want to herd swine with you."

"What's that? . . . What's that for? . . . What did he mean about herding swine and working for different masters?" drawled Márya Martýnovna in perplexity.

"That's just the point! If you don't understand, then don't argue with me!" replied Aíchka in a tremulous voice. A moment later she added still more angrily, "According to them consoling yourself with love is called 'herding swine.' "

"Ugh!"

Márya Martýnovna gave a loud spit of disgust and cried, "Swine! I swear, they are swine themselves!"

"Yes," replied Aíchka. "He said worse things than that . . . He'll pay for it . . ."

"For what, sweet, for what? What else did he . . . How did he insult you?"

"He insulted me terribly . . . He said I was not a Christian, that a Christian couldn't live with me and bring up children to be Christians . . . !"

"Ugh, he'll pay for that!"

"Yes, I told him that. 'I fast and take Communion,' I said, 'and you never do . . . Which one of us is a Christian?' "

"He'll pay."

"I can't change my character!"

"Don't try! Why should you spoil them!"

"I told him I would get embittered and that if I pleased, I would give away all my money, but I would do it the way I wanted and not their way."

"Well, now I understand you . . . why you came here! Of course, they'll carry you in their arms here!"

"A lot of use I have for that! But you don't understand anything at all!"

"No, now you've let it out."

"I didn't let it out the least bit. I'm simply going to test whether it is true that by praying here you can make someone's heart ache and fix everything the way you want it."

But Márya Martýnovna interrupted her at that. "My angel!" she exclaimed heatedly. "Here you can arrange everything by prayer. This place is just like Mount Tabor.[40] But you should know that God won't answer prayers for evil."

Aíchka lost her temper completely. "What sort of nonsense are you talking!" she shrieked. "What do you mean by 'prayers for evil,' when all I want to do is to lead him out of homeless loneliness into lawful matrimony and then fix it so that he will finally like the things everybody else likes?"

"Yes. That is, that he would not cleave unto the simple life, but should seek for himself not only what is of benefit to the soul, but also what is of benefit to the body?"

"That's all!"

"Yes, if that is all, then of course that is the blessed law of matrimony, and in that case God will certainly aid you."

"Yes, and now you please keep quiet, because it will soon be dawn and I am very upset and will look pale."

The Scheherazade was over. My neighbors said nothing more; perhaps they had gone to sleep. Following their sensible example, I too went into a brief doze just before morning. But I awoke soon after, left some money on the table to pay for my "expectension," and departed from Rome without seeing the Pope.

The trip had been of benefit to me after all; I felt more cheerful. It was as if I had grown rich on impressions. And now, whenever I happen to be returning late at night through streets where merchants live and see the multicolored icon lamps glowing in their houses, I no longer imagine there merely shameless hypocrites or the timid and hopeless snivelers of the "dark kingdom." I feel there the invigorating spirit of Klávdinka breathing upon me, a spirit providing resources for life in any situation in which the will of the Most High sees fit to perfect in the struggle against darkness that which is born of light.

(Translated by Hugh McLean)

NOTES FOR "NIGHT OWLS"
Introduction

[1] Quoted by Leskóv's son in Andréi Leskóv, *Zhizn Nikoláya Leskóva* (Moscow, 1954), p. 627.

[2] Hugh McLean, "On the Style of a Leskovian Skaz," Harvard Slavic Studies, II (1954), 93–108.

Text

[1] In the Greek Orthodox wedding ceremony the couple are "crowned" in church. Thus by Afchka's reasoning a true divorce would have to include an "uncrowning" ceremony performed in church. No such ceremony ever existed in fact.

[2] A runaway monk, pretender to the Russian throne against Borís Godunóv; reigned in Moscow under Polish protection as Tsar Dmítry Ivánovich, 1605–06.

[3] From *pomeránets*, "bitter orange."

[4] A pun on *krutít*, "to twist, spin," which also has the meaning of "to have amorous relations"; also *krutói*, "harsh, severe."

[5] A three-kopeck piece.

[6] The Russian, *plotéts Skopítsyn*, is a spoonerism for *skopéts Plotítsyn*, "the eunuch Plotítsyn." The allusion is to a famous trial in 1869, as a result of which one Maxím Kuzmích Plotítsyn, a wealthy merchant from Morshánsk, was banished to Siberia for membership in the outlawed *Skoptsý* sect, which preached salvation through castration.

[7] The normal Russian version of this name is *Makáry;* the Latinized form used in the Russian text is a further instance of Stépenev's "cultural" pretensions. He probably refers to Mikhaíl Petróvich Bulgákov (1816–82), whose ecclesiastical name was Makáry. He was Metropolitan of Moscow from 1879 to 1882 and a famous theologian and Church historian.

[8] Vladímir Monomákh, Prince of Kíev, 1113–25. Renowned in literature for his Testament to his children. It is unlikely that Stépenev knows exactly to whom he is referring.

[9] A reference to "The Cat and the Cook," a fable by Iván Krylóv.

[10] The pun on *tactical* and *practical* is a reflection of Leskóv's Russian pun on *reálnoe,* "real" and *royálnoe,* "piano," both of which were foreign-sounding words to Márya Martýnovna. A "real" education, according to usage in many European countries, was one that emphasized mathematics and the natural sciences; it was distinguished from a "classical" education, stressing Latin and Greek. In Russia the idea was popular in conservative and government circles that a "real" education filled students full of revolutionary and seditious ideas.

[11] Undoubtedly Shakespeare's *Othello.*

[12] The phrase as Márya Martýnovna uses it is a garbled quotation from Púshkin's poem "The Prophet" *("Prorók").*

[13] I.e., Meyerbeer's opera *The Huguenots* (1836).

[14] The reference is to a Supreme Executive Committee, headed by Count M. T. Lorís-Mélikov, which operated in the last years of Alexander II's reign.

[15] A proverbial formula traditionally used in announcing decisions of the peasant commune.

[16] During the nineteenth century the Russian government wavered in its policy on the distribution of modern Russian (as distinct from Church Slavonic) translations of the Bible and the Gospels, at times encouraging and at times forbidding or restricting it.

[17] A corruption of the name of Jacques Barbauld (1824–97), a French tenor who sometimes sang in St. Petersburg.

[18] Certain marriages performed by the Old Believers were not recognized by the state, and such couples were therefore living in sin from the point of view of the law. The porter or concierge kept legal records of people living in his building.

[19] Stépenev uses an invented word, *nabryúshnik,* instead of the correct *nabédrennik,* which was a rectangular piece of brocade worn on the side of the priest's vestments below the belt. It was given as a reward for meritorious service.

[20] One of the legends about St. Nicholas, bishop of Myra, states that he slapped Arius, the famous author of the anti-Trinitarian heresy, at the Council of Nicaea in 325. There is, however, no historical evidence of St. Nicholas's presence at that council.

[21] A corruption, under the influence of the word *pagány,* "dirty," of *Afganistán,* the name of a Petersburg restaurant.

[22] A corruption of *Angleterre,* the name of a Petersburg hotel, which incidentally still exists, under the more patriotic name of "Leningrádskaya."

[23] I.e., "Titular Councilors," the ninth in the table of civil ranks established by Peter the Great, equivalent to a captain in the Army.

[24] O. A. Petróv (1807–78), a famous Russian bass.

[25] I.e., Enrico Tamberlick (1820–89), a famous Italian tenor. His last appearance in Petersburg was in 1884.

[26] I.e., Enrico Calzolari (1823–88), a famous tenor in the Petersburg Italian opera (with a pun on *kaltsóny,* "underdrawers").

[27] Angelina Bosio (1824–59), a famous Italian soprano.

[28] E. A. Lavróvskaya (1845–1919), a famous Russian contralto.

[29] Weber's opera *Der Freischütz* (1821) is known in Russia as *The Magic Archer (Volshébny strelók,* here garbled to *streléc).*

[30] Garbled lines from Glínka's opera *A Life for the Tsar (Iván Susánin).* Nikolái Ivánovich has transformed the horse from "poor" (bédny) to "bronze" (médny) from a confused association with Púshkin's poem *The Bronze Horseman.*

[31] More garbled lines, from Lérmontov's poem "A Dream" *("Son")* There is a pun on "with a shot" *(s svintsom)* and "with a bit of wine" *(s vintsom).*

[32] A formula from a supplicatory prayer. Names of persons to be prayed for were written on a holy wafer used in the Mass.

[33] An allusion to the Swiss mercenary army that Marie de' Medici in 1614 placed in the charge of François de Bassompierre.

[34] The "Nine Sleeping Maidens" descend from *Twelve Sleeping Maidens* in a poem with this title by V. A. Zhukóvsky. "The decrepitation of St. Cropius' head" alludes to the beheading of St. Procopius in 303 A.D. Leskóv's original Russian pun is a dazzling affair that defies adequate translation: *"techénie golový Potókovy"* for *"sechénie golový Pokrópovy."*

[35] A drink made from fermented mare's milk.

[36] It was customary to kiss a priest's hand.

[37] Presumably this ironing board (a simple plank in the 1890's) was lying on the table mentioned at the beginning of the chapter, and the two women in their excitement stood precariously on the ends of the board that overhung the edges of the table.

[38] The diminutive has a pejorative connotation.

[39] It was a Russian folk custom for a bride to remove her husband's shoes.

[40] Mt. Tabor in Palestine, believed by some authorities to be the scene of the Transfiguration. The Russian form of the word is *Favór,* and it had apparently become identified through paronomasia as a place where prayers or "favors" were granted.

NOTE TO "A PRODUCT OF NATURE"

This is another example of what Leskóv called his "retrospective stories"—narratives so convincingly presented in the form of reminiscences that it is impossible to determine just where fact ends and fiction begins. Here once again we meet with Leskóv's Scottish uncle by marriage, Alexander Scott, for whom he worked as a young man in the years 1857–1860. It is not known whether the incident described in this story actually happened to Leskóv, but we do possess evidence from other sources that he helped his uncle resettle peasants from Oryól and Kursk Provinces on new lands to the east in the 1850's.

Leskóv wrote this story in 1893 especially for a book of contributions by various authors that was published for the benefit of peasants who were then being helped to resettle on new farms in eastern Russia.

Leskóv always prided himself on knowing the Russian peasants at first hand rather than picking up his information—as he once put it in a polemical article—from conversations with Petersburg cab drivers. He insisted that he knew the Russian peasants too well either to idealize them or to scorn them. "A Product of Nature" provides an illustration of his sober appraisal. It might be called an example of what Chékhov once said was his purpose in writing his short stories—not to provide any solutions or teach any morals, but simply to state the problem correctly.

A PRODUCT
OF NATURE

Taking one thing with another, perhaps few terrestrial Appearances are better worth considering than mobs. Your mob is a genuine outburst of Nature[1] . . . When so much goes grinning and grimacing as a lifeless Formality, . . . here once more, if nowhere else, is a Sincerity and Reality. Shudder at it; or even shriek over it, if thou must; nevertheless consider it . . . The thing they will do is known to no man; least of all to themselves.

Carlyle, *The French Revolution*

CHAPTER ONE

In the course of my life I have had occasion to observe how settlers are transported from place to place and what sometimes happens to them during their migrations. Here I would like to recount a minor incident which has remained in my memory all my life. This event took place not long before the abolition of serfdom. Well-founded rumors about "liberation" were already afoot, but nonetheless the buying and selling of human beings still went on freely. Taking advantage of this, certain notable personages were creating large settlements on their estates in the steppes with peasants bought for export in the central provinces.

One of my relatives, my aunt's husband, was a Russified Englishman. He was no ordinary man, and in one respect he anticipated by forty years the ethics of the *Kreutzer Sonata*. Fearing that in selecting a wife he might fall under the seductive influence of "the moon, a sweater, and a brooch," [2] he resolved to examine his prospective bride in the simplicity of her everyday life. For this purpose he dressed up as a peddler's "boy" and went about visiting the houses of neighboring landowners. In this way he saw all the young ladies in their everyday attire, and having gathered information about them from servants, he made an offer to my aunt, who was a delightful and charming woman. People generally said that he was a *practical* man. He managed the huge estates of a very important personage, and among other things had the duty of populating the steppes. There he was to establish new villages and introduce scientific cultivation of the fields. The peasants taken there were bought for export from various landowners in the provinces of Oryól and Kursk; hence the "export peasants" were divided into two categories: the "Oryól people" and the "Kursk people." The "Oryól people" were considered "more scoundrelly," while the people from Kursk, "real peasants,"[3] were regarded as "more doltish."

At that time people were transported to the steppes in large parties. As I remember from my childhood, people from our district were assembled for resettlement on two different occasions. This was called the "gathering of peoples." Both times there was great wailing in the villages, and it was pitiful to look at the people chosen as settlers, although there were quite a few of them who were not at all downcast, but would say, "It is all the same to us—it can't be worse!" In the courtyards of the people due to be transported there was selling of sheep, heifers, ploughs, harrows, and sledges, and while this was going on there were heart-rending scenes of "eternal parting" among the women.

Once nearly two hundred peasants, as I remember, were transported from our town in wagons. Many of the men escaped and returned home to hide out in the hemp fields and drying barns. When they were caught, they said that they had "run away from the lice and harmful waters." They were sent to the district police station and flogged. Besides the runaways, many fell ill on the road. For a while they were carried along in the wagons and then "dumped" wherever they might be. The emaciated nags fell in the traces, the harnesses snapped, the wheels broke, and in general there was a great deal of misfortune. The second transportation of peasants from our district was even more disastrous. A terrible "tearing dysentery" or "gut strain" broke out among them, and the sick had to be kept in houses and earth huts along the road for the whole winter. Half of the people died, and their owners suffered great losses. Therefore, the third time it was decided to send the expedition by water, or, as they used to say then, "by vessel," along the Oká and Vólga. And this third migration is the subject of my story.

The party of settlers had been assembled from various parts of the Oryól and Kursk provinces, all bought from petty landowners. Among the peasants to be resettled there were both house serfs and plain village muzhiks. The house serfs had no animals or carts of their own. They were brought to the dock—how I never knew—and placed on barges. A few peasants had carts and wooden ploughs; all this was loaded, or rather piled, on the barges, and the families were installed both on the carts and under them. Some of them, I remember, had chickens, and on one barge there were two or three sheep.

CHAPTER TWO

I was then a very young boy and had not yet decided on a career. Sometimes I felt like studying science and sometimes painting, while my parents wanted me to enter the government service. In their opinion this was "the most reliable course." I both wanted and didn't want to be an official: I knew that the service was a good thing, but I was already somewhat spoiled by youthful dreams. I had read Griboédov's *The Misfortune of Being Clever*, and to me all the military seemed like Skalozúbs and all the civilians like Molchálins. I didn't like either of them. My temperament demanded an active life. I told this to my aunt, who passed it on to her husband. The Englishman advised me to stay out of the government service and instead to train myself for a career in business. To give me some inducement, he told me:

"Right now we are resettling a group of peasants, and the Count is dissatisfied with the way it is being done. The people in charge of the settlers, in the opinion of the Count (his employer), are all very brutal. I partly agree with him. It is unpractical. Perhaps they are only a *product of nature*, but even nature can avenge herself. There is no sense in infuriating people and driving them to despair and desperation. But on the other hand thoroughly kind and soft-hearted people are also no good as chiefs. This has been proved by experience. The peasant will hang on the neck of a soft-hearted person and then begin to kick him. What are needed are Pizarros,[4] and I have just the Pizarro I need. The man in charge of this expedition is a very trustworthy local fellow from Oryól named Peter Semyónov. He is a clever rascal, but a tyrant. His son is going with him—also very capable, and also on the vicious side. With them the peasants really squeal. But you can't get along without people like Peter Semyónov. There is a whole horde going with them, and with a horde you've got to employ the measures of the Tatar Horde. But this is an age in which you have to admit some influence of civilization; you must punish with one hand and show mercy with the other. Why don't you go with them? Pay attention to what is going on, don't get in Peter's way, but make things easier when you can. I will give you power of attorney as chief, with authority to grant any sort of amnesty."

I agreed.

"That's excellent! Your official status will be far above Peter's, but you take care not to ruin things. Rule, but don't govern. Let Peter bear the brunt of their complaints. Your job is to *show mercy*."

In Oryól I made the acquaintance of our Pizarro. He was a dark, curly-haired peasant of forty-eight or fifty, muscular, strong, and lively, with fiery black eyes, black brows which grew together above his nose, and a small, thick black beard. The expression of his face showed strength, daring, and decision, plus a certain amount of cruelty. His son Dorósha came along as his assistant. He was a youth of twenty-two or three, extraordinarily like his father.

My uncle introduced me to Peter Semyónov and asked him to teach me the ropes. He told me to keep on good terms with him. We were both directed to deliver the "product of nature" entrusted to us in good order to its destination.

My uncle was in an excellent mood and spoke to us in a very friendly way. Pizarro answered him in a caressing tone, but with an almost imperceptible undercurrent of irony and hostility. My uncle was arguing that the Russian peasant was the most long-suffering of all nature's "products"; he was unspoiled and would not be exhausted by a long journey.

"Only give him something to stuff his belly with, so there is no rumbling there, and he will knock off thousands of versts like dancing a cotillion."

This remark appealed to Peter Semyónov. He smiled with the corners of his mouth and observed, "Exactly so: we'll dance there like a cotillion."

"Dance away," answered my uncle. "Dance away." And in an overflow of good spirits that was perhaps somewhat excessive he failed to notice Pizarro's malice, and contrary to his custom, made the sign of the cross over us with his hand. "Guard the product and dance the cotillion!"

The peasants to be transported were already aboard the "vessels," and the most painful process, the embarkation, I did not see. I was told that there had been heart-rending scenes, especially when the resettled peasants were bidding farewell to their relatives and neighbors. Many of them supposedly "sought to revolt," but Peter Semyónov forestalled any rebellion. He sent Dorósha to the police station, and he brought back "three police Cossacks with lances," and everything was over. The "product of nature" was loaded, and the barge immediately shoved off from the bank and anchored in midstream.

CHAPTER THREE

Peter Semyónov took me around to show me how the people were "installed" in the barges. Two of them contained the "scoundrelly" Oryól people, and the third, the "doltish" people from Kursk. Each of these groups had "elders" appointed from their own ranks. The Oryól elder was a wheelwright named Fefyól. Peter informed me that he was a valuable man, but that not long before he had killed a man with a wagon shaft. The man had come to invite him to supper. This crime was not reported, but "just in case" Fefyól was sold soon after for a low price.

"The Oryól scoundrels need just such a man over them," Pizarro would say.

The Kursk people were led by an Oryól peasant named Mikháilo, a kind and moderate man.

"The Kursk people are like little chicks!"

I remember my first sight of these "peoples" and their leaders.

We left home for the Oká in a small cart driven by Dorósha. Peter Semyónov and I sat on the bench. The barges were anchored five versts from the town. When we arrived, Peter Semyónov gave a whistle, and a small boat put out from the shore. It contained Mikháilo, the overseer of the Kursk people, who took us out to the barges. We mingled with the peasants, and I did not notice anything especially harsh or oppressive. The people were sitting barefoot and half-naked—in short, just as pitiful and wretched as they ordinarily look in the Russian villages. At that time I still thought that peasants everywhere must look just as we were accustomed to see them in Russia. Their usual submissiveness was also apparent. Peter Semyónov dealt roughly with them; they were a mere "product," not worth good treatment. They behaved obsequiously toward him, calling him "bátyushka" [father] Peter Semyónovich and making various requests of him, to which he gave short and curt, but to tell the truth, always very businesslike answers. I had no occasion to employ my high powers of pardon, and I was in no hurry to do so. I was sure that such an occasion would arise during the journey, and then I would give vent to my authority as a dispenser of mercy, and the "peoples" would bless my clemency.

CHAPTER FOUR

When we had transferred from the first barge to another, Peter Semyónov showed me his cabin in the stern. It was a tiny room made of deal planks, containing two cots, his and Dorósha's, a minute cupboard with a tea set, a small yellow trunk, a wooden abacus, an account book, and in the corner an icon with a candle. This room was kept locked, and the elder Fefyól kept the key. Peter Semyónovich offered to make me a cabin just like this on one of the other barges.

I will skip over the account of our departure and of the voyage itself, since that would take too much time, and I cannot remember it all now. By and large, one day followed another in the same tedious and dull way, without anything to do. The favorite occupation of all the passengers was "louse-hunting."[*] This was something like a sport. Men, women, and children—everyone was constantly on the hunt, and this was not only to pass the time, but was brought about by the most urgent necessity, since the lice were mercilessly devouring the "peoples."

I do not know the name of the disease caused by lice, but I do not

---

[*]There are reports that this was also the chief occupation of the Russian settlers transported on an ocean liner from Odéssa to Vladivostók in 1892. But these people, besides their "lice," also had *playing cards*, which we lacked. (*Leskov's note.*)

think it could be more terrible than what I saw on these transport barges. No amount of effort to get rid of the insects was of any use. Although peasants are generally far from fastidious about cleanliness, in this case they set up a howl:

"The lice have eaten us up . . . ! Have mercy—have pity . . . ! They are crawling into our eyes: they want to drink our sight!"

It became unpleasant and frightening to walk about the barges. Especially at night or during the heat of the day, when the people were overcome with lethargy and wanted to sleep, the itching caused by the insects prevented them from sleeping soundly. In mute frenzy they all kept scratching themselves, squirming about in one place or rocking six inches from side to side and then suddenly jumping up, sitting down again, and looking around with dull eyes. Sometimes they wept, but they all constantly and eternally scratched. As soon as this started in one part of the barge, it went through the whole boat "like a cotillion."

The people were not in the least ashamed of their foul and horrifying filth; how could they feel shame when they were suffering so terribly? They were afraid of Peter Semyónov, but they thrust their louse-infested children with their disgusting sores right in my face and shouted:

"Look at the Count's peasants! Look! Write to him: see, the lice have eaten holes in this child of God."

There was no remedy whatever, and neither Peter nor his son nor the wheelwright nor Mikháilo did anything to ease the people's sufferings.

There were no baths, and it was impossible to disinfect clothing by holding it up in front of a fire, because on the barges it was too dangerous to build a fire big enough so that all the people could strip in front of it. They simply had to stand it. But as day after day went by, they just *couldn't* stand it.

Peasants from Oryól and Kursk wash themselves rarely and badly, because at home they have no bathhouses for this purpose. But at home they do occasionally steam themselves in the same stoves in which they bake their bread. On the barges even this was impossible.

"We are lost!" they would cry with despairing sobs. "The lice have eaten us to death!"

And even so we could do nothing for them.

To be sure, they were permitted to bathe in the river, but this the "peoples" did not want to do. Peasants consider river-bathing a good way of cooling off. But to wash in cold water is impossible. Even if you use soap it comes to nothing.

"And on the barges there is no place to go swimming: the men will see the women . . . A real disgrace, and besides, in cold water the lice will only multiply still more."

In short, they did not want to bathe in the river. Then Peter and his son decided to "oblige" them to do so, but they refused to undress. The men said that they were "shaking with fever," and the women claimed that they "had the sickness," and the like.

Peter Semyónov called my attention to this and said:

"You must put a stop to this. Don't you hear how they are beginning to shout in chorus? It is bad when they shout in chorus!"

After this Peter Semyónov began to use measures of compulsion in the form of pushes and slaps. I resolved to intercede and did so, trying to offend the touchy vanity of the chief as little as possible.

He heard me out and turning pale, replied calmly:

"Oh, so you don't want me to stir up the 'product' any more?"

"Not that way."

"How then?"

I didn't know how . . .

But I had come to the defense of the peasants, and they understood and appreciated it.

CHAPTER FIVE

In this way we passed from the Oká into the Vólga. In Nízhny Nóvgorod our lousy peasants again made a disturbance: they suddenly went up to Peter Semyónov with the "unheard-of" request that he put them ashore for a bath! Of course he refused, and then both "peoples," Kursk and Oryól alike, began shouting and making noise. I was again summoned to frighten them, and again I failed to do this as it ought to be done. And when I said that I was sorry for them, Peter Semyónov answered:

"Sir, a person who is sorry for peasants should never go on a resettlement expedition."

And he turned his back on me. I felt that he had told me the truth, and my conscience actually began to hurt.

In order to assuage my feelings a little, I bought a pood of soap. With the aid of Mikháilo I cut it up into small pieces and distributed it to the women with children. The women were very grateful to me for it, but they soon announced that "the lice were just the same," because "we need lye." And both stoves and lye were lacking.

In the next town I bought two more poods of soap and again gave it out to the women with children. But this time Peter Semyónov was angry with me: he believed that if we were to give out soap, we ought to supply a great many other essential things besides, and then there would be no end to their needs.

I began to feel that I was somehow doing harm and that at any minute Peter Semyónov would manage to get rid of me by some method known only to him and would go off alone as leader of the whole "cotillion."

These forebodings were quite justified.

CHAPTER SIX

Two or three days after Pizarro's insolent remark to me, an original and daring act of sedition was discovered on our Oryól barge. A tiny hole had been bored in the wall of Peter Semyónov's cabin and a piece of straw inserted in it. This device was invented by one of the "Oryól scoundrels" for the purpose of forcing lice through the straw into the cabin.

Peter and Dorósha were terribly insulted at this and wanted to "hunt down the guilty ones" at any cost. But since no one confessed, they threatened to "flog people at random," but I opposed this. Then on the following day there were three new passage holes in the wall.

Peter was even more insistent in his demands that they all be given "a good thrashing," but I refused to consent. In this state of mutual dissatisfaction we arrived at a small settlement where we anchored. Here an incredible and amazing event occurred.

It was the eve of some holiday, I no longer remember which. It was a big holiday, and Peter Semyónov, who had to buy some provisions, was afraid that he would not find any in the market on the next day. For that reason he headed for the shore with his son and three peasants. I remained on the barges. At this point the "peoples," seeing no intervening wall between themselves and me, surrounded me and began to ply me with complaints against Peter. He had supposedly not given them their full ration of bread and salt, had wrongfully restricted their freedom, and had unjustly accused them of boring holes and pushing filth into his cabin.

"That's all lies, and the holes were bored by Peter's own son, Doróshka, and nobody else. He wanted to get even with a peasant whose wife he is 'sweet on.' "

Directly after that I heard from the midst of the "peoples" a single-voiced and terrible wail. These people, my brethren, weeping, cried out for me to take pity on their sufferings and let them go ashore to the bath-house to wash off the filth that was covering them with sores . . . They were in torment, they tore their hair and had hallucinations of a "nice little bathhouse."

Ought I or ought I not to have hearkened to this agony and these prayers of my louse-ridden brethren?

CHAPTER SEVEN

I cannot say whether there really were bathhouses being heated on the shore or whether they were only the hallucinations of people who longed to wash above all else. But the peasants did assure me that there were bathhouses being heated on the shore, that they cost almost nothing, and that if I would let them go, they would wash and be back within an hour. Then I would send the others. I looked at the wheelwright and at Mikháilo. The wheelwright only gave his customary smile, and Mikháilo was silent, but the wailing was intolerable, actually loud enough to reach the ears of God. To cap off this scene and to exacerbate my feelings still more, some miserable peasant came forward and thrust into my eyes a dying little boy. Every nook and cranny of his body was crawling with insects like a living string of beads.

"Here!" shouted the peasant. "Here, look at this." And then he threw the child on the floor like a stick of wood and bared his own rag-covered ribs. Under his arms and between his caved-in ribs I saw a sight which I can no more describe now than I could endure it then. I said:

"All right! . . . I will have to answer for you, but I will give you money for a bath. Make your arrangements, go ashore and get washed."

We sent forty men in boats and put them ashore for a bath under the trustworthy command of the good Mikháilo, who was to set them ashore and send us back the boats with the oarsmen.

On the shore the bells for vespers or midnight mass were still ringing, and it seemed to all of us that the breeze from there brought with it the smell of steam and of the bundles of twigs used for lashing people in bathhouses.

I stood on the deck and watched our boats arrive at the bank and saw the men disembark. Very quickly, one after the other, like sparrows, they leapt out of the boats with a liveliness quite out of keeping with their usual awkwardness. And then . . . the boats remained at the bank and did not return . . . There were no other boats to send for them, and we heard not a murmur from them . . .

An amazing thing!

We waited for half an hour, an hour; it began to get dark. Still no sign of them, when suddenly we heard the plash of oars in the darkness and . . . like Satan there appeared the haughty and malicious Peter Semyónov.

CHAPTER EIGHT

I felt that something had gone wrong, and I was not mistaken. What had happened was that all the long-suffering people I had sent ashore to the bathhouse, who had assured me that I would not "answer" for them, had not gone to the bathhouse at all, but as soon as they leapt ashore, had *set off for the province of Oryól.*

"Our lousy brethren have rendered us good service, and you did well to take pity on them!" concluded Peter Semyónov, but he at once altered his jocular tone and said with great seriousness:

"Well, we can't wait for them! Allow me to take your power of attorney with me, and we'll go ashore. I have already notified the police captain, and he is ready. We must catch them right away! This bath will cost us dear!"

Things had taken such a turn that everyone was to blame; only Peter

Semyónov was in the right. Therefore all the weight of justice was on his side, and we had to obey him and obey him quickly and without argument. Pizarro had conquered me and had already begun to celebrate his victory. As we were walking to the boat, he went ahead of me with a lantern. Stopping alongside a young woman who was feeding a child at the breast, he took his lantern and with shameless insolence turned it so that its light fell on her naked breasts. Her breasts had a gray glint like a piece of tulle, and this tulle was moving, mingling at the nipple with drops of blue milk which had fallen from the baby's lips.

Pizzaro's mouth twisted in a contemptuous smile. He pulled away the lantern and said:

"How could my son fail to be attracted by such a charming sight?"

We rowed on in haughty silence, but as soon as we reached the bank, Peter at once asked insistently for my power of attorney. He demanded that I refrain from interfering in the matter at all; I was to wait for him in the tavern. He now came right out and told me that I might ruin the whole business.

I believed him, and he went off to the police station. The status of the official he had talked to was not clear to me; Peter sometimes called him the "District Captain," sometimes simply the "Chief." Soon after this he set off in pursuit of the runaways with this official and three Cossacks. They caught them easily five versts away, turned them around, and brought them back to town under the guard of those same three police Cossacks. Just as in Oryól, only one of them was armed.

Despite the darkness I could see how they were "driven" back. Some rain had fallen, and the soil was clayey. It was both ridiculous and pitiful to watch them ploughing through the mud. Their feet stuck and slipped from under them in the wet clay, and when a couple of peasants in front slipped and fell, all the others did the same—just as if they were repeating the figures of a cotillion.

Peter Semyónov came back in a droshky with the police captain, bearing himself with great dignity. He introduced me curtly:

"This is the man with the power of attorney for them." He uttered not another word.

After this the police captain, who was wrapped up in a cloak, bent over and whispered in my ear:

"Please come to my house right away . . . I must have a talk with you. Please, this very minute!"

He wrapped himself up again, and I noticed that he had some sort of star under the hood of his cape. He drove off, and I went to his house and waited for him for quite a while in the most unpleasant frame of mind.

"Lord!" I thought. "What a mess I have made! But how could I expect grown people to be so foolish as to abandon their wives and children and try to run away to a place they quite obviously could never reach! You can allow a tame badger to go hunting in the woods if you keep the female and the offspring locked up at home, and the badger won't run away, but will return to his mate in captivity! . . . And after all, these are human beings!"

CHAPTER NINE

I had plenty of time to think of how ashamed they would be when they were put back on the barges . . . Yes, and I would be ashamed to look at them the next day . . . And still no sign of the police captain . . . I was very bored in his office, but it was awkward to leave, because the soldier who had brought me there had gone off and locked the door behind him, so that I was under arrest.

In this unpleasant situation I tried to divert myself as best I could. Fortunately, there were books there, and ones at that time very popular; for instance, the lectures of the Moscow professors Granóvsky,[5] Kudryávtsev,[6] Heimann,[7] and Roulier[8] *(On the Urban Swallow)*; Herzen's *Letters on the Study of Nature* with the memorable opening passage ("Glory to Ceres, Pomona and their kin!"), and a Russian Bible with an official wax seal on its cover.

The Bible must have been put there for some special reason; it could hardly have been "under arrest" in the police captain's library!

Since that book was at that time a great rarity,[9] I began to leaf through it and did not notice my host's arrival.

CHAPTER TEN

The police captain, or, as it turned out, the police non-captain,[10] was a young man, apparently one of the "educated noblemen."

When I saw him in the droshky, wrapped up in his cloak with a strange medal gleaming from under his hood, he had seemed to be a man of solid respectability, as befits a police captain. But now, when he took off his cloak, there appeared before me a mere "whippersnapper," and moreover this whippersnapper conducted himself in an extremely offhand way. In the first place, this youthful individual ran into the room all out of breath, singing "Hear me and love me!"; and in the second place, he seemed surprised at my presence, and then began to apologize and burst out laughing.

"What can you do?" he said. "You do what you can, but you forget things. Anyway, thank God, it's all over: I have flogged them all!"

"Whom did you flog?"

"All forty of your rebels . . . Of course we ought to have found out who the instigators were, but your old fellow told me that it was better not to try, and to give it to all of them. And anyway, how could you ever find out?"

"But wait a minute . . . There must have been a misunderstanding! All forty . . . ! After all, they didn't go very far, and they all came back here without a murmur . . ."

The young man roared with laughter.

"Oh, yes! Don't say any more! Blockheads! I will tell you frankly, our peasants are blockheads! . . . Imagine an Englishman in my position! He would have lost his head, I'm sure. But I really know these people, and I know how to deal with them. Why? Because I was born and grew up here! When your fellow came here and said, 'Help me! Forty men have run away,' I thought: what shall I do? My boss is away; I myself have no rank and no authority; I am only a clerk, a secretary, nothing more. But I know these people. Therefore I took three old cripples, put on a cloak with a big buckle pinned on it, chased after them, and ordered them, 'Back, you swine!' And I brought them all back and flogged the whole lot. My buckle has an amazing effect: I chase them all back, bring them here, and have them all whipped. And don't forget this: I whip them with their own generous and benevolent assistance. They hold each other by the arms and legs and sit on each other's heads. Then I pack them off to the barges, and it's all over. They sail off, and I stand on the shore and think: 'Oh, you filthy Slavs! You worthless Russians!' Let someone with three helpers try to do that sort of thing to forty Frenchmen! . . . There'd be hell to pay! But here everything goes just fine . . . And don't forget, this was done with just my buckle; but if I had had a real medal! . . . Oh, if I had had a medal! With a real medal I could flog all Russia by myself!

"Your things are all on the dock. Everything is there. You can't stay with the settlers . . . Your Peter says that otherwise he won't answer for the success of the expedition, and I agree. He is right. He has taken your power of attorney along with him, and he did well to do so. Otherwise he would have had to send in a report on you."

"What sort of report?"

"Well, that you got the peasants all stirred up."

And then he explained to me that the group of rebellious peasants I had set ashore might have set off a general revolt for which a lot of people would have had to be banished to Siberia. Now, thanks to his resourcefulness, all that had happened was that forty men had been flogged, and I had been left behind . . .

I could only express my gratitude.

CHAPTER ELEVEN

Much time has passed since the adventure I have described, and much has changed. Some things have even changed considerably for the better.

But the rumors which reach the capitals about the movement of settlers still tell the same familiar story. One can draw the conclusion that two stimuli remain unchanged: (1) the "peoples" rebel without any definite aim and come back without knowing why; and (2) during their entire journey the "peoples" still "itch" and "go louse-hunting," because they are "devoured by lice." The latter fact is so disgusting that no one has the courage to speak seriously about it; it is only mentioned in passing. And perhaps for this very reason the matter of the "hunting" remains in its former terrible state. Yet this is a great national evil, which it is both shameful and cruel to overlook in the press. Filth is revolting; you don't sing songs about it while sitting at the piano, and you don't write ballads on that theme. But we must put squeamishness aside and speak out determinedly on the subject of filth, so as to do away with it once and for all. This is a real *Egyptian plague!* The settlers in the expedition which sailed to Vladivostók in 1892 were scratching themselves all over in sight of Colombo, but no one gave them any assistance, and they sailed on to scratch some more . . . ! Let it be known in what state our people go to pay visits! But at a meeting in Petersburg of the Society for Aid to Settlers on March 14, 1893, there were announcements and speeches about the insufficiency of funds for aid to settlers. There is no money even for "the most crying necessities"; "the extreme concentration of settlers furthers disease," and consequently "they infect the barracks in which they are housed." Therefore the Society calls for "the support of the zemstvos." [11] I considered it appropriate to relate here, in this *Settlers' Almanac*, the things I saw long ago on a settlers' barge, to remind the patrons of the wanderers that *the greatest cause of the settlers' suffering is the filth which devours them.* Why are they not met with charity on the road and given a chance to bathe? They infect everything they touch! Heine was right when he said, "He who loves the people should take them to the bathhouse." [12] This is the first thing that should be done everywhere when the "product of nature" descends.

(Translated by Hugh McLean)

NOTES FOR A PRODUCT OF NATURE

[1] In the Russian translation used by Leskóv, Carlyle's "outburst of nature" is rendered as "product of nature," which is the source of Leskóv's title.

[2] A somewhat garbled quotation from Tolstóy's *Kreutzer Sonata*.

[3] The phrase Leskóv uses to apply to the Kursk peasants is a reminiscence from the twelfth-century *Ígor Tale*.

[4] Francisco Pizarro (1471–1541), the Spanish conqueror of Peru.

[5] Timoféi Nikoláevich Granóvsky (1813–55), professor of universal history at the University of Moscow; a well-known liberal.

[6] Peter Nikoláevich Kudryávtsev (1816–58), professor of history at the University of Moscow, author of monographs on Roman and Italian history; also a liberal.

[7] Rodión Grigóryevich Heimann (Géiman) (1802–65), professor of chemistry at the University of Moscow.

[8] Karl Roulier (Rulyé) (1814–58), professor of zoology and medicine at the University of Moscow.

[9] Russian, as distinct from Church Slavonic, Bibles were indeed scarce in Russia in the first half of the nineteenth century.

[10] There is an untranslatable pun here. The word for "police captain" *(isprávnik)* is given a negative prefix *(neisprávnik)*, punning on *neisprávny* "careless, heedless."

[11] Elective bodies with limited powers of self-government in such spheres as education, medicine, etc., established in 1864.

[12] An inexact quotation from Heine's article "Confessions" *("Geständnisse")* 1854.

NOTE TO "ADMINISTRATIVE GRACE"

Leskóv wrote this story in 1893, but it did not appear in print until forty-one years later, when his son published it in Moscow in 1934. The long delay was no accident, for the story is one of the most biting satires in all Russian literature.

Like many of Leskóv's other satires, including "Choice Grain" and "Night Owls," "Administrative Grace" is told in approving terms by a character who turns out to be himself a target of Leskóv's attack. To the highly placed government official who relates it, this story of officially inspired character assassination, engineered by an archbishop and leading to the suicide of a professor, is nothing more than a clever joke on the liberals; but the reader sees for himself that the story is in reality a powerful indictment of the Tsarist Russian "establishment." Leskóv does not allow his reader to stop here, though; for the whole point of his story is that the Russian officials scored their victory over the liberals only by exploiting the petty human weaknesses, such as vanity, jealousy, love of gossip, and the tendency to run with the herd (their own liberal herd) that most liberals share with everybody else. Despite the topical allusions that would be lost on modern readers without explanatory footnotes, the satire in "Administrative Grace" is confined neither to Russia nor to the 1890's, nor to any particular social or political institutions, but may be easily translated into the language of any society made up of human beings.

ADMINISTRATIVE GRACE

(Zahme Dressur *in a Gendarme Arrangement*)

For wickedness hath exceedingly
polluted the whole earth, and
their hurtful works are fulfilled.
II Esdras 15:6

In our stinking times one cannot get away from the defects and deformi-
ties of our native politics even in the quiet of the Mérrekyul beaches.[1]
Among the generals' wives who were there last summer there was a frightful lot of alarm and confusion over their "inexperienced boys." That·is
the term that some of them applied to their sons, others to their nephews
(of a somewhat questionable brand), and still others simply to those *jolis
garçons* at whose powerful shoulders they had only to glance in order to
warm their withered hearts and dull eyes with the flames of former passions. The generals' wives were upset because the times were troubled
once again, and it was easy for a young man to make the kind of misstep
that "you could never get him out of." The ones in the biggest dither
were those whose *joli*-darlings were studying at Moscow University, from
which the authoritative arm of the Armenian enlightener of Russia had
thrown out Professors Múromtsev and Kovalévsky. The majority of the
"darlings" preferred ice-skating and dancing lessons to lectures, but youthful fervor requires courageous heroism, and when the authorities removed
these "rulers of men's minds," the darlings began to protest, to *faire des
bêtises*, and in this way to grieve the generals' wives.[2]
  One of them became disturbed especially passionately, and shaking the
array of false curls hanging over her carefully made-up brow, she would
squeal:
  "I couldn't endure it, and at *ma cousine* Barbe's I interrupted Mikhaíl

Nikíforovich himself with 'Pas de zèle, pas de zèle,' but he is still afraid we'll be cut off from Europe at the Nárva, and he only rubbed his hands and simply couldn't say anything sensible . . ."[3]

Hearing these attacks on Katkóv, a high-school principal from Volhýnia—either a Croat or a Czech by origin—who was vacationing on those same Mérrekyul beaches boiled up with righteous patriotism and arose in defense of the apostle of Strastnói Boulevard who was so dear to his Croatian heart. Squealing every bit as well as the general's wife, he began shouting at her that she did not understand the fundamental instructions about state policy according to which it was necessary tó remove not only Múromtsev and Kovalévsky but all others of their ilk.

"Let us get rid of the evil root and branch!" howled the principal, raising his skinny finger toward the wan Baltic sky.

"But that means irritating Europe!" howled the general's wife.

"Then we *will* irritate Europe, we *will*, but we won't allow riff-raff and false teaching at home," the principal kept saying.

When they had withdrawn some distance from the bench beside the monument, still arguing furiously, a dignitary of great prominence who had so far kept silent looked after them in scorn and summed up the significance of their quarrel in edifying fashion:

"It's not right to allow false teaching, but it won't do either to irritate Europe. The whole trouble is that people of our day and time don't know how to hew the line; they may even hack at the right spot but they'll do it awkwardly, without grace. It's just the way these very same Czechs play the piano: they won't strike a single false note, but no matter what they do they can't get the kind of touch Antón Grigóryevich Rubinstein caresses you with."

"And so, Your Excellency," someone asked the dignitary, "you think the administration needs an artistic touch too?"

"By all possible means! And I can show you with an example out of my own personal experience that the administration used to have this grace in politics.

"Up to the time I was called to the capital as a member of the highest institution in the Empire, I governed a university town in the South. The times were troubled. The Turkish War and Chernyáev's volunteers, to the accompaniment of Aksákov's playing the fool of God, had stirred everybody up, and my predecessor had been shot in his carriage in broad daylight in the most crowded part of the city.[4] Such a fate was not to my liking, and from the very first day I began keeping a sharp lookout. I saw that the center and summit of the whole disturbance was the university and the veterínary institute: the students were mainly Ukrainians—hot-headed and stubborn. The professors who egged the young people on were birds of the same feather—the stupider ones openly, in their lectures, and the cleverer ones on the sly, during walks and at evening gatherings. One tribune in particular was famous among them—as bright as they come, and an orator as good as Gambetta, so that the short-haired jokers came right out and named him the Khárkov Lassalle, and were waiting for him to lead them in serried ranks, like Spielhagen's Leo, to the 'final, decisive battle.'[5]

"I sized him up, collected everything I needed to know about him through the colonel of the gendarmes, and saw that we could expect no good as long as he was around. I decided to get rid of him.

"In my previous government service I had never had to handle the scholarly crowd, and I thought long and hard about how to keep from pulling something awkward through my lack of experience; but in military school they had taught us that every horse takes a particular snaffle, and the most important thing of all is to know which one to use to pull which horse. I was sitting once at twilight in front of the fireplace, thinking about what kind of snaffle I needed to catch him, when suddenly my adjutant announced that the archbishop was favoring me with a visit. My archbishop was a very shrewd fellow, brought up under the wing of Metropolitan Filarét of Moscow,[6] and after giving me his blessing he noticed at once that I was lost in thought and asked what the matter was. I told him the whole story in confidence—about the home-grown Lassalle as well as my search for a snaffle for him. His Eminence listened, counting his amber beads, and then asked whether I had apprised the academic authorities of my thoughts relating to this matter. 'No,' I answered, 'you are the first one, Most Holy Father, to whom I have revealed my thoughts.' 'Well, in that case,' he said, 'the matter is very simple: just leave it to my humility. Our Count Dmítry Andréevich Tolstóy, you know, is in charge of both the Holy Synod and the teaching department, and it meets with his strong approval when we members of the cloth see to it that he is not left uninformed about the teaching branch as well. Now, in a few days, at Easter, I shall send my Father Superior to him with communion bread, and on that occasion I will dispatch a little note about your Lassalle. My Father Isíkhy is a faithful slave, and in the postal service the hangers-on of the nihilists read all the most secret papers and let the news out everywhere. Pay me a visit in a few days after vespers for a glass of tea with my lime-blossom honey, and by that time I shall very likely find the leisure to prepare a rough draft of my epistle.' I thanked His Eminence, dropped in to see him two or three days later, and added a few flourishes to his exposition; but in general the archbishop had represented everything very appropriately—not a word about me, but only that his archepiscopal conscience was troubled by this tribune who, like unto a lion, did seek to swallow up the uncomprehending sheep in the flock that had been entrusted to his pastoral rod.

"Father Isíkhy took the letter along with the communion bread. He came back again; a good month and a half went by; and from on high no attention at all to my Lassalle could be observed. I made inquiries through the superintendent of education, who had also taken a trip to Petersburg for New Year's. It turned out that the Count only asked him why this professor was getting elected president of all the organizations and invited to make speeches at all the evening parties. In other words, I could see that the archbishop's letter had reached the Count, but I was all the more surprised at his inaction and his failure to take any measures along the line of 'sanitizing the roots of society,' about which Katkóv's zeal was already aroused at that time. I concluded that either our Lassalle was supported by a powerful hand in the capital or else those were right who howled that 'the reins had slipped from the hands of our leaders.' And so another two or three months went by in the midst of this uncertainty, and then suddenly I found out that like a bolt from the blue Lassalle had been thrown out of his post as president of the most progressive organization there was, and a week later from a second one, and then from still a third. And the superintendent of education reported in astonishment that the professor's students at first hooted him down in his lectures at the university, and then the very next evening broke out all the windows in his little house. We couldn't make head or tail of it. Where had the storm come from that had blown up against Lassalle? In the newspaper where until recently every remark he made, no matter how trifling, had been printed in large type in the most prominent spot, suddenly a notice from the editors came out saying that in accordance with the unanimously expressed will of the contributors so-and-so would henceforth take no part . . .

"In a word,

> *Where a table of viands had stood,*
> *Now there lay a coffin . . .*[7]

"That is the way the superintendent and I joked with Derzhávin's verses, but actually the coffin did arrive: a week later the professor was found on a highway just out of town with a bullet in his temple and the kind of farewell note that suicides leave on them. To be on the safe side I ordered the police chief to prepare a strong guard for the funeral, but except for his old nurse and two elderly colleagues not a soul showed up. In a word, 'dead and gone, buried and forgotten.'

"The funeral took place on Easter Thursday, and at Matins on Easter Sunday, after his Easter greeting in the cathedral, the archbishop whispered with a certain amount of pride: 'Father Isíkhy didn't deliver that little note for nothing.' It would not have been fitting to argue with him at that moment, but I thought to myself that the archbishop was completely mistaken if he gave that letter credit for what had simply taken shape to our mutual satisfaction by itself.

"After Easter there came a very troublesome spring and summer in the political line: even in our part of the country the kind of gossip started buzzing that was reflected in Lípetsk not by Prince Shakhovskói's comedy but by a very serious matter,[8] so that I simply forgot to think about the Lassalle who had killed himself, sitting as I did for whole days and nights at my desk. I worked so long over those alarms that my daughter and the office manager would all but throw me out of the house by force in order to give me a bit of fresh air. It would have been a sin even to think of a vacation that summer, and in order to get away from them I decided one day to look in on the circus, especially since the police chief kept going into raptures over the marvelous lady lion tamer who put on her act there. And it really was worth while: the lady lion tamer's legs in her riding breeches were highly remarkable, and she tamed the lions with staggering boldness, so that there was no cause to lament the loss of an evening. As I left, I couldn't help sharing my enthusiasm with the colonel of the gendarmes, whom I invited then and there, taking advantage of the opportunity, to come with me to the palace on urgent business. As we rode along, he said:

" 'I am astonished that Your Excellency found that Hungarian woman to your taste. It's true that her legs are supernatural, but her method of work, it seems to me, ought not to suit you . . .'

" 'But what kind of method has she got?'

" 'You noticed how she tamed her lions! How much powder she burnt up with her shots, how many firecrackers she threw, how many whips she cracked! For us military men all that shooting and branding with red-hot irons is pure pleasure, through force of habit; but for civilians' nerves, and especially for women's, it is nothing but a burden, and an almost unbearable torture . . .'

" 'But isn't that the way all animal tamers act?'

" 'By no means! They have two schools or methods: the wild one—*wilde Dressur*—the method you've just seen, with fire and iron; and the tame one—*zahme Dressur*—which not only has no shooting but even includes cracking of whips only for outward show, and yet they get the most brilliant results: the animals obey as meekly as lambs, and the public sits there full of peace and good humor. In good circuses, for example, at Renz's in Vienna, this barbarism was dropped a long time ago. It is still used for entertainment only somewhere in Linz or Cracow, where there is no refined audience. But since you yourself, Your Excellency, are such a rare master and expert in *zahme Dressur*, why, I thought—'

"But at this point I didn't let the colonel finish. Since I understood absolutely nothing, I asked him to show me just when and where I could have displayed my talent for taming, and in what style and taste.

" 'Why, in the case of ——,' (and here the colonel gave the full name of the professor who had committed suicide). 'Isn't that a model? Isn't that the most perfect *zahme Dressur?'*

"I saw that the man was giving me completely unmerited praise, and I asked the colonel to explain in detail just how it had taken place (seeing that the horses had brought us to the palace at that moment)—deliberately pretending that I didn't remember all the details. According to his story the matter turned out to be a lot more subtle than I had assumed.

"Here for the first time I learned that, according to the rules of their agency, whoever heads the government in university towns is obliged on his annual visits to Petersburg to report to the Minister of Education. Count Dmítry Andréevich had spoken to him in general terms about the archbishop's letter and had ordered him to work out a plan of action on the spot with His Eminence and to carry it out according to his blessing. As a Lutheran the colonel felt awkward about discussing such worldly affairs with the archbishop himself, and in order not to deflect him from his Godly thoughts he took his whole strategy from that same Father Isíkhy who had carried the letter to Count Tolstóy at Christmas along with the communion bread.

"According to their plan it was necessary to find out first of all who was the most jealous rival Lassalle had in town. Finding out this was actually no work at all: the whole town knew that Boleslàv Konrádovich Parasólka had it in for him. Parasólka was a first-class lawyer and also an attractive personality. Formerly he had presided everywhere and contributed to everything; but after the professor's arrival he had been obliged to move into the background and step aside—which Parasólka could not endure.

"And so the colonel sent for this same attractive personality. He arrived at the colonel's office, of course, looking as if he had drunk vinegar that morning instead of coffee, and they had scarcely begun their conversation when an orderly—by prearrangement with the colonel—called him out of the office. Ever since the time of the unforgettable Leónty Vasílyevich Dúbelt,[9] gendarmes have been models of delicate behavior; and as he left supposedly for a moment, the colonel made profound apologies to Parasólka. In reality he walked over to his housekeeper to drink the extra cup of coffee that she customarily sent to his office at that hour by that same orderly. The colonel drank his coffee without haste, then smoked a cigarette, and then, returning after all that to his office and Parasólka, made very special apologies, explaining that important business had detained him. But he noticed at once that his guest would willingly have forgiven him an even longer absence: the vinegar of his visage had disappeared without a trace under the radiance with which the whole of his aristocratic Polish countenance now shone. Using some utter trifle as the pretext for having called him in, the colonel very quickly sent him on his way in peace; and Parasólka had not yet left the anteroom before the colonel threw into the fire the paper that had so brilliantly served its purpose, as the countenance of Parasólka had made perfectly clear. Just before he came in, the colonel had interrupted—in the middle of a word—the draft of a secret report to the capital recommending that a financial reward beyond the regular budgeted amount be given for special services to our Professor Lassalle, whose first name, patronymic, family name, rank, and address were put down with complete exactness. When he went out behind his orderly, the colonel left this paper on his desk as if through absentmindedness. The whole plan had been constructed on the calculation that Parasólka would not let such a chance go by, and would become so curious while he remained there alone that he would be unable to resist the temptation to read a paper 'going out from such a place.' Parasólka's countenance, radiant with delight, confirmed that the calculation had been completely justified. There had fallen to his lot the highest joy that is accessible to a progressive intellectual: he had learned of some filth about his neighbor.

"This paper, written as if it were merely a test of the ink, without the slightest foundation or desire to send it anywhere, had fulfilled its purpose with the departure of Parasólka, and it had to be burned at once. The same calculation taught that Parasólka, like the barber of Midas,[10] would not bury his secret in a pit but would sent it out to wander over the world. Knowing our progressive society, it was possible to calculate the whole action just as accurately as an experienced billiard-marker with a slight tap of his cue sends the ball rolling into the pocket he has selected— which is what the note beside the body on the highway outside of town turned out to be.

"The colonel really seemed convinced that the whole plan that the crafty monk had thought up and that he himself had carried out exactly was really my product, and that it had at most been completed and worked out in consultation with the archbishop. And so this is indeed a sample— and a very high-grade one—of *zahme Dressur* in its application to a political task: they had tied up and removed a dangerous beast without even loading a pistol. The colonel was touched, and he praised this act also for the way in which it had proved fruitful over and above its primary purpose—through inertia, as you might say.

" 'Our society is always strong in hindsight,' the colonel continued. 'They at once believed Parasólka blindly, and only after allowing their god of yesterday to be buried so poorly and miserably did they start checking up on the substance of that vile rumor. In the colonel's office were such vile creatures that they would show things now and then to the nihilists—under his direction, of course, and of course for big money—and now in return for an imposing sum they proved beyond doubt by reference to the record of outgoing documents that no such paper had even been sent anywhere from their office. This also served the purpose of thwarting the exaltation of Parasólka, and cast upon him a rather dark shadow along the line of slander, and he was obliged to go away for good to the banks of the Vistula, which were so dear to his aristocratic Polish heart.

"And so with one crack of the whip in the air they first got rid of the beast, then neutralized the 'attractive personality' of Parasólka, and finally allowed the colonel's bureaucrats to earn a little something-or-other and to do a favor to the nihilists, which entangled them in another noose of confidence. Most important of all, the administration displayed genuine grace in its own line: for as we know, whoever eats even the greasiest pie or gravy with grace will violate the whiteness neither of his tie nor of his cuffs. Likewise grace helps a skillful administrator to settle the most unpleasant affair in such a way that no stain will appear on his department and all the dirt will remain on the plate—that is, on society itself.

"To this very day," said the dignitary, getting up from the bench, "I don't know whether that plan was sketched by Count Dmítry Andréevich or whether it came to full maturity in the quiet of our archbishop's monastery cell; but I am certain that the Múromtsev affair too could have been settled quietly according to the method of *zahme Dressur*. But this would have required the now forgotten grace of administrative devices, and the Armenian shepherd of Russian youth would have needed either to possess the intelligence of Count Dmítry or to call upon such intelligent and shrewd assistants as my archbishop."

NOTES FOR "ADMINISTRATIVE GRACE"

[1] Mérrekyul (Estonian: Mereküla) was a summer resort on the coast of the Baltic Sea.

[2] "The Armenian enlightener of Russia"—Count I. D. Delyánov (1818–97), a man of Armenian ancestry, who was Minister of Education from 1882 till his death. S. A. Múromtsev (1850–1910), a professor of law, and M. M. Kovalévsky, a professor of history, were forced in the 1880's to resign their positions at Moscow University.

[3] Mikhaíl Nikíforovich Katkóv (1818–87)—the powerful conservative editor and publisher of the *Moscow News (Moskóvskie védomosti)* and the journal *The Russian Herald (Rússki véstnik)*, with whom Leskóv broke off relations in 1874 because of his arbitrary changes in publishing Leskóv's narrative *A Family in Decline (Zakhudály rod)*.

[4] General Mikhaíl Grigóryevich Chernyáev (1828–98) was closely associated in the 1870's with the Russian Pan-Slavist Iván Áksakov (1823–86) and at the invitation of the Serbs commanded their army, including a group of Russian volunteers, when Serbia went to war against Turkey in 1876. The allusion here is to the assassination on March 9, 1879, of Prince D. N. Kropótkin, the Governor of Khárkov, by a member of the "Land and Liberty" terrorist organization.

[5] Léon Gambetta (1838–82)—a French politician and leader of the Republican forces in their struggles against the French conservatives in the 1870's.
Ferdinand Lassalle (1825–64)—the founder of the Social-Democratic movement in Germany.
Leo—the hero of the German novel *In Reih' und Glied* (1866), by Friedrich Spielhagen (1829–1911).

[6] Filarét Drozdóv (1783–1867)—the powerful Metropolitan of Moscow from 1821 till his death, whom Leskóv often mentioned in guardedly uncomplimentary terms.

[7] From the poem "On the Death of Prince Meshchérsky ("Na smert Knyázya Meshchérskogo"), by Gavríla Derzhávin (1743–1816).

[8] A reference to a meeting at Lípetsk in June 1879 of the revolutionary group "Land and Liberty"; and to the comedy "A Lesson for Flirts, or the Lípetsk Waters" ("Urók kokétkam, ili Lípetskie vódy"), by A. A. Shakhovskói (1777–1846).

[9] Dúbelt (1792–1862) was appointed head of the Russian gendarmes in 1835.

[10] A reference to the legend about King Midas of Phrygia, who was given ass's ears by Apollo as a penalty for deciding a musical contest against the god. Midas hid them under a turban and swore his barber to secrecy. Unable to keep the secret to himself, the barber finally dug a hole in the ground and told the secret there. On that spot reeds grew up and betrayed King Midas' secret by constantly whispering the barber's words in the wind.

NOTE TO "A WINTER DAY"

In all the corpus of Leskóv's literary works two stories are unique. One is "Lady Macbeth of the Mtsensk District," a sober account of illicit passion and brutal murder that in both theme and style resembles nothing else Leskóv ever wrote. The other is "A Winter Day," which stands alone among all of Leskóv's works not because of its theme but because of its remarkable structure.

"A Winter Day" is so similar in construction to a play that one is tempted to wonder whether Leskóv may have actually considered the possibility of writing it for the stage. It strictly observes the classical dramatic unities of time (a single afternoon), place (a single house), and action. Its plot is developed largely through dialogue, and much of the narrative and descriptive material that accompanies the dialogue sounds like stage directions.

Leskóv's contemporaries almost uniformly condemned "A Winter Day." The liberal editor M. M. Stasyulévich, who in earlier years had joined in the attacks on Leskóv for his allegedly reactionary writing, now proved too faint-hearted to publish Leskóv's bold criticism of Russian society. "It is an excerpt from Sodom and Gomorrah," he wrote in his letter of rejection, "and I dare not bring forth such an excerpt into God's world." When a more courageous editor published the work in September 1894, it met with almost uniform disapproval from the critics, who accused Leskóv of cynicism, exaggeration, and lack of proportion.

What everybody overlooked in the general hue and cry about "A Winter Day" was the striking originality of its form, which can perhaps be more justly appreciated today in the perspective provided by such critical works as Joseph Frank's well-known article on "Spatial Form in Modern Fiction" than it could be when the story was first published. The plot is essentially a plot of discovery rather than a plot of action, and the complexity of its intricate design will become more evident with each successive reading. Through the medium of words, which can only be perceived sequentially, in time, Leskóv presents an instantaneous picture, as it were, of a complex web of human relationships in which each element is dependent upon all the others for its full meaning. Step by step the reader discovers that the strands in this entangling web include spying, blackmail, theft, forgery, various kinds of sexual affairs ranging from ordinary seduction to the perversion and debauchery of young boys, and veiled hints that a number of persons entangled in this web are secret agents of one kind or another in the pay of the Russian government. The only ray of light penetrating this family kingdom of darkness emanates from the teachings of Leo Tolstóy, which are represented on two levels in the story by a Tolstoyan servant girl and by the attractive, independent-minded niece of the mistress of the house in which the story has its setting.

Two kinds of elements provide the clues to this drama of discovery: those which find their ultimate explanation within the story itself, and those which depend for their meaning upon the acquaintance with contemporary Russian society that Leskóv could expect in the readers of his day. These latter elements naturally require explanatory footnotes for present-day readers of English.

In a private letter on August 21, 1894, to V. A. Góltsev, Leskóv listed a number of persons whom he said he had used as prototypes for the characters in "A Winter Day." Most of the names on Leskóv's list are too uncertain to be worth mentioning, but three of them are exceptions. Lydia, the attractive Tolstoyan girl, was so closely modeled on two school girls of Leskóv's acquaintance named Makshéeva and Lörberg that their schoolmates recognized them; and Olympia, the powerful woman with high governmental connections who travels back and forth between Russia and Western Europe, was modeled at least in part upon Olga Alexéevna Nóvikova (1840–1925), a well-known Russian political journalist who lived much of her life in England.

The criticisms of Tolstóy's more dogmatic followers that Leskóv put into the mouth of Lydia have led some scholars to argue on the basis of this story that Leskóv during the last few months of his life turned away from the teachings of Tolstóy. This argument is not only a misinterpretation of "A Winter Day"; it also flies in the face of the evidence in Leskóv's letters and articles that he remained a devoted (though undogmatic) follower of Tolstóy's religious teachings up to the very end of his life.

Both "A Winter Day" and "Night Owls" bear the characteristically Leskovian subtitle *"Paysage and Genre."* For all the differences between the two stories in structure and tone, the subtitle they share does suggest certain parallels. In both the exuberantly comical "Night Owls" and the somber account of "A Winter Day" we find a corrupt and hypocritical society challenged by an attractive young Tolstoyan heroine.

o o o o o

THE TRANSLATOR'S CAST OF CHARACTERS

The Mistress of the House—an older woman, the mother of Arkády and Valéry.

The Guest—a woman past her prime.

Olympia—a cousin of both women, who spends most of her time abroad.

Victor Gustávych—a man of influence, who never appears on the scene.

Lydia Pávlovna—a niece of the Mistress, Luke, and Zakhár; aged twenty-four, an independent follower of Leo Tolstóy.

Fedóra ("Kátya")—a Tolstoyan servant girl.

Luke Semyónych—a brother of the Mistress and Zakhár.

Zakhár Semyónych—a brother of the Mistress and Luke.

Arkády—a son of the Mistress.

Valéry (Valerian)—a son of the Mistress.

The doorman.

The yard man.

The maid.

The cook.

The grocery boy.

A WINTER DAY

(Paysage and Genre)

*They meet with darkness in the
daytime, and grope in the noonday
as in the night.*
Job, 5: 14.

*At the Church of the Savior the clocks
strike, in the Church of St.
Nicholas they ring, and at old
Egor's they talk.*
V. Dal (A proverbial expression).

I

It is a wintry northern day with a slight bit of thaw. It is two o'clock. Daybreak had scarcely had time to look around before night began to fall.

At a table in a second-rate living room there sits the mistress of the house and a guest. The mistress is old, and her appearance could be called respectable if her face were not marked by too much fawning and solicitude. She has once seen better days and has not yet lost the hope of bringing them back, but she does not know what this requires. In order to let nothing slip through her hands she is ready to be anything on earth: she is a vessel molded for honor and serving now as a vessel for shame. The guest whom we meet in the home of this mistress is not young either. In any case she has reached the age when one can give up playing with feelings, but evidently she has not yet made up her mind to do so. This woman was no doubt remarkably good-looking, but now that her former beauty has faded, there remain only the *"beaux restes"*; her figure, however, is still supple, and her facial features have kept their regularity, but what predominates in her expression is a remarkable ambivalence: at times she looks like a gentle doe, and then suddenly this doe will rise up like a kicking nanny goat.

One could no longer be carried away by this lady without some ulterior motive, but something along this line might still be possible if she phrased the question differently. In her manner of conducting herself in relation to the solid mistress of the house the guest reveals something warm and respectful, one might even say filial, but these ladies are in no way related. They are united by a friendship that has as its basis not merely agreement in tastes but also unity in goals: they are united by their *métier*.

Now they are drinking tea that was served in a Harrach china pot covered with a knitted tea-cozy; and the guest is telling the hostess about what has happened that is worthy of notice and about what "people are saying." People are talking about the rivalry between two wonder-workers, and something has happened that is even more interesting and worthy of attention: yesterday Cousin Olympia arrived quite unexpectedly from abroad. She is a well-known personage. For a long time she has devoted herself to "problems" and lives permanently in foreign lands; but when she comes here she brings with her a whole heap of news and she "makes things lively." Her life is something astonishing: she is not rich—oh, not rich at all! She even has positively no means whatever, and yet she never borrows from anybody and never complains about her situation, and is even very useful to her country.

Nowadays, God be praised, there are several such ladies, but among them Olympia occupies the most prominent position. She has a large and excellent family. She is also related to the two women who are talking about her here. In all eyes Olympia is a very sizable figure, and everybody believes her, in spite of the warning that Dickens issued against all persons who live on unknown income.

At home, in her native land, Olympia always turns up suddenly and for a short time: she will arrive, glance around, meet one person and another, "refresh her resources," and then leave again. Many people say she is very talented, but what is most important of all is that she is completely indispensable.

The mistress is somewhat disgruntled with her and calls attention to the draft through the window. In addition, she says that Victor Gustávych is still sorry Olympia will not "make up." Otherwise she would unquestionably become most indispensable.

"For that matter, it doesn't in the slightest keep Olympia from behaving excellently," the mistress concludes, "since Victor Gustávych himself is not sure about anything. That means a great deal."

The guest looks with her doe's eyes and with this look answers that she agrees, and at the same time she makes a little movement like a kicking nanny goat and glances at the chaise longue placed in front of the fireplace between some latticework and a screen.

Off to one side and behind the lattice an attractive-looking young girl of twenty-three or four reclines in a deep armchair with her eyes closed and her arms folded across her breast. Apparently she is not at all interested in what the ladies are talking about: she is tired and is resting, or perhaps even asleep. This girl is the mistress's niece; her relatives simply call her Lydia, but others call her Lydia Pávlovna. She is disliked in her own family, because she does not behave as her mother and brothers wish her to. Her brothers are brilliant officers, and one of them has even fought a duel. Lydia is likewise not in favor with her aunt, on whom she has dropped in for one of her rare visits, but then she too does not hide the fact that she does not feel at home here.

The mistress looked at Lydia and said:

"She's asleep. Besides," she added, "even if she were not, it wouldn't make any difference to her; she's not at all interested in society. Anything that's not connected with her studies doesn't matter to her. But Olympia—and I don't deny that she's got intelligence and connections—has certainly taken a tumble since her last visit, when she tried to get a scandal started about the beating of those Bulgarians.[1] You remember what nonsense came close to getting out in connection with that. They got wind of her visit and crowded in here in swarms, and they all claimed that everybody in their country was getting beaten and that they themselves had all been beaten. Olympia wanted to make use of them, but she got carried away, and when she ran into the argument that they were bragging, she declared that they had been given a physical examination here in some editorial office; and afterwards, in order to raise their prestige, she wanted to give a ball especially for them, but then people started saying that foreign ladies probably wouldn't go, because—you know how it is—some ladies don't dance with men who have been thrashed."

"I remember that. And you can say what you want, dancing with beaten men—it's . . . it's very irregular!"

"Why, of course!" the mistress went on. "And afterwards somebody found out that there was no point in even starting all this, because it seems that these gentlemen had been beating each other in some alley so that it would be easier for them to attract attention. They say that Olympia knew that herself. God alone knows what it's all about! And then after that it turned out that even this wasn't so, because even though they did get beaten in some alley, it was not for that reason at all, but because some fellow countryman of theirs was giving them a treatment, sort of like a massage. God knows what to make of them—where the truth ends and where the lies begin."

"Yes, it all turned out to be so mixed up that you can't make out anything except that they got beaten over there and they've been beaten here."

"That's just it—puffed up with pride! And it led to a great loss, because brother Luke got mad and not only stopped giving money for the Slavic causes[2] but wouldn't even listen. You know, he's as stubborn as a donkey, and he said right out: 'It's all a swindle!' And he not only gave orders to keep the Slavs out, but he wouldn't let Olympia in to see him, and he sent her a feather to make fun of her."

"What kind of feather?"

"I don't know what kind. They said it was a magpie's feather, for her hat."

"You don't say!"

"Why, of course! Just as though he said, 'Here you are, magpie—now fly off!' And now he won't receive anybody."

"How is it that Luke Semyónych puts such store by who he will receive?"

"He's rich and he's not trying to get anything out of anybody else— that is why he doesn't have to receive people he doesn't want to see."

"But hasn't he got any kind of influence besides that?"

"None at all. But everybody is afraid of getting turned away by him."

The guest nodded toward the lattice and smiled.

"To receive Lydia Pávlovna—that I can understand. To turn away people of substance and importance and shower affection on a niece who is a medical assistant, and who flies in the face of social conventions—that is just to his taste. And so Luke Semyónych turns up his nose at those who would like him to receive them. But why should the second exception among all his relatives be Zakhár Semyónych? Our dear general is the same poor sinner as the rest of us."

"The old man spares Zakhár: 'Our brother Zakhár,' he says, 'has been punished aplenty for hobnobbing with bad people. May God forgive what he has done to himself.'"

"You don't say so!"

The girl behind the lattice began stirring. The ladies noticed this, and the guest said softly with a smile: "Do you suppose she'll go back to sleep?"

"Probably," answered the mistress. "She's that way everywhere. She'll come and sleep a little and then run off to her pigsty to 'do her duty there, no doubt, by cutting some corpse's innards out.'[3] But you have to admit that Bertenson has done a fine job of keeping them in line, especially ever since they caused him that trouble."[4]

"But you know, he taught them a lesson after that."

"That's true, but just the same, they put up with a lot from him."

"Buy why doesn't Lydia Pávlovna sleep at home?"

"Her family is in chaos; they all dislike each other; it's unpleasant for her to hear her brothers talking about horse races and duels, and unpleasant for them that she cuts up corpses, and unpleasant for their mother to hear about what she spends her time doing—that's the way the whole house goes—everybody pulling in different directions . . . But then brother Luke shows her a lot of affection and even sends flowers to her at the pigsty."

The guest nodded toward the sleeping girl and asked in a whisper: "She'll soon be through, and be a medical assistant?"

"Yes."

"I seem to remember she was learning how to make bandages a long time ago, wasn't she?"

"Oh, there's no end to her studying: high school and then teacher's training, and then the university—she's been through it all. Her earrings are gone, and her corset is taken off, and the girl is living in complete simplicity."

"Like a Tolstoyan?"

"Hm . . . Well, you know, as far as Tolstóy is concerned—the young people are already turning away from him completely. I always said it would happen, and there was nothing to worry about: 'The devil is never as terrible as his urchins.' "[5]

The guest smiled and remarked: "That's true. He has bored everybody with his moralizing. But, you know, there was a time when you wouldn't have agreed with that proverb: you yourself were partial to him then."

"I? Yes, I've changed, and I'm willing to admit it. I have always loved to read, and at that time I was for Tolstóy in every respect. His Natásha, for example![6] Wasn't she a delight? She was my idol and my divinity! And it was so fascinating that I didn't notice where he gave vent to all his extreme realism—all that about the diapers and the baby's stains. After all, babies do mess themselves up. They couldn't get along without that, and it didn't seem repulsive to me, the way it did to other people. And then do you remember how he described Alexander the First?"

"Of course! The way he dressed?"

"Yes. You remember, the way he fastened his suspenders?"

"Oh, it was divine!"

"Yes. But was it only his suspenders in that part? Because, you know, he stood there before you just as if he was alive all over! I can see him, I can feel him!"

"Napoleon was well done too, with his dark eyes."

"Napoleon had gray eyes."

"But they gave that sort of impression . . ."

"I won't argue with you about it. Tolstóy has no equal in all that. There's no question about it. But when he started getting ideas, and dropped his real work, and began writing rubbish, like telling people they couldn't eat meat or get married, and telling young girls to keep covered up to their neck and never take a husband, then I said straight out that it was nonsense! In that case we might as well send them all off to the Castrates[7] and be done with it, but as an Orthodox I won't side with him."

Here the guest quietly remarked that Tolstóy *in reality* had never *forbidden* anyone to eat meat, and had said, she understood, that some people might even need to marry.

"Yes, I know that he hasn't yet forbidden anything *in reality,* but *still,* why did he write about it so powerfully and majestically?"[8]

"Well, he did write boldly, of course; but in our country, thank God, he himself still doesn't have the right to forbid anything."

"Of course, thank God! But why does he keep harping on the same thing? Just why is that? He tries to argue that you mustn't offend the wicked, or simply tries to prove that you can't serve without faith, and all that is fine, but then he suddenly breaks off and starts writing nonsense again, like 'what good is soap?' Now, please tell me—does he really not know what soap is for! Let me ask you: how could we get along without soap—how could we wash our face and hands, not to mention our linen? Does he want us to boil it in ashes? But still, I could forgive him all that for the sake of his past. To tell the truth, all men are stupid when they meddle in things that don't concern them. What all they don't say! Even the best of us slip up now and then. 'Freedom to the free and paradise to save us.'[9] And the same thing about meat: let whoever likes fish or flour do without meat. Whatever the form of government may be, nobody ought to put pressure on anybody anywhere in this matter. For goodness' sake! Then maybe a top-grade filet will be cheaper for us. Isn't that right?"

"Of course."

"That's just it! All the same, let those who don't want to get married stay any way they please. You know, even the Gospels talk about them: 'some are eunuchs . . .'[10] You understand, they are madmen!"

The guest nodded her head in agreement.

"When my sons were boys," the mistress went on, "they had a student from the seminary as a tutor, very ambitious, but comical, and he was getting ready to become a monk, and when we told him, 'You'd do better, Monsieur, to get married!' he answered straight out: 'I don't see any need to.'"

The lady turned slightly toward the lattice and said: "Lydia, are you awake or still asleep?"

"Yes, *ma tante,*" answered a sleepy contralto.

"But what does that mean—that you've had your sleep or that you're still sleeping?"

"You probably want to talk about something, *ma tante*, that I am not supposed to understand, and so you want me to go?"

"I wish you would go, only not go out of the room, but finally go to the altar."

"And I will only ask you the same question the seminary student did: to what purpose?"

"Well, if only for the purpose of being able to talk about everything in your presence without feeling embarrassed because you are there."

"Why, it seems to me that you don't feel embarrassed at all."

"Well, we do!"

"You mean I don't know enough yet. Well, just assume that I am married and know everything you know."

"Just listen! Listen to what she tells on herself! But I wanted to tell you something . . . Oh yes . . . You've probably heard everybody telling about how a relative, some sort of hussar, came in his tight-fitting uniform to see the Count, and the Count took the nurse's apron and tied it around him before he would let him into the drawing room."[11]

"Yes, that's what they say, and they say it's the truth."

"Oh yes! And if you want to know my opinion, a hussar's uniform really isn't—entirely modest."

"Yes, but it's very beautiful!"

"Beautiful—yes. But then that apron—you know, that too is impudent! A hussar in an apron! But that is just what I can't forgive him—his unbearable insight! There is harm in that for society."

"That's just it! And of course we can't allow any harm to society. Now tell me, what do you make of all this?"

II

"Why, the trouble is, what right has the Count got to spoil our servants? If he has trained himself to do everything for himself, why, that's just fine for him, but we don't yet aspire to that. Isn't that right?"

"Of course."

"So why in the world does he try to thrust on us that impossible life of fraternizing with the servants, who are coarse as well as depraved?"

"It's stupid."

"Of course it's stupid! I gave Arkády the idea of putting it into some comical verse and reading it. You know, a lot of people in society like his talent."

"Yes, everybody says that, and he is so ingratiating . . . Oh, he'll get on!"

"Possibly—in fact, even probably. But we can't judge like that about the future; the future, as they say, is 'in the hands of Almighty God.' But of course he will be helped along a great deal in his success by his attractive talent. My second son, Valéry, is entirely different. He is a practical man!"

"Oh, to be sure!" the guest answered with a little embarrassment, and she hastily turned the conversation in another direction. "In just what way does Tolstóy spoil the servants?"

"Just let me tell you!" answered the mistress. "We will talk about the servants just like real bureaucrats' wives, but it is not an idle question. Even Schopenhauer talks about servants. Servants can calm you and they can upset you. I won't quote you all of Tolstóy's preachments on servants, but I will give you just one ready-made illustration about how it has its effect. I had an upsetting incident with my maid . . . Lydia hinders my telling you *everything*, but I can't restrain myself and I am going to tell you some of it."

"Please, *ma tante,* tell whatever you want!" the girl called out. "I'm going to sleep just a bit more and then I'll leave."

"I'll be brief," the mistress went on. "Just before the holiday I had to fire the worthless wretch. Well, you know how our common people are before holidays, and how hard it is to find replacements. They're all greedy, they all expect gifts, and they haven't got a trace of love for their masters. It's all right to look at the Russian common people from afar, especially when they pray and believe. Take Répin, for example, in his 'Religious Procession,'[12] where, you remember, he showed how all those officials of the various classes gathered together . . ."

"Yes, or the watercolors of Peter Sokolóv . . ."[13]

"Yes, but there is a little too much blue in them."

"That is true; he overdid it."

"In general, our artists don't understand moderation."

"Yes, but you know, it's all a matter of impression . . . Now, I have an acquaintance—you know her—we all call her 'the Apostle.' I'm sure you know her!"

"Of course I do. You are talking about Marie?"

"Yes. Now there are several unfortunates like her, but I won't compare her with the others. She is not like the others, and besides, she goes back to prehistoric times, when we all still spoke French, and neither Zasétskaya nor Péiker were in fashion, and even Radstock himself had not yet arrived . . . Oh, how remote! Vasíly Páshkov was still an army officer, and Modést Korf crossed himself with both hands, and in the presence of everybody in the cathedral held prayer services in the uniform of a gentleman-in-waiting. And as for Alexéi Pávlovich Bóbrinsky, why at that time he was still a Galician warrior and shouted so loud that the windows shook in the ministry. Seryózha Kushelyóv even sketched all this very nicely in a caricature and took it around and showed it to everybody, and they all laughed."[14]

"I remember all that."

"Yes, it's all unjust, you know, to claim that Tolstóy started the fashion of going barefooted and working with your hands. Marie was the first, and started doing that before everybody else. She scrubbed the floors herself and carried out even the most disgusting things for the sick. She even went a few times with Nikolái Andréevich into beer halls and tried to save some unfortunate girls there, and the girls themselves laughed them out of the house. You can't save them all, of course—that would be stupid: they are necessary. But still there was good will on Marie's part . . . And since Ánnenkov headed the police at that time, he smoothed everything over and no scandal came out of it." [15]

"I remember. It was funny the way they told it."

"Oh, it was most interesting, but all the same Marie has not changed to this day: 'Mother Sophia grieving over them all.' Before God she felt no jealousy toward either Radstock or Páshkov, and she feels none toward Tolstóy now. They all seem kin to her somehow, and even about her it's impossible to say anything except that even though she is a sectarian and a lost sheep, still she's full of goodness and sympathy for people. That is better than all her faith."

"Yes, it really does seem to be."

"Of course, just what is their faith? You know, a great many of these girls are thoroughly pitiful. Men will lure them away and then abandon them . . . You remember how Berton did that? [16] Carried her off and then threw her over, to live the best way she could. And Marie spends her whole life taking care of somebody. If you want to find a good person, go to her. She always has a supply of the 'insulted and injured.' [17] I went and asked her to recommend me a modest, upright girl, so that there shouldn't be any bad example and hypocrisy at home. The main thing was to have no hypocrisy, since I despise hypocrisy. And Marie was actually pleased. 'Oh, how glad I am,' she said, 'to hear you speak like that! Lies are the vice that Satan used to begin corrupting man. He *deceived* Eve, don't you remember?' (Yes, yes, yes, I thought to myself; you're very well read, but you've gone back a long way with all that about our ancestors and Satan, and all I'm asking you for is a chambermaid.)

" 'Oh yes, I have such a girl!' Marie answered. 'Just that kind of excellent girl has taken shelter with me till she can find work.'

" 'She's not a hypocrite, and she doesn't run around?'

" 'Oh, how could she! She's a Christian!'

" 'Well, you know, everybody in our country is baptized, and even Orthodox, but they've all got frightful morals and principles.'

" 'Oh no, how can you say that? Christians have excellent principles! Besides, this is a girl who is always busy, working and reading, "Intermediocre books." ' [18]

" 'Aha, so she's a Tolstoyan! But that's all right, I despise all utopias, but to have a servant aim at non-resistance to evil actually sounds excellent to me. Give me your non-resister. I will let her off for prayers. Where do they get together for their prayermeetings? Or don't they pray at all?'

" 'I don't know,' she said. 'That is a matter of conscience; it's not something to ask questions about.'

" 'Of course, I don't care—that's up to her. What is her name?'

" 'Fedórushka.'

" 'Oh, what an ugly-sounding name!'

" 'Why so? It is very good! Call her Feodóra, or even Theodora. What could be better?'

" 'No, that's theatrical. I'll call her Kátya.'

" 'But why?'

" 'Well, that's just my way of doing things,' I said.

"Marie made no protest and sent me her non-resister, and just imagine, I really liked the girl, and I hired her."

"For how much?" asked the guest.

"Seven rubles a month."

"How very cheap!"

"Yes. But she didn't ask more. She herself didn't even ask anything at all, but said, 'Just pay me what I am worth.' And so I named the figure. But excuse me, that wasn't what I was telling about; I liked her very much then, because she really did look so clean and modest. But I must admit that when I heard she was a non-resister, I did get worried about her cleanliness, since there is all that against soap in their books, and I remember how my nurse read how a shameless blackamoor threw himself on a certain saint, but since she never washed with soap, this Faublas fairly jumped back from her."

"That's awful!"

"Yes. All the others had to submit, but she didn't. But I really don't understand whether that can be why Tolstóy is against soap."

"Oh no! Have you forgotten what soap is made out of?"

"Out of meat juice."

"Well, there's the answer."

"Auntie!" the girl called from behind the lattice. "Why aren't you ashamed to talk such rubbish?"

"What do you mean?"

"Soap is not made out of meat, and a great deal of soap is not made out of animal fat, but rather out of vegetable fat. And then there is the egg soap that you yourself buy."

"Oh, that's right, that's right. It's true, there *is* egg soap. That's in Kazán, where Skaryátin was governor,[19] but I don't buy it now. I bought it for a long time and washed myself with it a lot, but I haven't liked it every since the Persian Shah was here and I found out he washes his feet with it, and I don't buy it any more." [20]

"Why should you want to know about that?"

"Well, why not? We weren't taught that kind of haughty airs in the institutes. And in my opinion it's better to be interested in people like that than in dirty slobs . . . I remember, when Arkády was finishing his studies, all sorts of people would visit him, and those non-resisters came too, and they were all in that uniform of theirs, all colorless and wearing muddy boots."

"Terrible 'urchins'!" said the guest.

"Yes, they're all like that—all with their fat little sheep's-tails. They would fasten their belts, and invariably it would make a sort of sheep's-tail behind, and they wore no galoshes on those clumsy feet and would leave dirty footmarks everywhere. Now there was untidiness for you! But the non-resister girl came to me in completely tidy shape and was an excellent worker, but still she turned out to be impossible in practical affairs."

"Why?"

"Yes, yes, yes! There are many sides to practical affairs, and she turned out to be the worst of all the non-resister girls."

"Did some non-resister boy turn up?"

"Oh no! Not at all. You'll never guess."

III

"I may as well begin with a trifle. I looked through her passport and right there once again I ran up against the name Fedóra. I said to her: 'Dearie, I don't like your first name, and I'm going to call you Kátya.' And she answered right back with the argument that 'If it so pleases you to have a servant called something else in your home, it is all the same to me: *those are man-made customs.*'"

"How funny!"

"Awfully funny. 'Man-made customs' . . . That's because they have their 'direct obligations to God.' But I myself grew up in the country, and I like to talk with the servants now and then. So I said, 'I'm going to call you Kátya, and you must answer to it.' And she answered, 'Yes, ma'am.' 'And one more thing,' I said, 'I forgot to tell you that your duties also include helping the cook wash the dishes and wiping up the painted floors with a damp cloth in the back rooms.' But what do you think? She wiped up the floors, and she answered when I called her 'Kátya,' but if any of my friends asked her what her name was, she would stubbornly answer, 'Fedóra.' I told her: 'Listen, dearie. You've been told already, and you've just got to remember that now you are Kátya. Why do you keep contradicting me?' And she began to argue: 'I respond to the way you call me, since you told me that was the way things were done at your house, and it doesn't harm me, but I myself *cannot lie* . . .' 'What sort of nonsense is that?' I said. 'No,' she said, 'I cannot lie; that would harm me.' "

"Well, would you ever!" the guest exclaimed. "She won't harm herself!"

"Oh, I should say she wouldn't! There was something punctual about her, something narrow and stubborn, just like Martin Iványch Luther himself. Oh, how I hate that dry Lutheranism! And how good it is that they are going after them nowadays in our country. So I asked her: 'What harm is it to you? Will your belly start hurting or will it be your head?'

" 'No,' she said, 'my belly may not hurt, but there are things that are more important than your belly or your head.'

" 'What are they, then?'

" 'Man's soul. I want to keep my conscience always in good order.' Now there's a cockleburr for you!"

"It's plain insolence!"

"Yes, but as brother Zakhár says, 'even though it's not pleasant, still, ever since our blessed Nineteenth of February it's been inevitable.' " [21]

"Yes, ever since that February they've had us where they wanted us."

"And especially right before a holiday. After all, we can't go to our own door and tell our visitors we are not at home. In general, it hasn't yet come to that, but that's just what that non-resister girl did at my house."

"You don't say so!"

"It's a fact!"

"Well, our only hope really is the city governor."

"Yes, he'll take them in hand. On the holiday I explained to her: 'Kátya, guests are coming. You must tell them all that I am at home and receiving.' And she received them all right, but then Victor Gustávych came. You know, a man with his position and his power, and me with two sons, and both of them so different in character: my Arkády—he's just plain lazy; and Valéry—you know how he is, squirming with life. You can understand that I am concerned for them, and I wanted to have a talk with him about Valéry, who didn't follow along after Arkády, but got into that—university. He'll finish next year, without connections, without anything . . ."

The guest made a barely noticeable movement.

"And so I got Victor Gustávych settled in a chair and ran out to her and said, 'Kátya, if anybody comes now, you must say *I have gone out* and *I am not at home.*' You'd think any stupid wench could get that straight!"

"What is there to get straight?"

"Of course, the most ordinary thing. But just imagine; she told every-body that 'I had *ordered* her to say that I had gone out and wasn't at home!' "

"Oh, good Lord!" the guest exclaimed and burst out laughing.

"But imagine, everybody did just what you did and only laughed about it. Nobody got angry, because they all knew perfectly well that everybody tells lies in those cases . . . It's taken for granted . . . But the young peo-ple started telling me, '*Ma tante*, your non-resister seems to be a big fool.' But I rightly understood that it was just her faith working on her, and I explained to everybody that was just Count Tolstóy sticking out of her, powerfully and majestically thumbing his big nose at all educated people, as if to say, 'Visits serve no purpose at all! They are all stupid: there's no point in wasting time with horses; when you need exercise, scrub the floors.' "

"Without soap?"

"Yes, just like that!"

"And what did you do with your non-resister after that?"

"I had it out with her. I told her, 'Look here now, you were recom-mended to me as a very good girl and a Christian, but you're a sly and stubborn type. What sort of prank was that on your part to make me out to be a liar?' And she made a simpleminded excuse:

" 'I couldn't say anything else.'

" 'Why not? You poor, unenlightened lame-brain! Why couldn't you say anything else?'

" 'Because you *were* at home.'

" 'Well, what's the harm in that?'

" 'I would have lied.'

" 'Well, even if you did lie a little, what of it?'

" 'I can't lie at all.'

" 'Not a bit?'

" 'Not a bit.'

" 'But after all, you're a *servant*. You've hired yourself out, you get a salary. With notions like that how can you hire yourself out and take a job?'

" 'I am hired to do work, and not to lie. I cannot lie.'

"No matter which side you started from, she would always come back to her 'I can't lie' and wouldn't budge from it."

"What narrow-mindedness!"

"It's awful! 'But after all,' I told her, 'you have to know how to make distinctions. There are lies you must not tell, and then there are the kind you can tell. Just ask any priest.'

" 'No, no, no!' she answered. 'I don't want to make those distinctions—you can have them. I won't go and ask about them. There's nothing said about them in the Gospels, those distinctions. Everything that is not true is a lie, and Christians must not tell lies.'

"Then I remembered that when I hired her I had thought that 'non-resistance' would be all right and wouldn't do any harm in servants, and in the lower classes in general—it might even be useful for them. But it didn't turn out that way at all! It turned out to be unsuitable here too, so that we've got to oppose it everywhere!"

IV

The mistress knit her brows seriously and said she had talked about this "arrogance" with the priest, and he had explained to her that this was "the fruit of a free and *personal* interpretation."

"Yes, but what kind of freedom is it when it's so terribly narrow?" the guest put in with a learned air.

"I agree with you, and besides that, not everything is good for everybody."

The mistress rapped on the table with her hand, so that the turquoise rings on her fingers started jumping, and she went on:

"I remember very well, you know, when Evropéus and Unkóvsky were in their glory.[22] It was very different from these days, and once it happened that we were at dinner together in a certain home and somebody brought Shevchénko—you remember, that Ukrainian.[23] He had played some sort of prank and got into a lot of trouble for it. And there all of a sudden at supper he took a drink of vodka and let loose such an impromptu remark that nobody knew where to turn his eyes. Somebody finally had the wonderful presence of mind to say, 'Believe me, what is good for a few may not be suitable at all for everybody.' And that saved all of us, although we found out later that it had already been said by Púshkin, and Shevchénko can't even be compared to him."

"Just suppose Púshkin started talking like that!"

"Of course, he wouldn't have thought of it," the mistress chimed in. "He lived in society, and the Decembrists knew they couldn't start anything with him. But Shevchénko hobnobbed with all sorts of people, and who knows whether it isn't really true that Peróvsky himself punished him in the military fashion—you know, that's how the times were: he was a soldier, and so they thrashed him, as was proper.[24] But Púshkin knew how to give just the right turn to that, too, when he said, 'What is excellent for London won't do in Moscow.' And it stayed just the way he said it: 'In London it is good, but in Moscow it won't do.' "[25]

"In Moscow there is nobody any more—Katkóv is dead."[26]

From behind the lattice there came the sound of a stifled laugh.

"What is so funny to you, Lydia?"

" 'Katkóv is dead.' You said that as if you meant, 'The great god Pan is dead.' "

"And your eyes 'flashed' like Diana's."

"I don't remember how Diana's eyes flashed."

"But it was so beautiful!"

"I don't know how to get away from all that beauty. I do remember, though, that Diana protected the common people and slaves, and that a fugitive slave who had killed a priest was a priest in her temple, and that she herself was a virgin but helped other women when they gave birth. That was beautiful."

"Beautiful!"

And the mistress shook her head and remarked, "You are completely without shame."

"*With* shame, *ma tante!*"

"Now, just what are you saying. What do you want?"

"I don't want young girls to feel bored with nothing to do in their girl-hood, and I want them to help whoever is suffering."

"But why when they are giving birth?"

"Because it's frightful when they are giving birth, and a lot of women suffer through it without any help, while young society girls make eyes at the men. Let them help others and they'll see plenty of what awaits them when they stop guarding themselves like Diana."

"Just a minute," the guest interrupted. "I wasn't talking about that Diana at all; I was talking about the one whose eyes flashed in the forest on an island when she got news from a ship that 'the great god Pan had died.' That was in Turgénev, wasn't it?"[27]

"I've forgotten how it was in Turgénev."

The mistress went on. "Nowadays they forget what is good and rave about what the 'Intermediocre books' say."

"Have you ever called Victor Gustávych's attention to those books?" asked the guest.

"Oh, he looks down on them, but you know, he's a Lutheran, and in his opinion anything is all right if it talks about goodness."

"But still, your non-resister was not actually good, was she?"

"Well, I can't come right out and say that. She was not spiteful with anybody, but I noticed that after you had kept answering her back for a while, something really would flash in her eyes."

"You don't say!"

"I assure you. You know, if you teased her in a joking way, her eyes would start flashing . . . and . . . it was just like fire."

"My God! And why did you keep her?"

"Oh, yes, I myself thought: 'Uh-oh, so you're full of fire,' and I let her go. But naturally, I wanted to find out first just what you could expect from such people; so I put her through an interrogation."

"That is interesting."

V

"I asked her: 'So tell me, dearie,' I says, 'if you saw something happen in a house that ought to be a secret and kept hidden from everybody, would you still refuse to hide somebody's shame or sin?' She got embarrassed and started babbling: 'I've never thought about that . . . I don't know!' I took advantage of that and said: 'And suppose you were called in and questioned about the people you work for, surely you must . . . You know what good and faithful servants there were in the old days, and yet when the pressure was put on them even they told whatever was demanded.' Just imagine how she answered:

" 'Whoever brought them to that point was the guilty one.'

" 'And suppose it was done on orders?'

" 'That's all the same.' "

"What a girl!"

"I should say! I told her, 'People can suffer for that.' And she answered, 'It is better to suffer than to ruin one's way of life.' "

"What non-resistance!"

"Well, you see for yourself!"

"Although if you look at it from their point of view and stick to the Gospel, she's not entirely in the wrong . . .'

"Why she's even very much in the right, but after all, society is not organized so that you can do everything according to the Gospel. They can't demand all that from us at once."

"Yes, it's very sad. But if you overcome it and spoil it, what will you put that is new in its place?"

"The nihilists used to say *'nothing'*!"

The mistress lapsed into silence and twisted a strip of paper in her fingers, and in her mind's eye she seemed to be surveying something long past; and then she said:

"Yes, *nothing*. All they knew how to do was lead women astray and teach them how to drink tea with two persons at once and not feel ashamed of it."

"And how did that non-resister behave in those circumstances?"

"You probably mean the circumstances we can't talk about in front of Lydia?"

But by this time Lydia was no doubt completely refreshed after resting behind the lattice, and she broke into the conversation with words that by no means sounded sleepy.

"When you are talking about such a woman as Fedórushka you can say anything in front of anybody," said Lydia. "And besides, *ma tante*, when will you finally get used to the fact that I am not a child, and that I know better than you not only what soap is made of but also how a baby is born?"

"Lydia!" the mistress said in reproach.

"Yes, *ma tante,* of course I know it."

"Oh Lord! How can you know that?"

"So that surprises you? I am twenty-four years old. I live, I read, and finally I'm supposed to become a medical assistant. So what do you expect—that I should pretend to be a stupid lying child who claims to think storks bring babies in their beaks?"

The mistress turned to her guest and said significantly:

"There you have Jonah the Cynic in feminine form.[28] And besides that she's a Diana, a puritan, a Quakeress, she reads and reveres Tolstóy, but she doesn't share a lot of even his opinions, and she won't live in peace with anybody."

"I don't think I quarrel very often."

"At the same time you don't become close friends with anybody."

"You are mistaken, *ma tante,* I do have friends."

"But you've thrown them over. For instance, the non-resister boys were once in your favor, but now you've grown cool towards them."

"There's nothing to be done with them."

"But still, you used to like to listen to them."

"Yes, I did listen to them."

"And you got fed up with listening to them, didn't you?"

"No; why should I? I'm ready to listen now to whatever they say that is well thought out."

"You used to stand up for them to the point of tears."

"I stood up for them when your sons—my cousins—got them together and made fun of them. I can't bear it when people are ridiculed."

The mistress burst out laughing and said:

"There's no sin in laughing at what is laughable."

"Yes there is, *ma tante,* and I always felt terribly sorry for them . . . They themselves are good-hearted, and they want goodness, and I wept for them . . ."

"And then you yourself got angry with them."

"I didn't get angry, but I saw that they only talked and talked, and what they accomplished wasn't worth a hill of beans. It was all very boring. If those who used to be forever getting ready to 'work on Buckle'[29] were tiresome, these people today are just as tiresome when you see that the only thing they know how to do is take a stick and muddy the waters. Both do harm to the very thing they try to teach people to approach with respect."

"You're just irritated because they crusade against science."

"Yes, that does irritate me."

"But I am for them! After all, why should you keep on studying for so many years and standing up for what you believe, when it's clear that all your learning will end by your getting a job as an assistant to some stupid doctor who will stand you in the corner?"

"Now, *ma tante,* you know that's nonsense."

"Well, then, maybe he'll stand you in the vestibule. He himself will go inside and eat his meat pies, and he'll tell you, 'Just stand there, my dear, in the vestibule.'"

"That won't happen either."

"And if it does happen, then what will you do?"

"I will pity the person who treats me so crudely because I have no greater rights, and lack them only because they have not been given to me."

"And won't you be offended?"

"By somebody else's stupidity? Of course not."

"But wouldn't it be better to get married like everybody else?"

"Not for me!"

"Why not?"

"I don't want to marry."

"You *are* talking strangely, after all. That's a law of nature."

"Well, it hasn't got to me yet."

"And religion requires the same thing."

"My religion doesn't."

"But after all, Christ was in favor of marriage."

"I've never read that."

"Then why did he bless the bridegroom and the bride?"

"I don't know when that happened."

"Read it in the Gospels."

"It's not there."

"What do you mean, it's not there?"

"It just isn't, and that's all there is to it."

"Oh Lord! What's the meaning of all this? So you've crossed it all out!"

The young girl gave a quiet laugh.

"There's nothing to snigger about. I know there *was* something about that, and if it wasn't in the Gospels, then it was in the Wisdom of Paul. In any case, he was in Cana of Galilee."

"Well, what of it?"

"It shows he blessed marriage."

"And didn't he also visit the publican?"

"Yes."

"And talked with the prostitute? Does that mean he blessed what they did too?"

"You're a terrible arguer."

"I am only answering you."

"And Peter's mother-in-law! After all, you remember, Christ healed her!"

"Surely you don't think he would have refused to heal her if she hadn't been somebody's mother-in-law."

"You have a most disagreeable mind."

"Yes, a lot of people say that, *ma tante*, and that convinces me more than anything that I must not marry."

"Now there you go, wriggling and twisting exactly like a snake so that nobody can corner you."

"But just why is it necessary to corner me, *ma tante*?"

"I'd certainly like to . . ."

"But what's to be done, my dear? You can't arrange everything just the way you would like."

"No, I don't mean that. I would like to know what kind of catechism teacher you have, and how it is that he doesn't see that you are all godless."

"We all get straight A's from him."

"Do tell! And what does he give you straight A's for?"

"He can't do otherwise; we all learn excellently."

"And just look at what kind of character you have developed!"

"Oh, do leave off, *ma tante*! What does that have to do with character? Characters come, characters develop—but they are still in the future, and we can't hold a candle to them. And they will come, they will! 'There comes the sound of spring, the joyful sound!'[30] The healthy mind will come, *ma tante*! It will! We live by that faith! Live by it yourself, and—everything will be all right with you, always, no matter what they may do to you!"

"No, thank you, my dear."

"Don't be angry, *ma tante*," and Lydia Pávlovna suddenly turned to her aunt's guest and said: "And would you like to know whether Fedóra ever had a romance? I can tell you about that. She was engaged to a watchmaker, but Fedórushka turned him down, because she had a sister who had 'given in to life.' She had farthingales and a brooch and earrings and two children. She kept the earrings and the brooch, but she wanted to send the children off to an orphanage. Fedóra took pity on them, though, and spent almost everything she earned on them."

"But didn't she ever have any great passion herself?"

"That *was* her own great passion!"

"Yes, but it will be hard for her to pay for it. With her character and the kind of rules she has, she'll never stay in one place very long."

"Others will help her."

"Don't you see? They're real sectarians, they work together like a peasant commune," the mistress declared. "Persecute them and they don't fear anything—they even welcome it!"

"That's just as it should be, of course," said the girl.

"Nonsense!"

"But it is written that we must rejoice when we suffer persecution for righteousness' sake, and in actual fact this greatly helps the spread of our ideas. They drive us off, and we go further and keep on talking about the good to more and more new people."

"But now you just listen a minute: just what kind of belief do you yourself have?"

"That is such a delicate question, *ma tante*, that I don't allow anybody to touch on it."

"Just listen to how they've taken to answering questions about their faith! That is certainly different from the likes of us."

"Yes, it *is* different from the likes of you," Lydia answered with a laugh. "For the likes of you 'it is seemly to ask of every man that entereth: speak forth, my child, what is thy faith?' "

The mistress struck the table with her fan and threatened her niece: "Lydia! This time I won't count what you have said here; we'll let it pass. But hereafter remember that you have a mother, and you must not be a hindrance to your brothers in their careers!"

"Who can forget that, *ma tante!*"

"Then there's no reason for you to keep playing the liberal."

"But 'what is thy faith?'—is that really liberalism?"

"It's unreasonable."

"Do forgive me, *ma tante*, but after all, life is given to us only once, and it is very imprudent to adapt it to any kind of season. That will soon change."

Having said this, the girl got up and came out from behind the lattice into the middle of the room. Now it could be seen that she was very beautiful. She had a well-proportioned figure of remarkable strength and grace, which did indeed remind one of the little Tanagra statue of Diana,[31] and her face, with its big and fearless eyes, had a pleasant and chaste expression.

VI

Her aunt looked at her, and her face took on an air of artistic satisfaction; she beamed and said softly:

"I'd like to know where people's eyes are who dare to say anything against high birth. Lydia, are you going around without a corset?"

"I never wear one."

"And as shapely as a goddess. But Valerian told me you have a lot of depraved girls, and all of them have now taken off their rings and decided not to wear earrings or any other kinds of jewelry."

"What concern is it of his?"

"Why not? Everything interests him. Now, isn't that the truth?"

"Yes, it is."

"And you'll see that very likely many of them won't hold out."

"That's very likely."

"Whoever looks good in earrings won't hold out—she'll put them on."

"Well, what of it? If she doesn't hold out, then at least she will get a little practice in holding out, and that is worth something. Good-bye, *ma tante*."

"And whoever has a really ugly figure had better wear a corset."

"Really now, *ma tante*, what do we care about such trifles? Good-bye."

"Good-bye, my beauty—oh, what a beauty you are! Only, I can't help being uneasy for fear you'll end by going off and living with one of those non-resisters."

Lydia gave her a cool but tender smile and said: "*Ma tante*, how can you tell what may happen to anybody? But in any case I won't run off with an opera singer."

"No! God forbid! Better anybody you like, only not a non-resister. Those 'urchins' with their little fat sheep's-tails—there's nothing nastier than that."

"Oh, *ma tante*, I just don't know what is not nasty!"

"Well, better let everything be nasty, only not like these people who talk against marriage and baptism. Get married, and then may God preserve you according to His will."

And the aunt got up and started making the sign of the cross over her, and then accompanied her to the vestibule and whispered to her there: "Don't condemn me for being so sharp with you. I had to in front of that woman, and I would advise you to be careful around her after this."

"Oh, nonsense, *ma tante*! I'm not afraid of anybody."

"You're not afraid? Don't talk about things you don't know about."

"Oh, *ma tante*. I don't even want to know; there is *nothing* for me to be afraid of."

Saying this, the young girl began hastily reaching about with her hand for the door knob and went out to the stairway in embarrassment, with a crimson face that simultaneously reflected shame, anger, and pity.

As she went past the doorman she let down her veil, but the keen, observant eyes of the doorman saw just the same that she was weeping.

"They're always rakin' that one over the coals," he said to the yard keeper, who was standing at the gate.

"Yeah, you can see she caught it for something," replied the equally observant yard keeper.

Meanwhile the mistress went back into her "salon" and asked, "How do you like that little character?"

The guest merely lowered her doe eyes and answered, "It's impossible to make it out completely, but you can see the same red thread running everywhere and through everything."

"Oh, today she was very quiet, but last time we came near having a scandal. Somebody recalled our good old days and told about the match-makers there used to be—the kind that nobody would dare turn down. Then she said straight out: 'How good it is that nowadays at least that isn't done any more.' "

"Nowadays girls come out of the high schools so practical that they haven't the slightest comprehension of institutional warmth."

"Not the slightest! I came right out and asked her then whether she really wouldn't be touched if we brought her a bridegroom, and she just flared up and snapped, 'I'm not a serf-girl.' "

"I keep telling you—the red thread everywhere. And such insolence—she talks so self-confidently about the personal passion of that Fedóra's wretched sister!"

"She has a lot of sympathy for children."

"But what can be done when children don't fill a woman's whole life?"

"Oh, there's a lot of trouble with children!"

"Yes, and even the simplest, crudest people try to forget themselves in love regardless of the children. I have an excellent woman who has lived here as a laundress for seven years, and she always struggles with herself, but just the same the result is that she sends a new inmate to the children's home every year. And the anonymous author still keeps on, without signing his name, and won't hear of anything; he just comes and knocks her about, and strips her clean of everything she's got. And that's the way they all are. There's a gigolo streak in our way of life. And when I said to her, 'Throw them all over or else turn to religion—that will help,' she listened to me and went to Kronstadt;[32] but on the way back she bought some Vyborg cracknels and dropped in to drink tea with the scoundrel, and now once more she's carrying a load around, and she's very happy. What can you do about it? 'I can't help it,' she says. 'The devil is stronger than I am.' When a woman admits her own weakness, you just put up with it."

"Yes, you put up with it, because that's our simple, native, Russian way."

"That's it! That's it! That's our poor Russian womanly flesh; not at all the same thing as those others, those English oilcloth dolls—clean but cold."

"Oh, how cold! Now *she,* you know, takes up for children; but mark my word, she doesn't love them either."

"You don't say!"

"I'm positive. She looks after children in a general way, but she never makes a lot over them and doesn't even kiss them."

"If she doesn't kiss them, that's very fine."

"Of course we can assume it's unhealthy, as they say—but she just doesn't like it!"

"Really? But it's natural for all women to want to pamper children."

"Pampering—no. The only thing she'll allow is caring for them, but as she puts it you should love only those who themselves have love for people. And babies are not capable of that."

"But can anybody know how a little one will turn out?"

"That's just what she says. 'I don't like unknown quantities; I like what I know and understand.' "

"What philosophizing!"

"I keep telling her: that doesn't sound like the heart but like mathematics. She doesn't believe other people love children. 'Otherwise,' she says, 'there wouldn't be such scoundrels who make a laughingstock of a Russian name among intelligent people.' They don't give a very high rating to our glory and power. And just imagine, they prove it by Máikov:

> *A nation's greatness lies in no small part*
> *In what that nation bears within its heart.*"[33]

Both the mistress of the house and the guest exchanged glances, and at once they both sank into thought, and their faces took on an unwomanly, official expression. The guest recovered first, and she remarked:

"At the same time that we Russian women sign Madame Adam's declaration,[34] it wouldn't be bad if we also protested against institutions that do not inspire respect for Russian principles."

The mistress began nervously twisting a bit of paper in her hands, and knitting her brows she whispered in perplexity, "But who will take the first step?"

"Isn't it all the same who does?"

"But still . . . My brother Luke used to . . . He's independent and never was a liberal, and he has nothing to fear for himself . . . It used to be that he would start up a conversation about anything at all, but now he wouldn't for anything in the world! He has turned his back on us in the most serious way, and he has taken Lydia into his good graces, and that is frightful, because he acquired his whole fortune himself and he can leave it to anybody he wishes."

"Do you mean to say it could all go to Lydia Pávlovna?"

"Nothing would be easier. Brother Luke doesn't approve of my sons, and he thinks Brother Zakhár is a spendthrift and a 'sink hole.' He supports Zakhár's whole family, but he won't leave them anything."

The guest stood up and walked over to the open piano, and in a moment she asked, "But where are Zakhár Semyónych's wife and daughters now?"

"His wife—I don't know exactly . . . She's in Italy or France."

"Something detained her in Vienna."

"Oh, but that was over long ago! Such detentions as that you couldn't count up if you took all evening. But now she has only three daughters with her. Nina, you know, the youngest, was married a year ago to Count Z. He's terribly rich."

"And terribly old?"

"Of course, he's over seventy—some say even more—and she's about twenty. There are a lot of them, you know—four girls. And the Count, the old man, married to spite his relatives. He still hopes to have children. We took the trip to ask a blessing for him."

"May God help him!"

"Yes. At the wedding Brother Zakhár told him, 'I drink a glass to your health and when my daughter presents you with horns I'll drink a whole bottle to her health.' "

In answer to this the guest turned away from the piano and faced the mistress, and her face no longer exhaled the gentle kindness of the doe but had the expression of the kicking nanny-goat. In a way that apparently had no connection but in fact was shrewdly to the point, she said, "It is obvious that you are the one to begin the action."

"But Lydia is related to me."

"That is just why it is necessary. It will show your impartiality and your readiness to sacrifice everything for the sake of society, and she'll be kept out of the inheritance."

The mistress looked at the guest with the look of one bewitched. The case was worked out correctly, but in the old woman's soul something dangled loosely, and again she twisted the paper and whispered: "I don't know . . . Let me think about it. I will ask the priest."

"Of course, ask him."

"Good, I will."

VII

At that moment the door swung open, and in came a gray-haired, cheerful, rotund general with a scholarly badge and merry, penetrating gray eyes in his big smooth face, which was capable of taking on the most varied expressions.

This was Brother Zakhár.

The hostess held out her hand to him and said, "Speak of the devil and there he is. We were just talking about you."

"And what for, exactly?" asked the general as he sat down and rather drily greeted the guest.

"What do you mean, *what for*? We were simply talking about you."

"Among us, people never simply talk about people; they always criticize them for something or other."

"But there *are* exceptions."

"Only two: Père Jean and Père Onthon." [35]

"You insist that it ought to be pronounced Onthon, and not Antoine?"

"That's the way it is pronounced by those who know more than I do on this subject, and believe more ardently. As you know, I'm weak in faith."

"That's shameful."

"But what can you do about it when you can't believe anything?"

"That used to grieve our mother."

"I remember, and I used to obey her but I couldn't pretend. She would say, 'May your guardian angel be with you', and I would go everywhere with my guardian angel—and that was all!"

"Olympia has arrived."

"I always thought she was called Olympiad. For that matter, I am not especially interested in her."

"She has a lot of news, and some of it concerns you. Your daughter, Countess Nina, is pregnant."

"Really! No doubt the rascal is performing Boccaccio's 'Magic Tree' in real life.[36] Still, I'll drink my bottle of champagne today and telegraph my congratulations to the Count. By the way, the other day I met an old comrade of my son-in-law and learned that he is only fourteen years older than I am."

"And what are the details about their life?"

"I don't know anything."

"But haven't you been to Olympia's yet?"

"I? No, my guardian angel didn't take me there. I saw some lady rushing along in a carriage, and in front of her the coachman had a clock tied behind him over a bustle. I thought to myself, What sort of vulgar old woman has turned up now? Then suddenly I guessed that it was she. And immediately she played me a dirty trick: I tried to get away from her and ran right into a Jew that I owe a devilish pile of money."

"Poor little Zakhár!"

"But God be praised, my guardian angel was looking after me, and it happened right in front of the cathedral: I darted into the church at once and went up to the altar, and the kike got cold feet and stopped at the doors. But what amazingly inconvenient rules they have in the churches! Imagine, they open only one door and keep the others shut. Why should they be shut? In Paris all the temples of God are open all day."

"In our country, my friend, things get stolen. There have been several thefts . . ."

"What pranksters! Well, just imagine—because of this I stood through several services in succession, but finally I left the Jew holding the bag after all. He was waiting for me at the main entrance, but I slipped out through the holy altar with a priest I know and just at that moment came across Lydia. She was upset, and so as to cheer her up I told her how I had run into Olympia, and then the kike, and then barely got away at last through the sanctuary. She cheered up and went along with me to drink a cup of chocolate."

"So you tried to console her? What a dear uncle!"

"Yes, but I had another purpose here too. Where we were there was a—ballerina who never quite succeeds in looking like a goddess. I showed Lydia to her and said, 'Look, you idiot, there's a goddess for you!' But who offended Lydia, and where?"

"That's something I won't try to tell you. 'The scythe struck a stone,' as the saying goes. But she herself said here that she *couldn't* be offended."

"Oh, that's nothing more than those disgusting Tolstoyan *bêtises!* You can be sure that it's Leo Tolstóy who is tangling them all up with all these stupid tricks. 'Da ist der Hund begraben!' [37] I simply cannot understand what that old man wants. They shout to him from the ends of the earth that he's the greatest of wise men, and it's just turned his head. But I simply cannot understand what people see in him that is so wisemannish."

"I can't either."

"And nobody can; it all comes from abroad. He and I once lived on the same street, and I didn't notice anything particularly wise about him. And I remember, once he was at the theater and then afterwards visited some friends of us both and when tea was served to everybody he said to the servant, 'Brother, bring me a glass of vodka.'"

"And he drank it?"

"Yes, he drank it, and he ate a ring-shaped roll, or a crust of bread—I don't remember now. And it was all the most ordinary affair—and later suddenly he started acting strange and joined the wise men. He had it made! But even though I don't share his Christianity, which would be the death of culture, still I do respect him for himself."

"But why?"

"Not for his wisdom, of course. That's all trifles. But I love all those non-resisters of his; it's so good to talk with them over coffee."

"I don't see that."

"Oh, it is! They have original views about a lot of things. I don't agree that any of their fantasies could be put into practice. This is not the time. But why not talk about them? Even Bismarck, you know, liked to talk with socialists. But these 'urchins' run counter to the socialists."

"Run counter? How?"

"Well, it's like this. The non-resisters, you know, always refuse inheritances in favor of their relatives . . . That's the very thing Peter the Great tried to achieve through primogeniture . . . That needs to be encouraged, so as not to keep splitting up property. Tolstoy himself is devilishly proud, but on the other hand he has a lot of character. That is rare in our country. You can't make him knuckle under and start bleating like a sheep—'Baa! Baa!'—for the sake of some shiny decoration."

The general squeezed his throat with his fingers and gave out such noises that the mistress of the house and the guest burst into laughter.

"But why must he have that unbearable insight and why does he keep preaching that there is no need of anything?"

"Well, that is nastiness, but I console myself with your Russian proverb, 'The devil is not as frightful as his urchins.' "

"I always say that too; he is off there, I don't know just where, but these 'Figaro ci, Figaro là' have scattered in all directions like baby chicks."

"That's just what they are—baby chicks . . . What makes them strut around so, as if they were growing their tail-feathers?"

"They really ought to be examined, so that it could be confirmed."

"What can be done to upset them?"

"They won't stop at anything to upset religion."

"My religion can't be upset. In arguments about religion I'm a follower of Byron; I eat my oysters and drink my wine, and I don't give a hang who created them—Jupiter, Pan, or Neptune! And I don't blaspheme about that, but his unbearable insight into our affairs—it's nasty! And then why must he keep denying that 'Cast not pearls before swine' was said to warn people not to go and blab everything in front of just any filthy brute? That's plain stupid. Some people are angels, and some are swine."

"Except that I hope those dear animals are found in their proper places, where they belong."

"Yes, they need to be kept in their pigsties; but sometimes it happens otherwise—there are cases when the pigs sit down in parlors."

"Oh Lord, what horrors!"

"Oh yes! There are a lot of horrors."

"But on the other hand, *are* there any angels anywhere?"

"Why, yes, there are. Such as our Lydia, for example."

"I don't see it—silly girls who don't know what sort they are."

"You people torment them and torture them in a downright godless fashion."

"How do you mean?"

"You badger them and tease them, and when the poor girls finally reach their rope's end and blurt out something to you, then you shout it from the housetops and cause them harm. To tell the truth, that is vile."

"I've never heard of such a thing."

"Well, I can tell you *I* have. They say that when Lydia came to you at the ball in a high-necked bodice, you made cutting remarks to her."

"It's not so!"

"You made fun of her in an offensive way. You told her that when she became a lady she would very likely present herself to her future 'Adam' as a Carmelite nun, dressed in a double hood, and she is supposed to have answered that she might go to her *own* Adam dressed like Eve, but she refused to show off her shoulders to bystanders at a ball."

"And just imagine, that's right—that's just what she said!"

"She said it because you ought not to have kept badgering her. Byron said it excellently: 'Even a broken-down nag will kick if the harness cuts her flesh,' and Lydia is not a nag, but a young and brave and beautiful girl. May the devil take me, but an Eve like that is worth giving up all these privileges and becoming a student again."

"Do you mean you're just running after her?"

"I'm not very much, but you should listen to what our elder brother Luke says about her! He says he spent the happiest summer of his life with her. And you know he's getting on toward seventy. And in actual fact, what miracles she did perform at his place last year! He had a peasant named Símka who would drive in the bears for the hunters. He was a man of forty-eight, and he had come down with sciatica. He had been sweating and he sat down on a frozen stone—that's how he got sciatica—it's an ailment of the nerve in your seat. You understand where the place is?"

"No details, please."

"And so the doctors had been trying to cure him for three years, and our brother kept paying; faith healers would try to heal him in one place after another, but they couldn't heal him either, and only took his money for their prayers. And our hero's whole enormous family went to rack and ruin. Then Lydia came to her uncle's for a visit and said, 'It's possible to try to cure that man, only it will have to be done with patience.'"

"It certainly wasn't proper for her to undertake that!" remarked the mistress with restrained irony.

"Well, she started laying out that big old peasant twice a day on his belly and kneading him below the waist. Do you understand? With those marvelous classical hands of hers, and on that sort of place on the peasant! I took a look and said, 'How can anybody kiss your hand after that?' She answered, 'Hands weren't given to us so that they could be kissed, but so that they could serve people's needs.' And Brother Luke—you know he's become a delicate, nervous old man—when he saw that, he broke down and cried. The priest came to him to beg him for some firewood, and he grabbed Símka and dragged him in and showed him to the priest. 'Look!' he said. 'Do you see that?' The priest answered, 'Yes, Your Excellency, I see it.'

" 'And you understand it?'

" 'Yes, Your Excellency,' he said. 'I understand it. Those of little faith are slothful only where the temple is concerned, but in practical affairs they do right well.'

" 'You bet your life they "do right well"! Now you go and pray for them in that temple. That's your business. And in return I will order some firewood to be given to you.'

" 'Yes, sir, Your Excellency,' he said. 'I will make a great effort.' "

"And I dare say he didn't make any effort at all?"

"Oh, of course not. Do you think he's fool enough to make an effort when the firewood is already delivered? But Símka is now walking around again and earns a living for his children, and whenever he sees Lydia he bursts into tears and squeaks: 'Don't ever die, Miss Lydia! Let me croak in your place. You're a mother to us!' Yes, whatever you say, these girls are marvelous."

"Only, the human race will come to an end with them."

"How's that?"

"They won't get married."

"Nonsense! Let the right kind of men for them come along and they'll marry them. And besides, that would be still better, because, to tell the truth, men like us have become such filth that it's not worth any sensible girls' while to marry them."

"Even if they become old maids!"

"What's the harm in that?"

"Old maids always turn sour."

"Only the ones who wanted very much to get married and are troubled by their temperament."

"It's not at all a matter of temperament, but rather that old maids are looked on as if they hadn't made the grade."

"That's the way blockheads look on them, but intelligent people, on the contrary, even look with respect on an elderly spinster who never wanted to be married. As you know, spinsterhood evidently has the approval of the Church. Or am I wrong? Is that not right, perhaps?"

VIII

The mistress smiled and answered, "Yes, that's right. But what is most curious, my sinful Zakhár, is that *you* should be taking up for spinsterhood!"

"But what's to be done, little sister? I too am not the man I once was; and now, in my sixty-fifth year, at times the thought of death slips in to me instead of some high-spirited *grisette*, and that sets me thinking. Don't you laugh at that. When the devil himself gets old, he'll turn into a hermit. Just look at our Old Believers, not here but out in the backwoods. They all live and sin, you know; but what an excellent custom they have out there! As soon as an old man hits sixty, he withdraws from his mate in the women's corner, and often even moves entirely out of the house. He will build himself a "cabin" in the garden, something like a little bathhouse in appearance, and he'll settle down there with a chosen youth, a sort of "Gehazi," and spend his time reading the Evangelist or the *Key to Understanding*.[38] He will have nothing further to do with money or business, and in general will not get in the way of the young people, who still have their duties to perform in life. To tell the truth, I commend that. I don't care how much they claim that the old hermits go back to their old women in the back room once a week, on Saturday nights, for old times' sake; I believe they go back only to get their clean laundry . . . Those dear old men and dear old women! How happy they'll be in return for all that in eternity!"

"Poor little old Zakhár! Perhaps you'd like that too?"

"Oh, without a doubt! But what could that mean for us unbelievers? Oh, by the way, what is that I noticed your Arkády had—another new boy, is it?"

The mistress knit her brows and replied, "I don't understand what business that is of yours."

"It's none at all. I just asked in connection with Gehazi, but if it's forbidden to talk about that, let's go on to something else. How about Valéry—is he going to knock off his university all right?"

"But why should he 'knock it off'?"

"Well, then, 'finish it,' if you want. Isn't it all the same thing? He hasn't got bitten by any kind of Jacobin bacteria, has he?"

"My son was brought up on healthy food, and he's not afraid of bacteria."

"Don't bank on it too much. Home training is like home temperature. The warmer it is in the room, the greater the danger that children will catch a cold when it strikes."

"Plague take you for saying so! But I'm not afraid for Valéry. God preserves him."

"Oh, yes, yes, yes, of course—he's an ardent believer."

"That is no laughing matter. We Russians all believe ardently."

"Yes, we're ardent fellows! But I must tell you, ladies, I have seen Ge's painting!"[39]

"More hash?"

"No—it's absolute *butchery*! It's a fright to look at!"

"I'm very glad they are getting him out of the exhibits. He himself was pointed out to me, and—Lord! What trousers! What a coat!"

"That coat has swallowed up a lot of sun's rays—but that is not so serious."

"And you think his paint-slinging is serious?"

"I'm not talking about his paint-slinging but about his coat."

"What nonsense!"

"It's not nonsense. He was supposed to be presented, but he couldn't because he had given his dress coat to a servant he knew."

"But how did the news get out?"

"He told it himself."

"How stupid!"

"And insolent!" the guest said in support.

But the general concluded, "It is *remarkable*! That's all they say nowadays: 'remarkable!' "

"But why is it remarkable?"

"Why, it's remarkable because these—what do you call them?—'non-resisters,' or 'urchins,' are all resisting something, whereas those of us who think we are 'resisters' and adults—in reality we're not worth a damn except to lick up the scraps from the plates."

"There he goes again," said the mistress in a joking tone. "He'll keep on tramping around till he has stepped on somebody's toes!"

And saying this, she sighed indulgently and went out as if to look after some household matter.

IX

The general and the guest remained alone in the parlor, and the tone of the conversation changed at once.

The general knit his brows and began a curt speech to the guest: "I preferred to see you here, because your sick husband came to me yesterday and was relentless. Allow me to tell you, it's cruel beyond all measure for you to send a sick old man on such errands!"

"On what kind of 'such errands'?"

"The kind that has no name in the language of respectable people."

"I don't understand at all. But I wrote you a letter, and you in your carelessness failed to answer it."

"I beg your pardon, but in order to send a satisfactory answer to your letter I had to supply you with a thousand rubles."

"Yes."

"That's just it! But I'm not a Persian shah, who has only to grab up a handful of diamonds and settle the whole affair."

The lady turned green, and glaring at him in anger she asked, "What is the meaning of that? For what reason is the Persian shah mentioned in my presence for the second time?"

"How should I know why he is mentioned in your presence? I simply think there are some people for whom I have long been doing everything I could and even what I could not do, and would not have done on any account if only the threats of unpleasantness had been aimed at me alone and not at other people."

Evidently the general was angry, and he spoke with some vehemence: "Twenty years have gone by since your husband so astonishingly found out that I had been with you, and—I saved myself and saved you, but I didn't save my notebook, and now I keep protecting people . . ."

"Oh, are you coming back again to that tale of woe?"

"Excuse me, but I certainly am! I'm not a scoundrel, and that is why I keep coming back to it and keep doing vile things for you—so as to take it all on myself. I make requests for you of people I would rather have nothing to do with, but you still aren't satisfied. Tell me, now, when will you finally get enough?"

"Others get more!"

"Oh, look now, why do others get more? You must forgive me—I don't know that business—who gets how much and why among you people. Maybe some are more clever than you; or else they work harder and do greater favors."

"Nonsense! Nobody can do any kind of favors. You can't make fish soup without fish."

"Oh, I don't know . . . 'Without fish'! Good Lord! Have you completely run out of poor fish?"

"Just imagine, we have! It's a fishless season!"

"Well, I don't know now what you will get under way. I've told you I don't understand anything about this business of yours. I'm guilty of all sins, all of them—but this is one kind of filth I have never got into."

The general raised his hand high and fervently crossed himself.

"There!" he said, nervously taking an envelope out of his pocket and handing it to the lady. "There, take it, please, and be quick. There are exactly a thousand rubles in it. I'm a poor, ruined man, but I never steal other people's money. A thousand rubles. That is the allowance I have begged for you twice in one year. Only, please, please—don't thank me! I am doing this with the greatest loathing, and I beg you—"

The lady started to say something, but he cut her off. "No, no! I beg you, don't send your wretched husband to me again. I implore you! I do have nerves and the leavings of a conscience. You and I once deceived him basely, but that was a long time ago. At that time I could do it, because he himself was deceiving others then in his turn. But now? That soft-headed look of his and those tottering legs—oh, Lord, preserve me! For God's sake, spare me that! Otherwise I myself will fall on my knees before him some time and confess everything."

The lady burst into laughter and said, "I am certain you will never do anything so stupid."

"Yes, I will!"

"Well, I am not afraid of him."

A smile flitted across the general's face, but he suppressed it and said, "Aha! So that means it wouldn't be news to him. Oh, Lord! Pray smite us down and put an end to our accursed corruption!"

"Oh, you really are a windbag!"

The smile reappeared on the general's face, and he stood up and replied, "Yes, yes, I'm a great windbag—it's 'remarkable'!"

With unconcealed scorn for the guest he put on his cap and went out, bestowing upon her a barely perceptible nod as he left.

In the vestibule a servant with the slanted eyes of a Chinese and the figure of a porcelain doll came out to attend him. She quietly nodded to him and gave him his coat.

"*Merci*, dear friend," the general said to her. "Tell my sister I couldn't wait for her because—I took medicine today. And here," he added in a whisper, "take this for yourself as a souvenir."

And he dropped a rolled-up ten-ruble note into the bodice of the girl's dress; and when she bent over to keep the paper from falling, he kissed her on the neck and said softly, "I am old and I don't permit myself to kiss women on the lips."

As he said this he squeezed her hand, and she squeezed his.

Downstairs at the door he put on his galoshes; and, feeling around in his pocket, he pulled out two kopecks and gave them to the doorman.

"Here, brother."

"I thank you kindly, Your Excellency," said the doorman gratefully, raising his hand to the peak of his cap in military fashion.

"Real ones, brother . . . Not made in Peskí . . .[40] You can take them right down to the shop and get a pound of rotten coffee for them. But be careful—it'll ruin the juices in your belly!"

"Yes, sir, Your Excellency!" replied the doorman, buttoning the general into the lap robe of the sleigh. But while he was joking so gaily, the general carried out a "thorough search of his premises" with both hands and convinced himself that he had not a farthing left. Thereupon he quickly stopped the driver, jumped out of the sleigh, and started off on foot.

"I'm going to take a walk," he said to the doorman. "It's splendid now."

"Remarkable, Your Excellency."

"That's it, brother—'remarkable'! Charge up a ruble to me for your wit!"

He wrapped himself up in his moth-eaten beaver coat and turned the corner of the street on his tired, superannuated legs.

When he had disappeared, the doorman nodded after him and said to the yard keeper, "It's nearly three months since he borrowed two rubles for the coachman and he keeps on forgetting it."

"A useless needle with a broken-out eye!" the yard keeper answered, scratching his back.

"It don't matter; whenever he's got any, he shoves it into everybody's pockets."

"Then wait for your chance."

"I sure will."

X

As soon as the guest was left alone she opened her velvet handbag; and hastily taking out the money, she started counting it. It was a full thousand rubles. The lady folded the notes more neatly and was about to close her handbag again when someone seized her hand.

She had not noticed that a well-fed, rosy-cheeked young man with a twitching Adam's-apple and an open smile on his lips had tiptoed into the room. With an agile clutch of his hand he seized the bronze fastener of her velvet bag and said, "This is confiscated!"

At first the guest shuddered, but her momentary fright disappeared at once and gave way to another feeling. She lighted up with joy and softly exclaimed, "Valerian! Where were you? O God!"

"I? As usual—everywhere and nowhere. Or rather, I've come straight from heaven so as to carry away this bag of earthly filth."

The lady started to say something to him, but he pointed to the closed door of the neighboring room, took the bag out of her hands, removed the money, and put it into his pocket.

The guest seemed not to notice all this. Watching her, one would have drawn the conclusion that she had long been used to such treatment and even found it pleasant. She held onto Valerian's free hand with both of hers; and looking him in the face, she softly moaned, "Oh, if only you knew! If only you knew how worried I was! I haven't seen you for three days and nights! They seemed like an eternity to me!"

"Really? What could I do? I won't soon forget those days myself. Where haven't I gone to try to get this stupid thousand rubles! Well, now I'm convinced that the surest way to get money from everybody is to go in for doing good to the poor! It's really a blessing from heaven that there are still some fools on earth like *Oncle Zacharie.*"

"Don't say anything about him."

"Oh, of course not. I'm grateful. This is the second time he's given us a breathing spell."

"But don't let this happen to you a third time, darling."

"If I lose as stupidly as this again, I'll hang myself."

"What sort of nonsense are you talking?"

"Why not? They say it's a very pleasant death. Something like a sort of—look, I've got the string from a sugar sack here in my pocket, just in case. I've tested it. It will hold."

"O God! What are you saying?" And lowering her voice, she whispered, *"Avancez une chaise."*

The young man made a comical grimace and once again pointed to the curtained door.

The lady frowned and asked in a whisper, "Who?"

The young man put his hands to his mouth and answered in her ear: "*Maman* is listening there!"

"That is not true either! You very often slander your own mother!"

Valerian crossed himself and softly assured her: "Honest to God, it's the truth. She always listens."

"How is it you're not ashamed?"

"On the contrary, I *am* very much ashamed for her, but I don't condemn her, I only warn others. I know she does it through the best of motives . . . A mother's sacred feelings . . ."

"*Approchez-vous de moi*, darling!"

"In other words, you don't think she is listening? All right, I'll call her right now . . ."

"Oh, please—none of those experiments!"

"You'd better go home at once, and in twenty minutes—"

"You'll be there?"

He nodded affirmatively.

She pressed his hand and asked, "That's not a lie?"

"It's the truth, but there's no need to scratch my hand with your fingernails."

"But I can't stand it!"

"Nonsense!"

"Kiss me just once!"

"Now what next!"

"But why not?"

"Oh, all right."

The young man kissed her and got up from his seat. He very much wanted this lady to get up and leave, but she did not get up, and whispered something else. Her further presence here was agonizing for him, and this could be seen in his face, which was distorted with anger. And in return he took her hand and pressed his lips to it, saying:

"*Lilas de perse*—that's delightful. I love that scent!"

The lady jumped up and, clutching her forehead in her hand, gave a lurch.

"What's the matter with you?" Valerian asked her. "Hurry out into the air!"

"That's base! It's vile! It's dishonorable! After I had explained it to you frankly . . . You have no right . . . No ri-ri-ri-right! . . ."

"For God's sake, no hysterics! You need air, quick!"

"Air—nonsense . . . I *had* to carry it all out . . ."

"Oh, yes—and you did carry it out . . . Now go home in a hurry, and everything will be fine."

Hearing these cheerful words she took his hand and whispered, "Oh yes . . . Oh, God! But since I had already told you all about why it was necessary, why did you have to say *'lilas de perse'*? That was vile! I will tell everybody—yes, I will!—how vile it was . . . And I will not leave here . . ."

"Yes, yes, please stay! *Maman* will be here in a moment."

And he got up from his seat, but she held him back.

"I'm really going out of my mind!" she said, putting the backs of her chilled fingers on her throbbing temples. "Help me! I'm truly going out of my mind!"

Valerian took fright at the martyred expression on her face and began to make the sign of the cross over her. She pushed him away in indignation and whispered, "Baptizer!"

"What do you need then?"

"Me? Humiliation and new insults! I need to have you with me!"

"But I *am* with you!"

"Oh, but of course not here!"

"Well, go home immediately, and I'll be there in a moment, and then you can fall any way you wish."

"How I wish—I deserve to be struck dead!"

She started to say something more, but instead she kissed his hand; and he, for his part, bent over her and touched the curly hair on the back of her neck with his lips.

The woman's distorted face lit up with a glow of sensual ecstasy, and she hastily covered herself with a veil and went out. Big hysterical tears rolled down her cheeks, her eyes were blurred, her lips and nose were red and stuck out, and her whole face became reminiscent of the protruding muzzle of a dog driven mad by passion.

She had surmised that she was repulsive and covered herself with a veil.

When she went past the doorman, he silently handed her a letter addressed to the "Squirmer" which he had kept under the cuff of his livery. She threw him a three-ruble note and sat down in the sleigh, silently tapping the driver with her finger.

"Can't even see the ground for the tears!" the doorman remarked to his companion. "And he couldn't care less!"

"Yes, nowadays the male sex don't lose its head over just any old thing."

XI

Young Valerian closed the door behind the lady himself, and going back into the parlor he took the crumpled money out of the pocket of his trousers and started counting it.

From behind the door that Valerian had pointed out to the guest there actually did come the voice of his mother. She asked, "Are you busy with something?"

"I've already finished."

"You can buy 'industrials'; everybody says they will double their value by spring."

"*Maman*, I know something a little more profitable."

"What, for example?"

"Oh, all kinds of things! Now, you know, they are sprinkling pawn-brokers with insect powder, and even our 'mutual friend' Michel has kicked the bucket . . . Something new is needed in their place."

"That's just it, but what?"

"Oh, *maman*! That is possible only for somebody like me who is considered a happy-go-lucky spendthrift without a kopeck to his name."

Behind the door came the sound of something being cut and of scissors being laid down.

"Are you sewing something, *maman*?"

"Yes, son, I'm patching up my holes, I'm putting myself in order . . . I'm sewing up the rags that I don't want to show to my maid."

"That is very reasonable, *maman*, and noble."

"But unpleasant."

The youth started to answer something but he kept silent, and only his Adam's-apple bounced up and down like a ball.

Again from behind the door there came the sound of someone cutting with scissors and then laying them down, and at the same time the mistress said: "I think you would gain a lot more if you helped Uncle Zakhár straighten out the infatuations of his youth. Luke would probably appreciate that and start receiving us."

"That's quite possible, *maman*, but you know I'm not vain and I have no weakness for boasting about where I am received."

"But he would simply give you a lot of money."

"In that case I'd be very glad, but how would I go about it?"

"You need to get the paper that Uncle Zakhár is afraid of."

"In other words, dear mama, I'd have to *steal* it!"

"You are so crude that it's impossible to talk with you."

"*Maman*, I say nothing crude, I merely spell out what has to be done."

"That's not true. That woman will do it all for you herself."

"Ow! You're wrong! That woman is an excellent agent and an excellent mathematician, but you can't take her in."

"Still, she thinks you're a gambler and a spendthrift."

"Yes, *maman*, but I'm making every effort to create that reputation only because it will be useful to me when things take a new turn."

"In all honesty, I don't understand at all why that is necessary."

"But to my mind nothing could be simpler. Everybody has already had a taste of the righteous life and is fed up with it. So what is to be done?

The human race is ungrateful and malicious . . . *Felicitas temporum* is taking its leave. A revenge is needed. A reaction is necessary . . ."

"And what will happen in the reaction?"

"That, *maman*, is unclear, but everybody knows that phenomena are not repeated. Sunshine comes after rain, and for that reason there *is* an advantage in having the reputation now of a wastrel and debauchee. That means you reveal a certain reliability which will very soon come in handy."

"So you people are ready for everything!"

"How could you want it otherwise? After all, you know, we are trained to be ready for everything."

"Oh, come on! How unwise your wisdom is!"

"But what is wisdom to us, *maman*? Even the journalists have read somewhere and keep repeating that 'wisdom and an inheritance are a blessing,' but you and papa got no inheritance together for us."

"Christian parents are not obliged to provide you with an inheritance."

"Yes, they are, excuse me."

"Where does it say so?"

"Why, in the Wisdom of Paul that people like to refer to so much; there it says, 'For the children ought not to lay up for the parents, but the parents for the children.' "

"That is something out of the Tolstoyan one, it's not in the regular one."

"I beg your pardon. Just take the trouble to look in the regular one at the twelfth chapter of the Second Epistle to the Corinthians."

"Where did you get all that—which chapter and where it is?"

"Ha! I'm just interested. I want to beat Tolstóy with it."

"Then beat away. That will show you in an excellent light."

"Just allow me—the time will come."

"Why must we wait? Everybody's fed up with him."

"Excellent, but there's no use doing something for nothing. You can't make a fur coat out of praise. Ever since banknotes were invented, all favors have had to be paid for: if I turn out a favor with this hand, you put a banknote in the same place."

"But *you* might receive an inheritance too."

"Oh, you still can't get Uncle Luke out of your head!"

"I certainly can't."

"Well, I will put your mind at rest. It's all over with that inheritance—'abandon hope forever'!"[41]

"You can't know that."

"But I do. I bought it, dear mother, from a notary's copy clerk. It's all given to 'feeding establishments' and 'Public instruction.' "

"You're joking!"

"Not a bit."

"But what about Lydia?"

"She doesn't need it. She doesn't want to stir up envy and quarrels, and she has refused it."

"What a fool!"

"And a harmful one! She didn't give it to her relatives."

"But that shouldn't be allowed!"

"It ought not to be."

"But what can be done?"

"Find a way out however you can—even through a miracle."

"And now you believe in miracles?"

"Oh yes, *maman* . . . ! I believe in anything you like—I want to live.

> *And truly I do feel that I shall live,*
> *E'en though by miracle—oh, in miracles I believe!*

I will even tell you something more, but this is just between ourselves."

"Please do."

"We must set up a new wonder-worker."

"What nonsense!"

"Oh yes, we must! And I have one."

"But what can he do?"

"Don't worry . . . ! He's already performing little things, and not badly at all, but we need to get him established and recommend him well. Oh, I know what it takes in life!"

XII

Mother and son fell silent. Both seemed suddenly fatigued by all the impressions they had been sorting out and by the weight of such a decision, after which each of them felt a need for some kind of stimulus or distraction from without, and it was not long in coming. At the very moment when mother and son were sitting in silence and horror at what they had resolved to do, there came from the street a steadily growing noise, which suddenly passed into a furious roar and drove out all the torment of their confession. Valéry was still buried in thought, but the mistress of the house became anxious and aroused herself. She ran into the living room dressed just as she was, dashed to the window, and exclaimed, "Look! What a mob!"

Valerian stirred lazily, as if half asleep, and murmured, "It's a stupid crowd, *maman*; it's not worth looking at."

"Yes, but still—it *is* touching!"

"I don't think so at all."

"Well, but just the same, it's real faith, you know."

"I don't know, to tell the truth."

"But now just consider our doorman; he must be a complete nihilist—"

"I understand he once had another kind of reputation."

"What kind?"

"He helped wipe out the nihilists. Your general knows about him."

" 'But really now,' I asked him. 'What does that mean?' And he answered, 'No-account people rush around without knowing why.' "

"He did give you a clever answer."

"Oh, please, that's enough. But what sort of idiots are they, really—why do they want everything at once?"

"They probably want to be thrown out and beaten."

"And how disgusting they are—all skin and bones, and in rags and tatters!"

"Oh yes—those who labor and are heavy laden. Very likely Jean or Onthon is down there somewhere."

"Just look—there's that upstart woman everybody complains about. Look, she's really scratching them!"

Valerian got up and became animated.

"Uh-oh!" he said with a smile. "There's one that attracts me. She is somebody with character; she is called something on the order of Elizabeth Sparrow;[42] she creates celebrities and then beats and scratches the very public that gave them fame. In my opinion she and Meshchérsky[43] are the only two who have understood what people need who don't know what they want. I'm going to see how she cracks those nuts."

Valerian went out to the vestibule, where it was dark; but at the lamp, fussing about with matches, there stood that same beautiful maid with the Chinese eyes who a short while earlier had so kindly allowed the general to kiss her on the neck. Seeing her, Valerian frowned and began putting on his gloves.

The girl threw aside the matches and started to leave, but stopped once again. She was uneasy, and her face was flushed and took on an insolent expression.

The young man noticed it. Slapping his cap on his head, he started putting on his overcoat himself, without any help.

The girl gave him a sidelong glance and decided to help him. She took the coat out of his arms; but just as he started to put them into the sleeves, she threw the coat on the floor and disappeared behind the coat rack, where a little door led into the cubbyhole that served as her living quarters. From this cubbyhole a little mirrored window, covered with blue taffeta, opened onto the main stairway.

"Pig!" Valerian whispered after her. Picking up his overcoat off the floor, he shook it and put it on without help from anyone else; and then, going out to the stairway, he hastily ran down the steps. But his speed did not save him, and from the little window behind him there resounded,

"Look-it how he's got that guilty backbone humped up! He thinks I don't know where he's running off to! The devil take you and your old women!"

But Valerian ran on and tried not to listen to what one may suppose he deserved to hear.

XIII

At the bottom of the stairway the two brothers met—Arkády and Valéry, the "Sluggard" and the "Squirmer." Arkády (the Sluggard) was older than Valéry (the Squirmer) by about six years, and was much more solidly built. He was also a pure-bred "half-breed": pudgy and with a big Adam's-apple, like Valéry, but looking as if he had just stood up on his hind legs. In his face he simultaneously resembled a puffy child and a performing wolf. He smelled of unusual perfumes that were reminiscent of the odor of apple seeds.

The Sluggard found that the door to his mother's apartment was not shut. It had remained that way after Valerian's recent departure. Arkády pointed this out to his mother in a scornful tone. She shrugged her shoulders and said, "What can I do about it? We are not even free to do as we please with our servants. Hiring and firing a servant is a complicated affair, and they know it and aren't afraid. They take every kind of liberty they like."

Arkády interrupted. "Valerian ought not to put himself in the kind of position where he's dependent on a woman!"

His mother threw up her hands and said, "Oh, stop talking against women!"

Soft, hysterical sobs, as if in answer to this, were heard coming from the little room behind the coat rack.

The mistress got up and locked the door and sat down again.

"I will always maintain that women servants are worth nothing at all," Arkády declared quietly.

"They are cheaper and more useful," his mother answered.

"But on the other hand you have to put up with her escapades."

"Oh, I really don't know whose escapades are the worst! I sometimes think all these experiences will drive me out of my mind."

"You always harp on that, *maman* . . . But why did you send for me?"

"My brother Zakhár was here . . . When will it all end?"

"Oh, come on, now! Uncle Zakhár never stops blabbing. Everybody knows he's a windbag!"

"He may be a windbag, but don't you spoil your career. I'm terrified about you!"

"There's nothing for you to worry about, *maman*. The time has passed when blackmail was well developed. Nowadays everybody in the lower classes knows that blackmail is punished by law, and besides, I myself refuse to stay here any longer, where there's no telling what that *fabulator elegantissimus* will make up about everybody. Aunt Olympia herself has offered to smooth it over with Gustávych. His son-in-law is being trans-ferred to the West, and I will get an independent assignment in the East."

"Oh, if only she would make up in this way for her sin against me!"

"What kind of sin is that?"

"What sin? The misfortune of my whole life."

"Oh, that must be something we children are not supposed to know!"

"You know nothing except what concerns you. But when will she get you settled?"

"Today . . . Perhaps right now! If I get the assignment, Aunt Olympia will stop in here . . . Why, there she is now," he added, looking out the window at the street. "I see her carriage at the entrance, and the coach-man with the clock on his back."

The Sluggard went to the vestibule and opened the door to the stair-way, up which there came an elderly, heavy-set lady wearing a cape cut in the diplomatic fashion—which incidentally is in great favor also with our cooks. Under her fur cape, which represented a kind of knightly cloak, there sparkled a beaded cuirass on the mighty chest of the lady. Breathing a little heavily but climbing briskly, the lady said with a smile to the Sluggard, "Look, I'm almost sixty-five years old, and my heart still beats as strong as a good blacksmith."

With this she took her nephew's hand and laid it on her cuirass; and then, going into the vestibule, she gave her cheek to the mistress to kiss and continued, "Excuse me, I've come only for a minute. I'll go in with-out even taking off my wraps. I've come only to bring you the good news: Arkády, you've got the assignment! Go at once, right now, and thank him! This will tie his hands and block the way against his changing his mind."

"This minute, *ma tante*," replied Arkády, and he started looking for his overcoat.

From behind the coat rack there appeared the maid, who had now recovered her composure, but Arkády convulsively turned away from her and hastily went out.

Olympia noticed this, and going into the parlor she said with a smile, "He's still the same as ever, the same buffoon—afraid of women."

"Ugh!" The mistress made a gesture of dismissal.

"Oh, my dear, don't give it a thought! . . . That is not at all uncommon nowadays! Still, it's good that *il ne met plus de manchettes*.[44] Now, after all, he looks just like all men. However, *adieu*! Maybe I'll get back for a heart-to-heart talk with you, but just now I've got a million things to do. You know, you've all fallen asleep here. That won't do! You're just saw-ing wood, as they say, and chewing your bast shoes! You've got to be awakened. Wherever you look, everybody needs to be aroused. Your slumber creates terrible difficulties for all of Slavdom. Holy Russia is the power of the world, and that will be its name in Russian—*Silamíra!* But as yet it is a dormant power. In time it will be otherwise! Then it will not be necessary to come from the West to stir you to action, as at present, when you begin to snooze and snore so scandalously."

"Yes, but now everybody among us is a believer!"

"In my opinion, even as believers you are weak. You believe in a sleepy sort of way, as if you were dreaming . . . as if you were barely able to keep your head above water and barely able to believe, and at any moment you may sink and forget everything . . . Farewell! Good-bye! You've already heard, of course, what Nina—Zakhár's daughter—has done?"

"They say she's—going to be a mother."

"Why 'they say'? It's a fact! Naturally, she'll be a mother . . . But how did it happen? The Count is so old, you know, and so stupid, that he got married to spite his own daughters Goneril and Regan . . ."

"Such immorality!"

"But you probably don't know the whole story. *C'est un inceste!* . . . They assigned her to the job of removing a nephew, who to this day is still a cadet, or something like that . . ."

"O God! O God!"

"Yes, a real criminal *conversation de Bysance!*"

And she waved her arms and shook her head and started toward the door, but the mistress held her back at the threshold and said, "You've done a lot in getting Arkády settled again, but I'm afraid—what if he really is crazy?"

"Stop that and don't worry," replied Olympia. "Remember what Oxenstjerna said: 'It takes no great intelligence to engage in politics.' "[45]

Olympia pressed her hand to her cuirass and added, "It is not our task at all to provide intelligence for the whole world; our *métier* is quite different: it consists only in putting salt on the tail of every creature that is pressing forward."

Having explained her vocation, the lady once more clinked her cuirass, and giving the mistress of the house an English handshake, she went downstairs, took a seat in her carriage opposite the clock that towered against the back of the coachman, and dashed off to *jouer un tour de son métier.*

XIV

The mistress remained alone and at once called for her coat and galoshes, put a flask of smelling salts in her pocket, and left the house, saying that she had some purchases to make at the shop for defective goods.

She felt the kind of terrible fatigue that can only be understood by an

actress playing a role that gives her no chance to leave the stage throughout the act.

She was very tired, almost exhausted, but she still had ample strength
left for such struggles. She would quickly recover in the fresh air and be
in shape to give the very best account at the proper place.

And while the cat was away, the mice at home began to play.

When the mistress left, the maid with the Chinese eyes and the figure
of a porcelain doll walked through all the rooms and opened the air vents
in the windows, and then drew back the door curtains and opened the
door from the parlor into the boudoir, which also served the mistress as
a sewing room and hiding place. Here the girl put everything in order,
then took a specially selected key out of her pocket, opened the desk with
it, took out a perfumed sheet of ivory-colored paper, lit a candle, and
started laboriously writing:

"If your propositions are substantial, then even though your years are
not similar, I am acceptable on account of your courtesy to having complete feelings for you, only not in your own house and not in the presents
of your servints."

She read through what she had written and added at the bottom, under
her signature:

"But please answer only by mail."

After writing the letter the girl took an envelope out of her mistress's
stationery set and began to spell out the address. At that moment the
curtains opened on the other side of the boudoir, and in came a tall
white-haired woman of forty-five, with a goose-like goitrous throat, an
enormous mouth, and a two-story chin. This was the house cook.

"Get me a couple of cigarettes," she said to the maid.

"Take them yourself," the girl answered and continued addressing the
envelope.

The cook took a few cigarettes out of a carnelian box and lit up one
of them. Sitting down on a padded velvet footstool in front of the mirror, she began to squeeze a pimple on her chin with her fingernails, and
then she powdered the spot with her mistress's powder puff and said,
"It's terrible the way these pimples are getting me."

"Then quit lapping up that black beer."

"But I've done quit."

"Then stop squeezing the grocery boys."

"How come—have you seen anything?"

"Of course! The boy that brought the fruit and vegetables yesterday—
I thought you were going to tickle him right off to his death, like a river
spirit."

"He's just a child—he don't understand nothing."

"And so I guess you'll hold off till he gets his understanding."

"Honest to God, I ain't done nothing—I just like to pet and tousle the pretty little kids. I had a godson was almost sixteen, but he went and died, and I get lonesome for him. And how about you? Who's that you are fixing to lead into sin? Who are you writing to?"

The girl did not answer.

"You think I don't know, but I do!"

The Chinese girl still kept silent.

"Want me to tell you?"

"Oh, go ahead."

"You're out for the general, that's who!"

"So now you know it's him!"

She began to seal up the letter.

"There you are, laughing at me for petting the boys, and you've fallen into something worse yourself."

"I haven't fallen into anything."

"Then what's all the howling for, and why have you gotten so ugly?"

"I howl because I was a fool—I thought people would be true."

"That's just it—and now anybody can see you're in the family way."

"You're a liar—nobody can see anything yet."

"Then why was it that when the priest was here he blessed me and let me drink tea out of his saucer and didn't give you none?"

"I had spit curls on my forehead, and he don't like them. And besides, it didn't matter—what he says doesn't come true anyhow."

The cook shook her head with a sigh and said in an edifying tone, "Yes, nobody knows just why he can pray away so many troubles for the merchants and can't do it for the other classes."

"He doesn't do it right!"

"You mustn't talk like that, dearie, because even if he don't do it right and it don't all come true, still we have to believe in God's mission, even though I myself—could pull all the hair out of that she-devil that scratches everybody."

"And they'd haul you into court," said the girl, whose disposition was mischievous but timid. But the cook, a woman of experience, answered her boldly:

" 'Disturbing the peace! Eight days in the clink!'—That don't mean nothing. By God, I'll give her a thrashing!"

XV

Just at that moment, all of a sudden, the doorbell rang. The cook and the maid both jumped up. The girl nimbly slipped the letter into her pocket and ran to open the front door, while the cook went down the corridor linking the vestibule with the kitchen and hid behind the door.

Valerian came in and asked in a low voice. "Who is at home?"

"Nobody," replied the girl.

"What about mama?"

"She's left."

"And has that stupid notion by any chance left you?"

"What's stupid about it? Tell me, please, have I no reason to have notions?" The girl spoke in the most quarrelsome tone.

"Here, take these, and stop pouting like a lady of the feminine sex."

"What's that?"

"Earrings."

"I don't need earrings. Get me some money."

"I'll get you some later."

"No, you're deceiving me! I'm not going to play the fool for you."

"Take these for now."

"I don't need them."

"Oh, what stupidity! Then who'll I give them to?"

"What business is it of mine? I don't want them! I don't want anything from you, because you are not a high-minded gentleman and a student, but the lowest and vilest sort of man!"

Valéry tried to stop her with a coarse gesture, but she jerked away and said, "Just you dare, just dare!" And she went off to her cubbyhole.

The young man dashed after her and started talking in kindly tones. "Now listen—you wanted them, you know. You asked for earrings. Go on and take them, now that they're bought."

"Bought! Where? In whose shop? Or did you just for a joke pull them off some wench on a bench?"

"Why do you say such common things?"

"But why not ask? Maybe I couldn't wear them!"

"And what sort of stupidity is that?"

"Well, that honeysuckle vine might see me and pull them off my ears."

The young man flared up. "What sort of 'honeysuckle vine'?" he shouted.

"That old woman—your Kamchátka. You know, she's like a honeysuckle vine . . ."

"What Kamchátka?"

"You don't know!"

"Of course I don't."

"Oh, that's enough of playing the fool!"

"I tell you, I don't know what a Kamchátka is, or what it's for."

"You just ask her why she is Kamchátka, or why other people are sent to Kamchátka on her account.[46] But I'm not afraid of her, and I say that she's the lowest of the low, and it's long past time she was dead, instead of taking on boys that are worse than any babbling girl."

"Really, now, you are forgetting yourself beyond all endurance!"

"What of it? I still can. On the other hand, when I become an old woman, I won't forget myself."

Valerian threw down his gift on the girl's dressing table and, squeezing her arm, whispered, "I hate you!"

"What could be more high-minded now than to hate me!"

"You yourself have brought yourself to the point where you are repulsive to me."

"If I'm so repulsive, why did you come here?"

"I only wanted to tell you that you're nasty."

"Oh yes! Do me the favor! . . . To be sure, I'm nasty! . . . For some people I'm not nasty, but you've said it, so now go away. Your pulse is pounding in vain . . ."

"You're lying! My pulse is not pounding."

"Yes, it is! I can see it."

"All right, I'll explain to you right now why it's pounding."

"Oh, no, brother, no you won't! I've already had so many of your explanations that I'm all out of shape now, and people are even beginning to notice it."

He said something, and she answered, "No," then again, "No," and then once more, "No, no, no! Wha-a-a-at? Aha! No! That gift you gave me doesn't count; you are guilty—beg my forgiveness . . . Again! . . . Once more! . . .

"Now, that's the way! And now be on your way . . . People like you have to be taught a lesson!"

Stealthily listening to these last words, the cook went into raptures, and, beaming with a joyful grin, she spat and whispered, "Oh, you rascal! So fresh from the country, and how she knows her way around! There she's got him on his knees again! By God, the devil himself puts honey in her mouth!"

And the cook held her breath in suspense so as to hear what would happen next, but no further lesson could be heard, because the door to the little cubbyhole was pulled shut, and from the other end of the corridor, where the usual preparation of food was taking place, there crept an unbearable odor.

The cook dashed to her seething altar and found the whole stove in complete disorder. One thing had boiled over and spilled, another had burned up, and the whole room was filled from floor to ceiling with a foul stench.

The cook flew into a rage and shouted, "Oh, the devil take you with all your pulses and lessons! You demons will have to go without feed today."

Full of wrath, she climbed up on the table, opened the vent in the window, and flung the back door wide open. But no sooner had she done that than she suddenly beamed with joy—her day had come too. On the very threshold there stood the rosy-cheeked grocery boy with a basket on his head, uncertain whether to walk in.

"Aha!" the white-haired woman welcomed him gaily. "So that's what I heard! I wondered who it was creeping and sliding along so fine and proud, and it was you—scamp, tramp, out without a lamp! Hello, Petie-boy!"

The young lad sulked in silence, and the curly-haired female burst into laughter. Pulling him into the kitchen by his apron, she went on glibly, "No more pouting! Don't be silly! You're still alive, ain'tcha?"

"I just barely got to you alive," the rosy-cheeked boy replied in a whining voice. Then suddenly changing his tone, he called out, "Take the basket in a hurry, won't you? I've got no time!"

"What's that to me? Don't put them down here! . . . Don't you see? It's smoky. Take them in there, to my room."

The boy started to move with the basket and then stopped again uncertainly, but the cook shoved him into her room, and a moment afterward there was heard a plaintive squeal.

The evening grew dark. Everything was quiet.

XVI

The air in the kitchen cleared up. The smoke disappeared. Looking around, the grocery boy timidly came out of the cook's room; on his head he carried the empty basket, upside-down. It covered his whole face, and evidently there was some convenience in this. The cook accompanied him and held him back for a moment at the threshold. She silently wagged her finger at him in warning, then poured out for him a handful of her mistress's dried fruit, and finally raised the basket above his head, took his crimson cheeks in her hands, and kissed him on the lips. During the kiss they both laughed.

Now the boy had thrown off his childish timidity, and she whispered to him, "Let's go to the festival together. You'll see what fun it is! I'll make you a blue blouse for the holiday. Just be sure to run back here tomorrow and try it on."

"I will," the boy replied.

She embraced him again and, pressing his head to her breast, she said to him with motherly tenderness, "And when they send you to the washerwoman at the laundry, don't you stop and talk to the girls at the ironing boards . . . Hear? They're empty-headed wenches—they could get you into trouble . . ."

"No-o-o!" the boy answered. "I already feel ashamed before all of them."

"So that's it! Now, all that don't mean a thing, dearie . . . But I'll bribe all the yard men, and they'll report everything to me right off."

He went whistling down the stairway, showing now that he really was "fine and proud."

The yard man met him with a bundle of firewood and asked him, "Pete, how old are you?"

"Thirteen."

"Just look at him—an old man! And are things going well?"

"They're all right."

"That means better days are ahead!"

Peter thanked him and walked on in expectation of better days.

He will be at the festival. She will give him the shirt. In time he will ask her to buy him a watch. Otherwise she can go to the devil!

Well-polished lamps have started glowing in the vestibule and the kitchen. On the kitchen stove the pots have been filled again and everything has been put back in order. The storm has raged and passed on, and cleanliness and order have ensued, as is fitting. Now it is time to get into uniform.

The cook turned on the faucet and sent a cold stream of water into the basin. She poured a big tin scoop full of this water and drank it down. She guzzled it greedily, like a steaming horse whose ears fairly jump with every gulp. Before she had finished washing herself, the maid also came into the kitchen; and she too silently took the scoop in just the same way, drank it down just as greedily, and her red ears quivered with every gulp.

After that she too washed herself in cold water over the very same basin, and waved her wet hands above her head, because she had forgotten to bring along a towel.

She did not feel like talking.

The cook understood her and threw her the clean end of her own towel. Greeting her with something like a curtsy, she said:

"I congratulate you on a pleasant *bonjour!*"

The maid answered with a playful grimace and said, "And you too on the same business!"

Apparently they recognized as real "business" only the business of nature, which multiplies life without worrying about its meaning and importance.

NOTES FOR "A WINTER DAY"

[1] This cryptic allusion to the Bulgarians is evidently connected with the vigorous propaganda carried on by Olga Alexéevna Nóvikova, the prototype of Leskóv's Olympia, in support of Russia's role as the protector of the Orthodox Slavs in general and the Bulgarians in particular.

[2] An allusion to Pan-Slavic campaigns among conservative Russians in the 1870's and 1880's.

[3] From the poem "Potók the Hero" ("Potók—bogatýr") by A. K. Tolstóy (1817–75).

[4] L. B. Bertensón (1850–1929), a prominent and civic-minded professor of medicine in Petersburg, who was active in encouraging the study of medicine by young women.

[5] Leskóv's use here of *ego malyútki* "his urchins" as a pun on *ego malyúyut* "he is portrayed" turns the Russian proverb into a commentary on the popular view of Tolstóy's followers.

[6] The heroine of Tolstóy's novel *War and Peace*.

[7] A Russian religious sect that sought escape from the temptations of the flesh through castration.

[8] "Powerfully and majestically"—an echo of a line from the Russian hymn to the Tsar.

[9] A distortion of the Russian proverb "Freedom to the free and paradise to the saved."

[10] An allusion to Matthew 19:12.

[11] According to his son, Leskóv heard this story when he visited the Tolstóy home in Moscow in 1887 (Andréi Leskóv, *Zhizn Nikoláya Leskóva* [Moscow, 1954], p. 601).

[12] A reference to the painting "A Religious Procession in Kursk Province," by Ilyá Répin (1844–1930).

[13] Pyótr Petróvich Sokolóv (1821–99), a specialist in watercolors whose favorite themes were drawn from the life of the common people and of soldiers, and who himself won the Cross of St. George for bravery in the Russo-Turkish War of 1877–88.

[14] Yúlia Denísovna Zasétskaya, Márya Grigóryevna Péiker, Vasíly Alexándrovich Páshkov, Modést Korf, and A. P. Bóbrinsky were all devoted followers of the English Protestant missionary Lord Radstock, who in 1874 began going to Russia every winter to conduct evangelistic meetings among the Petersburg aristocracy. In 1877 Leskóv published a book about him, *The Society Schism (Velikosvétski raskól)*. The Russian followers of Lord Radstock took the name of Evangelical Christians and in 1944 merged with the Baptists to form the largest Christian group in the Soviet Union apart from the Orthodox and the Old Believers. Sergéi Egórovich Kushelyóv (1821–90)—an adjutant general who was a gifted painter of watercolors.

[15] General Iván Vasílyevich Annenkov (1814–87) was chief of the Petersburg police from 1862 to 1867.

[16] Probably an allusion to the French actor Charles-François Berton (1820–74), who acted for many years on the Petersburg stage as well as in his native France.

[17] An allusion to Dostoévsky's novel *The Insulted and Injured*.

[18] A pun on "Intermediary," the name of the publishing house established by Tolstóy's followers in 1884 to make good reading matter available to the Russian masses at very low prices.

[19] Nikolái Yákovlevich Skaryátin was governor of Kazán from 1867 to 1880.

[20] Nasreddin (1831–96), the Shah of Persia from 1848 till his death, visited Russia in 1889.

[21] An allusion to the proclamation emancipating the Russian serfs, which was issued by Alexander II on February 19, 1861, the sixth anniversary of his ascension to the Russian throne.

[22] A. I. Evropéus (1826–85) was a member of the Petrashévsky Circle, along with Dostoévsky, in Petersburg in the 1840's and was condemned to death but saved by amnesty. At the end of the 1850's both he and A. M. Unkóvsky (1828–92) were leaders of the liberal nobility in Tver Province.

[23] Tarás Shevchénko (1814–61), the great Ukrainian poet, of peasant origin, who was also a gifted painter.

[24] An allusion to the unconfirmed story that Shevchénko, as a serf, was once thrashed on the orders of V. A. Peróvsky.

[25] A distorted quotation from Púshkin's poem "An Epistle to the Censor" ("Poslánie k tsénzoru"): "What is necessary for London is premature for Moscow."

[26] Mikhaíl Nikíforovich Katkóv (1818–87)—the powerful editor and publisher of the newspaper *Moskóvskie védomosti* and the journal *Rússki véstnik*, who grew steadily more reactionary from the time of the Polish Insurrection in 1863 until his death.

[27] A reference to "Nymphs," one of Turgénev's "Poems in Prose."

[28] An allusion to a character thus nicknamed who appears in Part II, Chapters 9–13, of A. F. Písemsky's novel *Troubled Seas (Vzbalamúchennoe móre)*, which was published in 1863 at a time when Leskóv was closely associated with the journal in which it appeared, the *Library for Reading (Bibliotéka dlya chténiya)*.

[29] Henry Thomas Buckle (1821–62), an English historian of the English empirical school whose *History of Civilization in England* (Vol. I, 1857; Vol. II, 1861) acquired momentary fame in England and was avidly read by progressive young Russians in the 1860's.

[30] A somewhat altered quotation from N. A. Nekrásov's poem "The Green Sound" ("Zelyóny shum").

[31] Tanagra, a province in ancient Greece.

[32] A guarded reference to John of Kronstadt, the same Orthodox priest who was the unnamed target of Leskóv's satire in "Night Owls."

[33] A quotation from A. N. Máikov's poem "Three Deaths" ("Tri smérti").

[34] Juliette Lamber Adam (1836–1936), a French political writer who traveled in Russia and whose numerous activities included working for an alliance between France and Russia.

[35] Père Jean—another guarded reference to John of Kronstadt. Père Onthon—possibly a reference to Archbishop Antóny (A. V. Vadkóvsky, 1846–1912), who was placed in charge of the Finnish eparchy in 1892; but possibly also an allusion to Antóny Khrapovítsky (1864–1936), who was hostile to both Tolstóy and Leskóv.

[36] A reference to the ninth tale of the seventh day in Boccaccio's *Decameron*.

[37] "That's where the dog is buried!" (i.e., "that is the cause of it all").

[38] Gehazi was the servant of the prophet Elisha in the Old Testament story that is related in II Kings 4–5.
Key to Understanding (Klyuch razuméniya), a collection of sermons published in Kíev in 1659 by Ioaníki Golyatóvsky (died in 1688), rector of the college founded in Kíev by Peter Mogíla and later archimandrite of the Nóvgorod-Séverski Monastery.

[39] Nikolái Nikoláevich Ge (1831–94) was a friend of Leskóv and a follower of Tolstóy. The controversial painting mentioned here may have been "What is Truth?" (1890), "Golgatha" (1892), or "The Crucifixion" (several versions).

[40] Peskí, a village in Moscow Province.

[41] An allusion to the inscription over the gates of hell in Dante's *Divine Comedy: "Lasciate ogni speranza, voi ch'entrate!"*

[42] The dead serf-woman whose name Sobakévich changed to a masculine form and entered in the list of male serfs that he sold to Chíchikov in Chapter VII of Gogol's *Dead Souls*.

[43] Prince V. P. Meshchérsky (1839–1914)—the editor of the conservative journal *The Citizen (Grazhdanín)*, to which both Dostoévsky and Leskóv contributed for a while. After the 1870's Leskóv frequently attacked Meshchérsky and his publication.

[44] "He no longer wears frilly cuffs"—a hint at the pederasty implied by the obsolete French expression *chevalier de la manchette.*

45 Oxenstjerna—a member of the prominent Swedish family by that name, probably Axel (1583–1654), who was one of Sweden's greatest diplomats and served for forty-two years as Chancellor. It is highly probable that the quotation Leskóv puts into the mouth of Olympia was here taken directly—if not too exactly—from the writings of her prototype. In Olga Nóvikova's book *Skobeleff and the Slavonic Cause* (London, 1883), page 229, she refers to "the maxim of Oxenstiern 'With how little wisdom the world is governed.' "

46 Kamchátka—a region in eastern Siberia used by the Russian government in the latter half of the nineteenth century as a place of deportation for persons it classed as dangerous criminals. The word here alludes to the guest's presumed connections with the police.

BIBLIOGRAPHY

I

The Russian Sources of the Stories in this Book

Except where otherwise noted, the Roman and Arabic numerals refer to the volume and pages of the following edition:
Н. С. Лесков, *Собрание сочинений в одиннадцати томах*. Москва, 1956-1958.

1. "The Steel Flea" «Левша (Сказ о тульском косом Левше и о стальной блохе).» VII, 26-59.
2. "The Archbishop and the Englishman" Глава 3, «Мелочи архиерейской жизни.» VI, 418-424.
3. "Singlethought" «Однодум.» VI, 211-243.
4. "A Journey With a Nihilist" «Путешествие с нигилистом.» VII, 125-132.
5. "Deception" «Обман.» Н. С. Лесков, *Полное собрание сочинений*, издание 3-е, XVIII (С.-Петербург: Издание А. Ф. Маркса, 1903), 91-123.
6. "Choice Grain" «Отборное зерно.» VII, 280-304.
7. "Notes from an Unknown Hand" «Заметки неизвестного.»
   "A Clever Respondent" «Искусный ответчик.» VII, 322-324.
   "How It Is Not Good to Condemn Weaknesses" «Как нехорошо осуждать слабости.» VII, 324-326.
   "Superfluous Mother Love" «Излишняя материнская нежность.» VII, 326-333.
   "Female Aspirations Toward Understanding Lead to Vain Distress" «Женское стремление к пониманию причиняет напрасные беспокойства.» VII, 339-341.
   "On the Harm That Exists for Many of Reading Worldly Books" «О вреде от чтения светских книг, бываемом для многих.» VII, 342-349.
   "About the Folly of a Certain Prince" «О безумии одного князя.» VII, 355-358.
8. "About the Rooster and His Children" «О Петухе и его детях.» VII, 381-398.
9. "Fish Soup Without Fish" «Уха без рыбы.» *Новь*, № 7 (1886), 352-358.
10. "Figúra" «Фигура.» VIII, 463-486.
11. "Night Owls" «Полунощники.» IX, 117-217.
12. "A Product of Nature" «Продукт природы.» IX, 340-355.
13. "Administrative Grace" «Административная грация.» IX, 388-396.
14. "A Winter Day" «Зимний день.» IX, 397-455.

II

A *Bibliography of Works in English about Leskóv*

BRIDGMAN, RICHARD. "Leskov under the Bushel of Translation," *Texas Quarterly*, IX, No. 3 (Autumn 1966), 80–88.

EDGERTON, WILLIAM B. "Leskov and Tolstoy: Two Literary Heretics," *The American Slavic and East European Review*, XII, No. 4 (1953), 524–534.

_____. "Nikolai Leskov: The Intellectual Development of a Literary Nonconformist." Ph.D. thesis, Columbia University, 1954.

_____. "Leskov and Russia's Slavic Brethren," *American Contributions to the Fourth International Congress of Slavicists: Moscow, September 1958* ('S-Gravenhage: Mouton and Co., 1958), 51–76.

_____. "Leskov's Parody on Gogol': *Otbornoe zerno*," *Lingua Viget: Commentationes Slavicae in Honorem V. Kiparsky* (Helsinki, 1965), 38–43.

_____. "Missing Letters to Leskov: An Unsolved Puzzle," *Slavic Review*, XXV, No. 1 (March 1966), 121–132.

_____. "Leskov, Paškov, the Stundists, and a Newly Discovered Letter," *Orbis Scriptus: Dmitrij Tschižewskij zum 70. Geburtstag* (Munich, 1966), 187–199.

_____. "Leskov's Trip Abroad in 1875: Four Unpublished Letters to I. S. Gagarin," *Indiana Slavic Studies*, IV (Bloomington, 1967), 88–99.

EEKMAN, THOMAS A. "The Genesis of Leskov's *Soborjane*," *California Slavic Studies*, II (1963), 121–140.

MCLEAN, HUGH. "Leskov and Ioann of Kronstadt: On the Origins of Polunoščniki," *The American Slavic and East European Review*, XII, No. 1 (February 1953), 93–108.

_____. "Leskov and His Enigmatic Man," *Russian Thought and Politics*, Harvard Slavic Studies, IV (Cambridge, 1954), 297–322.

_____. "On the Style of a Leskovian *Skaz*," *Harvard Slavic Studies*, II (Cambridge and The Hague, 1954), 297–322.

_____. "Studies in the Life and Art of Leskov." Ph.D. thesis, Harvard University, 1956.

_____. "A Contribution to the Revival of Leskov," *Slavic Review*, XXII (December 1963), 745–750.

_____. "Russia, the Love-Hate Pendulum, and *The Sealed Angel*," *To Honor Roman Jakobson* (The Hague, 1967), 1328–1339.

_____. "*The Priest and the Sorcerer*: Leskov's First Short Story," *Languages and Areas: Studies Presented to George V. Bobrinskoy* (Chicago, 1967), 90–99.

_____. "Leskov and the Russian Superman," *Midway* (Spring 1968), 105–123.

PRITCHETT, V. S. "A Russian Outsider," *The Living Novel and Later Appreciations* (New York: Random House, 1964), 420–426. (First published in 1946).

4/15/71

DATE DUE

GAYLORD   PRINTED IN U.S.A.